## Raves for The Annals of Drakis by Tracy Hickman

"Fans of Tracy Hickman's series, *The Annals of Drakis*, your wait is over. . . . The third book in Hickman's series, *Blood of the Emperor*, will sweep readers along for the ride as Drakis and his army approach the elven capital. Hickman strikes a perfect balance between action and intrigue, blending all elements of this story seamlessly into an epic conclusion that will keep fans guessing until the end."
—*San Francisco Book Review*

"In Book Three of *The Annals of Drakis*, readers will find treachery, hidden goals, betrayal, and victories among madness. The rebel army continues to grow as the elves of the Rhonas Empire finally begin to see the enormity of what is happening. Yet everything and everyone isn't what or who they seem. The stage is set and someone will be taking control. . . . A perfect ending for this trilogy."
—*Night Owl Reviews*

"The world imagined by Hickman is not your typical fantasy realm, with power-hungry elves that resemble aliens more than the traditional ideal and an empire based on conspiracy and lies, held together only by a powerful magic. The plot twists will keep readers guessing and completely enthralled in the story, while the imperfect characters are inherently likeable."
—*Sacramento Book Review*

"Bestseller Hickman . . . creates memorable characters and realms of immense richness, while holding the reader enthralled with exhilarating action."
—*Publishers Weekly*

"An exciting and extensive journey . . . . Readers are sure to get caught up in this adventurous and original story, which has a lot of twists and turns."
—*Romance Reviews Today*

"*Citadels of the Lost* is the exciting second book in *The Annals of Drakis* series, and like its predecessor, it does not disappoint. . . . Hickman writes with authority, masterfully and flawlessly switching between different points of view and keeping this novel flowing toward an epic conclusion that only promises more to come in the next book. A must-read for fans of the fantasy genre."
—*Tulsa Book Review*

*The Annals of Drakis*
by
Tracy Hickman:


# SONG OF THE DRAGON
# CITADELS OF THE LOST
# BLOOD OF THE EMPEROR

# Tracy HICKMAN

# BLOOD of the EMPEROR

*THE ANNALS OF DRAKIS:* Book Three

## DAW BOOKS, INC.

**DONALD A. WOLLHEIM, FOUNDER**

375 Hudson Street, New York, NY 10014

**ELIZABETH R. WOLLHEIM**
**SHEILA E. GILBERT**
**PUBLISHERS**

www.dawbooks.com

First Paperback Printing, June 2013
1  2  3  4  5  6  7  8  9

DAW TRADEMARK REGISTERED
U.S. PAT. AND TM. OFF. AND FOREIGN COUNTRIES
—MARCA REGISTRADA
HECHO EN U.S.A.

PRINTED IN THE U.S.A.

Dedicated to:
CPT Justin Cuff
and the service men and women of
B Battery, 2-17 Field Artillery, 2-2 SBCT
With our gratitude forever.

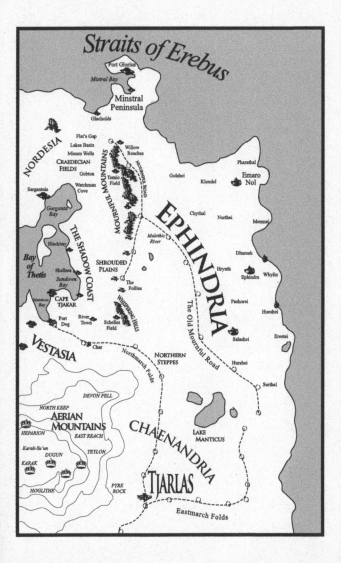

# TABLE OF CONTENTS

# Book 1:

## MAN OF PROPHECY

# CHAPTER 1

## Port Glorious

THEY WERE COMING out of the east.

The dust of their line of march was made a brilliant orange-red by the rising sun on the horizon behind it.

*It's an army,* Qistan thought, *and it's coming right at me.*

Governor-general Qistan Sha-Barethin, elven commander, stood on the wall of Port Glorious above Emperor's Gate sweating profusely beneath his armor. Perspiring was something that elves did only in intense heat or under extreme duress. This day accounted for both and so the gray-faced war-mage gazed out over the gently rolling landscape and reached up with increasing frequency to mop his brow with the hem of his cloak of office. It was a disgraceful act of disrespect for the symbol of his office, but Qistan was as far from the Imperial Courts of Rhonas as it was possible to be and still be considered within the boundaries of the Empire. It was one of the places where the Imperial Grace sent his sons who were better off forgotten. Qistan's previous offenses had earned him the longest road home possible. It was a road which he was certain now he would not have the opportunity to take.

Qistan offered up a quick prayer in his mind to the god Anjei—the god of all seeing and hearing—in the hopes that the god might pass along knowledge of his plight to someone—anyone—who might give him some aid. He turned around, looking over the port city and realizing that it simply was not important enough for the Emperor to care what happened to it. The seaside village known as Port Glorious came nowhere near living up to its name. There was his own Governor's House, which, despite being the largest structure in over a hundred leagues, proved to be the most modest of residences by elven standards. It was also the only building in the port town that followed the traditional elven design of a subatria foundation and the floating avatria above it. Clinging to the outer wall of the subatria were the hovels and ramshackle shops of the inner city, which appeared as though children had poured out toy buildings within the confines of the city wall and then dragged a narrow stick among them to create the alleys that passed for roads. The city wall itself was of elven construction and enclosed the city on three sides before projecting out into the waters of the bay and ending at a pair of towers surrounded by battlements. Proxis could mount the battlements to defend the city from an attack by sea while his own full Cohort of warriors—nearly seven hundred strong—could defend the city proper from atop the walls.

Or they *could* defend the city, Qistan thought grimly, if so many things weren't going wrong.

From the wall of the inner city and his perch above the Emperor's Gate, he searched the horizon. The wide expanse of Mistral Bay lay to the south, its waters lapping up gently along the long curve of the shoreline that ran eastward before turning south down the peninsula to the port town of Markrethold some twenty-five leagues away. There had been no word or ships from Markrethold in nearly a week and no communication with Glachold and the Willow Reaches for a week longer still. The elven supply ships out of Shellsea were also overdue and Qistan was beginning to feel truly isolated in his port.

If that were all, he still would not be standing here sweating. Ships were often late and messages from Markrethold and Glachold were tenuous at best. There were two things that truly concerned him.

The first was that the Aether Well was acting peculiarly. The Well had failed altogether two weeks ago. The avatria of his Governor's House had settled onto the subatria and threatened to fall over altogether. The Aether had returned to the Well, fortunately, but the Aether output was greatly reduced. It was barely sufficient to keep the avatria above the foundations and left precious little more for defense of the port. The few slaves that were in Port Glorious fell out of their Devotions and most of them had to be put down. Qistan had yet to determine what might be causing such a terrible drain of Aether.

He was still trying to coax the Aether to return when the second unnerving event had happened two days ago. The night watch had been drugged into sleep. The next morning, the Governor and all the elven warriors awoke to discover Port Glorious deserted except for themselves. The usual noisy bustle of the goblin shopkeepers, chimerian traders and gnome craftsmen as well as their brawling children and wailing infants had gone silent. The chimerian and gnomish ships in the harbor had all sailed during the night, leaving only the elven galleys tied up at the long docks. The smithy hammers were silent, the cooper's mallets still and the streets deserted except for the warriors of the elven Cohort. No children ran or shouted in the streets. No carts moved. Indeed, there were no carts or conveyances left to be found anywhere in the port town, either inside the crowded alleyways within the city wall or among the sprawling buildings outside. The goods in the shops were missing. The tools of the craftsmen were gone. Not even a dog had been left behind.

Qistan had sent out runners to discover where the townsfolk had gone with the idea of sending out a Centurai or two—no more than a hundred warriors or so—to round up the citizens of Port

Glorious and shove them back into their homes. Most of the runners came back no wiser than when they left but two of the three sent eastward returned with news of an enormous army possibly four thousand strong marching toward Port Glorious. In the lead were the manticores, but there were also goblins, gnomes, and even a few humans and elves observed by the two runners who made it back. The third scout did not return.

Qistan knew at once that they were about to be laid under siege. He commanded the Cohort to abandon the barracks outside of Centurai Gate and moved them all inside the city walls. He then ordered the shanties outside of the Emperor's Gate and Satja's Gate to be burned to the ground. The ruins still smoldered and smoked but Qistan now had a clear view of his enemy as they approached and knew that they would have to come at the wall exposed and in the open.

*Four thousand rabble against my seven hundred? We're in a defensible position of strength and I've already had the Proxis engrave fold marks into the approaches. We've the Aether on our side—what there is of it—and the manticorian tactics are easily countered. . . .*

Qistan mopped his elongated forehead once more with the edge of his robe. *So why am I still sweating?*

"Are your warriors ready?" Qistan asked.

"Yes, General!" It was Tribune Sha-Meihuen who answered him. Qistan trusted the Tribune implicitly. "There are two full Centurai on the walls with four Octia positioned behind each of the five gates. The rest remain reserved in the plaza adjacent to your home; each are organized in Octia with their Proxis awaiting deployment behind the siege lines at your command. We have a single Octia of war-mages but I've spread them as evenly as I could across the Centurai. Proxis are also in the sea-towers as a precaution against any attack by water."

Qistan looked down the line of the battlements. The elven warriors stood in their armor, black featureless eyes shining through the ports of their gleaming helmets. The morning breeze rustled their banners. The distant rhythmic sound of the approaching army rolled toward them across the landscape.

"Who are they?" Sha-Meihuen asked, gazing out toward the approaching battle line.

"The runners called them the 'Army of the Prophet,'" Qistan answered. "Word reached me from Rhonas that two Legions had been dispatched to annihilate them weeks ago. We were to be the rear guard against their escape."

"Escape?" Sha-Meihuen chuckled. "Escape to where?"

"The very problem I was contemplating," Qistan said quietly.

"It would seem that the Legions did not accomplish the Emperor's Will," Sha-Meihuen sniffed. "All the more glory for us, General."

"If we survive to claim it," Qistan observed.

The forward lines were moving quicker now.

The general could make out the shapes of the manticores bent over, the lion-men starting their charge toward the port town.

"Where is the House of your ancestors, Tribune Sha-Meihuen?" Qistan asked, his eyes fixed on the approaching battle line. The sun rose directly behind them, its rays obscured by the dust but the glare from its disk making it difficult to keep his eyes on his enemy.

"The House of my Ancestors is in Zhadras, General," the Tribune replied.

"Mine was in Tyrania . . . my father was a Baron of the Aethergus Coast," Qistan said with studied casualness. He could hear the manticores' roaring battle cries more than see them in the glaring haze. "We are both far from the memory of our wives and children, Tribune."

The manticores had nearly reached the outskirts of the town. The elven warriors shifted nervously on the wall to either side of him.

"Archers . . . READY!" the Tribune called out, raising his hand. The manticores were charging across the charred ruins of the outer city. Polished armor flashed on their backs in the rising dawn breaking behind them.

"You don't suppose they'll stop on their own, do you?" Qistan said with dry amusement.

"No, General," Sha-Meihuen chuckled under his breath. The howl from the charging army was overwhelming. "I don't suppose they will."

"Then we'll have to stop them . . . now!" Qistan said.

"FIRE!" the Tribune shouted.

Instantly, a rain of arrows flashed from the city walls, driving down into the front lines of the manticores. Some deflected from the elegant armor of the lion-men but more found purchase in flesh. Yet the manticores drove on, far fewer falling than Qistan would have expected. The Tribune shouted again, loosing another volley against the roaring charge. Then the manticores reached the base of the wall, charging the main gate with a battering ram as the Tribune released the archers to fire at will.

The Army of the Prophet continued its steady approach. Qistan could see from his position on the battlements that the army's battle line extended well to the north and was wheeling rapidly around the northern side of the city, well outside of the range of his archers.

"Keep firing," Qistan shouted at the Tribune over the din. "They're trying to flank us on the north and put us under siege but the brunt of the manticores seem to be here at the east gate. If we wait for the rest of their army to draw in toward the north gate, then we can fold in the reserves behind their lines on the north—devastate their flank and then pivot . . ."

The Tribune was not looking at him, his face filled with awestruck terror.

Qistan turned to follow the Tribune's gaze to the east.

Enormous, unspeakable winged monsters flew out of the sun. Leathery wings more than fifty feet in span glowed in the sunlight. Talons as tall as an elf, barbed tails and flashing scales all flew at him out of the sky with screeching cries so horrible that General Qistan thought he might lose his sanity. Though he had never seen one nor even believed in their existence, nevertheless their shape was familiar to him from the histories and legends he had long considered dead.

*"Dragons!"* Qistan screamed. *"They've got dragons!"*

One of the enormous shapes—a dragon with gray-blue markings—wheeled suddenly, raking its claws down the length of the battlements wall as it passed. Elves tried to escape but found no refuge. Most fell from the wall, some jumping outward in their terror, plunging into the battle-mad rage of the manticores below, while others were crushed or torn by the weight and edge of the dragon's claws. Two more of the dragons shrieked overhead toward the center of the town.

Qistan, in outraged wonder, saw figures riding on the backs of the dragons as they passed over his head. *Humans! Humans and dragons together? That's a legend we killed long ago!*

"Shift targets!" Qistan bellowed, pointing to the winged monstrosities filling the skies over Port Glorious. The creatures were plummeting down toward the plaza near the center of town. Qistan could see the massed numbers of his reserve Cohorts still filling the plaza in their prepared ranks. "Archers! Take them down! Take them down! Stop them now!"

The archers swung their bows around but it was too late. The black-and-rust-colored dragon with multiple raiders on its back dipped its head and a storm of fire rained down on the plaza, engulfing the massed troops in a devastating conflagration. Fire roiled upward, catching among the surrounding buildings, its greasy smoke curling skyward around the avatria of his floating home. The yellow-green dragon with its own set of riders wheeled around the avatria, its claws extended as its wings opened wide, slowing the beast in the air. The wings folded against its body as the dragon alighted on the subatria wall, the raiders on its back slipping down the leathery membranes into the garden within the walls of his home and . . .

*The Aether Well!* Qistan realized with a shock.

The Aether Well that supplied all the magic of Port Glorious was located in the center of his garden. It had been secure behind not only the city wall but also behind the walls of his home's subatria. The power of its magic could repel any assault from the ground . . .

But until this moment, Qistan had not considered the possibility of an assault from the sky. The Governor-general of Port Glorious suddenly realized that this Army of the Prophet had done to his Cohort what he had intended to do to them; bypassed his frontal defense and struck at his heart behind his own lines.

"Fall back!" the general yelled. "Fall back to the Aether Well! Protect the Well!"

Qistan could not see the Tribune. Chaos had exploded among the ranks of the elven warriors. The gray-blue dragon relentlessly ravaged the warriors atop the city walls, driving them down into the tight streets below. The black-and-rust dragon continued to pass back and forth across the city, breathing flames of death from the skies onto the troops as they fled in panic through the narrow passageways below.

"Captain . . . what is your name!" Qistan demanded.

"Neirah, General!" the captain responded, his sharp teeth chattering despite the warmth of the morning.

"Where are the Tribunes?" Qistan demanded.

"I don't know, General," the elf replied. "My own Tribune is dead, dragged from the wall by one of those dragons and dropped outside. We are without a Tribune, General."

"*You* are now Tribune, Neirah," Qistan barked. "Rally your Octian and anyone else you can find. We have to . . ."

A brilliant flash of light exploded from the sub-atria of his home near the center of the town. An expanding dome of energy radiated outward with terrible speed, passing over Qistan and dissipating across the hills and the waters to the south. The avatria rose upward with the wave, tumbling sideways before smashing down just to the north of Centurai Gate, falling sideways and collapsing the wall. The wave rushed outward, passing over the wall where the Governor-general stood. Qistan nearly fell, not from its impact for it passed over them like a sudden wind but from its *absence*.

He nearly stumbled from the sudden lack of Aether.

The magic was *gone*.

*How could this have happened?* Qistan's mind raced, trying to comprehend the incomprehensible. *How could everything have fallen apart so quickly?*

"To the galleys," Qistan said to the newly-minted Tribune Neirah. "We've got to get to the galleys and escape. Get word to everyone you can to converge on the galleys and set sail at once!"

"We are . . . abandoning the city?" Neirah blinked.

"Yes, if we can," Qistan said. "Tell everyone to rendezvous at Point Erebus in three days' time. *Then* we'll plan what to do next!"

"But, General, the Will of the Emperor is . . ,"

"Run, Tribune!" Qistan barked. "Or there will be none of us left to care about the Will of the Emperor!"

The Emperor's Gate of Port Glorious shattered beneath them. The manticores poured into the city.

Governor-general Qistan Sha-Barethin never made it to the harbor. His corpse was discovered beneath the blistered bodies of twelve elven warriors, including one agonized creature in charred captain's robes and armor still struggling for breath. He kept referring to himself as a Tribune and shouting for everyone to get to the ships in the harbor.

The manticores shook their heads and honored him by keeping their silence . . . never telling him while he breathed that the ships that had been his hope had all been burned at the docks by the dragons before any had managed to even cut their moorings.

# CHAPTER 2

## *Wary Travelers*

SOEN TJEN-REI STOOD on the city battlements, leaning on his Matei staff as he gazed down from above the Centurai Gate toward the sunset. The elf and former Inquisitor of the Iblisi had found his Drakis after all—but hardly in the manner that he had hoped and far from one that would help him return to the graces of his Order. Drakis' spectacular return on the back of a dragon was the perfect staging of a fulfilled prophecy, cementing the human's status as the chosen one of the gods to bring down the elven Empire.

*That's how I would have done it, if I wanted to convince the rabble that I had a divine mandate,* the elf thought, gazing down with contemplative contempt at the people below him. *A big mythic show, a public miracle or two, and the crowd will follow you. How did I come to this?*

He knew well enough how he had found himself on the wrong side of this war. The truth. It was always getting him into trouble. Truth was his profession—the studious and selective hiding of which was essential to the continuation of the elven Empire. He and all his Order were tasked to find the truth wherever it might be, evaluate its value, and then bury it deeply whenever the truth got in the way of the Imperial Will.

But then he had encountered Drakis and the Prophecy.

It had proved to be a rather larger and more difficult truth than he had imagined. The Iblisi had known about the prophecy for centuries and kept the knowledge from reaching the citizen elves of the Empire although the tale was rampant among other races. Moreover, the Iblisi knew that the prophecy was not so much a destiny mandated by the gods as it was a prediction of the Empire's fall. The seeds of the Empire's destruction were found within the Empire itself; it really needed very little in the way of a catalyst to start the Empire toppling.

Drakis, it seemed, had provided that catalyst.

Now the frustrating question for Soen was how he could use that to his advantage and, more importantly, would he have time to do so? Events since Drakis' heralded return argued against those odds. The Army of the Prophet and the Drakis Rebellion were already set to tear themselves apart long before the Legions of the Empire could arrive to do the job. Of course, anything could be changed with enough time. Mountains could be sundered by something as delicate as the rain given enough time. It all came down to how much leverage could be applied and just how far one had to move the mountain to get the desired result.

The large storage houses below him had been located close to the docks. Now the large doors of the warehouses were open wide and an anthill of activity bustled in and out of them, emptying the grain stocks and other larders of Port Glorious and distributing them throughout the camp. The efficiency with which Belag and his council had organized the effort was impressive and they had even declared a feasting day in celebration of their, well, glorious victory. Such feasts were taking place in each Centurai of rebel warriors but the majority of the stores were being loaded onto large wagons for transport. The War Council—a smaller assembly selected from the Council of the Prophet—had recommended that the majority of the pilgrims remain in Willow Vale. Those capable of warfare then struck northeast to raid the towns along the sweeping arch of Mistral Bay, swelling the ranks of the warriors as they went with the disaffected citizens of both Glachold and Markrethold who were all too anxious to cast their lots in with the Army of the Prophet. There were a number of humans in these communities who were naturally inclined to join with the pilgrims' cause. The goblins of these towns, by far the majority of citizenry, were sufficiently impressed by word that the Pajak of Krishu had allied himself with the Army of the Prophet that they surrendered their towns without complaint. These liberated families then set out to join the main encampment in Willow Vale while the more eager and idealistic of their young promptly took up arms and swelled the ranks of the army as it came at last to its objective of Port Glorious.

But from the time he had landed and through all of the subsequent battles, Drakis had largely stuck to his tent. As much as his return had sparked an influx of pilgrims, his subsequent absence was straining their faith.

*Where, in the name of the Dark Gods, is Drakis?* Soen seethed. Since his return, the Man of Prophecy had refused all Soen's attempts to meet with him—when it was so obvious that Drakis was in desperate need of help.

*Fools!* Soen shook his head, his arms folded across his chest as he watched the evidence parade back and forth below him. *What have they achieved? They are like locusts crossing the land, feeding on whatever they can claim and moving on. All this northern raid has bought them is a momentary reprieve from their destruction. They cannot see beyond their next meal.*

Soen shifted the dead Matei staff in his hands as he sneered. It had all been for nothing so far as he was concerned. He had come along to Port Glorious in the hopes of recharging his staff at the Aether Well here, but something had happened during the attack that made the Well utterly useless. He could draw no further magic from his staff but continued to carry it more out of habit than need. Even dead to the Aether it was still a considerable weapon in his hands.

*Like myself, in some ways,* he mused.

Soen heard the soft padding of feet approaching up the stairs behind the city wall. He already knew who it was before they spoke. "Good evening, Ethis."

"Is it?" the chimerian countered as he stepped onto the wall. "Greetings, then, Master Soen. I see the council has wasted no time in looting the spoils of their victory."

"They hardly had any choice," Soen replied. "The Army of the Prophet was running low on supplies when we arrived. They will consume most of it just getting back to the main encampment in Willow Vale—and their position will not have improved much."

"They have another victory," Ethis observed.

"Victories all end when your army has nothing to eat," Soen countered, shifting his Matei staff in his hands. "Every cause is only three meals away from revolution. But then, Ethis of Ephindria, I suspect you already know that."

"We haven't known each other long enough for you to suspect anything," Ethis said.

"And yet we know one another so well," Soen smiled with his sharp teeth. "I understand you do a rather remarkable impression of me."

Ethis' face was, as common for his race, completely blank and showed no reaction to the words of the Inquisitor—but the hesitation in his response told Soen that he had an advantage.

"I trust I have not offended you, Inquisitor," the chimerian responded. "No slight was intended, I assure you."

"Not at all," Soen continued. "But I think it is time that you and I came to an understanding with one another, Ethis of Ephindria. It is time there was some truth between us."

"It has been said that if an Iblisi speaks the truth, that's when you know he is lying," Ethis said in a neutral tone.

"Spoken with confidence by one who changes his face as often as the Emperor changes his mind," Soen answered, "but perhaps we could set all that aside and find a place of mutual benefit."

"My experience is that the elves take little interest in mutual benefit," Ethis said, his arms tightening. "They simply take."

"And my experience is that dangerous roads are often more pleasant when shared with fellow travelers," Soen countered. "Should our roads converge and our destination be the same, would it not prove better to aid one another in our journey? Besides I have such stories to tell that would be of great interest on our way."

Ethis considered for a few moments in silence before answering. "You have a story to tell me, Inquisitor?"

"Oh, yes, one that I think you'll find most entertaining," Soen continued speaking, his gaze fixed out across the sea of warriors encamped about the town. "It starts with a Queen of Ephindria who once ruled the families of her great nation with equanimity and an eye to the future . . ."

"Our nation is our family," Ethis replied in cool tones.

"Yes, but in this story it is a troubled family indeed," Soen continued. "The tale is told that Chythal—the heir and rightful ruler of all Ephindria—has become the Mistress of the High Council in Exile."

"Where would you hear such a story?" Ethis asked, shaking his head.

"It is a story told by the Lady of Whylin and the Lady of Surthal of the southern families in Ephindria," Soen replied with a slight nod of his head.

"If it is told by such liars, then your story is a tragedy," Ethis said quietly, "and a poor one at that."

"But a tragedy only in the beginning," Soen continued. "It begins with the dreadful surety that Chythal no longer presides over the families from the Light-towers of Ephindria. The unity of the families becomes a fading shadow across the land—all because four chimerian families allied themselves secretly with the Rhonas Imperium who have supported their usurpation of the Ephindrian throne by supplying them with just enough Aether to force their queen from her rightful rule."

"I do not like your story," Ethis said as he looked away.

"But this is the part that interests me," Soen continued. "Queen Chythal had a group of noble guardians in her service who were legendary in their powers. All chimerians are shapeshifters; their telescoping and flexible bone structure and malleable sinews allowing them considerable flexibility in the form they take. But there are only a few—a very select few—who have the training, talent, and discipline to *mimic* other forms. They were suspect in their own society, outcasts in many ways as their own kind found the extent of their talents unnerving but Queen Chythal took them in and made them into a formidable weapon at her command. They were called the D'reth and vowed to serve her as her sons. They were charged with the most unpleasant of tasks—all in the cause of reinstating her rightful rule."

"They do not exist," Ethis said, turning his blank face back toward the former Inquisitor. "They are only a myth."

"But a good myth," Soen said, turning to face the chimerian standing now a full head taller than the elf. "I wonder what one of their number would say to me if they knew what is known to the Iblisi Keeper in Rhonas—what every Iblisi who has studied the prophecy knows—about the Rhonas Empire and the Drakis Prophecy? What would one of the D'reth say if they knew that the Rhonas Empire was going to fall—that it was entirely rotten from within—and that the question was not so much *if* the Imperium would fall as it was *when*

and *how* it would fall? What would such an honorable and legendary chimerian say on behalf of his
queen, knowing that the means of choking her enemies was within her reach . . . that an army was
at hand just looking for an excuse to bring down
the empire whose Aether was keeping her from
reuniting the families of Ephindria once more?
What would such a trusted servant of Her Majesty
say? Would they purchase their Queen's rightful
destiny by lending her support in food and goods
to an army, say, like this one?"

Ethis stared blankly back at Soen. Chimerians
normally exhibited few features on their faces and
those they did maintain often changed. They had
no expressions except those they chose to convey
through conscious effort. It was the silence and its
length that told Soen what he needed to know.

"You tell very strange tales, indeed, Soen. But I
had nearly forgotten why I had come for you,"
Ethis said without preamble. "The War Council is
to convene this evening. Belag has requested that
you attend."

"Belag?" A wry smile flashed across Soen's face.
"Not Drakis?"

"Belag remains head of the War Council," Ethis
said, unfolding the upper pair of his four arms
and gesturing toward the stairs descending behind the city wall. "It is only right that he should
determine who should attend."

"And will Drakis be in attendance?" Soen asked
as he stepped down the stairs.

The chimerian followed him down. "Drakis is occupied with other matters."

"As always."

"He sent his regrets to the council," Ethis replied as they reached the bottom of the stairs and began moving through the twisting streets. The wreck of the avatria lay shattered on their left as they circumnavigated the subatria toward the plaza. "He also says that Belag will know what to do."

"Of course he will," Soen observed. "As always. And where is this council to be convened?"

"In the temple north of the bazaar," Ethis replied.

"Of course," Soen nodded as he walked. "A holy place for the Army of the Prophet to plan its next conquest."

They walked along in silence then, moving past the charred plaza and through the streets. They came to the market square. The tents of the commanders were aglow in the deepening evening. Flickering light spilled from the doorway into the temple. Soen was about to cross to the temple steps when Ethis spoke.

"You tell good stories," Ethis said carefully.

"Thank you, Ethis," Soen bowed slightly.

"I must wonder," the chimerian said without inflection, "why an elf of the Imperium would tell such a tale?"

"Because I have come to believe that the Imperial tree is going to fall," Soen replied. "And I want to ensure the direction it falls . . . so that it does not fall on me."

Ethis stared back at the Inquisitor with his expressionless face for another moment before he spoke. "Perhaps you would like to accompany me. We seem to be going in the same direction."

# CHAPTER 3

## *Spoils of War*

"SILENCE! SILENCE!" BELLOWED BELAG, his massive, hoary form straining forward on the throne of the Grahn Aur, his massive hands gripping the armrests so tightly that he thought the wood might snap.

Even the roaring voice of the manticore was having difficulty cutting through the tumultuous cacophony that filled the torch-lit hall. Belag had originally chosen the elven temple as the location for the council meeting partly because it was one of the few undamaged buildings large enough for the council to meet in but mostly because its thick walls would keep the sights and sounds of these proceedings hidden from the Army of the Prophet encamped outside the walls of the town. As it was the commanders of the various warrior groups had pitched their tents in the plaza just south of the temple and, no doubt, could not help but overhear the heated words of the Army's general leadership council as not even the stone walls could contain the rising sound of argument.

Jugar, red-faced, was standing on his chair, his fist striking at the air as though propelling additional force into his every word. Doroganda, the gnome representative, was literally jumping up and down on her own chair, her voice a shrill squeal above the discordant chorus of shouting. Hegral and Gradek—the warrior manticores in charge of the two Legion divisions of the armies— were gesturing wildly while shouting in demonstration of their displeasure. Neblik, the mud gnome, was trying desperately to get everyone's positions straight for his narrative and, in the process, only adding confusion to the argument. Urulani, Air Master, sat with her arms folded tightly across her chest as she tried to restrain herself from knocking several council members' heads together. Ethis sat next to Belag's throne, his face twitching occasionally although otherwise studiously blank. Soen sat on the ground between the arguing manticores in grim contemplation.

All eyes were focused on Braun, who stood in the center of the circle of chairs holding a scroll of parchment in his hand, attempting to read it aloud to the assembly while a human messenger stood next to him, growing more pale and sickly in appearance by the moment. This was the tenth such communication from Tsojai Acheran since the elf had been appointed Pilgrim Master of the council in the absence of the Grahn Aur; the last four of these scrolls had arrived within the space of the previous week. Each was dutifully read before the War Council that commanded the Army of the Prophet and each epistle had increasingly enflamed the rage of the council members both over the distant elf's governance of the pilgrim camp and due to the differences between the council members themselves.

Even the manticore's voice was having difficulty cutting through the din. Belag rose to his feet, roaring. "There will be silence in this hall at once! All of you! You will close your mouths this instant . . . or I shall be forced to close them for you!"

The general arguing died down enough for a few voices to be distinguished from the noise.

Jugar's remained indignant. "But, this is an absolute outrage to suggest that . . ."

Doroganda's rush of words continued. "The very idea is an affront to the glorious rule of . . ."

Hegral shouted. "He has no right to . . ."

Belag leaped up from his throne with a great roar. He turned and picked up the massive chair, pressing it over his head. Then, with all his considerable strength, he slammed it downward, driving it against the stone floor. The chair broke with a resounding crash, shocking the assembly into quiet. Belag snatched up a now broken armrest and wheeled to face the council, holding it like a club.

"I will *personally* push this down the throat of the next council member that speaks without my permission," Belag seethed. "Everyone will be heard . . . but each in their own time."

Belag's words hung in the sudden silence within the long, rectangular hall. The only sound in that moment was the fluttering of the torches and his own ragged breath.

"Continue, Braun," Belag pointed at the human wizard with the broken arm of the chair.

Braun cleared his throat before continuing. "And, therefore, we require direction in the form of a written missive from the War Council explaining that the use of occupied lands and the establishment of permanent settlements is contrary to the council's intention to move the camp in order to more effectively pursue the downfall of the elven Empire. We require this correspondence at once."

"Require? Demand is more like it!" Jugar snapped.

Belag shook the chair's arm menacingly in the dwarf's direction.

"Merely commenting," the dwarf grumbled.

Braun continued his recitation, "Seventh: In addition to these issues come the problems of support for the members of the encampment itself. News of our success has spread from Manticus Bay all along the Shadow Coast and across both Vestasia and Nordesia. This has brought a burgeoning increase in the number of pilgrims seeking the returned Man of Prophecy and the hope for a better life that his return offers them in accordance with his legend. At the time of our victory in Willow Vale, the encampment numbered nearly seventy-three thousand including the Army of the Prophet, their families, and those pilgrims unable to participate in the army directly. Our best count as of the date of my writing puts the number of pilgrims in Willow Vale to have swollen to nearly twice that number with almost a thousand more arriving daily. Those who arrive all ask the question, 'Where is Drakis? When might we see him? When might we hear his voice . . .' "

*When, indeed,* thought Belag as he rubbed his forehead with his free hand. *When will any of us see or hear from him?*

"Because of his absence, many of the encampment are even beginning to question his existence and the majority are threatening either abandonment or, in some cases, the overthrow of the council. Many of these issues can be traced directly to problems of supply and the difficulty of obtaining food and proper shelter for nearly one hundred and fifty thousand pilgrim souls. With burgeoning numbers of pilgrims arriving at the main encampment each day, the People of the Prophet require additional resources in order to sustain the Cause and to maintain the faithful in their support of the army and its goals. Therefore we require that the army turn over to the Council of the Prophet in Willow Vale all material goods, especially food, seized during operations by the Army of the Prophet. Furthermore . . ."

"Furthermore?" Gradek sneered. "That's not enough? What more does he want?"

"Furthermore," Braun read on, "we require an increase in material assistance from the Pajak of Krishu and the allied tribes of Nordesia, especially in the form of edible goods . . ."

"More?" screeched Doroganda. "The Pajak of Krishu is beginning to wonder if his alliance with the Army of the Prophet is worth the risks he is taking on behalf of his tribe!"

"The Pajak has nothing to complain about!" Gradek snarled. "You goblins take the first spoils of our conquests and you've been more than compensated for what you've delivered to the encampment so far!"

"The Pajak does not make war for profit," Doroganda asserted.

"No, he only complains when his profit isn't big enough when he chooses to go to war," Gradek countered.

"It's *your* war that we are supporting," Doroganda replied with an edge of disdain in her voice. "Your great prophecy-war against the Elven Tyranny . . . and how have you waged this so-called war? By boldly marching in the opposite direction from the Empire you claim you want to destroy! In the meantime, you expect us to feed this increasingly burdensome rabble of your encampment while you boldly continue to conquer outposts that are even farther from your enemy's armies than before."

"We have won every battle," Hegral boasted. "Conquered every stronghold."

"Well, hurrah for the Army of the Prophet," Doroganda mocked. "Hail its victorious retreat at the Pajak's expense."

Ethis shook his head. "With little help from you or your Pajak. The manticores charge against the enemy walls while the goblin troops hold back."

"And where is the great Queen of the chimerians and her ever-changeable nation?" Doroganda said, raising her chin in defiance. "At least our warriors stand on the field of battle. What honor is there in Ephindria when they lie silent and quivering behind their borders lending neither strength nor aid?"

"Our nation . . ."

"Is your family, we've all heard it before," Doroganda finished in disgust. "You all hide behind that easy answer. Well, *my* family is with me here among honest warriors pitting our blood against elven swords. Where is the blood of Ephindria on the battlefield? Where are their caravans of aid? What do they offer beyond empty words?"

"And for once I would like to hear the answer to the goblin's question!" Gradek asserted, turning toward Ethis.

"There is more still," Braun interjected, pointing at the long scroll parchment that draped over his hand.

"Of course there is," Gradek growled.

Braun nodded and continued. "Eight: The pressures of maintaining order over the rapidly increasing population of the gathering believers has caused the rise of a number of factions within the encampment—several of which demand immediate attention . . ."

"Everything is immediate in the eyes of an elf!" Gradek snarled.

Soen's eyes shifted but he remained otherwise still.

Braun pressed on. "The self-proclaimed 'Brothers of Drakis' are a human faction which has been growing steadily in strength over the last month and recently has become openly defiant of the Council of the Prophet, claiming that Drakis is being deliberately kept away from the camp. There have been several incidents between the 'Brothers of Drakis' and the Grahn Aur Guard—a faction of manticores who believe in their right to stand in the Grahn Aur's place to rule over the pilgrims in his stead. The Pajak has also decreed Willow Vale to now be within the boundaries of his domain as his just spoils for his assistance in the battle against the elven Legions. His warriors on wyvernback patrol through the camp side by side with the council's constabulary with tensions running high on both sides. The constabulary force is inadequate to oppose the goblin warriors and a number of incidents have been reported of goblins intimidating pilgrims—largely Hak'kaarin gnomes and humans as well as a number of chimerians—into surrendering their goods under threat of reprisal. These thefts . . ."

"That is a lie!" Doroganda shouted, her small

brick-red fist thrust defiantly at Braun with her thumb and first finger extended. "The warriors of the Pajak are no thieves!"

Belag saw Soen smile. The manticore also knew from his negotiations with the Pajak that the gesture was a supreme insult among the goblins although apparently among those present only Doroganda, Soen, and himself were aware of it.

"Which part?" asked Neblik, trying desperately to keep the narrative straight in his head.

"Which part *what*?" demanded the goblin.

"Which part was the lie," Neblik said. "The part about the 'inadequate force' or the part about 'goblin theft by intimidation'?"

"Both of them, you idiot!" Doroganda snarled.

Ethis shook his head impatiently. "Braun! Can we get on with this?"

"He lists a great number of other grievances," Braun said, unrolling the scroll further as his eyes scanned down the page.

"Pass over them!" Ethis threw all four of his hands up at once in frustration. "What does the councillor want us to DO?"

Braun continued scanning down the page, pulling more parchment from the roll twice before stopping. "Ah! Therefore, we require that the War Council return the Army of the Prophet, led by the prophesied Drakis, at once to Willow Vale with the intention . . ."

"Shades of Hchai!" Hegral swore. "Who is this elf to order our armies at his will? Let him move the encampment to us here! Then we can gather our strength, build our clans, and prepare properly to take on the Empire!"

"You meet and you talk and then you talk about meeting!" Doroganda spat. "The Pajak will not stand for it! We stand with warriors not with cats who sleep when the sun is shining and only hiss when danger is upon them!"

"You will swallow those words, goblin-whelp," Gradek growled, "or I'll tear them out of your throat myself!"

"And what will that profit you, cat-man?" Doroganda sneered. "I know you and your kind! You would count yourself happy to be rid of the Pajak of Krishu and his goblin warriors. The warriors of the Pajak will walk with their spoils, take their mighty wyverns with them and you would not care—until your belly was hollow and your mewling whelps were without suck. If our warriors walk from your army, big cat-man, we walk with our grain and our meat and our stores. We walk with your lives. How long will the pilgrims remain? How long before this great army of yours starts eating itself?"

"It is late," Belag said. "We will convene again tomorrow at dusk to consider our response."

A silence descended on the hall.

Belag stepped forward, turning around as he spoke to the now silent council.

"We have forgotten," he said, his deep voice resonating through the hall. "We have forgotten our destiny. We have forgotten that we are the Children of the Prophecy."

Doroganda leaned back in her chair with a sigh. "As I understand this fairy-tale prophecy, you're supposed to be led by some great human who will bring down the elf oppressors and avenge the fall of his people. He shows up on the big, nasty dragon and everyone is impressed but where *is* he now? No one seems to have seen him since he arrived and the Pajak of Krishu is becoming concerned that he does not exist at all."

Belag eyed the goblin then turned to look at where his throne lay smashed and in pieces.

*Where are you, Drakis?* Belag thought. *Where are you?*

# CHAPTER 4

## Upside Down

URULANI STRODE THROUGH THE SOUTHEAST Goblin Gate of Port Glorious as the morning sun rose behind her with salmon hues. Her appearance was acknowledged by the manticorian and chimerian warriors working to clear the gate marketplace of the dead and debris with bows and silent salutes. Urulani was grateful for this change. When they had first returned with the dragons to find the Army of the Prophet and the pilgrim refugees on the shores of Willow Vale any sight of Drakis or any of those who had returned with him was enough to elicit wild cheers and thunderous acclamations. She had managed with considerable difficulty and the assistance of the Council of the Prophet to dissuade the warriors in the army from the practice of dropping everything to honor any of the "Drakis Chosen" as they had come to be called in favor of the quieter and subtler salute.

Yet they still looked at her with those same eyes. She could see the adoration and the hope behind them. It was a look the raider captain could not tolerate for any long period of time.

Now this dark-skinned captain of the Sondau Clan had been reduced to an all-too-glorified messenger. Ethis had come to her after the council disbanded the previous evening, begging her to present a message to Drakis on his behalf. He had rebuffed her suggestion that he run his own errands, claiming that Drakis would not see him but that he might see Urulani. She had tried that night to approach Drakis in his tent, believing it the best time to find him there but the manticorian guards had established a perimeter around his lodgings and had orders to let no one pass. She had attempted again at first light this morning and had been admitted—only to find not Drakis but a messenger with an urgent request from the Aether Master Braun that Drakis be brought to him at once. Urulani had dismissed the messenger, promising to fulfill the charge of the grateful man. She had been engaged in an increasingly frustrating search for Drakis ever since, discovering a number of warriors who claimed to have seen him but somehow their directions never seemed to get her any closer to finding him. The last had brought her through the southeastern gate of the town wall and into the carnage that lay before her.

It occurred to her to try another tactic. If Braun was looking for Drakis then perhaps all she really needed to do was to find Braun.

The destruction here near the former docks was bad enough but she knew that the plaza beyond the wreckage was much worse. There, the manticores had been working throughout much of the day to clear the slaughtered elven warriors from the charred square. That had been the place of greatest carnage, the dragon's breath descending like a deadly avalanche of flame on the tightly packed ranks of elven Octia. These warriors had been destroyed utterly before they had a chance to be deployed. The forward elements of the Army of the Prophet had breached three of the five city gates quickly which had allowed them opportunity to get the fires in the center of the town under control before the entire village—and its precious food stores—had been utterly destroyed.

The town and its buildings were unimportant. The food stores were everything in this raid.

However, Urulani found it difficult to think of food's importance at this moment. She had been a Captain of the Forgotten and as such had been a seasoned participant of many raids along the shores of Thetis Bay. Death had always been a part of her world but the stench from the still smoldering corpses in the plaza was almost overwhelming, even for her.

She spotted a human male hovering at the edge of the charred ruins, reluctant to help with the dreadful work at hand. His face seemed unusually pale even in the evening light.

Urulani approached him. "Pardon my question . . ."

The man turned, his scowl shifting at once into surprise. He fell to the ground in front of her, his arms stretched out before him as his face pressed toward the ground. "My Great Lady of the Dragon! Speak that I may serve you!"

"Oh, get up," Urulani urged, gripping the man by his arms and dragging him to his feet.

"Yes, My Great Lady of the Dragon," the man sputtered.

"What is your name?" she asked.

"Bartolem, my Lady," the man blurted out.

"I'm looking for Braun." Urulani dispensed with pleasantries. She knew diplomacy was not entirely her strong suit and when confronted with anything that made her feel awkward, she often reverted to being the commanding captain.

The man stared blankly at her.

"The Aether Master," Urulani insisted.

"The human wizard?" Bartolem asked.

"Yes! He asked to see me." That part was not entirely true. Braun had asked for Drakis but he was nowhere to be found so she had come in his stead. "Where is he?"

Bartolem gestured to his left. "This way, my Lady. I saw him on the fold platform by the eastern gate."

"The fold platform?" Urulani said with surprise as she eyed the narrow street to the north the man had indicated. "I thought Port Glorious had no folds."

"It doesn't," Bartolem confirmed, gesturing again to the narrow street. "Here, let me show you."

Urulani followed Bartolem as he made his way up the narrow, winding street, lined with watchful troops. Each saluted as she passed, their expressions conveying their pride and their support for her.

*It's embarrassing,* she thought grimly.

She followed the man between the buildings and across a small courtyard with a broken, dry fountain in its center. There were several exiting alleyways and Urulani hesitated for a moment but Bartolem urged her quietly to follow him into an alley on the opposite side. Within less than a dozen steps the narrow, winding canyon between the buildings on either hand opened onto the corner of what had been the main market square. The stalls were gone, replaced by a number of tents occupied by the field commanders of the army. There was a constant bustling through this area of manticores, humans, gnomes, and goblins relaying commands and results from the various units now operating throughout the occupied town. On her right hand rose what remained of the Emperor's Gate, its shattered doors laid askew. Gnome workmen were already busy rebuilding and shoring up the gates despite Belag's admonition not to bother with it. The army would not be here long enough to complete the job, let alone make use of the completed gates.

On the northern side rose a rectangular temple, which ran the length of the marketplace from east to west. Rows of statues stood along the outer temple wall.

"Elven gods?" Urulani asked.

"Yes, dedicated originally to Kiris," Bartolem mused aloud.

Urulani raised her eyebrows at the human.

"My former master in Blackbay was most devout and insisted everyone in his household learn and worship the Rhonas pantheon," Bartolem explained in haste. "See that row of statues lining the side of the building. Each of the statues depicted another aspect of the eye of the sun traversing the sky and the trickster moon dancing in chase. Kiris is the goddess of light and dark—she who sees the seen and the unseen."

"Let's hope she isn't watching now," Urulani muttered. "So where is Braun?"

"I saw the wizard down on the left, toward the Governor's old home."

Urulani nodded and started through the tents, leaving Bartolem in her wake. Creatures and humans stumbled over themselves to get out of the way and honor Urulani all at the same time. Ahead of her, to the west, she could see the subatria that had supported the Governor's House. The avatria no longer pierced the sky, but lay in a heap at the far side of its foundation.

Then, through the tents on her left, she saw it.

It was a low stone platform of the same design which, according to Braun, commonly supported nearly every elven fold throughout the Rhonas Empire and well into its provinces. In this case, however, it was incomplete as there was no fold established above it for the platform to support.

It was, however, supporting Braun and a rather agitated Jugar.

Urulani frowned. Having the dwarf and human wizards in any kind of proximity had become increasingly volatile and even dangerous over the weeks since the two had met.

Braun was still as insane as Drakis had described him but somehow knew more about Aether magic than even the mysterious dwarf Jugar. He had proved himself invaluable so far in the campaign and, if Belag were to be believed, had even proved adept at opening gateway folds more spectacularly than anyone—elf or human—of whom she had ever heard. Braun had even begun teaching some of the humans among the warriors the arts of drawing on the Aether and putting it to use in warfare. Yet despite these considerable skills to his credit, he still made Urulani uneasy.

"Air Mistress!" shouted Braun, waving from atop the platform. Fortunately, no one began a chanting chorus at the sound of her title.

Braun's face broke into a wide smile. He was a short man with a stocky build and a large, hooked nose. Dark hair streaked with gray had emerged from his head, still raggedly short, as it had not been growing long. His original Sinque mark still showed through its bristles, reminding Urulani that this man had once been enslaved by the elves.

Urulani climbed the stairs up the side of the fold platform and was immediately confronted by the dwarf.

"Well, it's about time someone came capable of talking sense!" exclaimed the gruff voice from farther back on the level stone stage. "Where's Drakis?"

*Where indeed*, Urulani thought, but she chose other words to speak aloud. "He is delayed. He asked me to come and find out why you called for him so urgently."

Jugar planted both his fists on his hips. "I've had to listen to this windbag bellow pointless noises for the last hour and, despite my most diplomatic efforts, I assure you, I've made *no headway* against his nonsense!"

"It worked, didn't it?" Braun countered.

"That's beside the point!" the dwarf sputtered.

Urulani looked at the dwarf and sighed. Jugar appeared to be in rather high dudgeon. He wore a padded leather coat that he had cut off at the arms and to a length to better fit him. The canvas trousers and linen shirt were a far cry from the original garish clothing that Drakis had first found him wearing as he emerged from the hiding place beneath the king's throne. Urulani had to admit that she missed the colorful costume although the dwarf had managed to retain his wide brimmed hat. "Jugar, what *is* the point?"

"The point is that this human charlatan shouldn't be practicing magic without a license!" the dwarf sputtered as the thumb of his left hand gestured toward Braun.

"There's no qualified authority to issue such a permit," Braun shrugged.

"Well, if there *were* such an authority, I would see to it that your license was revoked forthwith!" the dwarf spat back. "You're reckless—playing with all our lives!"

"We'll never learn anything if we don't experiment," Braun replied. "We need to grow. See a bit farther over the horizon than we have . . ."

"Are you casting aspersions upon my height?" Jugar grumbled, his fingers playing on the handle of his ubiquitous ax.

"Jugar! Please!" Urulani said, trying to remain patient. She was tired and the bickering was not helping her disposition. "What did he do?"

"What did he *do*?" Jugar exclaimed. "What *didn't* he do, more like! Did you know that this human charlatan leaped down from the dragon ahead of me? A feat in itself considering how anxious I was to get off that fell beastie!"

The titles that the Council of the Prophet had bestowed upon several of its members were supposed to help define the boundaries of authority between each but sometimes they were more of a nuisance than a help. Jugar was appointed "Master of Aer" while Braun was titled "Master of Aether" although he protested that Aether was what the elves called their magic and that "Anti-Aether" might be a better term. No one else understood the distinction and thus Braun became the "Master of Aether" anyway. All of this was of great distinction between the two of them but of little help to the rest of the army as the difference was completely lost upon the common warrior. It was all just "magic" to the army and whatever they called it was firmly in the province of the two "wizards" who were its masters. This left the two to bicker over the details between themselves with an animosity that had been building steadily ever since they were first introduced to one another. The War Council had decided it would be a good idea to have Jugar and Braun dropped into the subatria of the Governor's home in Port Glorious ahead of the ground-bound army to remove the Aether Well before the garrison of elven warriors could counter their attack. This, apparently, had ignited yet another argument.

"You were both assigned to assault the Aether Well," Urulani shrugged. Her head was beginning to hurt again. "He was just doing his job . . ."

"He was doing *my* job," Jugar interrupted indignantly. "More than that, he did it *wrong*!"

"Wrong?" Urulani chuckled. "It worked rather well for a mistake."

"No mistake that," Jugar sputtered. "He deliberately reversed the Well!"

Urulani shook her head, not understanding. "What?"

"I reversed the Aether Well," Braun said again with his cockeyed smile. "I listened carefully to the stories Jugar told upon your return. He is quite in love with the sound of his own voice and so wasted no time in regaling everyone with ears as to the details of your marvelous quest among the ruins of Drakosia. I was particularly interested in that part of the story where Drakis was in the Citadel of Light and how he opened the Aether Well."

*I was there. I tried to help Mala—only Mala found her own way to die and I could not stop her. Mala said she was going home and then the dragon Pharis ended her life. I fled through the resurrecting ruins of the ancient city, walls suspended in midair as they tried to reassemble themselves into the city that had died so long ago. How could I explain to Drakis what had happened to her? How could he ever forgive me for allowing it to happen at all . . . ?*

"Did you understand?" Braun concluded.

"Sorry," Urulani replied, returning to the present as she spoke. "Tell me again."

"As I was saying, that led me to believe that with the opening of the lost Wells of Drakosia, the drain on the Rhonas Wells has put a strain on them. I believed I could duplicate the opening of the Citadel Well with a Rhonas Well. It's not so much reversing as it is, how would you say, tipping it over and figuratively turning it upside down. The draw from the ancient Wells across the sea destabilizes the Well here in Port Glorious . . . makes it easier to reverse the flow from gathering to transmission. That's the essential difference between Rhonas Aether Magic and that of Human Anti-Aether Magic of old: elven Wells collect while human Wells disseminate. Of course, what I call the Anti-Aether magic was simply called Aether magic by the humans long ago, so perhaps it would be best if we actually called human magic Aether magic and elven magic—which was stolen from the humans by the elves—the anti-Aether magic even though they incorrectly call it Aether magic."

Urulani could feel her headache returning. "I still don't get it."

Braun nodded. "Think of human Aether magic as 'blue Aether magic' and elven Aether magic as 'red Aether magic.' They're both Aether but blue flows out of the Wells freely while red is drawn in and tightly controlled."

"Blue magic and red magic?" Urulani rubbed her forehead.

"Yes . . . or sweet and sour magic if you prefer," Braun grinned.

"The point is that we were supposed to break the Well," Jugar shouted, "and well he knows it! We were supposed to deny the enemy its greatest weapon . . . the magic of Aether . . . whatever color or flavor he wants to call it!"

"And so I have," Braun said breathing in deeply. "The Well here in Port Glorious is now flowing outward with the Aether—a fountain of mystical energy which *we* can tap but which is contrary to the understanding of the elves and will not function with any of their devices. We empower ourselves and deny the enemy at the same time. Take this fold platform, for example . . ."

"I thought there were no folds to Port Glorious," Urulani interrupted.

"They never were installed, let alone functional," Braun answered. "But the pride of the Imperial Will demands that there be two fold platforms created in every outpost whether they are utilized or not. Ah, the mind of the Emperor is ever forward thinking even when it is backward. There is another platform just like it on the other side of the town, is that not true, master dwarf?"

"You know very well that there is!" Jugar snarled.

"They exist here not only because some bureaucrat almost a thousand leagues removed from reality decreed that they must be built here but also because physical connection is at the heart of elven Aether magic. Staves, wands, rings, and platforms are the means by which elves store, focus, and conduct their magic. Without such physical objects they cannot work magic. That's why Proxis always carry staves and why the Iblisi do the same, though the two groups have radically different abilities. A connection between physical objects like these platforms is required before the Aether can flow through them. The efficiency of this power diminishes over distance but can be replenished again from physical bases like this one or through the interconnection of the Aether Wells."

"What are you saying?" Urulani urged.

"What if our 'blue' Aether magic didn't require physical connection to the Wells?" Braun asked, a gleam in his eyes. "What if you could access the Aether without having to be physically connected with it in some way? That's what reversing the flow of these Aether Wells makes possible! We can channel it outside the control of the Empire for our own use . . . and the more Wells we turn, the more powerful we become and the weaker the Empire becomes. We could command a trail of these reversed Wells in our wake . . ."

"And leave ourselves vulnerable from the rear," the dwarf added. "These Wells which he wants to keep intact could just as easily be turned back again. We already have an advantage with these dragon-beasties! We don't need to have a bunch of amateurs dabbling in magic that they don't understand."

"I understand it a good deal better than you," Braun said with an imperious air. "I've already proven that it works. That's what brought you up short."

"Short!" Jugar snatched up his ax.

Braun raised his hands in front of him, making a sudden circular motion with each. To Urulani's astonishment, a fold portal suddenly opened up in the stone beneath the dwarf. With a cry of rage, the dwarf fell through the portal.

The fold collapsed.

Braun lowered his arms and grinned.

Urulani thought she could hear the distant sounds of a dwarf swearing from the other side of the town.

*Drakis needs to see this,* she thought, biting at her lip. *Where is he?*

Suddenly, looking westward across the tops of the commanders' tents, she knew.

# CHAPTER 5

## *Haunted*

DRAKIS STEPPED INTO THE GARDEN of the Governor-general's home and shuddered.

The wall of the surrounding subatria was still largely intact. The avatria that had floated overhead was nowhere to be seen. The floating structure had been hastily blown aside when Jugar dealt with the font. Now, instead of the perpetual shadow of the avatria, an unobstructed view of a brilliant blue sky took its place, with low-lying clouds drifting quickly overhead and a column of smoke rising from the still-smoldering ruins of the city.

Where the avatria had fallen, Drakis had not asked.

The garden itself had escaped with little damage. Paths ran between the carefully cultivated flower beds and trimmed lawns. In an arrangement Drakis had not seen before, there was a reflecting pool surrounding the Aether Well in the center of the garden. The crystal of the Aether Well shone with a bright column of light extending upward along its surfaces, pushing the clouds aside into a ring around its light as it reached into the sky. There was a purple tinge to the edges of the light that reminded Drakis somewhat of lilacs that had grown in another garden . . .

"Drakis!"

The voice was bright and carefree in his mind.

*Another garden . . . another time . . .*

She smiled at him, the Sinque mark tattoo clearly visible on her clean-shaven head as she approached. She moved with light steps quickly around the Aether Well, touching on the Altar of House Devotions that now lay cracked and broken next to the Aether Well. She wore her slave's robe that was now unmarred, clean and whole as he remembered it. Her emerald eyes flashed at the sight of him.

"Mala," Drakis whispered as he smiled.

"So you *did* return to me after all!" His beloved smiled back at him as she had that day so long ago—when they were innocent and without memory of pain. He could hear her voice as though she were there as she turned her face up to look into his eyes again. "I prayed to all the gods each day that they would bring you back to me."

Drakis closed his eyes against the memory. She was happy and content then. Both of them were without care except for each other, caught in a dream from which he hoped never to awaken. But awaken they did when the dwarf shattered the Aether Well, released them from the enchantment of their elven masters, and made them *remember* the truth of their enslavement and that they were living a false life.

If only he could live that lie again . . . if he could go back to a time when his life made sense even if it was a dream from which he never awoke.

If only . . .

He opened his eyes again.

Mala was still dead. She had died because of a different dream . . . a false dream.

It had been her belief in him that killed her.

Since that day, color and taste had left his experience. Night and day were all the same to him. The celebrations and rejoicing at their return by the rabble Belag had assembled in his name were like the annoying sounds of pieces of tin banging together to his ears. For a time he had endured their council meetings, giving his opinions with diffidence only to watch his idle and disinterested observations become words of law and prophecy by the following day. He was a warrior by training and had marched their army northward around the Mistral Peninsula as a matter of basic tactics. He wanted to ensure that the elves of Port Glorious would not threaten the families and support in the rear of their column.

Mostly, however, he had simply not cared what Belag did with the Army of the Prophet. The manticores were flush with their victory over the Legion of the Northern Fist and were itching for another fight. The elf Soen had also been insistent about taking control of an Aether Well and Ethis suggested Port Glorious as the most likely place to take one. It was Ethis who had negotiated with the dragons, bringing them south across the Desolation and ultimately across the Straits of Erebus. It was largely his doing that the dragons had joined them in defeating the Cohort in Port Glorious.

All of this had been accomplished in Drakis' name.

He didn't give a damn for any of it. None of it mattered because it did not change the fact that Mala was gone and he did not know how to fill the well of his grief.

Drakis stepped down one of the paths. The blooms on either side were fragrant, their clean, sweet scent taking him back to House Timuran and the garden that was now a ruin but had once been so beautiful. He stepped up to the reflecting pool around the Aether Well.

*What have I done but destroy anything that I thought was worthwhile?* Drakis mused.

"If you've come for a bath, you're too late," Mala said, her shoulders just above the surface as she moved her arms back and forth through the water. Drakis could still smell the dense foliage and the dark earth mixed with the damp mists from the waterfall.

Her short red hair was wet and pushed back from her high forehead. Her emerald eyes had a playful look.

"I claimed this pool and it is mine by right. I will not share my private little paradise with anyone else—no matter how badly they need bathing—and you, most certainly, are desperately in need of a bath."

"It was all I wanted." Drakis smiled at the memory, pain playing at the corners of his eyes. "A life of my own to share . . ."

A cloud passed over the subatria, casting a shadow across the garden.

Drakis closed his eyes again but the sound filled his mind. Mala's voice again, now pleading in agony, not with him but with unseen demons. Her words scarred his soul. "You promised to keep me away from him most of all! The demons are nothing next to his pain! He loved me! He hurt me! I want him! I hate him!" Her voice dropped to a whimper. "Please take me home! I cannot live with what he feels. I cannot live with what *I* feel. I want to never know that pain again. I want to forget."

"Drakis?"

He opened his eyes to the sound of another voice. He lacked the will to turn and face the intruder into the garden of his despair. "What is it?"

"You are needed," she said simply.

Drakis turned and tried to focus his eyes on the figure that had addressed him. Urulani, daughter of the Sondau Clan and former captain of the *Cydron* appeared inside the main gates to the garden, the long fingers of her hands resting impatiently on her hips. Her tall, slender body stood casually, arms akimbo, as she looked back at him from large, brown eyes set above her pronounced cheekbones. Her skin was a deep black—as deep a black as the middle of the night and as smooth and unblemished as pure silk. Her thick, black hair was pulled back from the high forehead of her oval face and gathered into an explosion of curls at the back of her head. Her lips were thick and plump around her generous mouth—drawn slightly up at one corner as though being amused by some secret thought. She still wore the same buckskin breeches as when he had first met her but the vest had been replaced by a leather doublet more practical to her new status as a dragonrider and now as Air Mistress.

Drakis turned back to gaze into the still surface of the pool at his feet. "Who needs me?"

"Well, *everyone* it would seem," Urulani replied. Drakis could hear her approaching footsteps in the gravel of the path. "The War Council wants to convene again this afternoon. There's been another dire missive from Tsojai about the collapse of order in the pilgrim encampment. Jugar and Braun both have complaints for you about each other, and that elf Iblisi Soen keeps asking when you will have some time to hear him . . ."

Urulani's voice faded from Drakis' thoughts as he gazed into the pool. For a moment he saw himself with his head shaved, the Sinque mark clearly visible on his head and his patchwork armor strapped about his body. He saw the Impress Warrior once more who was confident in his clearly defined orders and responsibility only to his

House and his fellow warriors. But that image shifted in the water's surface and he saw the splay-haired refugee with the rough beard fleeing from his own memories across the Vestasian Savanna.

Then his vision cleared and the reflection sharpened in his tear-blurred eyes.

He did not know the face staring back at him.

His image was clean-shaven once more as it had been as an Impress Warrior of House Timuran but the hair was long and full now, trimmed and combed by a group of manticorian females each morning into a dark mane. He wore his own leather doublet similar to Urulani's but fitted with clasps at the shoulders and a rough, woven cape of bright crimson.

"Who am I, Urulani?" Drakis asked, gazing into the reflection as he spoke with unmeasured sadness in his voice.

Her footfalls in the gravel stopped nearby.

The face in his reflection did not change nor did it grow any more familiar to him.

"Who am I?" Drakis demanded, his voice rough and loud.

"You are Drakis," Urulani responded quietly. "You are the Man of the Prophecy."

"No. *That* man, perhaps," Drakis said angrily as he pointed at the reflection in the still water. "That illusion that they have created out of me . . . *that* is the Man of the Prophecy. They built him out of their dreams, wove him out of their suffering, and breathed life into him from their own dead legends. He's a phantom that they dressed up in this ridiculous cloak so that wherever he walks among the encampment the men, women, and children will all see his costume and know that the Man of the Prophecy has returned. They will know that he is real and hope will rise in their hearts that he will lead them to some paradise where every evil ever done to them will be avenged and their suffering will have meaning."

*Mala's face pleaded with him from the depths of the pool.* "There is a temple . . . on top of that rise . . . and a tower there—or there used to be a tower. I knew about the drakoneti attacking in Pythar before it happened. I knew about the river that brought us to the Ambeth before anyone.

*I know how the key was hidden and I know . . . I know where it is, Drakis. Please, please believe me this one time.*"

Drakis felt his legs grow suddenly weak beneath him. He fell to his knees at the edge of the pool.

*Mala's face held a soft smile. Her red hair fell about her face but there was peace in her countenance that he had not seen since the Devotions had been broken.* "One way or another . . . we are all going home."

Drakis gripped the edge of the reflecting pool, his knuckles white. He threw back his head, his mouth open wide, his lungs dragging in the air to fill his chest.

The cry that erupted from his throat was from the depths of his soul. Drakis felt suddenly detached from it, observing it as the wretched sound

vomited up the pain, despair, loss, anger, and outrage that overwhelmed him. Again and again he
drew the air into his lungs and screamed his fury
at the heavens, tears streaming freely down his
face. He felt his sanity unraveling, as though he
wanted to surrender himself to the madness of his
raw emotions in his grief and find release from
rational thought, contemplation, and regret.

*Mala is dead because of that man in the reflection . . .
that pretender . . . that hideous delusion . . . that monster that I cannot stop . . .*

Two long, dark hands touched him and called
him back.

Two willowy, dark arms wrapped around his
shoulders and calmed his grief.

"Peace, Drakis," Urulani said in soothing tones.
"Peace."

"Peace? What peace?" Drakis shuddered under
her hands. "She's gone!"

"Yes, she is gone," Urulani said softly. "I saw
her go. I was there."

"I wasn't there. I *should* have been there! If I
had been there . . ." Drakis' voice trailed off then
he continued. "She's gone, Urulani. Where did
she go?"

"Home, Drakis," Urulani said. "In the end she
said she was going home. Please believe me when
I tell you that is true."

"What home?" Drakis scoffed.

"A better home," she said. "A home far away."

"The gods again," Drakis hung his head, the
bitter laugh catching in his throat. "If they do ex-

ist, then I must be their greatest amusement . . . their most tortured plaything."

"Or their greatest weapon," Urulani said. "The best blades are forged in the hottest of fires, Drakis. You know this . . . and the gods know you. I did not believe it before we walked among the fallen Citadels but I know it now."

"Don't you see? Don't you understand?" Drakis shuddered again, gritting his teeth as he fought for control. "This isn't *me*. I'm not the man everyone wants me to be—some champion of the gods who will fix everything that has gone wrong in their lives. I can't even fix what's wrong in my *own* life! And the gods are only laughing, Urulani . . . at their joke of a hero."

Urulani pulled him up by his shoulders, setting him to kneel upright. Then, leaving her steadying hand on one shoulder, she moved around him. She crouched down in front of him, taking his face in both her elegant, long hands and lifting his chin so that he looked into her dark eyes.

"Listen to me, Drakis," Urulani said, her gaze locked with his. "Whoever you believe yourself to be—this legendary Drakis is real. Maybe he isn't you. Maybe he is just a dream or an idea. Maybe he's out there right now walking the Vestasian Savanna or the Northern Steppes of Chaenandria. I don't know. All I know is that whatever and whoever the Man of the Prophecy is . . . the Drakis that all these people look to that they might be free again . . . *you* have to be him right here and right now."

Drakis shook his head, defiance in the set of his jaw.

"I believe in Drakis," Urulani said, her lips quivering slightly as she spoke. "And I believe in you, whoever you are. I believe the gods did send you . . . and in the end, Mala believed it, too."

*"One way or another . . . we are all going home."*

Drakis blinked, his eyes suddenly bright and focused. It suddenly had become so clear to him as though he had known it all along but had refused to see it.

Slowly, he got to his feet.

"So, the gods want a show, do they?" Drakis said, drawing in a ragged breath. His lips split into a strange grin. "Then by all means let us give them a performance to end all performances."

Urulani gazed up at him, her large eyes narrowing. "Drakis, what do you mean?"

"I mean to give everyone the Drakis they deserve," he replied, still grinning. "Perhaps even a good deal more. When does the War Council meet again?"

"At dusk tonight," Urulani answered, trying to look into Drakis' eyes as she stood. She could not fathom the sudden change in him.

"Is Soen still asking to see me?" Drakis continued.

"Yes," Urulani nodded, folding her arms across her chest. "In fact, Ethis has been asking me all day to arrange a meeting between you and the elf."

"Of course," Drakis nodded. "Tell Ethis that I

will meet with the Iblisi no later than noon today . . . in Xakzaz's Warehouse."

Urulani shook her head. "I'm not sure which . . ."

"It's the third warehouse on the right outside Trader's Gate," Drakis said. "Promise me you'll do it."

"I will," Urulani said, "but you have to promise me something in return."

"Do I?"

"Promise you will attend the War Council tonight."

"Why?"

"The council is tearing itself apart," Urulani said, her eyes fixed on his face. "Everything they have fought for—everything Mala fought for—will become meaningless unless you step forward and lead these people."

"To whatever end?" Drakis asked.

"To whatever end," Urulani replied.

# CHAPTER 6

## *Deliberations*

SJEI-SHURIAN, GHENETAR OMRIS OVER the Order of Vash, winced as the muffled roar of the crowd sounded overhead.

*Will these games never end?* he thought.

Fine sand drifted down into the vast space beneath the northwest end of the Great Circus. It had originally been constructed as a cistern to hold water for mock naval battles. Emperor Rhonas Suchas had ordered the Circus constructed for the purpose two hundred and thirty-seven years before in order to commemorate the destruction of the Manticorian Fleets in the Battle of the Meducean Straits. They had been used once and then the Circus was converted back to the more traditional display of gladiatorial battles and warrior races. But the old cistern remained, the fitted stones of the floor long dry and the columns rising

to arches thirty feet overhead to support the west-
ernmost end of the Circus.

Again, the muffled cheers of the crowd above
reverberated between the columns and into the
darkness that veiled the distant walls. Fine sand
sifted down from the arched ceiling above. It
drifted down between the six globes of light that
floated about the small cluster of elves as they
waited listlessly in the forgotten darkness.

*Let them cheer, the fools. They have no idea what is
coming.* Sjei, the elder elf warrior, commander of Legions, scowled at the four other elves standing with
him. Kyori-Xiuchi, the Tertiaran Master of the Occuran looked decidedly uncomfortable, constantly
mopping his elongated head. The precipitous fall
from Imperial favor of the Myrdin-dai—rivals of
the Occuran for control of the essence of magic—
had restored Kyori's status at court but it was a
question as to how long that favor might last. Liau
Nyenjei and Ch'dak Vaijan, the Ministers of
Thought and Law respectively, both had their arms
crossed tightly; the tips of their long ears were quivering noticeably. Each looked as though he would
have preferred to be anywhere but with this company. Worst of them all was Arikasi Tjen-soi, the
elven Minister of Occupation who fidgeted with his
robes constantly and could not seem to keep still.

The cheering resounded above once again,
shaking the stones and the air in this hidden cistern.

*Keep cheering,* Sjei admonished grimly in his

mind. *There may come a time when your cheers will be needed and all your fervor put to the test. There may come a time when the games you play are no longer confined to the arena and the Circus and the blood being spilled is no longer that of someone else. Then we shall ask you why you no longer cheer or are amused.*

"Where is she?" Arikasi barked through his carefully sharpened teeth. "Bad enough that we must hold our sessions outside of 'Majority House' in this gods-forsaken place but that we should have to wait for the woman at all is intolerable!"

"She'll come when she can," Kyori snapped back. "She is now the chosen daughter of the Imperial Glory. She has her duties to perform . . ."

"As do we all," Liau Nyenjei grumbled. "The Devotional alterations alone to keep this quiet have been . . ."

The muffled roar above rose in a sudden crescendo drowning out Liau's words and forcing him to stop speaking. Sjei lifted up his head, listening carefully. The noise did not die down immediately but gradually subsided. "There! She will join us shortly. Then we can more properly begin."

"I do not see why she needs to be included in this deliberation, let alone this decision," said Ch'dak Vaijan. "She was our excuse for our actions . . . not the crafter of our policy."

"She is to be included for the same reason that she was initiated into our Order," Sjei said as though it were a fact. "She is the ward of the Emperor, his chosen daughter and, as such, has become our best eyes and ears regarding the Imperial Will—and how we may not so much shape as reinterpret that will to our advantage. That has been the purpose of the Modalis down through its centuries of existence; to quietly influence the interpretation of the Emperor's utterances to our mutual profit and that of the Empire on the whole. Each of you comes from a different position in government—each of you brings your own unique talents and powers of influence to our collective. How better to accomplish our designs than to bring into our confidence the woman who now has the Emperor's eye and heart? It was most fortunate that there was an open seat on our council . . ."

The cheers overhead had not stopped and suddenly they surged once again. Each member of the Modalis looked up as the sifting dust settled around them.

"She is popular with the Fourth Estate," Liau acknowledged.

"She is dangerous," Ch'dak said quietly. "She could be difficult to control and if she decided to turn against us . . ."

The noise of the cheering escalated as a square column of light suddenly cascaded down the long stair at the far end of the cistern. A single figure in a white robe descended the stairs, the light from above casting her features in shadow. Just as quickly the light was choked off, the stairs and its figure vanishing with it. They could hear the footsteps approaching. Sjei watched as each of the members of the Modalis around him waited in silence.

The young elf woman drew into the light of their floating globes overhead. Her robe was of the finest weave, with a carefully crafted jagged hem in the "torn" fashion that she had personally made so popular among all the estates of the Empire. She let fall the hood from the back of her elongated head, revealing the carefully coifed rim of white hair around her tapered bald crown. Her face had a pinched, angular look that most elves found comely.

"Tsi-Shebin Timuran," Sjei bowed slightly, followed after a moment's hesitation by the rest of the group.

Shebin had taken the place in the Modalis Council previously held by Wejon Rei, the Fifth High Priest of the Myrdin-dai—but Wejon was no more, acknowledged by no one and his name was never spoken aloud. He had been one of the most powerful of the Modalis in his time and had even challenged the authority of the council itself until it was no longer convenient or profitable for anyone to remember him. Now Wejon Rei was dead—whether in fact or in memory it really did not matter—and Shebin, the cunning engineer of his fall, now assumed all of her rival's authority and power.

"Sjei-Shurian," Shebin smiled, her sharp teeth gleaming in the light of the globes. "The Games of Triumph are underway and my presence is commanded by order of the Emperor. What urgency requires that we meet with such haste?"

"My question precisely," Ch'dak chimed in. He had been recalled urgently from his own plans at his villa on the shores of Lake Bra'an and was resenting having to attend to business during an Imperial holiday.

"We have received troubling word regarding events on the northern frontier," Sjei responded to Shebin, ignoring Ch'dak. "The Blade of the Northern Will and the Legions of the Northern Fist . . . we have received the testament of a survivor."

"*A* survivor?" Ch'dak said, raising an arched brow above his featureless, black eyes. "You called us here in this privy for only one report?"

"It will apparently be the *only* report. Arikasi received it," Sjei said, moving the discourse over to the uncomfortable Minister of Occupation.

"There will be only one report because, so far as we can determine and according to the report itself, there was only one survivor," Arikasi said, his voice echoing along the columns and into the black distance.

"Impossible!" Liau sneered. "Two Imperial Legions and only a single warrior survived?"

"His name is Tasjak Sha-Tsaria," Arikasi said, reading from a scroll wrapped around a field baton. The head of the baton was tarnished and bent yet was still recognizable as that of a Legion commander. "He was a Cohort commander under General Ch'pakra of the Legions of the Northern

Fist. His family is of the Fourth Estate with their House rooted in Shellsea."

"Sha-Tsaria?" Kyori asked. "I believe I know that family."

"You should," Arikasi said impatiently. "That family is the master of trade all along the Benis Coast. Tasjak was one of ours—a loyal member of the Modalis ranks. A group of gnome traders found him four days ago on the outskirts of Char."

"Char?" Kyori asked. "Where in the Void is Char?"

"It's a small town on the Northmarch Folds," Arikasi explained, impatient to get on with his report. "It's more than three hundred leagues south of where the battle took place. We believe that goblins from Nordesia were responsible for bringing him that far south. His eyes had been put out and both of his legs broken but he could still speak."

"We have a treaty with Nordesia!" Ch'dak said.

"We *had* a treaty with the goblins," Arikasi corrected. "They appear to have decided to side with the revolt."

"Never mind the dirty little creatures! Where are the Legions then?" Kyori demanded.

"Gone," Arikasi replied.

"Gone? What do you mean *gone*?"

"They were slaughtered," Arikasi said. "Commander Tasjak was in the command tent directing the battle from the southern elevation looking down on a place called 'Willow Vale' which no doubt was what the locals called that depression in the sand we saw in the Battlebox. It was a classic Imperial position and initially worked predictably well against a mixed force of manticores, humans and assorted others. The battle was being executed just as we observed in the Battlebox that day and looked to be a decisive victory for the Emperor's Legions. Then, again according to Tasjak's testament, magic died."

"Died?" Kyori sputtered. "What do you mean *died*?"

"The Aether failed completely is what I mean," Arikasi grumbled. "It vanished from the Proxis and the war-mages alike all at once. It was as though it had been pulled back into the ground and had never been. It was bad enough that the spells of the war-mages could not be cast but the folds no longer functioned either. The manticorian line charged against the Imperial Legions and the Legions could not fall back quickly enough to defend themselves, nor could they use their fold markers to attack the rear lines. It was as though warfare had been thrown back to the barbarity of the ancients—and the barbarians destroyed us because of it. The manticores rolled up the valley like a tide. General Ch'pakra tried to flee with his guardian Cohort under the command of Tasjak but the goblin armies joined in from the east and cut them off. After that, it was madness."

"I can hardly believe it," Kyori sputtered. "Is it possible that these anarchist fanatics have found a way to rob us of the Aether? It's the foundation of our Empire! Without it, we're . . . we're . . ."

"Calm yourself, friend Kyori," Shebin said, resting her long, elegant hand on the arm of the old Aether mage. "They are barbarians. What do they know of Aether?"

"This is terrible," Ch'dak said, shaking his head. "With the defeat of both Legions our northern borders are vulnerable."

"We can reposition some of the southern Legions but it will take time," Sjei said but he knew that it would most likely take a few weeks. Furthermore there was the problem of the missing Legions and how that might be explained in such a way as to make this debacle sound like a victory.

"I trust not too much time," Arikasi said, reexamining the scroll. "This is the only information . . . and I mean ONLY information . . . that we have secured north of Char. Port Glorious has not reported since before the battle. Trade and communication from all along the Shadow Coast has stopped. The seaport towns of Cape Tjakar and Port Dog are reportedly deserted—their inhabitants said to have fled either to Port Melthis or northeast to join up with the revolt. North of River Town there is a great silence and it is as though a veil had fallen over that land. We know practically nothing of what is going on in the northern reaches except the rumors being spread in Port Melthis about a legendary human returning from across the sea who is gathering everyone gullible enough to follow him into some kind of holy army."

"Drakis?" Shebin asked, a chill in her voice.

Sjei winced. Shebin was a bright and cunning

woman but on occasion he would prefer that she ask him her questions in private. Sjei never started an argument whose result had not been predetermined nor asked a question to which he did not already know the answer.

"Yes," Arikasi replied, looking down with puzzlement at the scroll. "How did you know?"

# CHAPTER 7

## The Secret

"**I** AM COUNTING ON YOU, INQUISITOR," she said in a raspy voice that echoed in the long, wide chamber of her lair. "I have chosen you for this task. Do not fail the Order. Do not fail me."

"You may depend on me," answered the young Iblisi elf through a wide, needle-sharp grin as he bowed slightly, his hand to his chest.

"Then go with my blessing," the old woman replied, leaning back into her throne with a sigh. "And keep silent the truth you guard. Admit my next audience and close the doors behind you."

Ch'drei Tsi-Auruun, Keeper of the Iblisi, gave a dismissive motion with the back of her left hand. The young elf backed quickly away the required five steps before turning and striding toward the black, oiled doors at the far end of the Keeper's Hall.

Ch'drei closed her black, featureless eyes and

drew in a deep breath. Somewhere above her, she knew, there was a warm wind blowing across the Imperial Capital from the south, bringing with it great, towering clouds of moisture from the distant Aergus Sea. The heat would build them up in the afternoon into dark tempests with lightning that would never touch the Imperial Palace and rain that would never dampen its walls. Yet here, on her underground throne, Ch'drei suddenly longed for the exhilaration of the flash, the thunder, and the cascade of cleansing downpour on her face. Instead she was entombed in the darkness, buried beneath her duty that hung over her more oppressively than the black stone ceiling that was only a hand's breadth above where she sat.

Ch'drei's previous audience had barely begun to pull open the heavy doors before a female elf pushed through them. She was unusually tall for an elf and certainly tall for an Inquisitor as they were usually called for their lack of distinguishing characteristics. She had all the elements of elven beauty—elongated, elegantly tapered skull, finely pointed ears and prominent cheekbones above a pinched, narrow jaw with fine, sharp teeth and glossy black eyes. Yet despite the elegance of her individual features there was an indefinable something about the totality of them that was chilling.

"Inquisitor K'yeran Tsi-M'harul," the Keeper croaked in her scratchy, alto voice.

"Keeper Ch'drei," the Inquisitor responded as she stood before the open doors, her arms folded across her bony chest and her featureless eyes narrowed under a slightly furrowed brow.

*Is she actually waiting for me to cross the room to her?* Ch'drei thought.

"Close the door, K'yeran," Ch'drei said.

"I made it as far as Zhdras," K'yeran continued as though she had not heard the Keeper's command. "I *should* be in Port Dog—as you asked—to capture those 'Bolters' out of Char and get you the truth you said you needed. And yet here I am again."

"K'yeran," Ch'drei said with monumental control. "Close the door so we can . . ."

"I thought, 'Surely the Keeper of the Iblisi must have some special need for me,'" K'yeran continued in defiance. "I push my way back through the folds I had just traversed three days before because I was certain—absolutely certain—that my Keeper would not have asked me to toss aside the mission she had given me herself and told me was critical to the survival of the Order—unless she needed me particularly . . ."

"K'yeran, will you . . ."

"And what do I arrive to find?" the younger elven woman continued without pause. "Your outer hall is choked with my fellow Inquisitors who have all been summoned back here by you for reassignment and I'm just another face in the lowing herd waiting in line until . . ."

"Close your mouth, K'yeran!" Ch'drei snarled. "Close it now because if *I* have to close it, it will never open again."

K'yeran stopped talking at once but still made no move.

*The Inquisitors,* Ch'drei thought. *They are most useful when they are willful and independent—and at their most irritating.*

"Now, close the door and hear my council or you will *never* know why I have summoned you here and I'll find someone else for the glory which I believe is your destiny to fulfill."

K'yeran blinked.

Ch'drei waited. She knew that K'yeran would never let a secret pass by unknown and unexamined.

The younger Iblisi unfolded her arms and turned. She could, no doubt, see the faces of the other Iblisi still standing in the hallway beyond. She pushed closed the heavy doors, turned, and strode imperiously toward Ch'drei's throne.

"My apologies, Keeper Ch'drei," K'yeran said though there was still a touch of defiance in her tone. "I serve the truth, the Emperor's Will, and that of the Keeper."

"Better, K'yeran," Ch'drei responded with a cautioning undertone in her voice. "I have summoned all these Iblisi to the Keep and each one is being given an assignment which they believe is important and secret—but each of those assignments are a lie, a cover for the true mission which I have reserved for you."

"You honor me, Keeper," K'yeran bowed slightly.

"Then do not give me cause to regret the honor

I do you," Ch'drei said with an edge of contempt. "What do you know about an Inquisitor by the name of Soen?"

"History or truth, my Keeper?"

"Truth," Ch'drei affirmed.

"Soen Tjen-rei was an honored and feared Inquisitor of our Order," K'yeran responded at once. "As an Inquisitor in the field he was considered imaginative, resourceful, and dispassionate in his service to the Iblisi and the truth we protect. His methods were often unorthodox but always justified by their results. I have never worked with him in any Quorum but I did meet him once . . . nine years ago, I believe. And . . ."

The voice of the *Inquisitor* fell into silence.

"And?" Ch'drei prompted.

"It is known among the Inquisitors that he was favored by you," K'yeran responded. "I also know that he disappeared some months back as the result of an operation gone rogue. I know that you want him back."

Ch'drei closed her eyes. *Yes. Truth is spoken in this hall today. It is unfortunate that I am so constrained to lie.*

"What do you know of recent events in the Northern Provinces?"

"Is the Keeper asking for history or truth?" K'yeran asked, raising her right brow.

"In this room we never deal with history," the Keeper lied.

"Then the truth is that the Legion of the Northern Fist marched forth beyond the Northern

Steppes in pursuit of a growing army of rebels in the name of the Emperor's Will and for the reality of increased property acquisition by the Modalis," K'yeran said. "It might even have turned into most profitable war for the Modalis if something had not caused a failure of the Aether Wells all along the northern frontier at a most inopportune time. Now the northern Legions are missing— apparently permanently—and now there is no information coming from the north. That was, I believe, why you sent me there in the first place; to find out what the true conditions were in Nordesia before the Modalis could discover it."

"And you shall carry out that mission still," Ch'drei nodded, her long fingers clenching and unclenching the smooth, worn ends of the chair's armrests. "But that will be secondary to your personal mission."

"And what personal mission may I undertake for the Keeper of the Iblisi?" K'yeran asked with a slight smile.

*The best lie is leavened generously with the truth.*

"Soen Tjen-rei is known to be moving with the camp of the rebels," Ch'drei said.

"He has renounced his Order?" K'yeran said with surprise.

"No, he has not renounced," Ch'drei snapped. *Why this woman couldn't let her finish was beyond her understanding. Lies should not be interrupted in the telling.* "He has been enchanted with Ephindrian magic by the agents of their exiled queen. You need to find him . . ."

"And kill him?" K'yeran interrupted with relish.

"No!" Ch'drei leaned forward. "Killing him would be difficult enough, I assure you, but I want you to do something far more difficult."

"My Keeper?" K'yeran smiled broadly though there was no warmth in it. "How may I serve you?"

"You must bring him back to me here at the Keep *alive* and functional," Ch'drei said. "Say anything you must . . . do anything you must . . . but bring him here *personally* to me yourself."

"I am most flattered," K'yeran replied with an icy chuckle, "but from what I have heard of this Soen he will not come just because I smile at him."

"You will take one Quorum with you to assist," the Keeper said, running her tongue over her sharp teeth after she spoke. "Choose who you must but bury the truth of your quest in the lie. Only you must know of this."

"I am looking forward to it," K'yeran answered with another slight bow. "Where do you want me to start looking for this Soen?"

Ch'drei considered for a moment before speaking. *Where was it that I was to send this one? Oh, yes . . .*

"He was last seen north of Char," Ch'drei spoke.

"Char?" K'yeran laughed at the irony. "That *is* where I was going when you recalled me."

"Then you will know where to find it," Ch'drei said, her voice weary. *This will be a very long day.*

"Then I shall find this Soen for you," K'yeran

smiled once more. "And, though it goes against my better judgment, I will bring him back to you in a single piece so that you may convince him of the error of his ways."

"I am counting on you, Inquisitor," Ch'drei said softly. "I have chosen you for this task. Do not fail the Order. Do not fail me."

"I have never yet," K'yeran nodded.

"Then go with my blessing," the old woman replied, leaning back into her throne as she waved a dismissive hand at K'yeran. "And keep silent the truth you guard. Admit my next audience as you leave."

K'yeran swung open the heavy doors and stepped through, bumping shoulders with another Iblisi who seemed as much in a hurry to enter the room as K'yeran was to leave it. He snarled at her but she took no notice of him, passing in chilly serenity between the other Iblisi lining the hall beyond.

"Inquisitor Tsugai Xi-re," Ch'drei nodded in greeting as the next elven Iblisi entered the chamber.

"Keeper Ch'drei," the Inquisitor responded with a bow toward the Keeper.

*How many times must I play this scene?* Ch'drei thought.

"Close the door, Tsugai," Ch'drei said.

The elven Inquisitor turned, pushing the massive doors closed and then turned back to face the Keeper. "I serve the truth, the Emperor's Will and that of the Keeper."

"As do we all," Ch'drei said wearily. "You have noticed your fellow Iblisi gathered with you to the Keep?"

"I have, Ch'drei," Tsugai answered as he strode across the hall toward the throne, his boots echoing loudly against the stone floor. "It seems all the Empire is bereft of Inquisitors today by your will."

"I have summoned all these Iblisi as I summoned you. Each one is being given an assignment which they believe is important and secret—but each of those assignments are a lie, a cover for the true mission which I have reserved for you."

"My Keeper, I am flattered," Tsugai said, baring his sharp teeth.

Ch'drei thought of the rain as she spoke. "What do you know about an Inquisitor by the name of Soen?"

Ch'drei descended the ancient stairs alone. The corridors she traversed were unmarked and shifted through a maze of deception. Some of the more surface levels of the labyrinth utilized Aether-driven illusions to prevent anyone from gaining access but from the beginning this deepest region beneath the Old Keep had been designed to survive the end of Aether and the very fall of magic itself. Those who had hewn it out of the bedrock beneath the Old Keep were now centuries dead. Even in their day, no single group knew how they had arrived at the section that they were tasked to construct and their Devotions were such that they had no memory of doing so. In the end, only one person—the Keeper of the Iblisi—even knew of its existence or how to arrive at the final chamber of its twisting passageways and occasionally deadly turns.

It was the most secure place in all the Rhonas Imperium. It was known only to the Keeper and three other Iblisi. Those others were scattered across the Empire and had no memory of the place and would not unless the unthinkable happened.

Ch'drei turned the final corner. There she was confronted by three walls covered with intricate and ornate carvings. Death was imbedded in all three walls but in the right-hand wall there were a series of catches. She pressed them in sequence and the stone carving slid away with a deep grinding sound, its ancient mechanism groaning under the centuries.

Ch'drei entered the enormous chamber beyond, the glowing globe of light hovering above her upheld hand.

The illumination revealed a mountainous treasure piled in the center of a vaulted room nearly thirty feet tall. The light from the globe glinted off the facets of gems and the polished surfaces of gold and silver crowns, bracers, swords, and scepters. A cascade of Imperial coins, enough to buy entire provinces, lay here at the center of the labyrinth.

Ch'drei smiled and shook her head. This, too,

was part of her defenses. The treasure was real
and would distract anyone who managed somehow to access this place from the thing which it
was intended to guard.

Around the treasure room were several alcoves.
In the fourth alcove around the right side, Ch'drei
found the compartment and pried it open. Beyond
was a three-foot-square hole in the wall.

Within lay three scrolls.

Ch'drei selected one particular scroll from
among them and held it in her hands. It was comforting to her to touch it, to know that it was here
and safe from the eyes of the world so far above
her.

She thought of the rain.

She thought of Soen.

"This is the one truth you don't know, Soen,"
she murmured to the scroll. "This is the one truth
no one may ever know."

She placed it back in its secure place, closed it
up behind the stone and, leaving the treasure untouched, retraced her steps.

And she thought again of the rain.

# CHAPTER 8

## *Obligations*

IT HAD BEEN A SMALL WAREHOUSE attached to a goblin shop just inside the walls of Port Glorious. What few items that remained in the warehouse had been liberated earlier in the day. The original owner—a goblin by the name of Xakzaz according to a few abandoned parchment receipts—had done a thorough job considering the apparent haste of his departure a few days before the Army of the Prophet had arrived. Now that the army had finished ransacking the building, all that remained was the empty shell of the structure.

Drakis stepped into the large, open space, peering into the deep shadows of the room and wondering if the goblin would appreciate his building being restored to him cleaner than he had left it. The goblins had been instrumental in getting word to the townspeople in advance of his army's arrival and to his relief the town was emptied of everyone except the occupying elven garrison before the assault had begun. Word had reached him that the town's citizens were already turning around from their flight and returning to the port to take up, once again, the only lives they knew.

Drakis sighed. Life is so often a matter of momentum, he reflected. Would he have felt more justified in this sacking of the town by his army if the motives for doing so were more pure? The people who made their homes in Port Glorious knew better. The Army of the Prophet could tell themselves that they were liberators, freeing the town from the oppression of the elves but the truth was that they needed the food and supplies the port trafficked in and so they had come and taken it. The people who called Port Glorious home knew enough to stay out of the way between two armies and were now returning, substituting a new set of masters for the previous set of masters. They did not feel liberated so much as cautious about whether the change would help them or hurt them.

*We are the masters of sky and light*
*We are the doom of the night*
*Dawn we are seeking*
*Dawn and awakening . . .*

Drakis shook his head. The song of his dragon Marush often intruded on his thoughts at the most inopportune times and at such times made sense only after he could touch the dragon and know what Marush actually meant. It sounded like a triumph song but Drakis felt far from victorious. It was why he had come: to face down the Beast that had pursued him.

Hearing someone enter the warehouse, Drakis pivoted around.

"Ethis?" Drakis called. "Have you come alone?"

Ethis held out both sets of his arms, his palms forward. "Drakis, there is someone who needs to speak with you."

Ethis moved to the side, revealing an elf.

The elf Inquisitor stood not ten feet from Drakis, his Matei staff held casually across his body in both hands.

Drakis slowly drew his sword from its sheath. "I've had a lot of practice with this blade."

The elf remained still, blinking his lids over his dull, featureless black eyes. The elf tilted his elongated head, nodding toward the sword in Drakis' hand before he spoke. "Do you really think that would have made a difference?"

Drakis glanced at the sword then fixed his eyes again on the Iblisi elf.

"If I had any wish to harm you, Drakis of House Timuran, you would not be hearing my words now," the elf said softly. "You would either be dead or halfway back to the Empire."

"Tell me your name," Drakis said, his throat dry.

"I'm sure you already know." The elf drew back his thin lips into a sharp-toothed smile.

"I want to hear it from you," Drakis demanded, his sword still raised.

"Proper introductions? I am touched." The elf bowed slightly. "Then may I proceed. I am Soen Tjen-rei, Inquisitor of the Order of the Iblisi—or, more accurately, *former* Inquisitor of the Order of the Iblisi—and the elf who had been hunting you since the day you bolted from House Timuran. You've proven a most resourceful prey, Drakis."

"Somehow this is not helping me to feel any better about meeting you," Drakis said far more casually than he felt.

"But meeting you is precisely what I have been trying to do since you arrived," the elf continued. "When I first heard of you just after the fall of House Timuran, my obligation was to my Order: it was my duty to find you, learn the truth, and then kill you on the spot."

"Again," Drakis said. "Not feeling any better about this."

"But then my obligation changed," Soen went on. "My own Order determined that *you* were a truth that had to be hidden. Since I knew about you, my old, dear friend the Keeper of our Order determined that both of us needed to be 'hidden' well ... preferably deep in an unmarked grave far from any possible discovery. So my obligation became to the truth of myself; I was still looking for you, but now as a means of proving that I was still loyal to my Order. The only way I could do that was to capture you and bring you back in chains to our Old Keep in the Imperial City."

"This is why elves are not known for their diplomacy skills," Drakis said. The conversation was absurd. "Why are you telling me this?"

"Because since I came looking for you, I've come to learn a new truth," Soen said simply.

"Please do *not* tell me that you've become a *believer* in me," Drakis scoffed.

"No, not at all."

Drakis blinked, the tip of his sword dropping slightly. "What then?"

"I don't think you are the Drakis of the Prophecy," Soen said, shifting his Matei staff from the right to the left. "I don't believe this prophecy has any power at all. From what I have learned along the way, *you* don't believe it either."

"Then why bother with me?"

"Because, as I think you already know, it doesn't matter what you or I think," Soen shrugged casually. "What matters is what that *army* outside this warehouse thinks. What matters is what all the pilgrims in Willow Vale think, as well as the thousands that even now are swelling their ranks each day. What matters is what the Keeper of the Iblisi thinks and, for that matter, what the Emperor and his Legions think. Most importantly, what matters is what Nordesia, Ephindria, Chaenandria and Aeria think."

"Aeria?" Drakis shook his head. "The dwarves are gone—utterly destroyed. I was there."

"Driven from their strongholds? Certainly," Soen nodded. "But I believe they are still there, deep within the mountain, waiting . . . waiting for someone or something to unite them."

"And you think that the dwarves will rise up again and the entire Rhonas Empire will collapse," Drakis' eyes remained fixed on the elf, "because of some bedtime story?"

Soen bowed slightly as he nodded. "The highest ranking among the Iblisi know that the prophecy will be fulfilled. The Rhonas Empire *will* fall."

"Why?" Drakis shrugged. "You just said you didn't believe in the prophecy!"

"I don't believe the prophecy has any power of its own," Soen corrected. "But I *do* believe that the more people who want the prophecy to be true, the greater the power they give it. The prophecy is nothing but if enough people believe it is true, then they will *make* it true. And *that* is where my obligation now lies . . . to the truth that all these people's beliefs are forging into reality."

"That makes you a believer," Ethis chuckled.

Soen shook his head. "Let's just say that I believe in the power of belief. I remain loyal to my race, my people, my nation. If my nation is to fall, then I want to ensure that as few of its citizens are harmed as possible and that as much of what is good in the Empire—and there *is* good in the Empire—is saved from the chaos of the Empire's fall."

"So, you were first obligated to kill me, then you felt obligated to imprison me." Drakis continued to stare at the elf. "So what do you feel is your obligation now?"

"The one constant obligation in all of this has been to the truth," Soen answered. "But I know that war is coming—real war with all the horror and violence that entails. My obligation is to my people."

Drakis lowered his sword. "As is mine."

"As is mine," Ethis added.

"You wanted to speak to me," Drakis said, sheathing his sword once more. "I am listening. What have you to say?"

"Come, look," Soen said. He began moving his Matei staff, swinging the tip across the firmly packed dirt of the warehouse floor. The metal tip of the staff dug into the packed earth, inscribing lines in the dirt that quickly took the form of a great map at their feet. Complex coastlines emerged, rivers, and even symbols where mountain ranges were located.

Drakis and Ethis stepped closer, stopping just beyond the edge of the shorelines.

"Here is Rhonas," Soen said, pointing at a region on the map farthest from him with the tip of his staff, then shifting to regions closer to where he stood. "Here Chaenandria, the Mountains of Aeria, and the Plains of Vestasia. Over here to the east are the lands of Ephindria and up here is Nordesia and our little Mistral Peninsula. Willow Vale is here. For the time being, we are vulnerable— easily contained with our backs to the Straits of Erebus, short on supplies, and with nowhere to retreat."

"But the elven Legions were destroyed," Drakis said as he gazed at the map.

"The Legion of the Northern Fist, yes," Soen

acknowledged, "but there are many, MANY more Legions available to enact the Imperial Will and I can assure you that they are moving in our direction with every breath we draw. More importantly, they will come with Aether—pouring their magic into the northern frontier with enough strength to overcome this reversal of the Aether you caused in Drakosia. If you remain and wait for the Legions to come to you, you will lose your advantage."

"You're saying we must move," Drakis nodded. "That we have to strike while we can."

"Yes," Ethis agreed. "But where?"

"The Legions will almost certainly move toward us along the Northmarch Folds," Soen said, leaning on his Matei staff as he considered. "Part of their force they will deploy to guard the Shrouded Plain since they know that your army escaped them once there and will want to guard against your reemergence from that place again. Then they will send out scouting parties to the south, east, and west to cover the rest of the frontier while the main force continues to the north. Once their scouts and their spies locate your main force and the pilgrim encampment they will know where to attack."

"But they will keep marching north, won't they?" Ethis asked. "If they don't find the army they'll assume that we just haven't moved yet and keep coming north."

Soen nodded. "Yes. And with the speed of their advance through the folds, they could be deployed in Char before we even managed to reach the Shadow Coast. Then we would have the Bay of Thetis on our right with Ephindria and the Shrouded Plain on our left. That is why we have to move the army and the encampment as soon as possible toward Vestasia. We have to beat the Legions to the Shadow Coast. Perhaps then we can come through Vestasia around the western end of Aeria—Queen Murialis permitting. From there we could use the army against the Western Provinces, reversing the Wells there and progressively weakening the Rhonas hold on Aether from the west."

"That would be a long campaign," Drakis said. "And once the Legions knew where we had gone they would just shift to the west to intercept us."

"Yes, which is why you need to call for allies," Soen stated. "You must send out emissaries—in your name and in the name of the prophecy—to rally them now while you still can claim victory against the Legions."

"How?" Drakis asked. "There's no time . . ."

"You have just enough time," Soen smiled, his sharp teeth gleaming. "And you have the means that will not only bring your emissaries swiftly to the courts of all the subjugated nations of the north but in a manner that will ensure that they will be suitably impressed."

"What do you mean?" Drakis asked.

"Dragons," Soen said simply. "Send them on your dragons."

Ethis stepped from the warehouse door into the evening. He was already late for the council meeting but his thoughts were elsewhere.

Soen might be obligated to the truth and to his race, Drakis clung to his obligation to the pilgrims and army that followed him, but Ethis had his own obligations that he shared with no one.

Soen's analysis was excellent and his advice good but Ethis had formulated a plan of his own as he gazed at the map—one that could spectacularly serve his own duty to his Queen and crumble the foundations of the Empire in a single stroke.

All he had to do was convince his Queen to permit the impermissible.

And keep Soen from finding out about it.

Drakis stood once more at the edge of the subatria garden. The stars now appeared overhead but it was the faint blue light of the Aether Well that gave the space its dim, ghostly glow.

Drakis tried to hear Mala's voice, wishing for her council or some guidance but he was answered only by silence. If her spirit had been here it seemed to him now to have left and gone far away.

He was alone.

The entire world had robbed him. The elven Empire had robbed him of his dignity, his family, and his past. The faithful pilgrims had robbed him, too, of his freedom, his private hopes, and his future. The prophecy had even robbed him of his identity and remade him into a legend. Together they all had a hand in robbing him of Mala.

Yet standing here in the broken subatria, Drakis knew there was one thing the great, nebulous They had not taken from him in all their conspiracies of fate.

He owned his own soul.

It raged within him, screaming at the world that had so cruelly abused him. He held fast to his pain and his outrage. It burned with purifying fire and clarifying light.

And he believed that if he must endure it, then everyone else must endure it with him.

*"Drakis, do you know who you are?"*

The memory drifted up into his conscious mind unbidden from the place deep within him where it had lain dormant, buried beneath the House Devotions that had enslaved him seemingly a lifetime ago.

*He looked up at her with large, tear-filled eyes. He was a boy, hurt and fragile. His mother—his true mother—knelt in front of him.*

*"It does not matter what they tell you, what they force you to believe."* *She held him firmly by both shoulders, her eyes locked with his own in earnest instruction. "They can take everything from you but yourself."*

*She laid her hand on his heart.*

*"Do you know who you are, my Drakis dear . . . here inside where they cannot touch you?"*

Drakis caught his breath.

The memory faded behind his thoughts.

He realized that he did not know himself at all.

All his life, others had told him who he was supposed to be, which he suddenly realized was an entirely different thing. During the long nightmare of his Aether-enslaving Devotions to the Empire, it had been his elven masters who had told him and molded him into who they wanted him to be; an Impress Warrior fighting their battles for causes that were not his own. He had no coherent childhood that he could recall—even the memory of his parents and family were a confusion of different people at different times. Then the dwarf had broken the bonds of his Devotions and he knew his past was a fraud, an invention created to keep him docile and compliant to the will of his elven masters. Yet even when he was free, his identity lay with others—with the dwarf filling his mind with words of the ancient prophecy and with Belag, who so desperately wanted to find meaning in his brother's death that he clung to his faith in Drakis as though he had been personally sent by the gods to save him. Their journey into the ancient lands of humanity he had intended as proof against his identity as the Man of Prophecy but it had ended in tragedy and with him even more firmly hailed as the fulfiller of prophecy than before. Now the Council of the Prophet and their followers all wanted him to be someone he was not.

But, he realized, he himself did not know who he was beyond his desperate desire to be anyone other than the one man everyone else wanted him to be.

*"Do you know who you are, my Drakis dear . . . here inside where they cannot touch you?"*

He closed his eyes for a moment and drew in a deep breath, then he turned his back on the subatria and strode out through the broken gates into the plaza beyond.

He turned up the side street before the astonished manticores in the plaza had time to react. Ahead of him, the warriors of his army could see him coming and pressed themselves against both sides of the shattered, narrow street to make way for him. He passed them without a word, his strides finding their own military tempo as he walked briskly between the warriors. Without thought on their part, they fell into step behind him, excited to be following in his wake.

The street opened onto the western end of the former Bazaar. A large congregation of warriors—manticores, chimerians, and humans—stood milling about the wide steps leading up to the closed doors of the temple. They were all listening to the loud proceedings of the War Council within. One glance at their faces confirmed for Drakis that there was doubt and concern among them. At the sight of him, however, the crowd parted, closing ranks behind him as he dashed two steps at a time up the stairs.

He gripped the handles of the double doors. He could hear the dwarf's voice bellowing over a cascade of other voices in heated argument.

"To whatever end," Drakis muttered to himself.

He pulled backward on the handles and the

enormous doors to the temple swung wide as he strode into the hall.

A great cheer arose from within and was echoed quickly across the plaza, through the streets of Port Glorious and throughout the encamped army beyond its walls.

Drakis, the Man of the Prophecy, had arrived.

# CHAPTER 9

## The Quest

DRAKIS TURNED AROUND SLOWLY, taking in the spectacle and feeling more foolish by the moment. In every direction, the Army of the Prophet carpeted the landscape around the hilltop they had come to know as Dragon's Roost.

Drakis knew that the name was something at which the dragons themselves snickered once their riders had confided it to them. Dragons, as Marush had informed him, preferred mighty aeries either high among the sheer slopes of the God's Wall ranges in the north or within cliff-face caverns by the edges of river gorges or overlooking the sea. The rolling hills that undulated upward from Mistral Bay to look over Port Glorious could hardly compare to the sharp peaks of Drakosia. Adding to the humor of the great drakes was the idea that dragons would "roost" at all, as though they were some kind of domesticated fowl. A rather unfortunate cultural collision might have taken place had Marush not confided the problem to Drakis, who helped the great dragon see the humor in the strange ways of the manticores—who had no understanding of flight and were terrified of the dragons for the most part. Marush then helped the other dragons to understand the humor in the naiveté of these lion-men who were so fierce in battle and yet so uncertain before dragonkind.

Now, however, the entire army had assembled around the crest of the hill—if at a respectful distance. Marush lay on his stomach near the grass-covered crest, his wings folded down against his body. Ephranos, the white-and-gray dragon, lay in a similar position beside him. The Lyric stood to the side of Ephranos' head, idly scratching the dragon's skin just behind the turn of its jaw. Both of Ephranos' eyes were partially closed in bliss at her attentions—neither the Lyric nor her dragon entirely present for the proceedings.

The three other dragons stood opposite their counterparts. Wanrah, the black-and-rust-colored dragon of Ethis waited expectantly, her wings shifting in nervous anticipation. Pyrash, the cerulean-blue dragon with violet markings craned and stretched his neck, clearly bored with the proceedings and anxious to get into the air with or without Jugar. Kyranish, the gray-blue dragon of Urulani remained still except for her tail, which flicked anxiously back and forth.

Encircled by these dragons on the hilltop, members of the War Council stood to one side. Among the manticores, Belag alone remained serene while the ears of his generals Hegral and Gradek lay flat back against their manes, an obvious sign of nervousness on the part of these lion-men. Doroganda, the female goblin, had taken a part in the War Council partly on the insistence of the Pajak of Krishu that someone with the sensibilities of a true warrior race should be along to advise the humans along with their "cats" and "bendies" on how to properly conduct a raid. Doroganda had been perfectly happy in her role as combat critic until the dragons arrived. Now she stood unusually silent on the hilltop, her sharp tongue silenced and the tips of her long ears quivering. Among them, only Braun stood with a placid expression, cheerfully oblivious to the monstrous, winged creatures that surrounded him.

Soen, the Inquisitor of the Iblisi, had claimed a spot directly in front of the three manticores. He cradled his Matei staff in the crook of his arm. The thing was currently useless; it was completely discharged. The local Aether Well, having been "reversed" as Braun called it, was now useless in terms of recharging his staff. Not that it would have made any difference to Belag; the manticore seemed to be unfazed by the presence of a notoriously cunning member of the Iblisi elite. To the remaining manticores, however, it seemed to matter a great deal as they could not seem to decide which concerned them more—being surrounded by five dragons or having to stand within reach of the elf Inquisitor.

Drakis' crimson cape flapped annoyingly in the hilltop breeze. At last, he came to face his newly appointed Emissaries—one to the dwarves, one to the Forgotten humans of the Shadow Coast and, lastly, one to the Council in Exile of Ephindria. Jugar, the dwarf jester, stood before Pyrash, tugging at his brown leather coat even though it fit him perfectly well. Urulani looked striking in the long leather coat of her dragon-rider uniform, her arms crossed, with her gloves and a specially made helmet clutched in one of her hands. Ethis had refused the uniform, however, claiming that the cold of the higher air did not affect him the same way it did the others.

Drakis drew in a breath to speak but thunderous dragon song rang through his mind.

*Far from this place is a world apart*
*Far from the sounds of the heart*
*Thoughts there are sharing*
*Silent words telling . . .*

Drakis paused, then spoke quietly as he deliberately drew off his gloves. "My friends, before you depart, perhaps one last communion."

Drakis reached out, touching the snout of Marush.

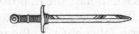

"What are they doing?" Soen asked, his black eyes blinking.

Each of the dragon emissaries had followed

Drakis' example, touching the snout of their dragon and bowing their chins to their chests.

"It looks as though they are offering a prayer to their gods," Hegral suggested.

"How odd," Soen said, his eyes narrowing.

For Drakis, the hilltop and its surrounding army vanished, replaced by a lush, verdant forest glade. The smell of flowers drifted over him on a warm breeze. He once again felt the peace that being in touch with the dragon gave him—and the strange, otherworld into which the experience always thrust him. This was a place where the dragon song became words of meaning and understanding— but it was more than just communion. It was a place removed where the everyday world could not intrude.

More important still, Drakis knew that what was shared in this special place remained outside the world.

Around him he saw the dragons in much the same poses as they had been before. Marush and Ephranos still rested side by side but now in the more verdant grass of this "other" place. The Lyric stood next to Ephranos scratching behind the dragon's jaw but her eyes were bright and focused on Drakis. It was a startling transformation that she exhibited each time they came together in this place. Drakis still found it unnerving: sudden sanity in a woman who he knew otherwise to be insane.

Wanrah, Pyrash, and Kyranish appeared on the other side of the glade. Urulani and Ethis appeared as well as each placed their palms against their dragons in the real world left behind.

"Where is Jugar?" Drakis asked.

Urulani opened her mouth to reply but as she did the dwarf appeared tentatively touching the scales of Pyrash's foreleg.

"Well, this is an unexpected gathering, Lord Drakis," Jugar said with thinly masked impatience.

"Some things need to be said that should remain between us alone," Drakis asserted. "I would have told you earlier but this is the first opportunity—or perhaps the last—that we'll have to speak privately."

"We're standing in the middle of your army," Jugar chuckled.

"In a place where they cannot hear our words or see what we do," Drakis affirmed. "To them, we look as though we're standing quietly beside our dragons. It won't be long before that will start to seem suspicious—so let me explain quickly."

"What is there to say that you did not say to the council last night?" Jugar asked. "Your speech inspired every member present to action and your words have spread throughout the army. They are prepared to follow you now against the Empire just as you asked them to do yesterday."

"It is what I have asked," Drakis said, "but it is not what I want."

"I do not understand your meaning," Ethis said with a tilt of his head.

"What he means," the Lyric said in her clear, high voice, "is that he has told them what they want to hear—but not what he wants for them. Just as he has given you a quest which they want to happen—but not one he wants you to perform."

"The Lyric is not making sense," Jugar shook his head.

"Here, Aer Master Jugar, you may refer to me as Karan," the Lyric replied. "And, on the contrary, I am making perfect sense."

"She's right," Drakis affirmed.

"Wait a moment," Urulani spoke up, her voice resonant in the quiet of the glade. "Our quest was to ride these dragons to the far edges of the Northern Provinces and rally support for our army against the Empire."

"Yes, that's what I told them," Drakis said in a husky voice.

"And now you're going to tell us that's *not* what you want us to do?" Urulani continued, her dark eyes narrowing as she looked at him, her voice rising in anger.

"I have something . . . something *more* in mind," Drakis said.

"Indeed?" Ethis asked, "What *more* would you have us do?"

"The Iblisi elf Soen believes we need to move the encampment and the army into Vestasia because it is the best place from which to launch an attack against the Empire," Drakis replied. "The War

Council believes him and it is important for the time being that they still believe that to be our goal. You will fly out as planned. Urulani, you will fly along the Shadow Coast and the ports there as far west as the Forgotten Humans of your Clans, if possible. Ethis, you will go to your homeland of Ephindria to try to make contact with the courts in exile there. Jugar, you will fly the farthest; to the Aerian Mountains to see if any remnant of the dwarven kingdoms remain under the mountain . . ."

"That's no change at all. So far your quest is the same charge as we were given by the council," Jugar shrugged.

"But I do not want you to ask for aid against the Empire," Drakis asserted.

"What?" Jugar sputtered.

"We are not going to attack the Empire," Drakis said flatly.

The dwarf glared at the human in disbelief. "Drakis, I know you have been feeling out of sorts this past month or so—it has been a difficult time for us all—but this is your destiny! You are fated to be the downfall of the dread elves of Rhonas!"

Drakis shook his head. "No."

"No?" Jugar gaped.

"I will not have one more person die in my name or for this insane prophecy," Drakis said firmly. "We're going to lead the pilgrims to a place where they can make a home . . . a place where they can settle in peace."

"Drakis, I don't see how that is possible," Urulani said though not without compassion. "Where could they go that the Empire would not hunt them as they have always done? Where could they settle beyond the reach of the Rhonas Legions?"

"To Drakosia," Drakis said, looking Urulani in the eyes as he spoke. "Across the Straits of Erebus."

"You think the sea will protect them?" Ethis shook his head. "It did not stop the elven Empire from destroying Drakosia once before."

"Drakosia fell because one dragon betrayed humanity and his own kind," Drakis answered. "We could go back . . . start again . . ."

"How?" Urulani demanded. "How do we cross the sea with the entire encampment? It would take nearly two thousand ships to carry them all!"

"Then we make as many crossings as required with whatever ships we have," Drakis responded, the volume of his own voice increasing. This was taking too long. "Your task will be to gather as many ships to our cause as you can from the ports along the Shadow Coast. Tell them that Drakis and his army are coming and need their ships for transport. Find out from the ship captains where a suitable anchorage could be found as far north up the shoreline as possible and have them all sail there to meet us. Then return and let us know where we are to meet this fleet of transport ships. The farther north the better, preferably on the east coast of Gorganta Bay. Then we'll sail around Nordesia past Cape Caldron just as we did before and north into Drakosia. Once there, we'll be beyond the reach of the elves."

"They will have heard of you in the port cities,"

Urulani argued. "They will think you are raising a fleet of ships to sail your army against the Empire!"

"They may think what they want," Drakis shouted. "Soen believes we are moving the army and the pilgrims into Vestasia to fight the Empire on their western frontier. Let him think that, too, as well as whoever he serves."

"This is insane!" Jugar seethed.

"The Rhonas will not leave us to be free," Ethis stated, his expressionless face shaking back and forth for emphasis. "It does not matter where you lead them, Drakis; so long as the Empire exists they cannot let us live."

"I will lead these people, but not into war," Drakis asserted in tones that defied contradiction. "These people don't need a cause or a crusade. They are already full enough of that. What they need is a home where they can forget all about me, revenge, and this prophecy. If we can do that, then perhaps we will have saved lives, and everything that we've done—that we've lost and sacrificed—will have meant something after all."

"These pilgrims are hungry for war." Ethis said. "And you mean to avoid it?"

"You may have no choice," Jugar interjected with vehemence. "The Legions are on the march as we speak."

"Which is precisely why you must hurry," Drakis asserted. "We have to move the pilgrims out of the path of the Rhonas Legions while we still can. The Lyric will fly to Willow Vale and convey to the council my order to get everyone there ready to move. I will return to Willow Vale with the army. But the day I arrive with the army, the encampment must be ready to depart. We will have little time to reach the sea before all of us are trapped in the Nordesian Peninsula."

"And just how long do you believe we have to accomplish this madness?" Jugar asked incredulously.

"No more than ten days, I believe," Ethis replied. "It will take that long even with a forced march to move the army back to Willow Vale from here. Besides, I doubt that the council could organize the encampment to move in that amount of time even were they to begin at once. And even if the encampment is ready to move by then, it may be too late to avoid the Rhonas advance."

"How long do you think before the Legions are here?" Drakis asked.

"Fourteen days for them to get as far north as Char," Ethis shrugged all four of his shoulders. "Depending on how quickly they can react to this defeat and where their other Legions are located. That's my best guess."

"Which gives us only four days to move the entire encampment past them into Vestasia?" Drakis shook his head. "That's over three hundred leagues from here. It's not possible."

"Wait." Urulani held up her free hand. "There may be a way we can shorten the distance for ourselves. Braun has discovered how to open folds."

"Belag said the Proxi saved the encampment from the Shrouded Plain by using Soen's staff as a source of Aether," Drakis shrugged, "but now it's useless."

"Braun has opened a fold without a staff," Urulani said as she turned toward the dwarf. "Hasn't he, Jugar?"

Everyone looked at the dwarf, whose left cheek was twitching.

"Is this true, Jugar?" Drakis asked.

"Well, after a manner of speaking," Jugar sputtered. "It is a completely untested effect of the ancient human magic and, if you are asking my professional opinion, it is dangerously unsafe as a means of transportation."

"He managed to send you from one side of Port Glorious to the other," Urulani chuckled. "He placed you squarely on the platform as I recall."

"Three hand widths above it, he did!" the dwarf bellowed. "And upside down, by the way, which I believe was entirely deliberate on his part!"

"Then I would say the fold was reliable, indeed," Ethis replied. "If Braun can train others in this ability, it would be a tremendous advantage. If enough pilgrims could be taught this ability quickly, then we might make the coast ahead of the Legions."

"I'll deal with Braun," Drakis said, though there was a dark edge to his voice as he spoke. "But for now, none of us should mention this beyond our group and Braun, of course—not even to the council."

"Why?" Urulani demanded. "Do you not trust them?"

"Let us just say that trust is earned," Drakis replied, "and that there is more advantage in a secret kept between friends than revealed between enemies. Tell no one what we've discussed here today."

"We are *secretly* going to move an entire nation?" Ethis nodded. "I rather like that idea."

"Yes but all of this depends upon the speed of the Rhonas advance. Look for them in your flight," Drakis said. "Report their movements when you return should you see them. Return to the Vale before ten days pass and then we'll know where to lead these people out of the way of war."

"So, you believe you can avoid the prophecy?" Jugar grumbled as he asked the question. "Just sidestep destiny?"

"For the sake of every pilgrim out there on the plain, I hope so with all my heart," Drakis said. "I don't want to fulfill this prophecy, I want to find something *better* for these people, and for all of us, too."

"It's a fine enough dream," Jugar pressed his point. "But you have no real idea how all of this is going to work!"

"Then help me find a way to make it work," Drakis answered. "Help me find a better fate for all of us."

"What do the dragons think of all this?" Ethis asked. "They have been particularly silent during our discussions. What of you, Marush? What do you and your kind think of Drakis' desire to thwart the prophecy?"

A great chuckle rose from the dragon. "Drakis is whom we have vowed to serve. He is the Man of Destiny and the Man of Prophecy—but we know that he is also a man. Humankind have always been mercurial, their ears not attuned to the whisperings of the gods and their eyes dim to the visions of prophecy. It is the great gift to men that they may choose their course through life. Their willful acts may change the path of a stream but the waters will come to the sea by one course or another. Drakis may choose his own path and perhaps he may find a better destiny than the prophecy foretells. It does not make him less chosen nor cause us to question the destiny before him. We serve him and humanity as we have vowed to do."

"Well, if I may choose, then I choose life," Drakis said. "I choose to save these pilgrims from themselves if necessary. Help me bring us to a place where we can all live in peace."

"Then let us be off," Jugar affirmed. "If I'm to ride this beastie so far, I'd just as soon do it sooner than later."

Each of them pulled their palms away from their dragons and the otherworld vanished. Once more they stood atop the windswept hill north of Port Glorious. With a smile, the Lyric leaped up onto the neck of Ephranos who vaulted into the sky, causing the army to cheer wildly as she flew westward. Jugar mounted Pyrash almost at once, feeling somewhat upstaged by the Lyric. Pyrash's magnificent wings extended and pulled him upward toward the southern sky as the roar of the army increased. Ethis swung up onto Wanrah's neck and launched over the heads of the cheering army, wheeling toward the southeast.

Urulani tarried. She turned from Kyranish and instead strode directly over to Drakis. She took his head in both her hands, holding his gaze with her own large, dark eyes. There was sadness in them as she spoke.

"To whatever end, Urulani?" he asked.

"To whatever end, Drakis," she answered, her voice husky as she spoke.

Then she turned, climbing the dragon's neck. Urulani pulled on her gloves, Kyranish took two quick strides, and they were off.

Five dragon-riders took to the sky that day. The Lyric flew to the west to prepare the pilgrims to move once more. Drakis rose above the army, leading them down the coast to return to their families as warriors laden down with the spoils of their victory.

The remaining three riders flew off on their missions. All three of them were charged with keeping their goals secret. Only one of them had any intention of keeping that promise.

# CHAPTER 10

## Initiatives

URULANI PEERED DOWN through the low clouds drifting eastward off the Bay of Thetis. She could just make out the coastline far below from her view over the base of the dragon's wing. It was difficult for her to see through the slits in her new helmet's faceplate, let alone from such a height.

She turned her head away from the wind rushing at her over the dragon's head, which bobbed up and down at the end of its long neck with every stroke of its enormous wings. The whistling of the air suddenly increased in her ears and once again she silently cursed the fact that there had been no time to try out the strange new headpiece she now wore before continuing on the journey they had briefly interrupted by stopping at Willow Vale. She supposed she should be grateful to have even this much protection.

When their flight from Port Glorious had almost immediately given the dark-skinned raider captain stinging, reddened eyes, Kyranish had suggested the stop at Willow Vale to have a flying helmet made by modifying a warrior's helmet. Knowing she'd be hard-pressed to complete her mission if she didn't find some way of shielding her face and eyes, Urulani had agreed. They landed at Willow Vale and she followed the dragon's instructions, finding an armor smith among the Khadush Clan of manticores and having him fashion the armored headgear as per Kyranish's description and her own recollection of some similar helmets she had seen among the carvings in the ruins of Drakosia.

The gnome leather artisans, not to be outdone in their service to the Mistress of Air, declared they would make her a saddle for her dragon so that her flight would be more comfortable. Kyranish endured their enthusiastic fitting process without succumbing to the growing desire to breath fire on them and end his humiliation.

While the smithies were beating metal and the gnomes were crafting the saddle into these strange new shapes, Urulani had managed to see the Lyric who, it seemed, had declared herself to be Drakis' mother—a woman she claimed was called Jerusha—and had set the entire camp into a frenzy of preparations for their great migration following the flag of Drakis despite Tsojai Acheran's efforts to keep the camp calm and organized. Urulani almost sympathized with the elf's frustration as the temporarily designated head of the Council of the Prophet but decided it would be Drakis' problem once he arrived.

She had her own set of problems.

Now, rushing through the chill air above the Shadow Coast, she wondered just how she might accomplish her portion of the quest in time. The War Council had publicly charged her as Mistress of Air to spread the word of Drakis and to call all who desired their freedom to support Drakis and his people in their cause against the Rhonas Empire. But then Drakis had told each of the riders in their communion of dragons' minds that he wanted them to avoid open war and find a means by which the Army of Drakis and their families could live in peace and avoid the Legions of the Emperor.

The more she thought about it, the more the former objective was needed in order to ensure the latter. She was most familiar with the lands in which she grew up—the region north of the Sentinel Peaks beyond Tempest Bay. It was remote enough that the Empire had not bothered them there for many long years until Drakis came. But Nothree was far down the Vestasian Coast and her charge had been to secure the cooperation of as many ships as possible from each of the port towns down the Shadow Coast. The most likely place to board those ships for the Drakis Pilgrims would be Watchman Cove on the northernmost shores of Gorganta Bay. It was actually a good deal larger than its name implied and could shelter a large number of ships simultaneously and, due in part to the cliff-guarded entrance to its anchorage, could conceal ships well. It also had the benefit of being the closest serviceable haven off the Bay of Thetis to Willow Vale although even at that it was still some hundred and six leagues from the encampment. Under the best of circumstances that put the encampment almost three weeks away on foot even if they had the supplies to keep them moving forward. It was clear to her that if their army and all the pilgrims were to make it that far, they would need more than just ships. They would need material help from the ports and towns along the Shadow Coast.

And wasn't their cooperation exactly what the War Council had asked her to secure?

*Down from the realms of the cold and ice*
*Visions of people and ants*
*Destiny falling*
*Their doom foretelling . . .*

She turned her head back into the wind. The shrill whistling lessened considerably but now the wind again dragged against her eyes through the faceplate slits. It was better than without the helmet but still troublesome and sometimes difficult to breathe if the dragon rose too high into the sky, something which Kyranish did too often out of habit. It was then that something caught her eye through an opening in the clouds below. She leaned forward in her saddle and laid her hand against the dragon's neck.

The clouds instantly vanished from the sky,

warm air flowing over her like a breath of peace. The coastline was perfectly clear beneath them.

*Why do the clouds clear from the sky only after I see it with my eyes in the true world?* Urulani wondered. The ways of dragons—and of magic, for that matter—were strange to her.

"It is Shellsea," Urulani said to Kyranish.

"What would you have me do, Urulani of Nothree?" Kyranish asked, the dragon's song replaced by understanding and meaning. "Shall I alight east of the city gates as we did in Blackbay?"

Urulani shook her head then smiled. It had taken them almost three days to convince the people of Blackbay, up the coast behind them, to let them in the gates let alone to listen to her message. In the four days she had been on her journey, she had only managed to contact Blackbay. The people of that northern port were skeptical at first but the presence of a dragon—which had caused the local militia to abandon their posts after the second day—ultimately impressed them with both her and the legendary Drakis whom she claimed to represent. But now she had only six days left on her quest and a number of ports ahead of her. Urulani had been considering a different tactic and was anxious to test it. "No, my friend. I think we might try something different this time."

The dragon's head actually craned around in the wind to look at her as it flew on. "What will you have me do?"

"Do you see that large market square that opens onto the quays?" Urulani said, as the dragon

soared around the town far below. She could see
that the sight of them had already attracted considerable attention. The distant, tinny sound of an
alarm bell drifted into her ears.

"Yes, Urulani," the dragon replied.

"I want you to land there," she said.

"Inside the city walls?" Kyranish questioned.

"Yes, exactly."

"And what shall we do when we arrive in the
center of this town, among all its armed warriors
and elven masters?"

Urulani grinned. "Why, *nothing*, if we can possibly help it."

Bells throughout Shellsea pealed madly.

Gardnephaus Pleu leaned out the window of his
Mayor's Residence to see his town in chaos. He occupied the entire third floor of the Shellsea Ministry; a fitted-stone building which also housed the
countinghouse on the main floor and the constabulary on the floor beneath his own. It was one of the
tallest buildings in Shellsea, situated on a slight rise
that allowed him an extraordinary view over the
large market square and the harbor quays beyond.
Normally the sight filled the fat goblin with inordi-
nate pride that he, coming from such a lowly clan
as Pleu, had managed to rise to the exalted position
of Mayor and Harbor Master of Shellsea. It was as
high a position as one might aspire to in the protected harbor town without actually being an elf.

It was this last limiting condition which Mayor Pleu had long been harboring some resentment over for his ambitions were much larger than those his Imperial masters seemed to permit him. Still, until he could conceive of a way to be rid of the elven garrison in the town and their fat Legion commandant, he would have to remain content with his title and put aside the grander ambitions which he dreamed of both day and night.

Now, however, the world outside his window had quite unexpectedly turned upside down. The goblins, gnomes, and even a number of chimerians and manticores were running madly about the marketplace while the warning bells tolled incessantly. Several crews at the quays beyond were scrambling aboard their ships—the square-sailed manticorian traders and a few triangle-sailed goblin ships—struggling to rig their vessels for sea. Several cut themselves clear of their moorings before their rigging was properly set, which resulted in a pair of smaller ships drifting up onto the southern beach and several more running into each other in the confusion.

The Mayor recognized one of his staff scampering about in the square below him.

"Kubis!" the Mayor called down from the window. "Kubis! What in the Dark God's name is going on?"

Kubis, a goblin master accountant with whom the Mayor had been working for years looked up and then simply pointed toward the sky.

A shadow passed over the Mayor as it rolled across the square below.

The Mayor looked up . . . and froze.

It was an unmistakable shape straight out of legend. The enormous leathery wingspan seemed to cover the entire inner township, stretching from city wall to city wall. Its large, horn-spiked head roared above the noise of the bells. Talons from its hind claws reached out, gripping a spire from the adjacent Chapel of Aquis Delve and pushing off it as it passed. The spire swayed dangerously but managed to remain upright. As the Mayor watched, the impossible monster rose, carried upward on the breeze from the sea and then wheeled back toward the town.

Toward the Mayor.

Gardnephaus Pleu's eyes opened wide as he ducked down behind his windowsill. He both felt and heard a terrible crashing sound from the marketplace below accompanied by the loud rustle of leather. Then a terrible quiet descended, broken only by occasional shrieks and the distant sobs of hysterical weeping.

The iron-banded door on the opposite side of the Mayor's office suddenly opened.

"Lord Mayor!" squeaked a goblin wearing a wide, golden ceremonial sash.

"Giblik, shut up and get down!" the Mayor whispered hoarsely. Giblik was his political adviser and liaison with the elf garrison commander. The appointment not only provided for a good living for his brother-in-law but meant that Gardnephaus did not have to deal directly with the Imperial occupiers of his town any more than was absolutely necessary.

"Giblik, you have to alert the garrison!" the Mayor grumbled. His voice sounded far too loud in the sudden quiet outside.

"They already know," Giblik replied. "They said something about regrouping to consider— then they left."

"Left?" the Mayor snapped then, suddenly aware of his own noise, lowered his voice to continue. "Left for where?"

"I don't know," Giblik replied. "Out . . . away. They opened up their fold portals with their Proxis and vanished outside the walls."

"So there *is* something that the mighty Rhonas elves are afraid of, eh?" Mayor Pleu considered with a sharp-toothed grin. His long, pointed ears began to quiver as he considered. "Get over here!"

Giblik scampered across the room on all fours, then came to sit next to the Mayor beneath the window.

"What's the dragon doing now?"

"I don't know, Mayor," Giblik replied. "I can't see from here."

"Well, then stand up and take a look!"

Giblik's face fell. "As your adviser I think I should tell you . . ."

A voice, deep yet feminine, drifted in through the window from the marketplace below. *"Where is the master of this town?"*

Giblik and Gardnephaus looked at each other.

"I believe they want to speak to you, Mayor," Giblik offered quickly.

"They don't have an appointment," Mayor Pleu stammered.

"Do they need one?" Giblik asked back.

Gardnephaus' eyes narrowed. "Giblik, stand up and tell me what is going on in the square! Now!"

The goblin quivered but stood up partway, crouching down so that his eyes barely cleared the windowsill.

"Well?" Gardnephaus demanded.

"Well, it's . . . it's not doing anything," the goblin reported. "I mean, it is a gargantuan, terrifying dragon in the marketplace but it's just sitting there. There's a dark-skinned human woman standing in front of it who keeps calling out to speak to the leader of the town."

The Mayor raised his thin eyebrows. "Do you see anything else?"

"No . . . nothing moving," Giblik reported. "I think they're all too frightened to move."

The distant woman's voice drifted upward again. *"I come with news of Drakis and his Army of the Prophet. I come to bargain in his name."*

Giblik looked suddenly at the Mayor. "Drakis? I thought those were just rumors!"

"That dragon in our marketplace is a rather persuasive rumor," the Mayor said, rising slowly to his own feet. "You say the elves have fled outside the walls?"

"Yes, Lord Mayor," Giblik answered.

"Then I think I should like to hear from this human woman what this rumor wants," the Mayor smiled. "In the meantime, I have a task for you."

"What do you want me to do?" Giblik asked in fearful tones.

"I want you to round up the constabulary—as many as you can convince to come out from wherever they are hiding," the Mayor said, adjusting his own tunic and silver sash. "You know those marks I showed you that the elven Proxis make?"

"The ones that anchor their transportation folds?" Giblik said.

"Yes," the Mayor replied as he moved toward the door leading out of his office and to the stairs that would take him into the square. "I want you and the constabulary to find every single one of those on the city wall and in the elf garrison compound. Then I want you to chisel them out flat. Once that's done close the gates."

"You mean to lock the elves out?" Giblik said with a wicked grin.

"We have both done well for ourselves being realistic about the elven occupation," the Mayor said with a nod. "But I think now there is more opportunity for us in this legend."

# CHAPTER 11

## Hammer's Fall

JUGAR WAS SICK to his stomach.

Dwarves loved the ground. They reveled in the solid feel of it beneath their feet. They felt comfort in its solid mass above their heads in their underground cities. Their hands took comfort in its touch.

Dwarves were made to be underground . . . not above it.

Yet despite the lurching protest of his bowels, Jugar flew on as though Dratjak, God of the Dead, were flying at his heels. Though he continued to apologize from time to time to Pyrash, the cerulean-blue dragon on which he rode, for the vomit that now streaked down one side of the monster's neck and to which he still occasionally added, Jugar nevertheless pressed on to the southwest over the skies of Vestasia. The savanna stretched all around him, its chaos of plains grasses, winding rivers, copses of trees, and the occasional Hak'kaarin mud dome city drifting far beneath him in a seemingly unending procession. When he could rally himself, he had to marvel at the distance it all represented. They had spent weeks crossing these plains in their journey northward from the borders of that presumptuous Queen Murialis' realm that brought them to the Forgotten Humans beyond the Sentinel Peaks . . . and then Drakis changed everything.

Jugar was not a human and so the dragon song did not come into his mind as they traveled together. The dwarf could communicate with his dragon through touch like the humans and could thereby be magically sent to whatever hideous otherworld place the dragons lived in in their minds. Drakis called it "communion"—a communication and a connection with the dragons—but Jugar found it unnerving. He was always afraid that he was "communing" more than just his spoken words to the dragon and, above all else, it was his true intentions that he needed to keep to himself. He could not afford for things to go wrong now; not with so much at stake.

And it had all been going so well, Jugar reflected. Not according to plan, of course, because no plan ever survives first contact with reality. That's why great leaders must remain flexible, open to opportunity when it presents itself and then have the will, strength, and vision to seize the advantage when it arrives.

And if there was anything that Jugar excelled at, it was seizing an advantage. He believed he could pull victory itself from between a dragon's teeth and had proved it more than once—perhaps even literally, he thought, smiling to himself wanly.

Pyrash craned his neck around, looking dolefully at the dwarf clinging to the harness Jugar had fashioned to secure himself to the dragon's back. Jugar knew that look and reached forward with his thick hand, laying it against the dragon's neck.

The sky turned suddenly into night in an instant. Stars shone overhead.

Jugar's stomach lurched once more.

"Dwarf Jugar," Pyrash's voice came to him. "You are not well. We have traveled far and you need rest."

Jugar raised his head. Beneath the star-filled false sky he could make out the razor-edged peaks of the Aeria Mountain Range to the south. There had been a time not two weeks before when he had despaired of ever seeing those formidable, glorious formations again. Now he could see them clearly from the strange, unreality of the dragon's otherworld. *Teylon, Hoglithe, Karak, Dugun, Madrikath, Heparion and Aradak* . . . he could name the sharp, snow-capped peaks as they thrust into the starry sky. Each called him on despite the distress in the pit of his stomach, beckoning him back to the halls of his ancestors.

His mind wandered for a moment to the dragon song. He could not hear it nor, for that matter, could anyone except those of humankind and then only those who had any descent from the Ko-rypistan region of Drakosia in the ancient days before the Fall. Yet he had heard a description of it from Drakis. Nine syllables, followed by seven syllables then two lines of five syllables each. Nine Crowns under the dwarven mountains, he thought, and seven peaks in the Aeria Mountains. It must be a coincidence, he thought. Dragonkind were of Drakosia as was the infernal magic of the Aether long since usurped by the elves. Aeria was the land of Aer, the magic of earth and sky. The true magic.

"Dwarf Jugar," Pyrash repeated. "You must rest. We will descend from the sky and stop for the night."

"No!" Jugar croaked out. "Fly on."

"But Dwarf Jugar . . ."

Jugar took in a ragged breath as best he could before he spoke. "Dragon Pyrash, do you see that tallest of the peaks before us in the distance?"

The dragon swung his head to look ahead once more. "Yes, Dwarf Jugar. It is the second to the right of our course."

"There are three canyons to the left of its peak," Jugar said, his watering eyes fixed on it. The warmth of the dragon against his chest was wel-come as he clung to it with both arms. "The far-thest leads up into a mountain bowl surrounded by three lesser peaks. Do you see it?"

"Yes, Dwarf Jugar," Pyrash nodded as he spoke.

*Karak-su'un,* Jugar thought closing his eyes. *The*

*Palm of the Sky.* He could imagine the glacial lake fed by the permanent ice sheet extending down from between Karak and Dugun peaks. It was the High Watch of the Nine Crowns and the place of last resort for the dwarven kingdoms. "Make for that place. You'll see a pillar of stone jutting up from the snow on the right-hand side. I want you to leave me there."

"I should like that," Pyrash purred. "Mountain stone and aerie caverns are the proper place for a dragon to perch. This pillar sounds to my liking."

"The Hammer of the Sky is not to be squatted upon by you or any other creature!" Jugar tried to shout but ended with a loud belch instead. "It is a stela on which is carved the history of all the Nine Dwarven Kingdoms and the roots of our race. If there are any dwarves to be found, they will be in this sacred spot."

"Sacred?" the dragon asked in surprise.

"Yes, sacred!" Jugar continued. He was not particularly cold on the dragon's back but he was shivering nevertheless. "Only dwarves are supposed to come near it and it is certain that no dwarf will show himself to me if an enormous beast such as yourself were settled on it like some impossible crow. You'll leave me there at the Hammer of the Sky and then go wait wherever suits you to the west of Heparion."

"West of where?" Pyrash asked.

"Heparion!" Jugar blurted out. "That tallest peak I pointed out earlier. You just stay out of

sight of the stela for three days then come back
for me."

"Three days?" Pyrash nodded although Jugar
sensed that the dragon was not happy at the
thought. "It will be bitterly cold in the mountains
without me there to watch over you. Do the
dwarves survive such weather regularly?"

*No, we do not but I don't intend to spend more than
a few minutes in that dreadful weather,* Jugar thought
to himself but he spoke differently to the dragon.
"We are a hearty folk and love the bracing joy of
places bereft of both heat and air to breath. But
most of all we are a shy folk who hide ourselves at
the very sight of dragons. If I am to find any remaining dwarves then I need you to be as far from
me as possible."

"Do you think your dwarven people will be
here?" Pyrash said with deep concern.

"No, they are no more," Jugar said quietly. "But
we have promised Drakis for his sake that we will
try. Three days will be enough and then we will
return with our sad news."

Jugar pulled his hand off the dragon's neck.
The night sky vanished once again into the reality
of day. The mountains ahead of them that had
been so clear a moment before that the dwarf felt
he could touch them were suddenly once more
obscured with haze and distance. Jugar gripped
the harness with both hands and despite feeling ill
smiled to himself.

Jugar knew that what he had just told the
dragon was a lie.

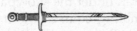

Jugar turned away from Pyrash as the dragon withdrew from near the base of the stela. The sweep of the dragon's enormous leathery wings beat the powdery snow into a white flurry that engulfed the dwarf, making it impossible for him to see. He turned away, shielding his eyes from the wind and ice swirling around him. Then just as quickly the gale abated, the billowing snow once again drifted back toward the ground.

Jugar lowered his arms. He was nearly shoulder deep in the high mountain snow and knew he could easily sink deeper with very little effort. So he stood still where he was and watched as Pyrash circled around the great bowl of the mountain vale, gaining altitude from the wind rushing up its steep slopes until the dragon lifted himself over the western ridge and vanished from sight.

Jugar shivered from the cold around him. He had rather hastily gathered warm clothing that would fit him from the encampment before setting off on their flight. His leather jacket he had lined against the cold and it was keeping his body warm but the gloves and boots proved inadequate despite their layers. He would have preferred to go about his business but Jugar was a patient dwarf—more patient than anyone knew.

As he waited, Jugar looked around the mountain bowl. It emptied to the north down a steep canyon. The outlet from the glacier lake was not visible as it ran under the snowpack but he could hear its tumbling course and crystal waterfalls rumbling from their cascades far below. Those waters would eventually make their way down to the Vestasian Savanna and follow a long, tortuous route to the sea. Other than this steep and narrow cleft, the bowl was surrounded by sharp ridges and cliffs. The Karak and Dugun Peaks shone in the waning light of day, their jagged pinnacles still aflame with the light of the late afternoon sun when most of the bowl was now cast in shadow. The long glacier ran down between those peaks. In late summer the snows would have all melted and the mountain lake at the base of the glacier would sit like a turquoise jewel near the base of the Hammer of the Sky. Now, however, the lake was largely frozen over and only the stela itself could be seen above the blanket of snow.

The Hammer of the Sky rose above him and he reveled in its sight. Here was the history of the dwarves laid out in intricate detail. The top of the stela reflected the very foundations of the world and its origins among the dwarven folk— powerful and glorious in the beginning of days. It was they who forged the other races in defiance of the gods and were cursed when the gods gave the other races their freedom to afflict the dwarves from those days onward. There near the top was the Age of Frost and the Omrash-Dehai—the 'Peace of Reasoned Thought' when dwarves, chimerians, and manticores all were united until the Bloodless War and its decline into the Age of Mists. He could easily read the descendants of kings down through King Brok of the Hammer and the Sundering when the descendants split into branching roots of the Nine Thrones under Aeria. Then the Age of Fire came after the Long Abyss and the War of Desolation in the north. It was here that the stela inscriptions vanished beneath the level of the snow. There was more below it, of course, it was a marvel of dwarven stonecraft that the stone of the stela extended as one piece into the roots of the mountain, being thrust upward and carved whenever new history was forged below. Jugar knew it by heart to its base and had every intention of adding to it in a most glorious fashion.

"Stay where you are!" a voice growled behind him. "Stand forth and be recognized!"

Jugar did not turn but he did speak. "Well, which one is it to be?"

"What do you mean?" the voice snarled. There was a nervous edge to it and Jugar thought it sounded young.

"If I stay where I am I can hardly stand forth to be recognized," Jugar's deep voice rumbled. "So do you want me to turn around or not?"

"Turn around!" the voice commanded less certain than its words would indicate. "Hands out!"

Jugar extended his hands out to either side, his gloved fingers splayed open, palms flat and facing forward to show that he had no weapons in them. He slowly turned around to face his captor, plowing his way through the snow, and smiling to himself at the thought of the guard's reaction upon seeing his face.

It was a young dwarf, as he had suspected. The helmet was a little too large for him which meant that no one had bothered to fashion a proper one for him. His beard was one hand's length long and the skin at the corners of his eyes was still smooth, which told Jugar that his challenger was young and inexperienced. His chain-mail armor overlaying his thick cloak against the cold was tarnished and several of the links were damaged which Jugar credited to the armor's experience rather than that of the young whelp who had somehow inherited it. Still, the halberd which the youth wielded remained steady in his hands and was held at the prescribed angle dictated by the "Book of the Guardians," which meant that the dwarf had at least been trained in combat. His eyes were gray and unblinking.

What both disappointed and astonished Jugar was that the youth showed no reaction at all upon seeing him.

"State your name and craft!" the young dwarf cited verbatim from the text of the "Book of the Guardians."

"You don't *know* me?" Jugar sputtered.

"You answer to me, thin beard!" the young guard demanded.

"Thin beard?" His once-glorious beard was still not nearly as long as it had been before the elves had shaved him for a slave but the insult was not about its length but its thickness, calling him decrepit and old. Jugar put both his hands on his hips, his voice commanding. "Who are you? What is your name and your section number?"

"I'm asking the questions here!" the guard sputtered.

"Name and section number . . . NOW!"

"Dalgrin, son of Vakinag," the guardian responded. "Section 31045318."

"King's Guard, eh?" Jugar chuckled. "Isn't that ironic? So did Wadex send you out here or is he no longer in charge?"

Dalgrin ignored Jugar's question and lowered his halberd menacingly. "You have trespassed upon the sacred dwarven realms—both you and the monster upon which you came!"

"Ah!" Jugar smiled. "So *that's* why Wadex sent you out here all on your own? The warrens of Hammer of the Sky must contain an entire dwarven Legion by now with more than a hundred warriors guarding the stela at any time and yet they send only you. You're the bait!"

"Bait?" Dalgrin blinked, confused. "You're my prisoner!"

Jugar stepped back, looking up at the Hammer of the Sky rising to dizzying heights above him and began shouting. "Let the Marshal of the Hammer come forth! Tell him the day is come and this night will his clan be called blessed as once it had been before the King of the Ninth Throne!"

The intricate carvings of the stela shifted just above the level of the snow. The snow around Jugar also shifted and suddenly he was surrounded by a phalanx of dwarven warriors.

From the opening in the stela, a barrel-chested dwarf strode onto the snowpack. His beard was interrupted on one side by a long scar and he wore an eye patch over his right eye. His arms, however, were still massive and powerful despite the streaks of age showing in his rust-red beard. He carried a double-bladed ax whose blade was etched with dark runes. His thick cape was trimmed in fur. The look on the dwarf's face was grim as he approached, his eyes narrowed in the glare of the snow.

"Marshal Wadex," Jugar said. "It was destined that we should meet again."

Marshal Wadex stopped in his tracks, gazing at Jugar for a moment before wonder and awe dawned on his face. In an instant, the old Marshal of the King's Guard Legions fell to one knee, bowing his head as he planted the head of his ax down into the snow.

"King Aerkan!" Wadex shouted.

Dalgrin's eyes went wide.

The dwarven guardians instantly followed Wadex's example, suddenly falling to their knees in homage.

"It is good to see you once more," Jugar said as he stepped up to where the Marshal knelt, lifting him by the hand as permission to stand.

"By the gods of the deep," Wadex muttered. He removed his cloak at once, wrapping it around Jugar. "We had received word that you were walking beneath the sky but there had been silence for the last two months. We feared you were lost to us forever. Yet here you stand with us once more." Wadex turned to one of the guardians kneeling near the still-open stela access. "Kelva! Run at once with all haste and spread the word throughout the warrens! The Last King has returned!"

"I have returned," Jugar said, gathering the warm cloak about him, "but not for long. I must walk under the sky a while longer, old friend. But we have three days before I must leave again and there is much that must be done in that time."

"Then let us waste none of it," Wadex said, gesturing toward the opening in the stela.

Jugar nodded. He took a step toward the entrance, longing to get below ground and feel dwarf-hewn stone about him once more, but he stopped as he passed Dalgrin. The young dwarf was bowing so low that his face was almost planted in the snow. Jugar reached down with his left hand and lifted up the chin of the dwarf.

"Cheer up, Dalgrin," Jugar said with a strange smile. "You are about to become a Hero of the Dwarven Thrones . . . if Wadex doesn't execute you first for insulting the last remaining of the dwarven kings."

# Chapter 12

## Dark Heart

JUGAR LEFT THE WORLD of light behind.

It was taking him longer to get used to the darkness again than he cared to admit, even to himself. Dwarven eyesight was particularly suited for the underground, capable of seeing clearly even in the dimmest of light. They were perfectly comfortable either aboveground or below but dwarves who had stayed aboveground for extended periods of time occasionally became "sky-blind" as it was known among those who dwelled beneath the mountains of Aeria. Their transition back underground took somewhat longer than those who moved freely between the world above and the world below.

*A king blind in his own realm,* Jugar thought grimly as he peered into the blackness ahead. He could hear the anxious voices echoing from the space before him. *Will they follow me blindly as well?*

Jugar had been traveling for nearly a day under the mountain, its tunnels, caverns, passageways, and chambers leading him ever deeper beneath the mountain. A single day's travel was all he could afford: he only had three days before Pyrash returned to fetch him. That left him only one day to accomplish his mission before he would have to start once again for the bright surface of the mountain bowl above him.

The dark was framed by the dim outlines of an ornate arch with a carved label above it proclaiming the space beyond to be the Council Chamber of a dwarven settlement called Fedrith-nar. The place could barely be called a village but it was within a single day's journey from the Hammer of the Sky. Its location, therefore, dictated that Fedrith-nar become the place where Jugar—here known as Aerkan, Last of the Dwarven Kings—would triumphantly appear before the surviving dwarves. The warrens immediately surrounding the stela were certainly grand enough for such an occasion as were three grander cities than this minor and otherwise forgotten town but each of those were too far for the dwarven Thanes to reach in a day's time. It had once served as a waypoint for dwarves on pilgrimage to the stela but this otherwise undistinguished dwarven township was now overflowing with dwarves rushing from diverse redoubts deep within the mountain to hear the will of the Last King. He would address them all in time but first he had one very important gathering to command.

"Thanes of the Seven Peaks," boomed the voice of Wadex standing just beyond the dark portal. "Gather to hear and be heard by Aerkan—King of the Ninth Throne of Aeria."

Jugar heard the Thanes rise from their chairs in the darkness, their boots stomping against the stone in perfunctory welcome.

The king almost did not recognize his name as he was announced. When he realized the stomping was for him, he smiled. He had been Jugar for so long that his true name was foreign to his ears. Jugar reflected that the original bearer of the name would have appreciated the humor in all this. He had, indeed, been the king's court jester; a position that doubled as his personal guard. It had been his greatest performance and his final joke to exchange clothing with the king as the elven armies assaulted the Yungskord. The king then hid in the secret treasure trove beneath the Ninth Throne while the jester took his place. It was the jester Drakis had killed atop the embattled throne while the king waited unseen beneath the carnage. The jester had been a trained and able warrior as well as a capable performer. The king missed his old companion but had all this time taken solace in knowing that the joke lived on in him.

A joke for which the king was determined to have the last, bitter laugh. *The Jugar is dead; long live the new Jugar!*

The last of the dwarven kings stepped through the dark portal. Still partially sky-blind, he could make out the extent of the room. It was a modest hall so far as dwarven craftsmanship was concerned, suitable for its town council duties without taxing the capabilities of the local community. It was round after the common practice of any dwarven meeting hall but plain to the point of embarrassment. The floor was slightly uneven and the wall carvings practically nonexistent. There were nine pillars evenly spaced against the wall of the curved room climbing only fifteen hands to the shallow dome overhead. Each pillar was topped by a carving of one of the nine kings as was typical for such ceremonial rooms throughout the dwarven realms but the figures were obscured to his eyes and Jugar could not pick his own out from among them. What he could see more clearly were the twenty-five Thanes who had gathered within the room, most still stomping their left feet against the ground.

*Most*, Jugar noted, *but not all.*

Jugar raised both of his hands above his head in acknowledgment of their welcome but his thoughts were troubled.

*Twenty-five Thanes under the mountain. That's five by five. Nine Kings . . . seven peaks . . . five Thanes by five . . . the rhythm of the dragon's song resounding beneath the mountain. A warning from the gods . . .*

Jugar shook his head and smiled brightly at the Thanes.

*It was no gods that made Drakis*, he told himself. *Only a fool believes a myth of his own creation.*

Jugar stood in the middle of the hall, turning around as he faced the Thanes who were seated in two rows around the room. At last he faced the empty throne that had been set in the hall by enthusiastic guardsmen. It was not as grand as the one he had last occupied in the Stoneheart but in many ways far more important. It sat on a platform just three steps above the rough-hewn floor. He climbed those short steps, turned, and sat.

The platform itself had been hastily erected and its surface was also uneven. The throne wobbled slightly as he sat on it.

*Thrones*, Jugar reflected, *can be particularly precarious perches to maintain.*

Jugar waited until the Thanes had all stopped their display of welcome and, no longer stamping their feet, had all taken their seats. Only then did Jugar address them. "Thanes of the Seven Peaks, I have returned from the lands beneath the sky but I cannot stay. I must return and finish what I have started—for your sakes and for the sake of all dwarvenkind."

"And what has our remaining king started?" asked Gorfend, Thane of Bekra, standing abruptly from the second row.

"I have started a war," Jugar answered simply.

"A war?" Gorfend tilted his head, the three braids of his long beard quivering. "Must I remind King Aerkan that we just went through a war—a war that cost us the thrones of each of our Nine Kingdoms and thrust the refugees from those kingdoms upon the outlying Thanes?"

"Does Thane Gorfend seek to educate me re-garding the battle," Jugar said. "I was there and do not recall his presence."

"I may not have been at the battle," Gorfend rejoined, "but I have born the burden of its results daily since. And now the Last King returns to us so that having lost our last war he may start an-other?"

"We will be victorious," Jugar stated. "We have the advantage."

"Advantage?" Evon, Thane of Osath scoffed as he stood up to join in the argument. Evon was a stocky, fat dwarf with a red, wide beard that he preferred to leave splayed out rather than braided. His region lay deep under Mount Heparion and had been largely untouched by the battles to the south. "What advantage? Our armies are but a fraction of their former strength, most of them filled with new and untrained warriors and the elven Cohorts continue to occupy and sack our lost cities. We are a nation in exile and you talk of advantage?"

"Yes, I say advantage," Jugar asserted. He reached inside his leather coat and pulled out an ugly, multifaceted stone that looked like onyx but seemed to absorb even the dim light of the subter-ranean room. Several of the Thanes cried out, hold-ing their arms up as though to shield themselves from the stone.

"It is an abomination!" Evon cried out.

"It is our salvation!" Jugar rejoined.

"The Aer Crafters have whispered about the

Heart of Aer," Thane Baldron of D'ras said in awe as he, too, stood to address the gathering, his luxuriously long, black beard separated into two braids that he had draped back through epaulets over his shoulders. D'ras was beneath Devon Fel far to the north, and it was where most of the dwarven Aer masters had congregated after the fall of the last city. "They spoke of how the kings had demanded their mages mimic the Aether magic, to channel the natural Aer of earth and sky as the elves now did and the humans did before them. It was in their sight a corruption of the natural power of Aer but they forged the Heart in a desperate hope to keep the elves beyond the dwarven gates. Now the wizards all believed the Heart to be cursed and to have caused the fall of the kings, dooming them for creating it in the first place! They said it had been lost but it . . . it exists still?"

"It more than exists," Jugar said, holding the stone high above his head. "It is the key to bringing the elves to their knees before us. I have used the power of this device, channeled its energies and seen its wonders. The Aether Wells of the enemy cannot stand against it. It shatters them utterly, robbing the Rhonas of the very Aether by which their entire Empire is ruled."

"It is an atrocity against the very nature of Aer," Evon asserted. "It should be destroyed."

"When the towers of the Imperial City lie in ruins!" Jugar shouted, his face suddenly filled with rage. "When the last elf takes his final breath!

When the souls of our dead can join their ancestors with their heads held high because their sacrifice has been avenged! Then . . . THEN you may do what you will. I am KING . . . and with the Heart of Aer we will bring down our enemies with a fall so great that its sound will echo to the very end of the world!"

"How?" Thane Evod demanded. "You would bring down the might of Rhonas with one magic stone and a decimated army of dwarves?"

"No, not with our army but with a gift," Jugar said, regaining his composure. "I have these last few months been busy in the world above. In this the gods have smiled upon us for they have brought us a human legend."

"Drakis?" Baldron scoffed.

Jugar raised his eyebrows in surprise. "You've heard of this?"

"We trade with the Hak'kaarin from time to time," Baldron said. "They have been full of tales of this Drakis-human coming back from the dead to free the world from the elves. We thought they had made it up."

"Not them, *I* made him up," Jugar's voice boomed proudly. "He was a slave—an Impress Warrior of a backwater elven household—nothing to anyone. But I started a small stone rolling down that most fortunate hill and it has grown into an avalanche. Most of the northern continent seems convinced that he is the fulfillment of their foolish prophecy. Now there is an army being raised in his name that is bent on doing exactly what we wish: to march on Rhonas and destroy the Empire."

"Then to vengeance and war!" Wadex shouted. "If the King commands it, we shall march with this Drakis and his army."

"No," Jugar said, shaking his head with a smile. "I most certainly do not command it."

"Then why have we been summoned here?" Thane Gorfend asked in astonishment. "You say you start a war and now you do not want us to join it?"

"That is correct, my good Thanes," Jugar stated calmly as he sat back down on his wobbling throne. "I will be leaving you again tomorrow. I will return to this Drakis and make sure that his devoted and fanatic army will march against the Rhonas Empire. I will help them destroy the Aether Wells as they advance, robbing the Empire of its magic. Without its magic . . . Rhonas cannot stand."

"And are our warriors to stand still and our blades to remain clean while war is waged?" Marshal Wadex sputtered.

"That is precisely why, my good Thanes, you will support me in this war," Jugar said, holding his head up with pride. "Because the manticores, goblins, gnomes, chimerians, and humans . . . all those who have come together against our common enemy, will fight our war *for* us. They will bleed in our stead. They will die for our cause. And when at last they have thrown themselves against the gates of Rhonas and both the Empire and this army of rebels are spent and wasted . . . only *then* shall our armies march from beneath the mountain and none shall remain to stand in our way."

Silence fell among the Thanes.

"All you have to do is prepare the army for war and await my word," Jugar said through a gap-toothed grin, "while others do our dying for us."

"And what will you be doing?" Thane Evod asked.

"Insuring our triumph," Jugar replied, "By destroying Aether magic . . . wherever it is found."

# CHAPTER 13

## Conjuration

WITH HIS CLOAK PULLED AROUND HIM, Drakis stood next to Braun on a windswept hilltop two leagues to the east of what the residents had started calling Pyris Camp. Before them stood a ragged formation of pilgrims, almost entirely human with a smattering of elves, three goblins, and a gnome mixed in.

"These are all there are?" Drakis whispered to Braun in dismay.

"Yes, Drakis," Braun answered with a soft smile in the morning light. The sun had drifted only a hand's width above the horizon, burning away a hazy low fog and leaving them all under a bright, if chill sky. "Sixty-nine that have the ability to command the magic."

"Sixty-nine?" Drakis said, shaking his head. "I count only fifty-three."

"There have been a few—incidents—during the

training," Braun said, his thick brows lowering as he spoke.

"Incidents?"

"There were some initial problems with fire and lightning that we're still working on and then there are the fold spells," Braun shrugged. "They can be a bit difficult when you first learn them. They require a lot of control even over short distances. Some of our acolytes have more talent than patience and decided on their own to attempt longer distance folds for themselves."

"Did they survive?" Drakis asked.

"If we ever find them, we'll know," Braun said then coughed.

Drakis turned to mask his frustration. He gazed at the vast encampment in the distance, spread as it was almost three leagues on a side spilling out of Willow Vale with columns of smoke rising into the bright sky from innumerable cook fires. An elven Legion would have to be blind not to spot that smoke from more than a hundred leagues in any direction.

*And Soen—the elf Inquisitor who has hunted me since the day I woke to this living nightmare—advises me to move* that *secretly into Vestasia?* Drakis gritted his teeth at the thought.

It was insane. He had barely managed to get the quarrelsome pilgrims under some form of order. The enormous and still increasing number of pilgrims that comprised the assembly had created a growing problem of segregation within the encampment. Manticores preferred to associate with their own by virtue of their common customs. Chimerians were recognized by every other race as reclusive even in the best of relationships. Humans were distrustful of other races and had begun to develop their own group called the "Brothers of Drakis." The elves that had joined the cause of Drakis felt shunned and marginalized. The presence of the goblins in the camp, ostensibly as a constabulary force operating side by side with the Grahn Aur Guard, had become a source of constant friction for everyone. Coercion, extortion, and intimidation were just a part of their job as far as the goblins were concerned, and they could not fathom why none of the other races in the encampment could grasp those simple facts.

Drakis spent most of the first day upon returning to the camp dealing with this mess. He first decided it would be better for him to proclaim a division of the encampment himself before other, more partisan divisions formed on their own. It was the Lyric who suggested that the pantheon of Drakosia would provide names for ten smaller camps. The names of ancient and largely forgotten gods were beyond the scope of any existing partisan disagreements. She even provided the names of the gods who now, it seemed, were remembered only by her: Abratias, Heritsania, Aremthis, Aegrain, Khorithan, Tyra, Pythus, Jurusta, Quabet, and Elucia. Drakis divided the Encampment into those ten individual camps and then appointed a council chosen from as best a balance of the different races as possible for each. Each camp council would appoint a representative to the Council of the Grahn Aur to convey their problems to the central council as well as the directives of the council to each of the ten camps. It had taken three days to accomplish this; much longer than he had hoped.

He managed to return to the column of his army that night on the back of the dragon Marush. He kept flying into the night farther and farther up the coast until he discovered them encamped just north of Markrethold. Their advance had not been as fast as Drakis had hoped and his meetings with the unit commanders lasted well into the night. He managed a few fitful hours of sleep before awakening again and, back on the harness fixed around Marush's neck, returned again to the southwest.

On the fourth day, Drakis had met with the Pajak of the goblins and convinced the goblin ruler—through his winning smile and the presence of an enormous, impressive, and hungry-looking dragon at his back—to have the Pajak's units on wyvernback conduct their so-called "security patrols" only *outside* of the encampment and leave the interior enforcement of the camp's law to the Grahn Aur Guards. It had still cost the coffers of the encampment dearly to purchase that agreement even with the threat of Marush eating the Pajak's entire court, but thereafter the incidence of theft and extortion within the encampment plummeted.

But as Drakis stood on the hilltop next to Braun and inspected the group standing before him, he was not sure how long the unity of the pilgrims would last.

"So your folds can't help us, then?" Drakis asked Braun.

"Oh, of course they can help!" Braun grinned. "We lost a few at first but we've gotten rather good at the folds since then. It's largely a question of the potency of the Aether as we draw on it. The more potency the Aether exerts, the farther we can open the fold. Unfortunately that potency falls off over distance. The farther we get from the inverted Aether Well in Port Glorious and, for that matter, the Wells you inverted across the ocean in Drakosia, the less potent the Aether we have to draw upon. The Rhonas enchanters surmounted this problem through the use of portable altars for their Devotions. They would gather the weak force from distant Aether Wells over a lengthy period of time and then discharge it in a powerful burst of Aether in a short period of time."

"Could such a device help us?" Drakis wondered.

"Absolutely," Braun affirmed. "As as soon as I can determine just how such a device can be built, we will make use of it at once. What would be most helpful would be an elven enchanter who could tell us how such a thing might be accomplished. Still, the Aether should be sufficient to help us reach the Shadow Coast. Once we are there we could invert one of their local Wells and that would solve many of our problems for us."

"So you believe this group of wizards can move

the entire population of the encampment, their wagons, equipment, and the army as well?"

"Undoubtedly!" Braun beamed. "We can with almost perfect certainty project a transport fold corridor a distance of ten leagues if we can see the destination—twice that distance if we have another mage at the other end. You remember the gatefold runes I used to inscribe as a Proxi? In this case, the mage acts as a living rune, anchoring the far fold and doubling the distance traveled."

Drakis turned his skeptical gaze back on the assembly before them. "And these are all the enchanters you could find?"

"Mages," Braun corrected.

"Mages and enchanters . . . what's the difference?" Drakis sighed.

"Mage is the latest appellation for the users of our Aether magic," Braun said with a smile. "A mage is traditionally someone who uses or channels magic. It's found in the old Drakosian language, or so the Lyric tells me. Those who use the elven method of Aether would more properly be called "enchanters" as their technique requires that the magic be channeled through a prepared physical object . . ."

"Such as a Matei staff," said a voice from the huddled group before them.

Drakis looked sharply toward the high-pitched, elven voice.

Soen stepped out from the gathered mages and approached Drakis and Braun as he continued speaking, his unpowered staff still in his hand.

"The Aether requires a physical property or conduit through which its power may be channeled. But the elven enchantments, as you call them, and your own sorcery, as you may more reasonably call it, are basically the same. Rhonas magic is channeled through exterior physical objects like staves, crystals, wands, amulets, and the like. Braun magic—and if it needs a name, why not your own?—also requires a physical resonant connection with the source of Aether but in your case the connection appears to be in your internal bones rather than external objects. Elven magical items resonate and are bound with the Aether with which they are charged which is why they retain the power over time. Your bones do the same—but it seems that only a very particular combination will work, is this not so?"

"Why are you here?" Drakis asked with thinly-veiled suspicion.

"Perhaps a better question to ask would be *how* I am here," Soen responded.

"You were with the Army of the Prophet when I saw you last," Drakis said, his eyes narrowing as they fixed on the Iblisi's Matei staff. "You should be more than a week's travel away."

Soen followed Drakis' gaze then shook his head, smiling. "No, Lord Drakis, my magic has not returned. My staff is still dead and my powers spent. In truth, you were the magician who conjured me here."

"He was selected," Braun groaned. "He's right, Drakis. You asked that we quietly find as many among the encampment as had a gift for the re-stored Aether magic and gather them for training. Whenever we found an acolyte—a novice mage—the first thing we taught them was how to use the Aether to detect others who had the gift and bring them here. Once the folds were more reliable, we sent several mages to search the army."

"And to bring them back here through your folds," Drakis sighed then glared at Soen.

Soen shrugged, smiling as he showed his sharp teeth slightly. "It seems I have an aptitude for this sort of thing."

"Get him out of here," Drakis said quietly to Braun. "He's done enough already."

Drakis turned his back to walk away.

"On the contrary, Drakis, I've done too much to stop now," Soen called out. "Rhonas Magic and Drakosian Magic—it's two sides of the same Aether coin. There are important, fundamental differences between them but there are significant areas that they have in common—and I know them better than any man here, including Braun."

Drakis stopped but did not turn around.

"Braun said just a moment ago that there were nuances of controlling the Aether that were diffi-cult to master but the elves had faced those prob-lems early on in their use of the Aether and developed methods of dealing with them—methods from elven enchantment magic that can be applied to human conjuration."

"Enchantment and conjuration!" Braun beamed. "Say, I like that!"

"I'm offering you knowledge that could take you years to develop and discover on your own," Soen said. "Knowledge you need now to help your people survive."

Drakis turned. He looked at Soen, considering before he spoke. "What do you want, Soen?"

"Teach me your magic," Soen said casually. "Just let me learn from Braun what everyone else you have brought here has come to learn as well."

"Our repertoire is limited," Braun said, almost apologetically. "You might be bored."

"You just show me your magic," Soen said, his featureless, dull black eyes still fixed on Drakis. "And I'll show you mine."

"Oh, I like the sound of that . . . and it seems rather fair," Braun nodded with a pleasant smile. "Edra! Kardan! Open a fold another league to the east and take half the acolytes with you. Jullan and Pheleg; you take the rest of the acolytes— including Soen—through a fold two leagues to the south. Pheleg you'll teach Soen the fold anchor summoning. Soen will anchor the southern group and Kardan will anchor the eastern. Then we'll practice folds between the anchor points."

A collective groan was heard from among the acolytes.

"I'll move between the two and we'll see what Soen has to contribute," Braun said. "Go now, we've got a lot to cover today."

Edra, a scrawny female human with her hair cropped raggedly short, stepped out from among the group and raised her hands. She formed patterns in the air in front of her as she spoke, the words somehow interacting with the gestures and causing the air to waver in front of her. Suddenly the space tore into a circular opening in the air with a different place beyond. Jullan, the sole gnome in the group, did likewise and a second fold opened leading to a rocky knoll presumably two leagues to the south. As soon as the openings appeared, the acolytes began filing through them to the other side.

Soen bowed slightly toward Drakis and then again to Braun. He turned, still holding his Matei staff and stepped through the southern portal.

In a moment both folds collapsed.

Drakis and Braun were suddenly alone on the hilltop.

"I know what you're going to say," Braun said before Drakis could speak. "But this really could advance our understanding of magic—of *conjuration*, that is—in ways that would take us years to stumble upon on our own."

"I don't trust him and you shouldn't trust him either," Drakis replied, biting at his lower lip as he considered the problem.

"But that's not really the question, is it?" Braun argued. "The question is whether we can get what we need from him before he gets what he is after from us. That is why I sent for him."

"*You* sent for him?"

"Certainly!" Braun smiled. "I need to know what he knows. You asked for magic that could move the camp. Soen can show me how. If you want any hope of moving the encampment in time, then Soen holds the key."

"This was your idea, Braun," Drakis said. "I don't like it. He's dangerous. We've managed to deny him elven magic—and now you're talking about giving him our own magic: the one advantage we have over the elves."

"Oh, you can leave Soen to me," Braun said with a confident grin.

"Why should I do that?"

"Because I'll be the one teaching him," Braun replied. "And what I don't tell him, can't hurt us."

Drakis turned again, his eyes on the encampment and the more than one hundred thousand inhabitants that depended on this gamble.

"Just make sure he doesn't learn too much," Drakis said.

# CHAPTER 14

## *Due Haste*

ETHIS SHOOK HIMSELF AWAKE.

He blinked the eyes of his featureless face. He was for a moment confused, uncertain as to how much time had passed in his sleep. The sky was still dark but he could see the faint brightening on the eastern horizon. Dawn would soon assert itself. He had flattened his body as much as he could against the back of the dragon's neck in an effort to increase the creature's velocity through the sky but speed had not been their enemy so much as the illusive nature of their destination.

And he knew that his time was running out.

Together, the chimerian and the dragon had pressed southward from Port Glorious along the shores of Mistral Bay. They left the coast at Markrethold where the shores turned more toward the west, driving hard through the clouds above the rolling hills below. As the sun rose toward its zenith,

Ethis set their course toward the eastern slopes of the Mournful Mountains whose dark, vague outlines grew more distinct with each beat of the dragon's wings. Ethis made sure that Wanrah kept well to the east of the range and when he could see that the village of Willow Reaches—a goblin trading post at the northern tip of the Mournful Mountains—was almost directly to the right of their course, Ethis pointed the dragon in a more southeasterly direction and over the carpet of forest canopy that was Ephindria.

The sameness of the treetops rushing by below him confused Ethis. Territory that he knew intimately from the ground was foreign to him when viewed from the unexpected perspective of the sky. Those rare occasions when he managed to get his bearings by spotting a clearing, lake, or waterfall he recognized were only of fleeting comfort as more often than not such locations flashed past too quickly for him to properly identify. As the sun began to set on that first, frustrating day, Ethis finally asked Wanrah to descend into a large clearing with a ruined tower so that he might get some feeling for where they were in his nation. The ancient bone tower was derelict and abandoned and, after instructing the dragon to wait for him there, Ethis moved on foot into the thick woodland. It was some time before he was able to discover any chimerians—most of whom had fled in terror at the dragon's approach. Even then it took him the better part of two hours to approach them—for if Ethis knew anything for certain in the Ever-changing Realm it was that you could never be certain of anyone.

In the end the local chimerians had fortunately proved to be part of the Chythal Family on the western reaches of their family lands near the Malethic River. They had heard that the Queen in Exile had taken her court northward into Klendel lands and cautioned Ethis about Shalashei and Pashorei Enforcers rumored to be raiding as far north as the Whitescar Canyon.

Ethis was surprised and chagrined; he had flown too far south and had come dangerously close to the lands being held by the Families of the Opposition. He hurried back to Wanrah, climbing up the harness and urging the dragon into the air before he had even settled into place.

For two days and nights, Wanrah crossed here and there over the tree canopy of Ephindria, repeating the process again and again. They would land, get their bearings and Ethis would again move into the woodland, seeking out the panicked chimerians and approaching them with caution. Twice along the borders of Dhuresh he encountered agents of the Opposition, barely escaping their snares and on one occasion even calling on Wanrah to come to his aid. Still, Ethis urged Wanrah back into the sky despite the aching in his four arms, the weakness in his legs and the lethargy that called him ever more insistently to sleep. Wanrah could fly without rest for days on end but had asked repeatedly if his rider wished to stop. Ethis had spurred him on without stopping.

He had to find her. She had to listen to him.

Ethis gazed at the brightening horizon. Was the dawn approaching him or was he approaching the dawn, he wondered idly. At last his eyes were fixed on his next destination that he could make out only as a dark shadow against the surrounding deep green. It was in the northern reaches of Nurthei lands which, by all accounts, were still loyal to the Queen.

*Emaro Nol,* Ethis recalled. *City of Steel.*

Ethis looked for a place where he might ask the dragon to make its landfall. He knew from experience that it was better to leave the dragon some distance from where he expected to find anyone. Taking the creature anywhere near a chimerian city wall would be more than cause for panic, and he was looking for cooperation, not fear. Besides, stealth was his business and the fewer chimerians who know what it was that he was trying to achieve the better it would be for everyone. He asked Wanrah to land in a clearing several miles down the ridge and then wearily descended the creature's neck until his feet at last found the ground.

Ethis placed his hand against the dragon's neck now lowered to the ground. He was leaning on it more heavily than he had intended. "Wanrah . . ."

The trees vanished around him as the landscape was replaced. The ridgeline remained but its trees had suddenly transformed into soft, grass-covered slopes. The towers of Emaro Nol remained visible, however, at the far northern end of the ridge. For a moment, Ethis wondered how it was that those towers should extend themselves into the dragon's reality. Was it that the dragons created this place from their own observations of the world or was this a more true representation of the world of their experience? He promised himself to ask Wanrah the next time he had the opportunity.

*If there was an opportunity,* he thought wearily.

"Wanrah," Ethis said to the dragon, "If I don't return by the time the sun sets on the second day . . ."

"Each time we land you tell me the same thing," Wanrah responded, a deep, resonant chuckle in his voice. "If you do not return to me in the time you set then I am to leave you and find a chimerian among the Drakis pilgrims of the encampment. I am to tell them through one of the other dragon-riders that they are 'charged to the whispered conveyance' . . . whatever that means."

"And," Ethis allowed his heavy eyelids to close.

"And to give them this message," the dragon continued. "That 'the sixth son of Chythal delivered her words but regrets he cannot attend. A new light shines in Drakosia where her grace should also shine.' And I am to use those words precisely as you have given them to me . . . on multiple occasions might I add."

"Thank you, Wanrah," Ethis nodded, too tired to form his face into any shape beyond its neutral blankness.

"You need rest, Ethis Windrider," the dragon rumbled.

"We will all rest soon, my friend." The chimerian could not even smile though he wished it with his heart.

Ethis pulled his hand off the neck scales of the dragon. The other world vanished at once and the trees sprang back into existence around the clearing just as he remembered them from a few moments before. He turned then and moved toward the edge of the clearing. A well-trodden path led from the tall grasses in the clearing and up the slope through the trees. His legs felt heavy beneath him as he moved, the slope a tortuous ascent.

The narrow path soon joined another, wider path and then a road where three chimerian women were walking toward the city. Each supported a basket atop her head with all four arms and all were engaged in animated conversation. Ethis strained to hear what they were talking about but was having difficulty concentrating. He could see the brilliant gleam of the sunrise glinting off the graceful curve of the steel towers to the north.

"Sisters!" he called out.

All three chimerian women turned with a start. One of them dropped several *manis* fruit from the basket in her haste.

"Please," Ethis said, his arms splayed open before him. It took concentration to hold them up; they felt so heavy. "I . . . I am a sixth son of Chythal and I charge you with . . . with the whispered . . ."

Ethis collapsed unconscious to the ground.

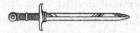

"You are a damned difficult chimerian to catch," purred the voice above him.

Ethis awoke with a start.

Four hands held him down—two at his shoulders and two on his chest. He tried to reach out, find some leverage so that he could gain an advantage against whoever it was holding him down.

"Relax, Ethis," the voice continued. "You've come home."

Ethis suddenly stopped struggling, his eyes focusing on the blank face above him.

To all other races, chimerians appear to be identical. It is nearly impossible for non-chimerians to know the difference between the males and females of their species just by their appearance, let alone to tell an individual chimerian from another without them either wearing some identifying article of some type or the chimerian volunteering a name. The differences were in the details which, of course, chimerians easily recognized on sight.

Ethis had no doubt who was looking down at him from the bedside even though to most people from beyond the borders of his nation the two of them would have looked identical.

"My Queen," Ethis said simply.

"My son," Chythal replied with pleasure.

Ethis relaxed back into the comfortable bed. The mattress was sculpted to his form, an extraordinary extravagance among the chimerians. The room was spacious and well appointed after the chimerian fashion at court. Wrought iron frames were set in polished walls of fitted stone veined through with polished steel. Chimerians, themselves so flexible, had a love of things that spoke of permanence.

Chythal tilted her head to once side, considering. "So you have decided to return to me at last?"

"My Queen, I . . ." Ethis tried to sit up but Chythal continued to hold him down.

"I am much vexed with you," the Queen said, the troubling sound of distant thunder intruding into her words. "You seem to have acquired a bad habit in your absence of distressing your Queen with the repeated reports of your death. First we heard of your distressing enslavement among our elven enemies . . ."

"A misstep on my part, Your Majesty," Ethis acknowledged. "The traitor was dealt with and shall trouble no dreams of the Queen's family any longer."

"All that is well and good, yet we were all prepared to mourn your loss," the Queen continued, "Then it was reported that you were gallivanting across the Vestasian wastelands in the company of humans, manticores, and, of all things, a dwarf. We wondered how it was that so loyal a son of the Queen, one of the D'reth, should not return to her side and report the gladsome news of his escape and the glorious completion of his task? Then we heard reports of you vanishing once again . . . and would have mourned you once more but for the reports that you had suddenly returned again from your presumptive death and this time upon the back of a tamed dragon."

Ethis stared up at the Queen's face. "He is not tamed, my Queen."

"Ah!" Chythal nodded. She released her hold on him, rising to stand next to the bed facing him. "And now for the last few days we have heard the most alarming tales of a cunning chimerian on the back of this untamed beast which my advisers tell me is only a myth and cannot possibly exist. Worse, every time we have sent our other sons out to where these strange stories have originated, this mysterious chimerian and his nonexistent monstrous mount have vanished . . . rushed into the night only to suddenly appear at a completely different place in my lands. I have dispatched members of my D'reth to be scattered everywhere across loyalist lands and in places no longer friendly to me in the hopes of catching up to this elusive phantom of a son and his dragon. If he had only stayed in one place long enough, he might even have been discovered."

Ethis closed his eyes and sighed.

"So, my Ethis," the Queen asked. "What drives a son of the D'reth so madly to every corner of my land?"

Ethis opened his eyes and sat up on the edge of the bed. "A desperate hope, Your Majesty. Tell me, how fares the war against the southern families?"

Queen Chythal frowned, folding the upper set of her arms across her chest. "You find me holding court in Emaro Nol; does that alone not tell you how badly our armies are failing and our lands being lost? I have not ruled from the courts of my ancestors in more than a year, Ethis. Salashei, Pashorei, Whylin, and Surthal . . . they were only the beginning of the disease that has infected our people. One by one the families of the south have been intoxicated by the heady drug of elven magic. Those loyal to us are either forced to withdraw before their magical onslaughts or fall prey to the temptations the elves' Aether offers in granting them their darker desires. They have bound themselves willingly in the golden chains of elven magic and count themselves rich in their captivity."

"But, my Queen, what if our nation could be rid of this elven magic?" Ethis asked, looking up earnestly. "What if the temptation of this power could be removed? What if the warriors of the southern families were no longer supported by the Aether flowing from Rhonas?"

Chythal stood perfectly still, considering the impact of Ethis' words before she spoke. "The southern families would collapse without the support of the Rhonas magic. The nation would be one. The family would be one. Is such a miracle possible?"

"I know of a man—a human—who could make such a thing possible," Ethis replied. "He has gathered an army in the north. They are a nation apart. Their warriors are twenty thousand strong and growing—manticores, gnomes, goblins, many humans, and even many from the family of Ephindria. I have seen their warriors destroy Aether Wells and render them useless even to the elves."

"And why would this human fight for the Queen of Ephindria?"

"He won't," Ethis said.

"Then why . . ."

"My Queen," Ethis interrupted, knowing that he was only one of a handful of Ephindrians who could do so and remain alive. "This human will fight for his people just as his people will only fight for him. They all will fight for one thing: land that they can call their own."

"They are a nation without land?" Chythal scoffed.

"They are a nation in search of a land," Ethis offered. "I believe I can convince this human to rid Ephindria of the Rhonas magic in exchange for a land of their own. I believe it is within the power of the Queen of Ephindria to grant this."

"This nation seeks land but I have none of my own to spare them," Chythal said, shaking her head.

"But if the southern families fall," Ethis responded. "Then the nation will be one."

"You say this human has an army at his disposal and that his people have the power to rob my enemies of the Rhonas magic?" Chythal asked to confirm what Ethis had told her. "Well, if this human and his landless nation are willing to fight our battles for our mutual benefit and give me back my land then perhaps I can spare a little of it in return."

"That hope has driven me to find you," Ethis nodded.

"Will this work, Ethis?"

He could hear both the uncertainty and the longing in her voice as she asked the question. "Can he bring down the Rhonas magic that is poisoning our people?"

"I believe he can, Your Majesty," Ethis said. "But for it to work, I must return to this human and convince him at once of this plan—for there are those who would take him down paths that will ensure the doom of our nation. And, above all, I will need to grant him a favor from the Queen of Ephindria."

"What boon do you ask, Ethis?"

"I need you to permit the impermissible," Ethis said. "I need your consent to their nation passing through Ephindria."

Chythal's eyes widened. The storm sounds had come back to her voice. "Our borders are closed. No outsiders have been permitted since the elves infected our people with their magic!"

"Nevertheless," Ethis insisted. "If any of us are to survive, you must open the Mournful Road."

# CHAPTER 15

## *Imperial Utterance*

T HE EMPEROR OF RHONAS SAT in serene still-
ness on his throne, his eyes fixed in a tranquil
gaze across the private audience chamber of his
Cloud Palace, seemingly oblivious to the war of
words being conducted at his feet.

The chamber, known as the Whispering Hall,
was an oval room at the boundaries of the Emperor's regal private suite of fifty-seven rooms. It
was nearly thirty feet from the entrance doors to
where the Emperor's throne rested atop a raised
dais in front of seven frosted glass panels etched
with the figures representing the first seven Em-
perors. The walls were a smooth rise of twelve feet
to a sculpted crown supporting a domed ceiling of
cerulean blue ornamented with golden stars. The
chamber was not nearly so grand in comparison
to the enormity of the Emperor's Court, where official state business was conducted and the general

proceedings took place but those grand affairs were largely meant to make public the decisions that had previously been concluded in the Whispering Hall. It was in this room that most of the actual business of the Empire had been conducted down through the years out of the troublesome earshot of the rest of the Imperial Court. This was because the room had one unique characteristic from which it derived its name: the acoustics of the room were such that anyone sitting on the fixed throne could hear even the quietest conversation within its boundaries with perfect clarity.

The Emperor remained immobile and impassive. He was a tall elf and strong beyond his years. The fringe of his white hair cascaded far down his back and, as always, had been brushed to a brilliant luster. His face had prominent cheekbones that gave him a skull-like appearance despite his long, prominent nose. His eyes were featureless black as were those of all elves but there was a quality to them that suggested they were watching everywhere at once. His sharp teeth remained hidden behind a determinedly serene and inscrutable half-smile. It had been said of him that he could accomplish more through his silences than most citizens of the Third Estate could accomplish in a year of talking.

Of those present, he alone was seated. There were chairs set against the walls on the right and left of the room facing each other, intended for those currently in audience with the Emperor though none of them were in use. Almost all of the courtiers in the room were on their feet in heated exchange.

The single exception stood next to the Emperor, statuesque in her long red gown, her narrow, pale hand resting on the back of the Emperor's throne.

Shebin, too, was serenely watching the fray.

"We must continue to maintain our Legions in Lyrania!" Ch'kar Meinok, the Ghenetar Praetus of the Nekara proclaimed. Praetus Meinok was an unusually broad-shouldered elf whose nose looked as though it had been pressed against his flat face. He, like the two other Ghenetar Praetus in the room, had worn his ceremonial armor to the audience with the Emperor with three purposes in mind: to honor the Emperor, to establish his authority with everyone else in the room, and to protect himself should the other two Ghenetar Praetus summoned to the council decide to escalate their disagreements to more direct persuasion. "The threat of the Lyranian rebels in that region has not diminished and withdrawing those forces could invite the Lyranian elves to bolder action. Beside, these warriors are simply not needed. You people talk about these rebels in the north as though they were actually of some concern!"

"They completely slaughtered the Legion of the Northern Fist," countered Ormai Betjarian. He was the Ghenetar Praetus of the Vash and, like the other Ghenetar Praetus in the room, the liaison to the Emperor's court for his own order, the Vash. He had a wide mouth that displayed his sharp teeth prominently when he spoke. He was gifted with words but those he spoke today were largely at the direction of his immediate superior, Ghenetar Omris Sjei-Shurian. "This was not some matched contest in the arena, Ch'kar! This was a full strength and supported Imperial Legion with superior numbers and field position that took on an inferior mixed force of manticores, chimerians, and the gods alone know what other rabble and were not just defeated but slaughtered down to a single warrior."

"Because of this Drakis!" inserted Tsukon Keiloi. He wore the draped purple robes of a senior Minister of Conquest though thanks to his repeated hand gestures he seemed to constantly be getting tangled in them. He had an elegantly long face and the tips of his pointed ears nearly touched the sides of his elongated skull. He was considered handsome by elven standards, an accident of birth that had helped his meteoric rise at the Ministry at the young age of fifty-six. "All the Northern Conquests are chattering about this human named Drakis fulfilling a prophecy and threatening the Empire with vengeance he brings from their ancient gods."

"The human gods are dead," scoffed Pakhar Kilan-soi, the fat Associate Minister of War. "We killed them centuries ago!"

"There were no human gods on the field of battle at Willow Vale," Praetus Betjarian said, shaking his long head. "That was no myth that obliterated our Legion!"

"*Your* Legion!" snapped Ghenetar Praetus Wei Ch'Kal. The warriors of the Krish Order of battle had no love for their fellow warriors of the Vash. "It was your Legion that was obliterated. I've read the battle reports from the archives—not those official releases, mind you—and interviewed your survivor myself though it took some doing to find him. Next time you try to declare one of your living warriors to have died, you might think of killing him before he can be discovered."

The corners of Shebin's mouth rose in an almost smile.

"What is your point, Wei Ch'Kal?" growled the Vash Praetus.

"My point is that none of you understand the real danger in the north," answered the Praetus of the Krish. "Your Legion set up for its attack with classic deployment and tactics against a ridiculously weak opposing force. It should barely have rated a victory worthy of writing in the War Journals. But in the middle of routing your enemy and pressing him back against the sea, the Legion advance dissolved and the Legion disintegrated completely!"

"The Aether failed completely!" Praetus Betjarian's face had grown even paler in his anger. "The Devotions of the Impress Warriors failed ... the folds failed ... the connection to the Proxis failed ..."

"That was a failure of the Myrdin-dai to properly supply the Legion with Aether!" chimed in Tertiaran Master Kyori-Xiuchi of the Occuran. "That would never have happened had my Order been given rightful authority to administer the folds and distribution of Aether to the Northern Provinces . . ."

"Your hindsight is clearer than your reasoning," snorted Minister Pakhar.

"The Aether distribution failed simultaneously all across the Northern Provinces at once," Minister Tsukon Keiloi affirmed. "Nothing in the experience of either the Occuran or the Myrdin-dai could have prevented it. Neither Order even considered it a possibility."

"Which is why I am urging that we avoid haste in addressing this northern threat," said Praetus Wei. "We are facing a threat to the Empire the extent of whose power we do not fully understand."

"You would have us cower under our bunks while an army descends upon us?" Minister Pakhar sneered.

"I would rather we showed more forethought in our deployment," countered the Krish commander. "The Vash have uprooted their eastern army—four Legions—from their postings along the Thetis shores and have them marshaling at Shellsea. They've also asked that we pull three Legions from our Army of the Imperial South and marshal them to Tjarlas—on the northern borders of the Empire!"

"As the mighty Ch'Kal so aptly points out," Praetus Betjarian interrupted, "We do not know the strength of our enemy in the Northern Provinces! Better that we should use an excess of force and crush this rebellion at once."

"But you've also asked for three additional Legions from the Nekara," complained Praetus Meinok. "This leaves our western frontier badly exposed against both Chronasis and Mestophia . . . let alone that Murialis witch."

"This war against these traitorous slaves will be swiftly accomplished," Praetus Betjarian insisted. "The general plan is simple. We rally all our armies north of Tjarlas. The Occuran assure me that the Northmarch Folds are now open and reliable. They have also assured me of their support in conveying our combined armies to the Northmarch Provinces. Then, using scouts and Proxis we will advance the armies abreast up the Shadow Coast. We'll deploy the Nekara forces on the eastern side to guard the borders of the Shrouded Plain . . ."

"As though anyone could pass through there!" Minister Pakhar exclaimed.

"Then advance northward with the armies of the Vash and the Krish until our scouts discover the enemy's encampment," Praetus Betjarian continued in a louder voice. "Our latest reports indicate they are traveling with their families, which will make them slow to move and easy to find. Once we have the location of their main force we can consolidate the armies against them, surround them, and crush them."

"Beyond avenging the complete failure of the Legion of the Northern Fist," Praetus Ch'kal asked, "is there any reason why we should mobilize all the armies of the Empire to deal with an untrained mob of rebellious slaves, their women, and their children?"

Minister Keiloi spoke up. "The Prophecy states that . . ."

"This prophecy *again*?" Minister Kilan-soi groaned loudly. "Does anyone even know who created this so-called prophecy in the first place? Where did it come from? What chosen receptacle of the gods received it? It seems that the entire Empire is falling over their feet, wringing their hands, and fretting about this human-slave fireside story for no reason at all! Some discontented slave generations ago—surviving son of a conquered and beaten race—makes up a comforting little story about how the utter defeat and destruction of the human empire will be avenged one day. That some long-dead hero whose bones have dissolved by now where the boots of our elven warriors drove them into the mud hundreds of years before will somehow rise up and make humans great again. Well, the Drakosian Empire is no more, its people are no more, and no wishful daydream by any slaves—no matter how many— is going to change that!"

"Whatever their mad reasons for rebelling, they have to be crushed," Praetus Meinok added. "Must we deploy so many of our forces?"

"It is the Will of the Emperor to do so!" the Vash Praetus blustered.

"The Will of the Emperor?" Praetus Ch'Kal mocked. "We stand in the presence of the Emperor! If the Emperor wants this war then he can tell us his Will!"

Shebin moved her hand from the back of the chair to rest lightly on the Emperor's shoulder. It was a common gesture and accomplished with such subtlety that no one in the room noticed it.

In that moment, the Emperor spoke.

"Much has been spoken," the Emperor hissed, his reedy voice silencing the courtiers at once. "Little has been said of that which concerns our Imperial view. Is not Shebin Sha-Timuran the embodiment of this threat? Did she not first suffer the depravations of this human beast Drakis who now threatens the whole of the Empire with the same? Was her debasement not the shadow of that which this army now brings against every citizen of Rhonas and against the embodiment of the Imperial Will? In defiling her, did not this Drakis defile a daughter of the Emperor, the Imperial House, myself, and the Empire I hold in trust?"

Shebin, too, looked down from where she stood next to the Imperial Throne, watching the faces of those whose gazes were fixed on the Emperor as he spoke.

"It is the Will of the Emperor," he said with all the calm that he might have used a few hours earlier in selecting his breakfast, "that every possible force of Imperial Might be directed against this Drakis, his army, and his followers. Bring him to me in chains if you can, bring his head to me if you cannot—and let all else who follow him be destroyed to the last child until there are none remaining to utter his name."

"Every possible force, my Emperor?" Praetus Ch'Kal asked.

"It is my Will," the Emperor stated firmly.

Shebin smiled.

# CHAPTER 16

## Shebin's Blessing

THE EMPEROR HAD SPOKEN. The Empire responded.

It answered from the Western Provinces, gathering two additional Legions from the Estates—all that might be spared after the losses from the Dwarven Wars. Outside of the three Honor Legions of the Vash, the Nekara, and the Krish who made their quarters within Rhonas Chas, these were the first of the Legions to arrive outside the confines of Tjujen's Wall on the fifth day after the decree. They came under many banners but were largely united behind the Krish under whose general command they fell.

The Empire answered with four Legions from the Chaenandrian Frontier—the entire army known as the Might of the Imperial East. It took them two days to decamp and four more to travel the Eastmarch Folds until they reached their rallying point just outside the gates of Tjarlas the Beautiful—the northernmost of the elven cities and considered the heart of art and culture for the Empire. There they made camp in the shadows of the city's many graceful, towering avatria, awaiting the arrival of the remaining elements of what would become the greatest elven army to march into battle in over two hundred years. Four Cohorts—a total of over three thousand warriors over half of which were Impress Warriors—continued their march beyond Tjarlas through the folds leading back to Rhonas Chas so that the Armies of Imperial Dawn might be represented in the Imperial City to receive the Emperor's blessing. These arrived in Rhonas Chas on the sixth day, exhausted but relieved that they were not the last to arrive.

The Empire answered from the southern coasts bordering on the Aergus Sea, gathering three Legions and mobilizing them within a single day. These Legions known as the Spear of Rhonas pushed relentlessly northward through the Southmarch Folds made clear by the Occuran, who removed all trade and other traffic from their path toward the Imperial City. They were only part of the large force commanded by the Nekara but nearly all that remained along the southern shores. The majority of their warriors and command staff were still across the Meducean Sea engaged in their battle against the Lyranian rebel elves. No folds had ever been able to cross the waters of any sea so word had been dispatched by courier on the earliest supply ship. The message would not reach the war-mages for nearly a week but it only commanded the armes in Lyrania to remain in place until further word was received. The Spear of Rhonas would represent the southern armies and answer the Emperor's command. Even so it took five days of forced march for the Legions to reach the western outskirts of Rhonas Chas, arriving on the seventh day of the issued decree, their banners proclaiming them as united under the Order of Nekara held high.

The eighth day was declared a day of feasting and celebration on behalf of the glorious assemblage of elven might. The entire capital city was caught up in a lavish festival that ended promptly at midnight—again by Imperial Decree. The following day—the ninth since the Decree—was ordained a day of reflection by the Emperor's Will. This had equal parts of honor and practicality, for it permitted the armies a day to restock and prepare for the culminating event: the Parade of the Emperor's blessing.

The Imperial City had never before seen such a display of the Emperor's Might, Will, and Conviction. Everyone within the city and as many of its surrounding regions as could manage the journey came to witness the processional of the united armies of the Emperor as they marched out of the city.

But no one among the teaming throngs filling the balcony of every avatria in the city, or barely contained to either side of the Vira Rhonas running through the city below, drew more satisfaction from the day than did a single young elven woman looking down from the Cloud Palace of the Emperor.

Shebin Sha-Timuran basked in the cheering roar that erupted from the city as she stepped onto the Emperor's Audience Platform and smiled with perfectly filed, sharp teeth. The dome of the avatria's foundation glowed especially for her, casting her in a light that was as gloriously brilliant as the perfect day beyond its shadow.

Shebin Sha-Timuran stepped up to the railing surrounding the oval platform, the train of her vibrant, red dress sweeping behind her as she moved. It was a stylized duplicate of her "defiance dress," as the Ministry of Enlightenment was calling it. It was far better fitting than the torn rag she had worn before the Emperor had adopted her into his House, clean but still sporting the simulated hole of torn cloth as a badge of pride and honor. The original dress had been white but this color was more symbolic according to the Ministry of Thought and also easier seen by the crowds.

The Emperor's Audience Platform, although situated off the central axis of the Cloud Palace, was actually the lowest point of the avatria, suspended below the curving base of the floating portion of the palace at the end of a great curving stone arm for occasions such as this.

Almost a hundred feet below her stretched the Garden of Kuchen now completely overrun by a sea of elves as was the surrounding roadway of the Vira Rhonas as far to the west as she could see. Their hands were raised toward her as they shouted their approval and adoration. It was the Emperor's Will that they love her, she thought, raising her hands in acknowledgment. *How could they not love me?*

Shebin glanced around the platform. Several elven mages stood at the edges of the platform, their lips moving in silent preparation. That the Emperor had not appeared at any such "Grand Audience," as they were called, in nearly a hundred years demanded a special use of Occuran Aether so that as many in the city could be a part of the pageantry as possible.

The crowd below roared again and Shebin turned.

The Emperor stepped onto a raised dais on the platform, his hands held upward, palms turned toward him as though in his gesture he was embracing all of the Empire. At once the Occuran mages at the edge of the platform loosed their magic and the image of the Emperor appeared to tower over the city, his features rising two thousand feet as he beamed down at them from his enormous face. As the Emperor moved, his colossal image mirrored his every gesture.

The Emperor opened his mouth and his words were repeated through the image that towered behind him into the sky in a voice that was heard throughout the city.

"Citizens of Rhonas!" The Emperor spoke quietly but his words rebounded through the city like thunder. "I am your Emperor!"

The deafening sound from below nearly overwhelmed the words of the Emperor.

"Citizens of every Estate! You are a part of our greatness!" the Emperor called. "Show me the fist and steel of the Imperial Will!"

Again the roar arose from the throngs filling the streets below as a sea of adoration. Trumpets sounded from somewhere above them in the Cloud Palace which were answered in turn by trumpeters standing atop the various subatria foundations above which the avatria of the buildings lining the Vira Rhonas floated. Soon Shebin could make out the martial drums approaching from the great plaza to the northwest that lay before the crush of buildings known as the Ministries. The citizens packing the Vira Rhonas began pushing to either side as the Herald Drummers of the Honor Legion of the Order of Vash led the parade. Their drums were enormous, nearly ten feet across at the top and almost fifteen feet tall. Each was fashioned out of polished copper with hides stretched across the top. They were mounted on a series of ornate carriages, each pulled by three ogres—prizes taken in Mestophia—while their drummers, in ceremonial tunics of the Vash livery, pounded on them with long-handled mallets.

Behind them marched the Honor Legion of the Order of Vash, to whom came the honor of securing the city for the procession. The front lines immediately behind the drum carriages marched to either side to line the Vira Rhonas with their raised halberds. Shebin could imagine this line of warriors extending behind the Vira Rhonas, down the Vira Coleseum, and through the Circus to Gladiator's Gate and beyond.

The drum carriages separated where the Vira Rhonas moved around the oval of the Garden of Kuchen, taking up positions on either side. Only those of the Third Estate or higher were permitted in the garden for this occasion and then by direct invitation of the Palace. Even so, there had been a number who had to be turned away or ignored in their requests—there was simply no place left to stand. The Honor Legion of the Order of Vash fell into place behind the drums on either side of the road, their remaining numbers the most honored of their Legion for their duty had brought them within sight of the Emperor for his blessing upon the army that was about to fight in his name.

Shebin gazed down the Vira Rhonas, her eyes filling with tears. As far as she could see down the broad avenue that curved slightly to the right from the view of the Emperor's Audience Platform marched a steady stream of warriors. The first of these was a Cohort of the Vash from the Eastern Armies that had come to represent their might all the way from Tjarlas in the north. Then came a Cohort—another eight hundred warriors—from the Order of Krish and yet another from the Order of Nekara. There were elven war-mages as well as warriors, and Impress Warriors from nearly every

race. Each approached in turn, filling in the street
and, halting their march, turning to face the Imperial Audience where she stood. This continued for
nearly twenty minutes until the streets were filled
with warriors as far as she could see.

And there were many, many more combatants,
she knew, that she could not yet see, waiting their
turn in the streets beyond to march past where she
stood. The last report given to the Emperor had
been one hundred and seventeen thousand warriors, war-mage Tribunes, Proxis, archers, Centu-
rians, Legates, and Praetus prepared to march
northward to destroy Drakis.

Her Drakis.

"Shebin?"

She realized that her name was being called. She
looked up.

The Emperor standing on the round, elevated
platform was looking at her, reaching his hand toward her.

Uncertain, she took it.

The Emperor drew her up onto the platform
with him. In that moment the enormous figure of
the Emperor was joined in the sky overhead by
the gaunt features and tapered head of Shebin
Sha-Timuran.

"Citizens of Rhonas!" the Emperor's voice
boomed from the sky. "I accept this Union of the
Imperial Might—but not in my name!"

A strange hush fell over the city.

"I accept it in the name of she whose wrongs
have inspired our indignation and stirred our

souls to act!" the Emperor said with strength and conviction. "I accept this—The Army of Imperial Vengeance—in the name of Shebin Sha-Rhonas, daughter of the Empire!"

The Emperor stood a step back off the dais. In that moment, only the cadaverous features of Shebin towered into the sky above the Imperial City.

The crowd erupted into deafening cheers and applause.

"Give them your blessing," the Emperor urged from behind her.

"My fellow citizens," Shebin shouted. Her voice blasted from the sky with deafening sound. It startled her as she struggled to speak. "I give my blessing . . . my blessing to the Army of Imperial Vengeance . . . *my* Vengeance!"

The approval roared upward from the streets below. She smiled from the platform. She smiled from the sky.

The enormous figure of Shebin vanished as the Emperor took her hand and led her to the railing of the platform. The drums had begun beating again and the army—the Army of Imperial Vengeance—was once more making their way through the city. They would parade past the foundations of the Cloud Palace and continue down the Vira Rhonas to the Meducean Gate, down the road past the sprawling buildings outside the city wall until they came to the fold platforms now prepared to take them on their first of many folds northward toward Tjarlas and the Northmarch Folds beyond.

The Emperor stood next to her, waving with her

to the crowds below. His words no longer thundered over the city but were for her ears alone.

"Enjoy the day, Shebin," the Emperor said. "Remember it well. If the army crushes this rebellion then it will be remembered as our victory but should it fail . . ."

Shebin's smile dimmed slightly. "Then it will fail in my name alone, my Emperor."

"Yes, my dear daughter," the Emperor nodded, still waving.

"Then I will ensure that it will not fail," Shebin replied, brightening her smile.

Ghenetar Praetus Betjarian marched at the head of the Cohort from Tjarlas in his ceremonial armor. The roaring of the crowds on either side of the road was giving him a headache and he longed to be rid of the worthless show costume he was wearing and get back to the business of war.

He was especially anxious to get back to Tjarlas with his Cohorts ahead of the Army of Imperial Vengeance. He wanted to be there to see the look on the other Ghenetar Praetus' faces when they arrived and discovered that two of his Legions had departed up the Northmarch Folds five days before this nonsense parade had even begun. They were most likely beginning their search for this Drakis rabble even now.

It had seemed a strange order coming from his

commander, Ghenetar Omris Sjei-Shurian, but the old warrior had never led him astray.

It was unusual, however, that he had insisted a Quorum of Iblisi accompany the Legions. Still, Sjei-Shurian had assured him that the Inquisitor in charge of the Quorum—some female by the name of K'yeran Tsi-M'harul—would not interfere with his command.

And his Legions would arrive on the Shadow Coast days before anyone would have thought possible.

# Chapter 17

## *Risks*

DRAKIS LAY EXHAUSTED ON HIS COT. He felt
the aching in his muscles and bones, the longing in his body for sweet rest and, in truth, he
wished to embrace it, for even in troubled sleep he
could not be free.

He was in this twilight of his mind when *she*
came to him.

Her memory stalked him at all times during the
day. In the urgency of his position he could bury
this pain in activity or divert his emptiness with
work. But it was in this time between consciousness and oblivion that she pounced from the shadows of his mind. She came bearing sweet talons of
guilt and regret that tore at his doubt and despair.
Her smile flashed with unbearable loss. A harsh
word he had uttered that had hurt her became
magnified a thousandfold in his soul, screaming
his blame. There, before the darkness took him,

her loss became a gaping wound in his soul from which his life seemed forever to bleed and for which no healing ever seemed possible.

Drakis shuddered, his breath coming quickly as he lay on the cot. He tried with conscious effort to relax the rising tension in his painful muscles, attempting to busy his mind with other thoughts . . . other memories . . . anyone but the woman that he had loved in a dream and lost so terribly in cruel reality.

*Mala.*

He shook again, turning his head so as to avoid the name that boiled up into his conscious mind.

She walked up one of the gently rolling hills surrounding their home. The stalks of grain through which she strolled were supple in the evening breeze, colored orange-gold by the setting sun. Her face was turned away from him, her attention on the avatria of House Timuran. Her head was bald as he had so long remembered it, the Sinque mark of her Devotions clearly visible on her exposed scalp. There was barely a trace of the auburn hair which . . . which . . .

His breathing came harder, his mouth suddenly dry. He tightened his eyelids, trying in vain to block the memories from his recollection.

*She stopped at the crest of this hill. Pink clouds floated in a deepening sky. Her skin seemed almost radiantly aglow. She started to turn, as though she just noticed him behind her. He could not see her face and suddenly wondered if she would turn to face him and there would be nothing there at all . . .*

*Before she turned around, she started singing to him, her voice distant and hollow.*

*"Mala of Drakis now walks the fields*
*Warmed by the harvesting sun.*
*Dead roads we're walking!*
*Destiny talking . . ."*

Drakis sat upright with a sharp cry. His forehead was beaded in perspiration despite the chill in the large pavilion that passed for his tent. He rubbed his eyes and swung his legs over the side of his cot.

Drakis heard the flap on the far side of the tent rustle open.

He held up his hand. "It's all right, Belag. Just a bad dream."

The figure staggered a few steps toward him.

Drakis tensed, reaching for his sword. The shadow in his tent was not nearly large enough to be the manticore.

"Drakis!" the voice said in a tense whisper.

"Ethis?" Drakis asked, his blade drawn, the grip cold in his hand. "What are you doing here? We weren't expecting you until . . ."

"Quiet!" the chimerian gasped, gripping the human by the arm. "Where's Braun?"

"His tent is with the rest of his acolytes about a mile from here," Drakis answered. "He's sleeping, with any luck."

"What Urulani said about opening folds," Ethis continued his questions, barely waiting for the answers before asking the next. "Can Braun and his acolytes actually make it work?"

"Yes. They had some disasters at first but . . ."

"Could they create enough folds to move the encampment?"

"Yes. In fact, we've already moved the rest of the army up using their folds," Drakis said.

"Then the army is already here?"

"Yes and the encampment should be ready to move by the time Urulani and Jugar return from their . . ."

"And that elf . . . Soen," Ethis continued. "Where is he?"

"With the other acolytes," Drakis said. "Why?"

Ethis' normally blank face shifted into a grimace. "Well, it can't be helped. Send word for Braun to meet you near Dragon's Roost. We need to talk . . . but not here!"

"One battle?" Drakis asked, an uncertain edge to his voice. "That's what she is asking of us—just one victory?"

"That is all my Queen asks," Ethis affirmed, "and all she needs."

Marush lay coiled about Drakis, Ethis, and Braun, his great bulk touching all the walls of a magnificent rotunda that had sprung up around them. Arched columns defined three tiers nearly thirty feet tall. The ceiling was an incredible dome of crystal panels fitted into an iron lattice. Beyond, a gentle, warm rain fell from a leaden sky. In the center of the room lay the uppermost curve of a partially exposed sphere protruding through a circular opening in the fitted stone of the floor. Its surface was etched with a map of Aeria extending southward beyond the Aergus Sea to the coasts of Oerania and as far north as the Siren Coast and Drakosia beyond. The rotunda looked as though it were kept in perfect condition despite the fact that there appeared to be no other creatures in existence beyond the dragon and his guests.

Even so, Drakis knew that the pilgrim encampment was situated not more than a dozen yards from where they stood and, were he not touching the dragon, their conversation might easily have been overheard. The gentle plains that moments before had surrounded them and the tents, lean-tos, and wagons where the pilgrims slept under a starry night sky were still there. Ethis, standing near him, had suggested this as the only place where they might speak freely—their discussion hidden from ears of the pilgrim followers even should any wake and spot them standing beside the dragon.

As for Braun, the third member of their party, the experience was completely new and distracting in the extreme. "Do you think this place is created naturally by the dragons from the Aether magic or do they act as Aether Wells themselves, channeling and refining Aer from the world into this higher form?"

"Braun!" Ethis urged in exasperated tones. "Focus your attention! We have little time and important matters to discuss!"

"Of course, but do you think this place actually exists?" Braun grinned, showing his gapped teeth in wonder. "Was it here before we came, and has it been magically reconstructed? Or is this tower from another place or time and has it been duplicated here? Or perhaps is it that we have gone to wherever or whenever it exists?"

"Braun!" Ethis shouted.

"Yes, of course," Braun said, rolling his eyes. "You've returned with a proposed pact from the Queen of Ephindria who offers to support Drakis and his merry pilgrims by ceding lands to our cause in exchange for us doing her a little favor."

"It's no small favor," Drakis said, shaking his head. "She's asking us to take down an entire elven city."

"Yes, but think of the possibilities, Drakis," Ethis continued. "This city is the key to Aether collection and distribution throughout Chaenandria and serves in support of the rebel houses of Southern Ephindria. You bring down the Wells in that city and it robs the Empire of nearly half of the Aether production from the Wells all along the Benis Coast. You choke off the flow of Aether from the Empire to the families of Pashorei and Surthal, and they cannot stand against Queen Chythal."

"Why not?" Drakis argued. "How does cutting of the Aether end your civil war?"

"Because it was the Aether that *caused* the war of rebellion in the first place," Ethis answered, anger creeping into his voice. "After the elves conquered Chaenandria they began trading with the southern families in Ephindria. Most of the elders saw the danger but the young were particularly susceptible to its allure."

"Indeed?" Braun asked with an eager expression. "Are chimerians seduced by the power of magic?"

"No," Ethis sighed as he allowed a pained expression to fill his features. "We are seduced by our desire to please."

"As they have always been," Marush said. The dragon rarely spoke to anyone but Drakis. "It is their greatest gift and their curse; their strength and their downfall."

"That makes no sense," Drakis said. "Everyone knows the Ephindrians are the most secretive and reclusive people in the known lands."

"We hide because we are too giving, too responsive to others' desires and needs," Ethis said, his words halting and coming with difficulty. "It is never spoken of outside of the family. All chimerians naturally desire to build rapport with everyone we meet. While the adults of our kind learn to be more guarded with outsiders, it requires discipline which the youth of our race often lack. Our ability to change our shape is greatly enhanced by our natural ability to become attuned with the emotions and even, on some level, the thoughts of others."

"Ah!" Braun said, his thick eyebrows rising with his understanding. "So Ephindrians do not just change their shape to suit others but modify their own thoughts to align with them. That is how you make yourselves so convincing to others; by not only mimicking forms but attitudes and thoughts as well."

"That has always been the danger to us," Ethis nodded. "The elves brought Aether magic to the young princesses of Surthal and Pashorei. It seemed innocent enough at first—indeed it was welcomed as a new convenience among the southern families, especially the young."

"But it didn't stop with the Aether, did it?" Drakis said.

"No, it did not," Ethis sighed, folding his upper arms across his chest while his lower hands remained in contact with the dragon. "The young chimerians in those southern families began to adapt to the thoughts and ethics of the elves. Soon they began placing themselves under Devotions to the Aether altars and desiring more of the Aether, became more and more like the elves in their thoughts and ethics. By the time the danger was realized in Chythal's court, the south was already poisoned by rapport with the elves. Chythal closed all the borders, trying to quarantine our nation from the sickness of the world but by then the southern families were too infected by the Aether to go back."

Drakis drew in a deep breath. "And your Queen believes that if we cut off their supply of Aether . . ."

"Then the illness will no longer be fed and the southern families may be redeemed," Ethis finished. "The elves are very jealous of their Aether.

They collect it in a vast field of Aether Wells that cover the Southern Steppes well into the Chaenandrian Plains and have begun establishing new Wells in the southern lands of Ephindria over the last few months. But the Wells do not supply the chimerian mages directly; all their power is drawn through their folds to the city. Only then is it distributed back for the use of the chimerian mages—but only a trickle compared to the river they pull from our lands. That is how the elves keep Ephindria balanced on a knife's edge—and too weak to challenge the elven Empire."

"A very inefficient system," Braun said with disdain. "Our Aether is a much better and more efficient system of distribution."

"Ethis, I understand your nation's—your family's problem," Drakis shook his head. "But taking these people into battle is exactly what I wanted to avoid!"

"But think of how many *more* battles you would have avoided," Ethis argued. "You would have won a place where your people could settle in peace with a newly strong ally between your people and the Rhonas. And consider your advantage . . ."

"My advantage?" Drakis almost laughed. "I'm outnumbered by the Rhonas Legions almost a hundred to one!"

"Legions who will not be there! Look!" Ethis turned slightly, unfolding his upper pair of arms and pointing toward the map etched into the curved surface next to them. "Here is where we are now, between Nordesia and Ephindria. Down here between Chaenandria and the Aeria Mountains is your objective. The elf spy . . ."

"Soen," Drakis said.

"Yes, Soen," Ethis continued. "He says that the Rhonas Legions will move up the Northmarch Folds and march up the Shadow Coast, hoping to catch us with the Bay of Thetis on our right and the Shrouded Plain on our left."

"You think he's lying?" Braun asked.

"No, I think he's right," Ethis continued. "But what if we accept this pact with Queen Chythal? What if we move the army and the encampment *east* instead of south and down the Mournful Road . . ."

"But that takes us back into the Shrouded Plain," Braun said. "That is, trust me, very much a dead end in every sense of the word."

"No, there is another road," Ethis said. "It is ancient and has remained unused since beyond memory but it is there nevertheless. Queen Chythal commanded its closure but for this pact she will permit it to be opened for the passage of Drakis and his people—if you will accept the risks involved in traveling it."

"What risks?" Drakis asked.

"They are minimal, I assure you," Ethis said. "All we have to do is push southward down the road and then west along the elf folds. The elves have pulled out their Legions here, intent on pursuing us to the north as quickly as possible. Opposition will be light all the way to the gates of the city itself."

"But to take an entire city!" Drakis shook his head.

"You took Port Glorious in a matter of hours," Ethis said.

"But this is entirely different!"

"No, not different . . . just bigger," Ethis urged. "The tactic is the same. Find the central Well of the city, fly Braun or one of his trained acolytes in on the back of a dragon, and bring down the Well. The elves are useless without their Aether. When the Aether dies in southern Ephindria, Chythal will move against the southern families. Your victory is accomplished swiftly. You will have won a land of refuge for your people and the face of the world is changed forever."

"Will it work, Braun?" Drakis asked.

Braun considered the possibilities with a half-smile. "Bringing the central Well down or, preferably, reversing it, would cause a cascade reversal of any of the Wells that were feeding it. You would be bringing down the Aether across Chaenandria and probably most of the Northern Provinces if what Ethis says is true. Yes, it would work, but might I suggest that there is a delicate problem to be addressed."

"What problem?" Ethis asked.

"We must find a way to reverse the Wells but keep the Devotions intact," Braun said quietly.

Drakis drew in a deep breath.

"I have heard from Belag the accounts of the fall of House Timuran," Braun said wistfully. "What would such madness do to an entire city?"

"Then find us a way," Ethis said. "Make it work,

Braun. The only question we need to address is whether your acolytes can be depended upon to move this entire encampment and its army."

"The distances involved are staggering, the amount of Aether required beyond calculation," Braun said. "I cannot guarantee that any of my acolytes would even survive such a repeated use of Aether and we'll need to reverse a number of Wells as soon as possible to make it work."

"What of Soen?" Drakis asked. "We cannot take him with us. Everything depends upon the elves not knowing where we've gone."

"I've got something special in mind for Soen," Braun smiled. "Something unexpected and simple that I've been holding back from him for just such an occasion."

"You plan on killing an Iblisi?" Ethis asked in astonishment.

"Kill him? Nonsense!" Braun answered. "That's all warriors think magic is good for; reducing the creature standing in front of you to a pile of ashes just because you disagree with him. We don't have to murder the elf; just get rid of him. I've been working him pretty hard lately and learned about as much as I think I can from him. I think he deserves a long, well-earned rest—long enough for us to slip away and the longer, of course, the better."

"Very well," Drakis said. "One battle, one victory, and then these people can settle in peace. How soon can you take care of Soen?"

"Tonight too soon?" Braun asked, cracking the knuckles on both his hands.

"Do it," Drakis said.

"It will be a masterful performance," Braun bowed. "Sadly, no one will be around who will remember it except your humble conjuror. I just need to know one thing more."

"What is that, Braun?" Drakis asked.

"How do I leave this most enchanting place?" Braun beamed.

"Oh, all you have to do is remove your hand from . . ."

Braun suddenly vanished.

Drakis sighed, turning toward the Ephindrian.

"He is dangerous," Ethis said.

"Which one?" Drakis rubbed his neck. He could feel another headache threatening to blossom at the back of his skull. "Soen or Braun?"

"Take your pick," Ethis replied. "I don't like depending on either of them. Soen is power mad and Braun is just mad. However you achieve it, for the plan to work, the Well of Tjarlas must come down. If Braun cannot do it . . ."

"Then we need someone who can," Drakis nodded. "A certain dwarf comes to mind who would delight in fulfilling such a quest but only if Braun fails. I'll speak with him about it—assuming he can find us again."

"Then you will accept Chythal's offer?"

"If I can save these people without having to take on the entire Rhonas Empire then perhaps it is worth a single battle."

"What about Belag and the council?" Ethis asked.

"They already know we're moving the encampment," Drakis shrugged. "Braun will just change the destination for the first fold and we'll explain the change in plans after we're well on our way to Ephindria. I don't want anyone knowing where we're going who doesn't have to know and no sooner than they have to know it. Will that satisfy the offer from your Queen?"

"Our nation is our family, Drakis, but it is now a broken family," Ethis said. "The Queen will be pleased. As long as the Rhonas armies are still moving north—we can be victorious."

In the jungle beyond the tower in which Drakis, Braun, and Ethis spoke lurked a second dragon, white with gray markings.

Next to it, listening intently, stood a lithe woman with her hand to the dragon's scales. If any pilgrims chanced to see her they might wonder why she and her dragon were not standing with Drakis and the rest.

The Lyric had heard everything the other three had said and knew exactly what she had to do— for she believed herself to be Drakis, the Hero of the Prophecy—and she would save her people.

# Chapter 18

## Uprisings

"LEGATE XHU'CHAN!" THE WAR-MAGE BOWED slightly as he stood at the threshold of the command tent for the Legions of Rhonas Steel and Blood.

The elven Legion commander stood up from examining the maps spread on the table before him and arched his back, cracking several vertebrae back into place as he did. They had been surging forward through the Northmarch Folds for the last four days, arriving at last at a miserable, dirty backwater called Port Dog at the southern end of Manticus Bay. Here he had given the twin Legions under his command a day to regroup while he planned his next move. The orders of Ghenetar Praetus Betjarian had been specific up to this point but now allowed the Legate some discretion regarding how to proceed. There was an army of rebels operating in Nordesia which, according to the wise and noble masters of Rhonas, would be marching down the Shadow Coast to challenge the elven homeland.

*Nonsense, of course,* Legate Xhu'chan scoffed. Still, any opportunity to take the army out of the monotonous flatlands of Chaenandria and their Southern Steppes was a welcome relief. The manticores had once been worthy opponents but the days of the great warrior clans were over. The presence of their army in that conquered region was largely an unnecessary result of over-cautious bureaucrats in the capital city. At least now he and his warriors were on the hunt for what he considered easy prey. Betjarian had warned him that this horde of warriors in the north had managed to completely destroy a Legion of the Vash but Xhu'chan had studied the report on that battle. He knew that the defeated commander had lost because of a freakish failure of Aether on the battlefield. It was a mistake he would not repeat.

The Emperor had decreed that most of his military might should march northward and destroy these malcontents before any more damage could be done to the Imperial pride. *Well, let them come,* Xhu'chan thought. He would manage the job with the two Legions under his command and then the rest of the army could watch as he returned triumphantly with the heads of this Drakis rebel and each of his followers at the end of his Legions' spears.

Or he would, he corrected himself, if K'yeran Tsi-M'harul, the Iblisi Inquisitor standing on the opposite side of the map table did not claim this Drakis a prisoner first. The presence of the Iblisi Quorum, appointed to advise the Legate on this campaign at the direct instruction of Ghentar Omris Sjei-Shurian, was both a mystery and an irritant to Legate Xhu'chan. The Inquisitor had never interfered with his command except for the occasional urging to press forward with more zeal. He knew that she was unnecessary to the military success of the campaign. He also knew that if she ever did make a request of him, he would do as she asked. To not honor her advice would be a mistake, possibly the last he would ever make.

Xhu'chan turned his gaze from the Inquisitor opposite him toward the war-mage and beckoned him inside the tent. "You are . . . ?"

"War-mage Kleidon," the elf in the armored robes said with a bow. Kleidon was old for his calling, his lips drawn back from his pointed teeth whose ends were worn down to rounded points. "I am assigned dominion over the sixth Cohort Proxis of Centurai Mehuin."

"The scout Centurai, of course," Xhu'chan nodded. He knew Kleidon as a modestly talented mage who was slowly aging beyond usefulness. The years tended to make him talk more and do less. "My apologies, War-mage. My command is a vast one and I am not yet familiar with every detail of its elements."

"We have spoken before," Kleidon said with an edge of insult.

"And if we are to ever speak to anyone again,

you had best state your business here," Xhu'chan said, the obvious implication just beneath the surface of his placid voice.

"An Octian of our third Centurai has reach Shellsea," Kleidon said. "Do you know it, Legate?"

"Yes, it is the next decent port city up the Shadow Coast from this wrenched backwater." Xhu'chan remained unimpressed. "What of it?"

"The Octian reports that they found the city garrison encamped outside the city walls and apparently unable to return to their barracks," Kleidon continued.

"Unable?" Xhu'chan snarled. "What could possibly have prevented them from taking the city again by force?"

"Word is that they fled the city, Legate," the war-mage responded.

"Fled?" Xhu'chan blustered. "Deserted their posts?"

"And why would they flee the city?" the Inquisitor spoke up suddenly.

The war-mage hesitated, his dull eyes fixed on the Legate.

"Don't be stupid, Kleidon," Xhu'chan barked. "Answer the question!"

Kleidon smiled, exposing his dulled teeth as he bowed. "The garrison commander reports that they were driven from the city by a dragon."

A long moment of uncomprehending silence descended on the tent. The Inquisitor stared at the war-mage. The Legate's mouth went slack. He tilted his head slightly to the right as though he had not heard properly.

"A *what?*"

"A dragon, my Lord Legate," the war-mage affirmed.

"There are no dragons in Aeria," Xhu'chan asserted.

"It seems there are now," Kleidon shrugged.

"They must have been drugged or enchanted," Xhu'chan said, shaking his head. "Some sort of trick by the rebels."

"The scouts report that every elven warrior they interrogated has given the same account," Kleidon continued. "An immense monstrous creature resembling a dragon descended into the central square of the city breathing out flames and destruction before it. The commander ordered the garrison to regroup outside the city walls and prepare to retake the city and attack the creature. However, once they were prepared they found that the fold runes they had planned to use to re-enter the city had been rendered useless. Several attacks by the garrison force were repulsed by rebel warriors, who had by then manned their abandoned defenses on the city walls. As the garrison commander was concerned that the dragon might return, he determined to make camp outside the city and send word for reinforcements."

"A brave commander indeed," Xhu'chan mocked, spitting on the ground in his disgust. "I suppose he's just been waiting for someone to come along and salvage his honor for him?"

"As it happened, Legate, a dragon *did* return," Kleidon said with a slight smile. "Not the same as the first–a *different* dragon."

"A *second* dragon?" the Legate exclaimed. "Not possible!"

"This one was seen both by the remaining garrison and the scout Octian as well," Kleidon replied. "And, might I add, that I saw it through the eyes of my Proxi who was there at the time. It was a most astonishing experience. It was a creature of unprecedented size with enormous leathery wings and a long fluked tail. It was light and dark gray in its markings. Its talons were taller than an elf. There was also a rider—human, I believe—seated just ahead of the wings on the creature's neck. It, too, descended into Shellsea and for a time vanished from view. Then it, too, rose up into the sky, only this time the northern gates of the city opened and a caravan left the city."

"A caravan?" Xhu'chan squinted slightly as he twisted his neck, trying to get his vertebrae comfortable again. "You mean a military column?"

"Hardly, my Lord Legate," Kleidon corrected. "Females, old males, children, wagons of goods, and . . ."

"Pilgrims," K'yeran laughed.

"We shall retake the city," the Legate affirmed. "Kleidon, inform my aide that I want to see each of the Legion commanders and their staff at once. We shall advance up the coast with both Legions, retake the city and . . ."

"No, Legate Xhu'chan," the Inquisitor said with a chuckle in her voice. "You certainly shall not."

The Legate turned slowly toward the Inquisitor. "And why should I not?"

K'yeran turned to the old war-mage. "You said this 'caravan' was being led by someone astride a dragon?"

"I saw it through the eyes of my Proxi," Kleidon nodded.

"Then, Xhu'chan," the Inquisitor said to the Legate, "there is no need to retake Port Shellsea. Our prize is not to be found behind the barricaded walls of an insignificant port. You can retake this outpost of Imperial Might later. Your orders were to search for and find this army of the rebellion so that you may avenge the destruction of your brother warriors and the honor of the Emperor. This army is not in Shellsea and you now know how to find them."

"And how is that?" Xhu'chan demanded.

"The same way you find an anthill, Legate . . . you follow the ants."

"You want me to follow ants?" Xhu'chan puzzled.

"The dragon knows where this rebel army is located," said K'yeran, her gaze falling onto the map in front of her. Her long finger reached out from her robe, pointing at Shellsea on the map then drawing northward along the coast toward Nordesia. "The caravan follows the dragon. All we have to do is follow the caravan. You should continue to move your army northward. In the meanwhile, you should be relieved to know that I and my Quorum will be leaving you for the time being on a little expedition of our own. If we find your rebel army . . . we'll let you know."

Urulani felt a chill run through her that was deeper than the cold of the thin air around her. She was struggling to remain awake. The last six days had been exhausting as she had moved from village to town along the shoreline of the Bay of Thetis. Everywhere she had gone, the people in the villages had rallied to her tales of Drakis and the great army's victories in the northland. Some had remained in their homes, many had balked at her call but many more had listened to her message. It was with satisfaction that she saw the lines of new believers heading eastward along the roads and sometimes by ship, all yearning to become a part of the Drakis Uprising, as they had called it. All were eager to do their part and entire caravans had moved along the coast toward Shellsea and the coastal road north toward Gorganta Bay. They sang songs as they traveled about the "Drakis Dawn" and the "War of the Prophet," their words unclear to her as she flew above them but the intent of their hearts evident. Urulani was exhausted and desperately in need of sleep but the sight below had brought her back to wakefulness.

She leaned out from the back of the dragon,

gazing down. They were flying amid towering clouds that rose around them. Kyranish rode the currents that raged between the canyons of white in the sky, drifting with his wings extended from updraft to updraft. It was a violent, rough ride for Urulani but the dragon appeared to be enjoying the respite from having to beat his wings constantly against the air. It was making Urulani uneasy, a sensation which was completely foreign to her on the deck of a ship regardless of the hostility of the sea.

It was not the sky but the sight below that sent a sudden shiver up her spine.

Urulani had gotten good at recognizing landmarks on the ground far below. She had little concept of how high she was above the ground. In her mind, each time the dragon rose into the sky, it was not so much that she was getting higher as the ground was shrinking beneath her. The landscape below became an incredibly detailed map. It was fascinating to her and she enjoyed keeping track of their progress as they flew, picking up more details of each place along the way.

It was the details she had just noticed around Port Dog, now ten thousand feet below her that had caught her attention. There were over a hundred patches of tents in rows and columns that were too neat and too square. Flashes from a fold portal winked at her again and again as columns of warriors—antlike in their movements—wound out from its maw.

"It's already more than a Legion in size," Urulani murmured. "They're coming for us."

Urulani reached down with her hand, placing it against the neck of Kyranish.

"Yes, Urulani, I see them, too," the dragon responded as the clouds vanished from the sky which had suddenly changed from midday to dusk. The warriors below them were changed, too, appearing as a dark blight spreading across the land. "The elves make war on us once more."

"They have already reached the coast," Urulani said, weariness and despair washing over her. "We've got to warn the pilgrims. We've got to stop them before . . . before . . ."

Urulani slumped forward in her harness, shock and exhaustion overtaking her.

Kyranish obeyed, pressing northward along the coast. Day passed into night as the dragon continued north, but Kyranish did not feel the need to awaken his exhausted companion. The dragon spotted the streams of refugees moving northward along the coast.

Kyranish had nearly reached Watchman Cove at the northern end of Gorganta Bay when, quite abruptly, he raised his head. Then, silently, he banked sharply eastward, changing his course.

He turned so smoothly that the sleeping Urulani never noticed that they were no longer heading toward the encampment.

# CHAPTER 19

## *The Gift*

K'YERAN TSI-M'HARUL STOOD on the open and vacant plain. Dust and thin smoke drifted past her in the evening breeze as she surveyed the great expanse around her. For as far as she could see, the prairie grasses were trampled flat, in many places no longer there at all. There were stone rings for campfires laid practically to the horizon. There were a number of wagons with broken wheels abandoned here and there as well as pieces of discarded items everywhere she looked. Broken pots, cracked skillets, empty baskets, and tracks everywhere representing every kind of creature from manticores to gnomes, and more humans than she thought still existed.

It was not the enormity of the abandoned encampment or its implications that held her attention. Rather, it was a single tent that remained standing in the southeastern area of the field of debris. Its canvas rustled in the breeze but it remained otherwise placid amidst the abandonment stretching to the north and west. K'yeran stood considering this single fragile dwelling from more than three hundred feet away. She fingered her Matei staff in absentminded rhythms with her elongated head tilted to one side. It was dangerous in its innocuous appearance and she was trying to decide how to approach it.

"Inquisitor K'yeran!" An Iblisi Assesia approached the Inquisitor, running toward her from the north.

"Yes, Jak'ra," K'yeran acknowledged without turning her attention from the tent surface shifting slightly in the wind. "Why do you disturb my musings?"

The Assesia came to a stop a few feet away from the Inquisitor. Jak'ra was a part of K'yeran's Quorum, dispatched northward on a mission for their Order. His respect for her included maintaining a reasonably safe distance. "The Indexia sent me back to report."

K'yeran smiled. Wheton and Chik'dai had followed the tracks northward on her instructions. Both represented the Indexia of their Quorum but it was telling that they would send one of the lower-ranking Assesia to give their report. They must have feared their truth would not be to K'yeran's liking. "By all means, then, report."

"The cart and foot tracks lead generally toward the north," Jak'ra said, planting the metal tip of his own Matei staff into the packed dirt at his side.

"There they all converge into fifteen locations in a fixed line and then suddenly vanish with no trace of them beyond."

"They are using folds then," K'yeran observed out loud. She always felt that she reasoned more clearly when she spoke her thoughts.

"No, Inquisitor," the Assesia responded.

K'yeran turned her head slowly to face the young Iblisi. "What do you mean . . . no?"

"I mean, Inquisitor, that there were no fold markings to be found."

"No runes? No inscriptions?"

"No, Inquisitor."

"Fold platforms then?"

"No, Inquisitor."

K'yeran turned her attention back to the sole remaining tent. "Where did they go, then? And now we don't even know how they got there . . . wherever *there* is. What about the rest of the Assesia?"

"Assesia Phagana is investigating large, strange tracks of two—perhaps three—creatures of monstrous size," Jak'ra continued, seemingly relieved that he had survived what he considered to be the most volatile part of his report. "These appear to end abruptly as well."

"Dragons," K'yeran mused aloud.

"Dragons?" Jak'ra blinked, startled.

"Yes, they must have taken flight," K'yeran nodded. "That's why they don't go anywhere but into thin air . . . however I have great doubts that this entire encampment followed suit, flapped their wings and vanished into the sky."

"Perhaps the dragons . . . ate them?" Assesia Jak'ra suggested.

"*Ate* them?" K'yeran barked in disbelief. "Over a hundred thousand manticores, chimerians, and the gods know what all else—many of them armed and seasoned warriors—and the dragons *ate them*?"

"Well," Jak'ra offered hesitantly. "Maybe they were *hungry* dragons?"

K'yeran bared her teeth. "Wouldn't that be a wonderful gift for the Emperor! All his problems solved by a ravenous group of dragons now bloated on the carcasses of his enemies."

"I suppose it would be an incredible gift . . ."

"Only I don't believe in *gifts*," K'yeran snarled. "Too convenient is only pretty wrapping that hides the real danger waiting to bite you with poisonous fangs. Don't make up stories, boy, you're no good at it. And speaking of dangerous gifts—I think it's time I unwrapped this one."

K'yeran strode suddenly toward the tent. The Matei staff spun in her hands, the head suddenly aglow and alive. Jak'ra, caught off guard, followed quickly, trying to catch up with the head of the Quorum as she quickly closed the distance to the tent. She reached out with the metal tip of her staff, flipping the door flap to one side.

Jak'ra nearly ran into the back of the Inquisitor as she stopped suddenly at the entrance to the tent.

"I *hate* this," she muttered. "I really *hate* this."

"What?" Jak'ra breathed, trying to look around her.

"This!" K'yeran seethed, pointing the tip of her Matei staff at the center of the tent's interior.

There, lying on a cot, was the sleeping form of Soen Tjen-rei. He was in his weathered and faded robes, his Matei staff—devoid of all Aether—held in his folded arms, rising and falling slowly with every breath.

"He's . . . asleep?" Jak'ra whispered.

"It's an enchantment," K'yeran wrinkled her nose in disgust. "A simple charm placed on a rogue Inquisitor of the Iblisi. It's *embarrassing* is what it is! Any barely trained initiate into the Iblisi Orders could have defended against it."

"But that's . . . that's Soen Tjen-rei!" the Assesia gaped. "He's the renegade we were sent to kill!"

"Yes, isn't he," K'yeran observed dryly. "But we aren't going to do that, are we, Assesia Jak'ra?"

"We aren't?" The young Quorum follower responded with doubt.

"No, I have overriding orders," K'yeran asserted. "We are to bring him back to the Keeper for special interrogation. The Keeper demands to know why this renegade is here."

"Inquisitor K'yeran," Jak'ra said in haste, "if he is still under the effects of this magic, we could enfold him in a suspension field, then gently transport him so as not to awaken him, using each of our staves in series . . ."

"Or," K'yeran huffed. "We could just ask him what he's doing here. Oblige me by holding perfectly still for the next few seconds."

K'yeran stepped forward into the tent, placed

one booted foot against the cot and kicked it over.

Soen fell against the hard ground, jolting awake. He at once leaped to his feet, his Matei staff in his hands as though prepared to deal death.

"Hello, Soen," K'yeran said casually.

Soen blinked. "Hello, K'yeran."

"Been a long time," K'yeran smiled.

"Not long enough," Soen answered in a calm, flat voice.

"You mind putting down your stick," K'yeran said, pointing at Soen's still-poised Matei staff. "We both know that's as dead as last week's fish."

"And you also know, I can still do a lot of damage with a dead stick," Soen observed.

"And I can do whole *worlds* of damage more with my *live* one," K'yeran pointed to the bright glow from the head of her staff, cradled casually in the crook of her left arm. "It would be such a shame if I had to demonstrate the difference to you."

"It's never stopped you before," Soen observed.

"Nor you, as I recall," K'yeran smiled, raising her thin eyebrow over her featureless left eye. "The price of fame, I suppose . . . or is that infamy? I'm always getting those two mixed up."

"Are we talking about you or me?" Soen asked.

"Why, you, of course," K'yeran laughed with a sound like a knife's edge on slate. "Indeed, one hears a great deal about Soen everywhere one goes these days. Soen, the mysterious traitor of the Iblisi, who has joined up with the army of the Drakis

Rebellion. Soen the dangerous man who sold his birthright among the elven castes for the lies of a human charlatan . . . or something along those lines. The details of the official story are still being worked out."

"And how does this story end?" Soen asked, straightening up.

"You know, that's the most astonishing part of all," K'yeran said, reaching up with her right hand and rubbing the back of her elongated head. "Ch'drei hasn't told me the end of the story yet."

"Which is why you didn't kill me while I slept," Soen observed. "The Keeper does not yet know how she wants the story to end."

"I believe that's why she wants to talk to you," K'yeran nodded. "She wants a very private chat with you. I believe she says she'll even provide the tea."

"And you've come not only to deliver the invitation," Soen folded his arms around his useless Matei staff, "but to make sure that I accept."

"More than just accept," K'yeran said. "I'm to escort you personally to the party."

"Which is why you managed with this inept adept at your side to infiltrate the pilgrim encampment and find me," Soen smiled sadly as he shook his head. "You disappoint me, K'yeran. You should have known that slipping into a camp of a hundred thousand rebels is one thing; managing to escape it is another altogether. We are surrounded by an army who now has access to power that I am only beginning to understand. Power which . . ."

Soen stopped, his black eyes widening.

"It's gone!" he murmured.

K'yeran flashed a broad, sharp-toothed smile. "Lose something?"

"The Human Aether," Soen stammered. "I used to feel it in my bones. It's . . . no longer there."

Jak'ra, still standing just behind K'yeran, somehow managed to find his voice. "Soen Tjen-rei! You are charged by the Keeper of the Imperial Order of the Iblisi to yield your person to the will of the Quorum . . ."

Soen stepped past K'yeran toward the tent opening, pushing the young Assesia out of the way without a second glance.

"Relax, Jak'ra," K'yeran said as she turned and followed Soen out of the tent. "I promise to let you deal with the formalities later."

She found Soen standing outside the tent, his shoulders and back stiff. He gazed out over the horizon, searching. "What day is it, K'yeran?"

"The fourteenth day of Kholas," the Inquisitor answered, fingering her Matei staff. The glowing color in the staff's head intensified, shifting to a deeper purple. "Is it important?"

"I lay down on that cot on the night of the eleventh," Soen sighed, pointing back to the tent. "I've been asleep all that time which means they left me here three days ago. We've got to find them, K'yeran. Where are they?"

"I was hoping you could tell us," the female Inquisitor sighed. "But it doesn't matter."

"You don't get it, do you, K'yeran?" Soen said, the anger building in his voice. "None of you get it! It matters a great deal—more than you can possibly know!"

"The Army of the Prophet?" K'yeran laughed. "Bolters and frontier rabble?"

"These 'rabble' present a significant threat to the future of the Empire," Soen responded. "They have the means and the will to rob the Empire of its Aether—its very lifeblood. And they are very quickly reclaiming their magic. They already are capable of creating their own folds without the need of platforms or staves or conduits. If they are allowed to go unchecked . . ."

K'yeran swung her Matei staff in a blazing arc. The purple flash from the head of the staff erupted around Soen. He stopped moving in the moment, his mouth frozen in the act of forming another word. The brilliant purple glow surrounded him.

"That," grumbled Jak'ra as he emerged from the tent, "is what I thought we should have done in the first place."

"Fortunately, what you think does not matter," K'yeran said as she walked up to where the frozen Soen stood, inspecting him to make certain the spell had completely engulfed him. Satisfied, she turned to the Assesia as she pointed to the top of a nearby rise. "Inscribe a fold rune up there then propagate thirty or so more down either side of the slope. When that's done recall the rest of the

Quorum. We'll be taking our friend Soen here back with us."

"But what if these rebels do have access to their own Aether?" Jak'ra asked.

"The problem is already taken care of, Soen," K'yeran responded. "The Army of Imperial Vengeance is marching this way as we speak. With your rune inscriptions we shall have graciously provided them the means to bring their warriors even farther northward. Let them deal with the battles. Keeper Ch'drei wants Soen brought back to the Imperial City and that is all that matters to us."

K'yeran turned again to face Soen's immobilized form. "Well, Soen, I think you'll be attending Ch'drei's party after all . . . though I don't recommend drinking the tea."

"I wonder what he was about to say?" Jak'ra moved next to K'yeran, also looking closely at Soen's face. "Still, he'll make a most excellent gift for the Keeper."

K'yeran frowned.

She never trusted gifts.

# CHAPTER 20

## *The Mournful Road*

U RULANI JUMPED DOWN from the harness
fixed around the base of Kyranish's neck before he had fully stopped near the crest of the
grass-covered knoll. Her feet caught slightly in the
soft ground and she fell, skidding across the grass
and moist earth. A few peals of hearty laughter
came at her expense but for the most part, the refugees at the base of the slope appeared too tired to
take any notice of the ignominious conclusion of
her arrival. She picked herself up, scraping the
mud from her arms and the front of her padded
leather doublet. She did not even look back at her
dragon as she strode purposefully across the
knoll. Her legs were shaky but she plunged onward, too determined to allow her body to stop.

Only one thought drove her on.

She had to find Drakis.

The ruin of a stone fortress or temple—she did

not care which—stood at the crest of the rise. It was being utilized by a pair of dragons as a place to sun themselves. They seemed unaware of the chaos that surrounded the hill beneath their perch. All about the base of the mound, angry, confused Drakis Pilgrims were making their way around the prominence from out of the thick woodland to the north before following a beaten trail back into the woods toward the south. Urulani noticed that Kyranish, the Lyric's dragon was absent. Pyrash—the dragon who carried Jugar—was curled around the warm stones of the crumbling construction and Wanrah, the dragon that Ethis rode, lolled on a shattered tier of the ruin. The one dragon she hoped to find here was also absent; the presence of the green and yellow Marush would have confirmed that Drakis was here.

*Dragon or no, he's got to be here*, she thought. *And he's going to have to explain* why *the rest of us are here, too!*

Urulani saw a familiar shape near the base of the far slope surrounded by a circle of excited and angry beings all vying for his attention at the same time. There were many manticores in the throng marching into the forest but this was the only one who bore the crossed-sash of a Grahn Aur and the unmistakable harvest-gold-colored robe. She could hear his hoarse voice above the crowd. "We have to keep moving! You know what Drakis said. We dare not stop now!"

"It's been two days since we stopped to encamp," Tsojai Acheran shouted, his featureless black eyes seeming duller than ever. "That's well enough for the manticores and the chimerians but the elves among the company need to rest!"

"There will be a time and a place for rest but it is not here!" Belag asserted, baring his teeth at the elven councillor. "You know that since we crossed the Malethic River we've been in Ephindrian territory. We are still moving somewhere between what Ethis calls Chythal and Hrynth lands. We were warned not to stop until we had passed beyond Pashorei lands and that's two more days ahead of us."

Urulani had reached the edge of the circle of seething creatures that surrounded Belag but they were pressed tightly against one another. The crowd moving around them jostled her as she tried to break through the circle to reach the Grahn Aur.

"Two *more* days?" Doroganda screeched. Her voice was shrill with displeasure. "You only *say* it will be two more days but I've seen the magic-ones and I have heard them talking! The distance breached by the folds is getting shorter with each move. They say that the power of the Aethereon grows dimmer as we move toward the Elven lands . . . and that it will fail us altogether in the face of the Rhonas Legions!"

"You are mistaken in what you have heard," Belag roared, his voice shaking the ground around him. "There will be Aether Wells aplenty when we have moved into the Pashorei lands from which the Aethereon may be replenished. There we shall have abundance. There we shall earn our rest. But we must not stop until then!"

"You are eloquent and persuasive, Grahn Aur, as always," Tsojai nodded his head as slightly as possible in acknowledgment. "Speak whatever speeches you want but there are pilgrims of this company who cannot go much farther, even among your own kind."

"They will have to get what rest they can while we organize our next fold transit," Belag said, shaking his head. "I hear your words, friend Tsojai, and I am most sympathetic to them but until we have our people safely through these dangerous lands we have to . . ."

Someone behind Urulani pushed her hard against Tsojai's back. She stumbled, reaching forward to steady herself.

"Belag!" Urulani croaked. Her throat was dry from the long flight.

The great manticore saw her. She could see the tired, slightly bleary look in his eyes but there was a smile on his wide, feline face. He reached his enormous hand through the circling crowd and pulled her toward him.

"Urulani, it is a relief that you have come," Belag said. "Welcome to the Great Passage."

"Where's Drakis, Belag?" Urulani demanded. "I've got to see him."

"I shall take you to him at once," Belag answered. He held her tightly to his side with his left arm while gesturing for an opening between the still-circling council members. "Excuse us. Sky

Mistress Urulani must meet with Drakis without delay."

"But we are not finished!" Tsojai snapped. "We have a number of pilgrims who have not reported in and may be lost! And the supply caravans have been complaining of thefts from several of their . . ."

"We shall convene the Council of the Prophet after this transit of the folds is completed," Belag said as he pushed his way past the still arguing council members. He pulled Urulani with him, merging into the jostling crowd of pilgrims. "Come together at the battle standard on the other side and we shall discuss the issues then."

*Battle standard?* Urulani wondered for a moment if she had heard Belag correctly.

The loud, irritated mass of pilgrims closed around them like the waters of a great, noisy river, carrying them southward down the channel of the trampled road. The canopy of trees closed over them as they flowed with the crowd that extended beyond the flattened road out into the woods to either side.

"Belag, let go of me!" Urulani snapped, shrugging his massive arm off her shoulders.

"As you wish but you would be well advised to stay close to me," the manticore replied. "Get lost in this panic and you may not be able to find Drakis."

"I almost didn't find the encampment," Urulani said. "And yet I found that a hundred thousand pilgrims were no longer there. I awoke on the back of my dragon flying through the Shifting Pass and all Kyranish would tell me is that we had been called to come this way. I *thought* I knew where we were supposed to be going. I *thought* we had a plan."

"Plans are always the first thing to change," Belag observed.

"Well *this* change is a problem!" Urulani snarled.

They walked with the ebb and flow of the crowd, pushing and occasionally stumbling forward through the trees. The ground began to rise in front of them. Urulani could see lights through the forest between the heads of the diverse horde as they pressed forward. As they approached the edge of the forest, the lights appeared to extend down the ridge in either direction. It was as though a wall of lightning were dancing before them, luring them like moths to a flame.

Quite suddenly they pushed past the trees. Urulani tripped over a broken crate, its contents of clothing spilled out over the ground and being trampled unheeded underfoot. They were moving quicker now, the packed mob giving way to open space and a threat of stampede. The vista opened up in front of them.

A line of fold portals ran in both directions along the crest of the ridge. They reminded Urulani of the folds she had seen among the ruins in Drakosia as well as the one which Braun had demonstrated to her in Port Glorious but these were larger and, in some way, more terrifying. They were rough at the edges, the circle of light marking the interior of each portal shifting as though bolts of lightning were striking at the center. She counted fifteen of these portals extending along the ridge to their right and a good many more disappearing down the ridge to their left. A line of warriors from the Army of the Prophet stood as a cordon thirty feet in front of the magical folds, directing the constant flow of pilgrims into lines before each of the folds. They shouted the same litany over and over: to keep moving forward, to proceed quickly through the portal, and to only worry about reuniting with their families on the other side. Wails of the children and the tired sobs of their mothers mixed with the warriors' shouts. The warriors stepped aside at Belag's approach and Urulani followed him into the open space beyond. There she had a clear view of the streams of refugees passing the warriors heading toward the folds in ordered lines, ranks of them on either side as far as she could see.

To the side of each of portal stood a figure, arms up-stretched toward the vertical circle of the fold, straining to maintain it. Each wore robes in various shades of gray. In the bright light of the folds she could see the lines in their haggard faces, the strain in their muscles and the redness in their eyes.

"What is that?" Urulani asked, pointing down the ridge to a strange device she had not seen before.

It appeared to be an oblong box fitted with crys-

tals along the sides and top. A large shard of blu-
ish crystal protruded from the top while the entire
assembly seemed aglow. Hovering about it was a
human figure also in a gray robe, watching it intently from different angles and occasionally raising his hand, palm out toward it.

"That is the Aethereon," Belag nodded. "It is
the symbol of our passage and our beacon that
guides us toward . . ."

"Belag . . ." Urulani's voice rose in warning.

The manticore chuckled and shrugged. "The
elves have something called a 'portable altar' to
maintain the devotion spells of their Impress Warriors. It allows the Aether to be stored and then
distributed while at a great distance from the
Aether Wells of the Elven Houses. Braun used to
be a Proxi in our Centurai before Drakis freed us
from the Devotions. He found a way to adapt it to
our purposes. It provides the Aether needed to
open the folds and move the encampment step by
step, fold by fold, toward our objective. Braun
never leaves it."

"He's worried, isn't he?" Urulani considered
the human mage moving anxiously around the
Aethereon. "The goblin was saying something
about the fold distances getting shorter."

"There is no cause for concern," Belag began.
"The Aethereon is a blessing from the gods whose
light . . ."

A sudden cry rang out behind Urulani and she
turned.

The human mage three portals down the ridge

had fallen to one knee, his arms quivering visibly in the light of the fold. He was screaming, his warning inarticulate.

The fold was collapsing.

The warriors rushed back from the cordon, cutting off the line of refugees and pushing them back. Those who were just entering the portal dashed forward in a panic, rushing through the opening as its edges became unstable, and its color shifted toward red. A young human male holding a baby in his arms leaped through the fold just as it slammed closed with a clap of terrible thunder.

The mage lay unconscious on the ground. A small group of warriors gathered around him, lifting him up and carrying him to a large tent set up beyond the folds just behind the ridge. A few moments later, they emerged with another mage in gray robes—this one another human who looked as haggard and weary as the one who had just fallen. He took the place of the first and forced his hands into the air.

Light wavered in front of him and then the portal slowly opened up once again.

"There's something wrong with the magic box," Urulani said, facing the manticorian leader once again. "Isn't there, Belag?"

"It is providing us the blessings of . . ."

"I'm too tired for this, Belag," Urulani said angrily. "What's wrong with it?"

"Nothing is wrong with the magical device," Belag said. "The problem is simply one of distance."

"Distance from what?"

"Braun turned the Well in Port Glorious," Belag explained. "I understand that you did something similar in Drakosia. This altar—this Aethereon—is tuned to that Aether and draws on it. The farther south we go, however, the farther we are from those turned Aether Wells. That means longer times for the altar to regain its strength and the weaker that Aether becomes."

"That is why the folds are not as far apart as they were earlier in your journey," Urulani nodded.

"So why are you in such a hurry?"

"Because there are dangers in staying in Ephindria," Belag said, leaning closer to Urulani so that only she could hear. "Because if we stop, there is a good possibility that we may never leave again."

# CHAPTER 21

## Best Interests

URULANI EMERGED FROM THE FOLD. She always found the first moments through a fold confusing. Stepping from one place into an entirely new place some distance removed from where she had been a moment before left her uncertain and confused. As a mariner, she had to rely on a keen sense of her surroundings and a mental image of where she was located relative to the coasts and landmarks that defined the borders of her seaborne universe. In her occasional treks across land, that same sense gave her an internal confidence regarding where she was at all times and a knowledge of her relationship to the larger world. All of that was lost when the Aether suddenly moved her from a familiar place to an entirely new location.

She could not stop to get her bearings.

"Keep moving! Do not stop! Do not block the

fold exits!" Travel Masters from each of the Ten Camps of Drakis stood thirty to forty feet out from the fold exits, each wearily waving a flag with the symbol of their particular camp. Each called out in a hoarse voice a litany made dull from overuse. "Move past the flag of your camp to the next flag of your camp. Keep moving! Do not stop! Do not block the fold!"

Urulani realized the folds had deposited them all in a broad valley between two ranges of hills. The sun was peeking above the crest of the knoll to the west, casting long evening shadows across the valley floor. The land grew marshy in that direction, giving way to a shallow lake. Tall trees with white bark and leafy tops grew thickly on the slopes to the east. They brooded over the valley floor as though their peace had somehow been offended.

Everywhere else was pandemonium. A succession of flags from each of the camps waved in the air, drawing members of that camp toward them and beckoning them to more flags farther on and to their allotted space across the valley floor. Angry shouts punctuated the murmurs of the frantic crowd around Urulani as each member of the pilgrim encampment sought desperately to move toward the flag of their designated camp through a sea of others trying to move in every other direction. This struggling sea of manticores, chimerians, humans, gnomes, and elves was further thrown into disarray by supply wagons and carts struggling to continue forward through the throng and the occasional goblins on wyvernback adding even more confusion as they charged unheeding through the mob, scattering pilgrims in their wake.

*Where is the army?* Urulani wondered, biting at her lip. *Where is Drakis?*

Something caught her eye.

The green and yellow markings of the dragon were distinctive. Marush craned his great neck skyward near the crest of a hilltop overlooking the valley from the east. Urulani could just make out the tent south of the dragon.

She set her jaw and started pushing through the horde of exhausted and disheartened pilgrims, her eyes fixed all the while on Drakis' tent.

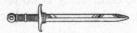

"We cannot stop now," Ethis argued. His face was contorted both by fatigue and rage as he planted all four of his fists simultaneously on the map table between them. "We've got to press on!"

"How?" growled Gradek, standing on the other side of the table. The manticorian commander swept his massive hand across the map laid between them. "How do we continue? The folds are getting shorter with each transit—the Aether magic of the humans is growing dim with distance. Without time for the Braun sorcerers to recover, we shall only grow weaker and may find ourselves in the midst of Ephindria without any magic and no means of escaping this place."

Drakis stood silently at the head of the map table, his arms crossed with his left hand resting over his chin.

"But if we stop, the consequences would be unthinkable," Ethis urged.

"You mean in contamination of your precious chimerian society?" Gradek snarled.

"I mean for us all," Ethis responded, his frustration showing in his voice. "Since we have entered Ephindria we have lost members with every transit of the folds."

"Is there a problem with the folds then?" Jugar asked. The dwarf stood next to Drakis on his left. He was wearing his leather flying doublet but had somewhere found a long strip of crimson with which to form a sash. "Perhaps this magic of Braun is at fault?"

"For the last time, we're not losing them to the folds," Ethis asserted. "It's when we regroup. For the first few transits, it was barely a noticeable problem but in the last three folds alone we have lost nearly a thousand from our company."

"Lost?" Jugar suggested. "As in misplaced?"

"No! Lost as in having been lured away," Ethis said. "The sirens have discovered we are here."

"Sirens?" Gradek sniffed. "They don't exist!"

"They have always existed," Ethis responded. "'Siren' is the name we give to the young and unwary of our race, those who are in that dangerous age between acquiring their shaping ability and learning how to control it. We protect them, shelter them from the outsiders not just for the sake of our young but for the sake of those who fall prey to them. Sirens naturally desire to empathize with those with whom they come in contact but are unable to filter those feelings and thoughts or control their reaction to them. These sirens, through no fault of their own, do everything they can to give or show to those whom they meet the heart's most secret desire."

"Well, now, that doesn't sound so bad," Jugar observed. "Sounds rather pleasant if you ask me."

"So everyone is tempted to believe," Ethis said, his words coming in a chill voice. "But the granting of these visions and wishes is unrestrained by the sirens. These fulfillments are rarely permanent or real: they are promises without substance. Our experience is that other races are consumed by their desires when they are so freely given but never fulfilled, ensnared by having their own dreams constantly just beyond their reach and ultimately imprisoned or destroyed by their own passions that are never truly sated."

Gradek drew in a deep breath, his lionlike face grown stoic but horror reflected in his eyes. "A golden curse most terrible! Can we not deploy the army around the encampment . . . protect the pilgrims from this danger?"

"I tried this in our last three transits," Ethis said, shaking his head. "We brought half of the army in to establish the forward boundaries of our camp and deployed the other half to guard the rear boundaries on the far side of the folds."

"And?" Gradek asked.

"And we lost three hundred and seventeen warriors before the folds were closed," Ethis said, straightening up from the map table. "The shorter the distance between the folds, the sooner the sirens are finding us and encroaching on the encampment. The longer we stay in one place, the more of them will come . . . and the more we will lose to them."

"But couldn't we reason with them?" Jugar asked. "Tell them to leave us alone or strike a bargain with them to go away and leave us in peace?"

"You don't understand," Ethis said, shaking his head, his face smoothing to its normally blank features. "It isn't a question of reasoning with them. They already understand that it is the Queen's command that we be left alone in our journey. But they are drawn to us, nevertheless, and cannot help themselves in their desire to empathize and please us. They do not understand the danger both to us and to themselves. They honestly think they are *helping* you when they lure you to your doom, Jugar."

"What can we do?" Drakis said.

Everyone around the table was so intent on their discussion that the question startled them.

"The sirens are following us, calling especially those who are tired and susceptible away from the camps," Ethis asserted. "The longer we stay anywhere and the shorter the distances of the folds, the worse the problem will become."

"So we must keep moving," Drakis nodded grimly.

"This isn't a trained army that you can force-march for days on end," Jugar said. "These are families with children and grandmothers. There are supply wagons and livestock to be moved. They've gone for three days without stopping. Soon they'll stop whether we tell them to keep moving or no."

"Then we need to find a way to lengthen the fold distances," Drakis observed. "Our Aether is being weakened by the distance. If we had a closer source of Braun Aether—a turned Rhonas Well—could we lengthen our folds and get through Ephindria sooner?"

"Certainly," Ethis nodded, pointing down to the map of Ephindria on the table before them. The details were necessarily sparse but the settlement was clearly marked. "There is such a Well located here in Shalashei. It is defended by a Centurai of Rhonas warriors but . . ."

The canvas of the tent rustled noisily.

Ethis looked up from the map table, nothing registering on his neutral face.

Urulani, her leather dragon flight doublet still streaked with mud, pushed through the flap of the command tent, her dark face taut with strain, her eyes bright and shining.

Drakis turned and recognized her. "Urulani! You've found us at last. I was beginning to wonder . . ."

Urulani's fist slammed into Drakis' face.

Drakis reeled, falling flat on his back from the fierce blow. Gradek reached instinctively for the hilt of his sword but was suddenly uncertain who to use the blade against.

"*Found* you? I *did* find you but not where you were supposed to be!" the dark woman raged over him, her fist balled up tight, ready to strike again. "I was *supposed* to have found you somewhere on the Shadow Coast! I was *supposed* to have provided you with an open road into Vestasia! I've spent the last ten days convincing half the population on the Shadow *and* Thetis Coasts that the Man of Prophecy has returned, that he's on his way to come and free them from the elven oppressors and now I find you *here*?"

"I know," Drakis said, raising his hands palm out in surrender. "There were changes ... opportunities which ..."

"Opportunities?" Urulani snarled. "Opportunities to leave those people on the coast defenseless against the elven Legions?"

"What Legions?" Ethis asked.

"I've seen them," Urulani seethed. "They were outside Port Dog not a day ago. They're marching northward along the Shadow Coast."

"That's good," Ethis noted.

"Good?" Urulani's voice nearly broke in her rage.

"Yes," Ethis continued. "It means they're moving in the wrong direction."

"It may be the wrong direction for you," Urulani countered, "but because I told those port towns about Drakis and his prophetic return, there are now an entirely new group of pilgrims making their way up the coast ahead of those Legions. They're expecting to join up with the encampment and its marvelous, victorious army! Instead, you're here in . . . where is this place?"

"Near the northern boundaries of Hrynth," Ethis answered.

"Where?"

"Deep within Ephindria," Ethis replied.

"Well wherever this is, it is *not* where the coastal pilgrims are ever going to find you," Urulani said. "The elven Legions will overtake them, Drakis! They will murder them, parent and child, unless we do something about it."

"What do you suggest, Urulani?" Gradek asked in a quiet, thoughtful rumble.

"I don't know." Urulani thought. "What about the dwarves? Couldn't their warriors at least feign an attack at the rear of the Legion? That would at least delay them long enough to . . ."

"There are no dwarven warriors," Jugar said.

"But you went . . ."

"I searched deep within the mountains of Aeria," Jugar affirmed. "There were no dwarves to be found."

"Urulani," Drakis said, slowly standing once more. His voice was heavy. "I'm sorry. Ethis returned with an offer from the Queen of Ephindria and we could not delay in accepting it. If we had followed our original plan—if we had charged toward the coast and Vestasia—then we would be facing those same Legions ourselves. The Lyric has gone north to see what can be done for your refugees. As it is, our situation here is not much better at the moment than theirs."

"I gave them my word, Drakis," Urulani breathed out the words.

"And I'm going to do everything I can to honor that," Drakis replied. "But to do that we have to take down a city of the elves . . . and to do *that*, we will need to find a way of surviving the land of our ally."

# CHAPTER 22

## A Place Called Home

"*D*RAKIS?"

"*I think he's coming around!*"

The sounds seemed far away. Drakis was struggling to place them.

"*He's breathing!*" came another voice, its familiarity playing at the edge of his conscious thoughts. "*It's a miracle of the gods!*"

Drakis drew breath painfully into his lungs; he pushed himself to sit up. His cloudy vision cleared.

The rolling hills of grain waved around him in the southern breeze. The sun was just cresting the top of the hill, casting long shadows across the landscape. Great shadowy clouds edged in brilliant salmon colors of the morning drifted through the sky above him. A low-lying mist stretched across the tide pools to the south, rendering the tall reeds in the shallows in shades of blue and gray. House totems lined the path to the east, winding around the hills toward . . .

Drakis caught his breath, holding it . . . afraid to let it go lest he should disturb the moment.

"We thought we might have lost you," purred ChuKang.

Drakis blinked at the enormous manticorian warrior. "Lost me?"

"There was no need to hold off the entire 'Blade of the West' on your own," chuckled Thuri, folding three of his arms across his chimerian chest and gesturing behind him with the fourth. "If Braun hadn't extracted us with a fold portal at the end, you might not have made it this far."

Drakis followed Thuri's extended hand and saw Braun, in his Proxi robes, looking back at him with a haunted and pitying expression.

Drakis glanced around him. Thuri pushed his blank face into the semblance of a grin. ChuKang, captain of their Centurai planted his enormous hands on his hips and let out a roar of joy. KriChan, another manticorian warrior stood beside him nodding with a fang-toothed smile. Next to them stood Karag, Belag's brother, still wearing his battle armor. The gnomes Onras and Druth Ophas were straining to get a look at him.

His Octia . . . His Centurai . . .

He looked down at the bier on which he was sitting. It was a hero's bier, draped in linen and covered in flowers.

"You thought I was *dead*?" Drakis grinned. He felt dizzy and euphoric.

"Well you gave a very good impression of dead," ChuKang bellowed and the rest of the warriors around them joined at once in the laughter.

Drakis turned. Behind him sat the familiar temple. Jerakh, Skyu'klan, Indrisi . . . the rest of the Centurai were pouring from the octagonal fold wavering between two crystalline pillars.

*Smoke and the shadow of fallen days*
*Welling from dreams that are dead*
*Familiar faces.*
*Lost from all traces . . .*

"We had thought to bear you back as a dead hero," Thuri said, "but given the circumstances, I suppose a live hero will have to do. I believe you have earned the right to present this."

The chimerian reached with his uppermost pair of arms back over his head and pulled a metal circle from his pack. He pressed it into an astonished Drakis' grip.

The Crown of the Ninth Throne of Dwarven Kings lay in his hands.

"A parade of triumph?" Braun suggested quietly. "Our hero is perhaps due a parade of triumph?"

"A parade of triumph indeed!" Karag called out. The Centurai cheered, raising their weapons into the air in acknowledgment.

ChuKang dragged Drakis off the bier, planting him on his feet, pushing him to the head of the column. "Form ranks! We've earned our pride. Drakis Sha-Timuran!"

"Yes, ChuKang?"

"Lead us home!" the Centurai commander ordered with a weary smile.

Drakis turned to look down the road across the familiar fields lined on either side by House totems. He could hear the Centurai of his brother warriors falling in behind him. He gazed down at his hands, his mind reeling as he contemplated the Crown of the Ninth Dwarven Throne in his hands. He knew the coolness of its metal and the heft of its weight. He could see the very top of the avatria of house Timuran shining in the morning rays. He knew that *she* would be there standing on the wall, searching for his return. Now he would come through the gates as a hero of House Timuran, just as he had dreamed he would so many times before.

So many times before . . .

"Wait," he turned to face the Centurai. "Where is Braun?"

"Here, Drakis," responded the Proxi quietly, his eyes averted.

"What . . . what about Ethis?" Drakis asked.

"He is coming later, my lord," Braun replied, still looking away.

"And Urulani?" Drakis asked. The pain in his head was unbearable.

"Who?" ChuKang asked.

"Urulani," Drakis responded. "She is . . . she is a dark-skinned human—a raider on Thetis Bay . . ."

"A dark woman warrior?" KriChan trumpeted with laughter. "That blow to your head must have been harder than we thought!"

"But she . . ."

"You need not worry about that right now," Braun urged. "The Centurai is waiting to present their victory to Lord Timuran. We must proceed quickly. They will be waiting and our masters will brook no delay."

Drakis nodded in dull agreement. He turned to face the path that was so familiar to him and so inviting. He breathed in the cool air, the fresh smell damp with the morning dew on the fields. He could hear the distant birds call down by the tide pools and from the woodlands on the far side.

Everything was just as he remembered it.

The thought brought doubt into his mind.

Then he gripped the prized crown in his hand and, raising it above his head, yelled out, "Brothers of House Timuran! We return in triumph at last!"

A great cheer rose from the warriors behind him. He marched forward, down the path toward the sunrise, climbing up over the crest of a hill. Before him, crowning the next hilltop, stood the glorious structure of House Timuran. The slender avatria rose up above the subatria wall, outlined in the growing light of dawn.

She was there. He could see her silhouette atop the subatria wall, her cleanly shaven head aglow. Already she was running along the wall toward the servant's stairs leading down into the garden, eager to greet him.

"Mala," Drakis said her name in a whisper, as though he were afraid to utter it, that somehow doing so would break the wonderful moment.

Thoughts tugged at his mind. Wide savannas and ocean voyages . . . vast deserts of sand . . . ruins obscured by foliage so thick as to nearly hide them completely . . . dragons breathing destruction and death . . . and a woman with skin as dark as midnight who was beautiful and terrible all at once. . . .

Mala waved at him and, smiling, he marched on.

The Centurai came to the gates of the chakrilya—the Warrior's Way—and found them thrown open at their approach. The household slaves were lining the curving passage, their cheers unrestrained. Drakis held the crown high once more as he marched through the gates, to even greater cheering from the Centurai that marched behind him.

Se'Djinka, the war-mage of House Timuran and a Tribune of the Imperial Army stood in the center of the chakrilya in his battle robes, his arms folded across his chest. The ancient warrior held up his arm, palm facing Drakis in salute.

"Victorious and bearing the greatest of honors," Se'Djinka proclaimed. "The warriors of House Timuran are home at last."

Drakis smiled broadly and bowed, extending the crown toward the war-mage with both hands.

Braun stepped forward, standing just to the right and slightly behind Drakis as he spoke. "May Drakis—champion of Timuran—present the crown before the altar of Devotions?"

Se'Djinka frowned, his featureless black eyes resting on the Proxi with disapproval.

"It would be his greatest desire," Braun urged.

Se'Djinka straightened up and turned, passing through the open gate between the chakrilya and the interior of the subatria. Drakis followed him, trailing Braun, and the rest of the Centurai marched behind him into the central garden of the House. The inverted dome foundation of the Timuran avatria floated above their heads, perfectly restored.

Drakis' smile diminished slightly. *When did it look any different? When was it that I saw it fall to the ground?*

The bowl of the garden lay before him. The altar of Devotions stood near the center, directly before the Aether Well of the House. By now the entire household had turned out to stand against the walls of the central garden. Slaves, free elven servants, craftsmen of every estate and all of the Impress Warriors from their Centurai watched in adoration, admiration and wonder.

Next to the altar of Devotions stood Sha-Timuran, tall and noble in his appearance. His wife and daughter were nowhere to be seen but he barely took notice of it.

Next to Timuran, stood Mala.

He could clearly see the Sinque mark at the crest of her shaved head. Her large eyes set in her heart-shaped face sparkled with joy. She held out her hand to him, beckoning him to come to her.

Drakis marched proudly down the path to the center of the garden. He stopped before Sha-

Timuran—the elf who had been like a father to him . . .

Drakis winced. He felt the blows on his back, the sting of the firereed whip across his flesh.

*It must have been a dream . . . a bad dream . . .*

"Drakis Sha-Timuran!" The high-pitched, nasal voice of the House Lord cut above the cheers of the household, calling them to silence.

Drakis looked up into the pinched face of his master. Then, without another thought, the human knelt down before the tall elf and, extending his hands above his head, offered the crown to Sha-Timuran.

"Never before in the glorious history of our House has any Impress Warrior performed his duty with such distinction. Of all the Houses of the Rhonas Imperium, you stand alone as victor. You hold the spoils in your hands of the defeated dwarven thrones. Your name shall be whispered with reverence and sung in songs of magnificent accolades for ages to come. Look upon me, Drakis Sha-Timuran!"

Drakis raised his face to the House Lord.

"I have pled your name before the Ministers of Imperial Estates," Sha-Timuran said, his voice raised so that all might hear in the garden. "By the Will of the Emperor, you are hereby granted your citizenship in the Imperium and your elevation to the Sixth Estate! Drakis Sha-Timuran is no more. Long be the life and great the fortunes of Drakis Sha-Drakon . . . first Lord of House Drakon!"

The tumultuous cheers rang across the garden as Sha-Timuran took the crown from Drakis' hands and then, extending his own, pulled the human to his feet.

Drakis barely noticed Braun moving softly behind Lord Timuran. *What was the Proxi doing back there?*

"Every House Lord requires a mistress of his house," Sha-Timuran observed, arching a thin eyebrow over his dull, black eyes. "Would you take a wife?"

"I would, my lord," Drakis turned his attention and gazed at once into the large, violet eyes of Mala, staring so hopefully up at him. "I would with every breath of my life take Mala to me in mine."

"Then as the Emperor has given you your citizenship," Sha-Timuran nodded, "permit me to give you Mala as my thanks for the honor you have brought to my House."

Tears welled up in Mala's eyes.

They threw their arms around each other.

Drakis drew in a shuddering breath. Mala was here. She was solid and real. He could feel her warmth in his arms, the brush of her eyelashes against his neck and her hot tears of joy.

It was everything he had wanted. Every desire he had ever dreamed.

Drakis lifted up Mala, spinning her around in his embrace. The cheers of the assembled servants, retainers, and his brother Impress Warriors rang around him.

Then he saw Braun standing next to the House Aether Well.

Dread suddenly overwhelmed him. Drakis quickly set Mala down, extending his hand toward Braun.

"No!" Drakis called out. "Please!"

Braun, with a look of infinite sadness on his face, reached up with his right hand toward the crystal of the Aether Well. He shook his head as he spoke. "I'm so sorry, Drakis."

Drakis tried to lunge toward the Proxi but Mala was still clinging to him.

Braun's hand touched the crystal of the Aether Well.

A blinding flash of light filled Timuran's garden, causing Drakis to slam his eyes closed. In that instant, a sudden blast of wind nearly pushed Drakis off his feet. A horrible chorus of screeching voices from every direction filled his ears with pain. He reached both hands up, trying to cover his ears from the sound but realized even as he managed to do so that the sound had already fled.

He stood in an elven garden far different than the one he had stood in moments before. No avatria could be seen overhead—only the unobstructed sky filled with stars. The Aether Well remained, but its once blue glow now pierced the sky in a column of purple-tinged light.

Braun, his dark face fallen into a thoughtful frown, stood next to the Aether Well, pulling his hand away.

Braun, who had started all of this in the first

place, Drakis thought. It had been this same Braun, mad as moonlight, who had abandoned Drakis and his brother warriors at the worst possible time. He had robbed Drakis of his victory and the greatest prize of the Battle of the Ninth Throne. It occurred to Drakis then that losing the crown as he had was what caused him to remain behind at the dwarven throne. If he had not lost the crown, he would never have met Jugar—and he might still be a slave.

*And she might still be alive today . . .*

Drakis had thought Braun dead in that battle for the dwarven crown deep beneath the mountains—had even thought that he had discovered his corpse among the dead. But it had been Braun who had been the first to welcome him when Drakis had slid down from the back of Marush on the shores of Willow Vale. Drakis had been too shocked to kill him outright at the time and had been conflicted about the man ever since.

One thing remained at the center of Drakis' thoughts regarding the human mage: more than anyone, Braun was responsible for what had happened to him.

"You," Drakis reached for the hilt of his sword, his hand shaking. "You did this to me!"

Braun glanced at Drakis. "No, Drakis. This was *your* plan, remember?"

"*My* plan!" Drakis yelled, drawing his sword. "I had everything—*everything*—and you robbed me of it. Worse, you showed it to me, let me taste it, and then tore it away from me!"

"Everything you ever wanted," Braun said, stepping back from the Aether Well.

"Yes!"

"And the sirens," Braun continued, stepping to the side of Well. "What is their danger?"

Drakis blinked, his mind trying to see past his pain.

Braun raised his arms up, shifting them in the air as he murmured strange sounds. A circular fold tore open in the air, the light at its rim intensely brilliant.

"Think! You know," Braun said again to Drakis. "What is the siren's danger?"

"That . . . that they give you what you want," Drakis said, his voice ragged with emotion.

The edges of the fold grew slightly, its light brightening into an unbearable purple that was uncomfortable to observe. Ten of Braun's mages moved through the fold as quickly as their weary legs could take them. As each stepped through, their faces brightened as though life and renewed strength were flowing into them.

"Marun!" Braun called out. "Take four other mages with you toward the south. Klestan . . . take the other half with you to the north. Establish the fold link with your paired mages back at the encampment. There's more than enough Aether now. Belag should have everyone arranged in their ten camps by now . . . one fold per camp."

"Are we waiting for a signal?" Marun, a voluptuous human female mage with wide green eyes asked.

"No!" Braun answered. "Don't wait for anything! Just start bringing them through!"

The mages moved with lighter step, rushing toward the open gates in the subatria wall.

Shaking, Drakis fell to his knees. He could see now that the subatria was much smaller than he had thought and that there was no garden here at all. The avatria never existed.

*Everything I ever wanted . . .*

Braun continued to hold open the fold gate. As the mages dispersed, Ethis stepped through the fold, followed by an Octian of manticorian warriors rushing to follow the mages to their assigned positions beyond the subatria wall. A second Octian followed, moving to the edge of the subatria and climbing the stairs to the top of the wall surrounding the Aether Well.

"The camps are ready," Ethis said to Braun, then spotted Drakis pale with shock, still shaking where he crouched on the ground. "What happened?"

"Corruption, that's what happened," Braun answered. "It seems that the Rhonas Imperium has been doling out their magic to your southern cousins just as you believed. Your youth—your sirens as you call them—have been using it to enhance their powers of persuasion. They appear to have become illusionists of more skill than we thought."

Ethis moved quickly to Drakis, dropping to one knee and examining him closely. "What happened to the sirens?"

"They fled when I inverted the Well," Braun said, watching another Octian of warriors—these almost exclusively human—emerge from the fold he continued to hold open. They ran with their blades drawn toward the western exit from the subatria. "It seems that they have an aversion to the Aether of an inverted Well. Now, with an inverted Well of our own, we have the Aether we need to secure the encampment and to send the army west just as you promised your Queen Chythal . . . and the world will never be the same."

"I take it the plan worked, then?" Ethis said.

Drakis bowed his head to his chest.

"Too well," Braun grimaced. "The sirens concentrated almost exclusively on Drakis. They were so intent on satisfying his desires that they paid little attention to me. It was the diversion that we hoped for—it certainly allowed me to reach the Aether Well and invert it—but it was worse for Drakis than he expected."

"Why?" Ethis asked.

"Because they gave him the one thing he can never have," Braun sighed. "They gave him back his home."

# CHAPTER 23

## *In His Name*

SHE CAME IN THE NAME OF DRAKIS... and they followed.

She came on the back of a great dragon, whose markings were gray and white. Manticores, chimerians, humans, goblins, gnomes of every station, both free and under elven Devotions—all trembled before the power of the enormous drake and the lithe woman who rode it. Elven Governors and their Legions of the Occupation abandoned their posts at her approach. The liberated towns gathered at her call. She told them that Drakis, the Man of Prophecy, had sent her for them so that she might lead them back to join with him and his army to forge for each of them a better life free from the cruelty of the elven administrators and their Legions. She told them to shake from their shoulders the burdens that had been imposed upon them and follow her to a better life in the name of Drakis.

She sat astride a monstrous creature of power and majesty that had been nothing more than a legend before her arrival. The elven oppressors fled from her and her creature. How could they not believe her? Word of her and her call spread eastward with every merchant ship.

So in the cities, ports, and townships from Tempest Bay to Cape Tjakar and up the Shadow Coast, those who could packed up what little they had to call their own, filled their carriages, carts, wagons, and wheelbarrows, harnessed whatever beasts of burden they could acquire and set off to answer the call of Drakis and the promise of his return in power to lead them to a better land.

They formed a stream of refugees making its way up the Shadow Coast and toward the wilderness. As they traveled, the refugees gravitated into small groups for their mutual protection. Each of these small collections of refugees followed in the footsteps of the refugee group that had gone before them. None of them suspected that two full Legions of the Rhonas Imperium were ahead of all the refugee caravans.

All, that is, except one.

"Excuse me?" A human by the name of Gyorg raised his hand from where he stood at the forward edge of the gathering. Nearly all of the fifteen hundred persons who made up the caravan had gathered together at a cautious distance from

Ephranos, the white-and-gray-marked dragon sitting regally upright on the north side of their camp. The remains of the original pilgrim encampment stretched for several leagues in every direction.

The Lyric, now arrayed not only in her padded leather flying coat but in assorted pieces of mismatched armor as well, stood before the dragon facing the caravan with her arms folded across her chest. "Yes, friend, what is your question?"

"Where are they?"

"They who?"

"Your army, miss," Gyorg answered at once. "You said they would be coming toward us."

"Look around you," said the Lyric as she gestured toward the horizon in every direction. "Do you see the remains of our encampment? Not just a city but a free *nation* made its home here not days before us. You have seen their tracks in the dust heading to the place of the magic road. Have I not opened up that same road to you again and again, crossing great distances to bring you to the very spot where they lived?"

"Yes . . . but they are not here!"

"I have moved them," the Lyric said with a wave of her hand. "They are now in a place of greater abundance and safety from which we may strike against our oppressors. That is where we will join them in only a day or two more. Our return will be one of triumph and celebration at your coming."

"Yes, as you've told us before but, begging your

pardon, miss . . . I thought Drakis was a man's name?"

"So it is, friend," the Lyric said, pitching her voice unusually low and husky.

"Well, then," Gyorg went on hesitantly as his glance shifted between the young woman and the dragon towering behind her, "no disrespect but . . . how is it that *you* are Drakis?"

"I am glad you asked that question," the Lyric said, pacing back and forth before Ephranos as she spoke. "I am, indeed, Drakis . . . the Drakis of the prophecy that was long ago foretold. That is because Drakis is not a man or a woman for that matter; Drakis is a calling and an ideal to which we all aspire. I am the embodiment of that idea and it is in that name to which I dedicate my life that I am Drakis. To the extent to which you dedicate yourself to that ideal, then Drakis is a part of you, too. We are all, therefore, each in our own part and our own way, Drakis. Does that make sense?"

Gyorg smiled wanly, nodded his head a couple of times, and then said, "Uh . . . no."

"Drakis is before you," the Lyric continued, her wispy hair blowing about her narrow, delicate face, now red from the sun and sky. She pointed behind her toward the north. "Out there is where my army awaits us! My thousands of the encampment long to accept you as their family in the fulfillment of your greatest destiny! Here stands with me a dragon of the north—the very symbol of Drakis and the future that he holds for you. For

tonight, rest and be at peace. We shall soon be
with our companions in this great cause—though
the road is long and difficult. I shall open the fold
in the morning and we shall continue toward the
north."

Gyorg and the rest of the company looked up at
the dragon towering above them.

"Yes, Drakis," Gyorg said. "So we shall do in
your name."

"Legate Xhu'chan!" shouted the elven Centurai
captain as he banged the hilt of his sword against
his armored chest in salute. He had been given
barely sufficient warning of the approach of the
Legion's commander to don his ceremonial armor.
The fringe of hair around his excessively pointed
head would not stay in place. "By the Emperor's
Will!"

The canvas of the captain's tent flapped and
snapped in the strong wind blowing across the
plain. *At least here inside the tent*, Xhu'chan thought,
*they would find some respite from the blowing sand
and howling noise.* The nosy War-mage Kleidon
had followed him into the tent as well as his
aide . . . a young elf by the name of Tsaj. He was
Xhu'chan's sister's son who had pretentions of
making the military his career since his father had
believed him unsuited to any other work.
Xhu'chan knew better. He doubted his nephew
would last more than a week in the field.

"By the Emperor's Will," Xhu'chan returned halfheartedly. Unlike the captain, who had had warning of the approaching commander, the Legate was dressed casually in a simple tunic, a cloak, and breeches tucked into his knee-high boots. "What is this place called, Captain . . ."

Xhu'chan let the sentence hang in the air like a question.

"Captain Zhan'sei Sha-Jadi, Lord Legate," the captain prompted with his name. "To be accurate, Legate, this specific place has no name. We are currently encamped on a plain known locally as the Craedecian Fields. We are seven leagues north of an abandoned village once called Gobton."

"And the pilgrim caravan?" Xhu'chan asked at once. "Where are they currently?"

"The pilgrim caravan is spread along a trail stretching from the eastern edge of Cape Tjakar up the coastal road through Shellsea and Blackbay Township then up toward Gorganta Bay, and then there is a large gap between . . ."

"I'm not interested in the stragglers, Captain," Xhu-chan huffed. "Where is the most forward element of the caravan?"

"They were last spotted here, my Legate," the captain replied, pointing down at the map unrolled on the table before him. "It's called Minum Wells. The locals say it is a good place to replenish water and has been a trade crossroads as long as any of them can remember."

"I did not ask where they *were*, Captain. I asked where they *are*," Xhu'chan said.

"We have not had any further reports from our scouts, my Legate, and therefore I regret that I cannot tell you with any precision where the caravan is located," the captain managed to get to the end of the sentence although the last words had nearly exhausted his breath.

Xhu'chan grimaced. He was striving to keep his temper in check. He knew that this pompous captain was just trying to be accurate not only in his report but in the words by which he chose to make his report. Still, he felt that getting information from this posturing commander would take more effort than was necessary. "Captain, do you have a *guess* as to where the caravan might now be?"

"I would hesitate to offer an opinion, Lord Legate . . ."

"Then offer a guess."

"A guess?"

"Yes, a guess," Xhu'chan said, his voice rising slightly as though the captain were hard of hearing. "As in, where would you *guess* the caravan is now?"

The captain frowned. "We have a scout Octian detached to follow the caravan. They sent word back to me this morning that the caravan has moved away from Minum Wells in a north-by-northeast direction. I have ordered the scout Octian to continue to follow the caravan and to report back daily or as often as the situation demands. As soon as word returns from them, I can give you a more accurate report."

"Just GUESS!" Xhu'chan yelled.

The captain swallowed hard. "I believe they are headed toward what is called Lakes Basin. It is a natural gathering spot about forty leagues north of the Wells."

"They should have made contact with the Drakis main force by now," War-mage Kleidon observed.

"Unless their army is moving southward slower than we expected," Xhu'chan said, considering the map. "This human is not just moving his army but all of his support and supplies. That would be nothing compared to moving the entire rabble of families that are following them as well."

"It would appear that the fears of the Emperor were exaggerated," responded Kleidon.

"Or perhaps misinformed," Xhu'chan said, straightening up. "It is certain, however, that he will be caught between the waters of Thetis and the Mournful Mountains. If they retreat into Nordesia with the aid of the goblins then we chase them all the way to the Westwall Cliffs. If they retreat into the Mistral Peninsula then we'll chase them back to Port Glorious."

"Then we have them," Kleidon hissed with satisfaction.

"Yes, all we have to do is find them," Xhu'chan nodded.

"And perhaps not even that," said an irritatingly familiar voice behind him.

"Just when I thought you had left me, K'yeran," Xhu'chan said as he turned.

The Inquisitor smiled as she entered the tent.

Captain Zhan'sei straightened a bit more. Xhu'chan noted beads of sweat forming near the point of his elongated skull as the Iblisi operative came closer.

"I'm only pleased that I found you at all," K'yeran said in a dangerous purr. "But I'll spare you the requisite pleasantries. I am only here in transit to the south and will be continuing my journey within the hour. I am leaving these military matters in your capable hands as I have other duties to attend. That said, however, I thought you should know that I and my Quorum have visited the remains of the main encampment of this phantom army that you have yet to see."

"Where is it, K'yeran?" It was formed as a question but Xhu'chan spoke it as a command.

"As you were so disposed as to ask then I shall gladly be disposed to answer," K'yeran said, stepping toward the map on the table. "I passed the caravan you have been tracking and it led us, as you suggested into an area known to the goblins as Flat's Gap. It is a wide plain of flatlands that sit between the Goblin Peaks on the west and the Mournful Mountains to the east. We've rune marked it for you in several places. March northeast from this Lakes Basin and, if you can manage to get within fifty leagues or so of our marks, you should be able to find it. That caravan you've been tracking certainly did. They should be there by now."

"They're that far north so soon?" Captain Zhan'sei blurted out. "That's not possible!"

"Possible or not, they were approaching that place when I passed them," K'yeran said.

"Tsaj!"

"By the Will of the Emperor, Legate!"

"Find the runner and send him back with orders to bring up the Legions," Xhu'chan said, his eyes still fixed on the map.

"All this way, Legate?" Tsaj asked.

"Do you have a problem hearing, Tsaj?" Xhu'chan shouted. "Yes, all this way! The entire Army of Imperial Vengeance is coming this way as quickly as the folds will bring them. Our two Legions of the Imperial East are days ahead of them all at least for the time being. Perhaps you would rather I sat around waiting for the rest of the army to catch up to us and rob us of the glory of capturing this Drakis renegade?"

"No, Legate!" Tsaj said as he bowed stiffly and backed out of the command tent in a hurry.

"If you will excuse me, Legate," K'yeran said with a needle-toothed smile, "I must return to Rhonas Chas and deliver the truth of our investigations to the Keeper of my order."

"Of course," Xhu'chan said with a dismissive wave of his hand.

"I wish you the best of luck in finding your war," K'yeran nodded as she stepped out of the tent.

Xhu'chan barely noticed her departure. "Captain Zhan'sei! Prepare to move your command. We've got to press north! Much farther north!"

# CHAPTER 24

## *Below the Horizon*

URULANI STOOD ON THE WALL of the conquered subatria and gazed out over the tree-tops of the jungle below. Through the canopy she could make out the fires of the encampment, glittering as though she were looking down on the stars. These ranged toward the horizon as far as she could see. She could hear the sounds of laughter, music, and conversation rising from below.

The encampment had found a home.

*Not a real home,* Urulani thought as she frowned. She knew it could not last. After the tumult of moving all the pilgrims, their families, and their supplies on the incredible forced march from the Mistral Peninsula down the length of Ephindria, setting up camp for anything more than a single night had the feeling of permanence. Each of the various camps—from Abritas to Quabet—settled in the locations assigned them by the Council of the Prophet around the conquered subatria and its inverted Aether Well. Each camp quickly began to settle and some, for the first time in many weeks, began to talk about the wood, grasses, clay, and stone around them with an eye toward building a more lasting life for themselves and their families.

This optimism continued to grow with the successive flipping of five additional Aether Wells located in a rough perimeter between two to three leagues of the first inverted by Drakis and Braun the day before. Braun's conjurers moved through all the camps mending items, purifying water, and using their renewed strength to lift everyone's spirits. Now, with the coming of evening and the labors of the day completed, the rising relief overwhelmed the camp. Music, dancing, and feasting spread through each of the camps.

There was no music in Urulani. No song.

Those who comprised the Army of the Prophet would be departing from this newly settled land the next morning through the reinvigorated folds of Braun's conjurers. Warriors would be separated once again from their families and strike once more toward battle and death.

Urulani turned and walked along the top of the subatria wall. She stopped at last facing the fading sunset to the west.

"What do you see, Urulani?" came the quiet voice behind her.

"The setting sun," Urulani answered. The voice behind her was a familiar one although she could not place it at the moment.

"That is what is there but it is not what you see." The voice was that of another woman, deep and slightly sad.

"One last battle," Urulani answered, her dark, bare shoulders slumping at the thought. "There beyond the horizon lies a city and everything depends upon our taking it. The lives of all these people . . ."

"And so many more beyond your sight," the woman interrupted. "The lives of all those in the city you seek to take. The lives of all those nations watching what will happen to Drakis and his warriors as they charge against the walls of Tjarlas. The lives of the elves as well as those who oppose them. There is much that you see, Li-li—but so much more beyond your sight."

Urulani turned to face the woman. She stood on the subatria wall about four steps away from the warrior woman. She wore a dress of deepest blue covered in a hooded cloak. The woman's face lay in shadow yet Urulani felt no distress at her presence.

"Who are you?" Urulani asked quietly.

"An old friend, Li-li," the woman answered. "You see the battle that is to come but you do not look far enough. You see victory and you see defeat but you do not look far enough. Can you see how victories right before you often sow the seeds of a bitter fall beyond your sight? Can you take comfort when tragedies unseen, hidden from your notice have laid the foundations of a triumph you claim for yourself? The world continues on, the sun rises and sets, and the stars march their predetermined courses through the sky in that time and place beyond the victors and the fallen."

"I don't understand," Urulani said.

"Look to that place, Li-li," the woman said. "Look to a place beyond where you have seen. Your success will not be found in the battle, Li-li, but in the world you choose beyond it."

In that moment, the woman was gone.

"Drakis," shouted Gyorg. The human barely had any breath left in him as he ran toward the Lyric.

"Yes, General Marshal Odelm," she replied, scrambling to her feet. She stood as tall as possible in her leather flying coat and cobbled-together armor. She had been sleeping on the ground in the shade of her dragon as she believed any good warrior of the prophecy should do among her warrior army.

"It's the elves!" Gyorg gasped out the words between gulping breaths. "They've come! It must be their entire army! I've sent out scouts and they haven't found any end to them, Drakis!"

The Lyric nodded with a slight pout. "It is as I have expected, Gyorg."

"What can we do?" the General Marshal whined.

"We do what we must, General!" the Lyric replied firmly. "And stop that sobbing. It is unbecoming in an officer of the Drakis Army! I shall consult with the gods!"

"Gods?" Gyorg blurted out. "*What* gods?"

But by then, the Lyric had placed her hand on the dragon's neck and closed her eyes in silent reverie.

Ephranos felt Karan—the Lyric—come into his inner world. Today he made his home in a place of endless warm sands under a warm blue sky. It was one of the dragon's favorite places and he held it for his own enjoyment on rare occasions. For some reason be felt it appropriate to honor Karan with this place today and experience it himself again although he did not know why.

The dragon could see the voices in Karan's mind fade away as she reclaimed herself. He craned his neck around to look at her, anticipating that she would direct a question to him. He was surprised, however, that Karan seemed to be considering something far away.

"Is it time?" she asked the wind.

Ephranos waited to hear a response but if the wind answered her, the dragon did not hear it.

"Thank you," Karan said, her eyes welling up with tears. "I've seen more than I should see. I would like very much to sleep but I must finish this one last chore first."

The wind moaned over the sands in reply.

Karan nodded and then turned to the dragon. "We have to ride into battle, my friend. I do not believe we are coming back."

Ephranos raised the lid over his right eye in astonishment. "Our dragonkind fear no death in the world; our souls live in this place and will come again into the world of mortal men, but I fear for you, my Karan. Why must we battle?"

"For the sake of my own soul," Karan answered with a wistful smile. "For the sake of all our souls."

Ephranos raised his great horn-covered head. "To whom were you speaking just now?"

"And old friend," Karan replied wistfully. "One who is telling me it is time to come home," Karan replied.

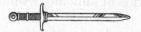

"General Marshal, are the warriors prepared for battle?" the Lyric shouted from the back of her dragon.

"Well, yes, Drakis," Gyorg answered nervously. "But there are only about seven hundred of us. You asked that the caravan continue to the north and these were all that could be spared."

"You have done well!" The Lyric stood up in the stirrups of her flying saddle, calling out to the warriors around her. "You are warriors of legend! You are warriors of the Prophecy!"

A ragged cheer rose up from the thin ranks.

The Lyric, from her perch on the dragon's neck, could see across the Flats toward the south. There came the advancing line of the Rhonas Legions—an army of perhaps eight thousand against her seven hundred.

Her seven hundred, and one dragon, she corrected herself.

Drakis would consider the problem from a military standpoint, she realized, and since she currently *was* Drakis she was determined to do likewise. The approaching army would be staffed with Proxis and the war-mages controlling them. Their combat spells were oriented toward ground battle and should not be nearly as effective against a flying target. Of course, they did not necessarily need to hit the dragon to damage it and, if the Proxis pushed enough fireballs into the air at once then their odds of inflicting wounds went up significantly.

All of this made absolute sense to her—but being without any real military experience, she had no idea what to do about it.

Except, perhaps, to reach some high ground and defend it as long as possible.

"Do you see that mountain commanding the land around it?" The Lyric pointed to the south. A low knoll rose above the plain. The Rhonas Legions were already making their way around it. It was a nameless bump on the otherwise featureless expanse. "That is where we will make our stand!"

"There?" Gyorg gulped. "It's in the middle of the Legions!"

"We will take that mountain, my warriors!" the Lyric cried out, drawing her sword. She brandished its notched blade in the air. "There, in our darkest hour, victory will come! Today begins the battle that will cast down the mighty and bring justice to you, your families, and our generations to come. Your names will be whispered in reverence and your deeds sung in every corner of every land where people live free of tyranny! Charge, my brothers! Charge the Legions and break your shackles! Charge beneath my wings and by one name will you be united and immortal... Drakis!"

"Drakis!" came the ragged shout back.

"Drakis!" the Lyric shouted again, her sword held high as Ephranos reared back, his wings spreading in the evening light.

"Drakis!" the warriors echoed back louder still.

"For Drakis!" the Lyric cried as Ephranos clawed into the air on his enormous wings.

"For Drakis!" Gyorg cried, his blade flashing in the evening light.

"For Drakis!" roared the warriors as they began their charge southward, following beneath the dragon's path.

The dragon climbed higher and the Lyric could see the extent of the Rhonas army. For a moment her resolve failed but then she heard again in her mind the comforting call to home and her courage returned.

She put her hand to the dragon. Ephranos responded at once, diving downward. The ground shook beneath them as they flew barely twenty feet above the plain. She could clearly see the astonished faces of the warriors on the Rhonas battle line, their ordered ranks panicking at this audacious approach.

*They will close behind us like stalks of wheat before a strong wind*, the Lyric thought. *Perhaps we need a more permanent path.*

Ephranos drew in a deep breath.

A river of fire poured from the dragon's maw, engulfing the elven warriors in its path. Ephranos shook his head from side to side, blazing a wide swath through the warriors whose carefully arranged columns made it impossible to escape the flames.

The small knoll rose up before them.

Ephranos banked low, his wing tips nearly touching the ground. Several more spurts of flame cleared a circle around the low mound which the dragon expanded in two more quick turns.

The Lyric glanced to the north.

Her warriors were charging up the charred path Ephranos had created for them, rushing toward the hill over the smoldering grasses and burnt bodies of those elves who had not managed to avoid the dragon's fiery breath.

The dragon vaulted skyward, twisting in the air before plunging back toward the hilltop. Gyorg was already atop the hill, the Army of Drakis setting up its defense. Pikemen on the exterior, warriors behind them, and archers back farther; they formed successive rings around the knoll.

As the Lyric watched, the flanking Rhonas Legions poured onto the charred ground, sealing off the escape of the Lyric's warriors.

"Find the war-mages and their Proxis," the

Lyric said. "We need to deal with them as quickly as possible."

"How long must we fight?" Ephranos asked her.

"As long as we can," the Lyric answered.

"Then let us fight well," the dragon roared.

"For Drakis!" shrieked the Lyric.

# CHAPTER 25

## *Tjarlas*

"**D**ID YOU JUST TELL ME THAT I CANNOT pass?" K'yeran glared at the Occuran Fold-master facing her at the base of the fold platform. "Is it possible that I actually *heard* those words spew from your lips?"

"It is most regrettable," stated the Occuran Foldmaster in charge of the fold shining on the temple pedestal behind him. His robes were dull with dust and the wizened elf looked as though he had not slept in several days. "But is the express Will of the Emperor that we move these final Centurai through the fold at once. There has been a misunderstanding in the transportation of this Legion and it must be cleared up before I can permit any other traffic through this fold!"

"But I am . . ." K'yeran began.

"I know perfectly well who you are, Inquisitor," the Foldmaster responded. "I have no doubt that your mission is vital and that the cargo you transport is of the highest importance. I assure you that I will accommodate you as soon as possible but that will take some time. We have nearly two full Legions in the city awaiting transport from the Northreach Fold but we can only effectively operate one of the city folds at a time."

"Why?" K'yeran demanded. "Is there a problem with the folds?"

"No, not at all," the Foldmaster said, frustration rising in his voice. "We are experiencing a drop in Aether from the eastern Wells that is slowing our recovery. When that is corrected . . ."

"It's been three days and you haven't corrected it yet," K'yeran shouted. "How much longer is this going to take?"

Yet another Octian in a seemingly endless series of Impress Warriors marched out from the shimmering octagonal frame of the Emperor's Fold. One of four permanent portals within the walls of the city of Tjarlas, this ancient platform was situated just inside the Emperor's Gate. It was linked to a series of fold platforms arrayed southward leading to Zhadras and Rhonas Chas beyond. This fold, therefore, had become the main route through which the Army of Imperial Vengeance arrived while passing northward. For nearly a week the warriors, supplies, commanders, warmages, Proxis, and anything else associated with the Army of Imperial Vengeance had been moving through it and through the city itself until they came to the Northreach Fold on the opposite side of the city and passed through it to continue their campaign northward.

Only they had stopped leaving the city three days ago.

"I give you my oath and my honor, Inquisitor K'yeran," the Occuran Foldmaster assured her. "I will send word to you the moment I can accommodate you and your worthy Quorum."

K'yeran nodded in reluctant surrender. She knew this Foldmaster of the Occuran and, for that matter, this fold very well. The Iblisi Inquisitor had come to Tjarlas originally on assignment from Keeper Ch'drei, only to be called back to the Imperial City through this same gate. She had barely arrived in the Imperial City before she had an audience with the Keeper, who then immediately dispatched her *back* through this same gate northward in pursuit of the infamous Soen Tjen-rei. Having captured him quickly—a feat that still left her ill at ease—she now found herself back at this same gate trying to pass through it yet again and complete her mission.

This was the first time she was actually interested in passing through this gate throughout this entire sorry affair.

And now events had conspired to keep her from using the fold at all.

"You may get word to me at Serenity House," K'yeran said. "It is located at . . ."

"I know where it is," the Foldmaster said with a dismissive wave of his hand. "Relax in the joys of Tjarlas, Inquisitor, and I'll give you the word as soon as it is possible."

K'yeran turned away from the elven Foldmaster without another word. She stepped from the foundation of the fold platform and onto the Vira Agrath, the wide avenue that ran from the enormous arch over the Emperor's Gate in a northwestern direction toward the thicket of towering avatria that defined the skyline at the center of the city. She could see the walls of the Nekara Barracks rising up on the opposite side of the avenue. There were a few guards at their entrances—no doubt listless from being left to such inglorious duty—but those buildings had otherwise been emptied of their occupants. At the same time, K'yeran knew that the warriors of the Vash were piling up inside the city walls and were being billeted not just in the Vash Barracks near the Northreach Gate but in the adjoining arena and on the training grounds as well. It was a waste of resources, K'yeran thought, but the divisions between the Warrior Orders of the Imperium were too great to be bridged by anything so inconsequential as reason or practicality.

K'yeran turned and began striding up the Vira Agrath toward the grand forest of floating avatria above the center of the town. The street was packed with citizens of the Fifth and Fourth Estates as well as Impress Warriors making their way across the city. She passed the twin temples of Agrath and Wedrath on her right. She rather admired the columns that decorated them. There were a number of patrons—all of them from the Third or Fourth Estates—who were making their way in or out of the temple. The gods were not a part of her personal life. K'yeran had given up those beliefs long ago but she knew the political practicality of espousing a belief in the gods. Still, she found their buildings comforting, as they spoke to the deep roots of the elven traditions and the history of the Imperium. They seemed so solid and timeless, their stones prepared to last into eternity whether their gods were remembered or not.

It was not the future that concerned her so much as the present.

The Vira Agrath ended near the center of the city at the Heroes' Circus. This great oval was not a true Circus; its size was far too small for the races that were associated with the name. It was, however, an elongated oval in the middle of which a carefully trimmed garden space surrounded several columns supporting statues of various heroes of the elven Empire down through the ages. The statues were supposed to have been placed there by the Emperor himself three generations before and were, by decree of the Imperial Will, never to be replaced.

The Heroes' Circus began and ended at the Vira Planesta. This broad avenue formed a vastly larger, rough circle around the center of the city. It touched on or crossed a number of plazas and gardens and was the quickest way to reach most of the outer parts of Tjarlas.

On the far side of the Heroes' Circus, rising high above the Hero statues, floated the avatria of Farlight Palace. It was a glittering spectacle formed like a closed flower although the exterior curved panels glittered with the flash of stars visible even in the brightness of the morning sun. The light from the Aether Well shining upward from the subatria beneath glowed against the bottom of the floating structure above it. K'yeran knew that the Aether of all the Northern Conquests was gathered through this Well and, more importantly, the numerous Aether Wells the elves had convinced the rebel chimerians in Ephindria to allow them to construct ostensibly on their behalf. Ephindria was rich in Aether and those Wells proved to be a tremendous boon to Rhonas. True, they had to trickle back a little of that Aether to the chimerians to keep them in line but it was never so much as could be used against the Empire—just enough to keep the Ephindrians out of the Empire's way. The result was a huge boon from a series of Aether Wells on the Ephindrian frontier, all of which Aether was then conducted southward through the fold portals to the glory of the Imperial Well beneath the Cloud Palace of the Emperor.

And that made Tjarlas glorious indeed. The city had been little more than an outpost village centuries ago but the Aether flowing from the north and, more recently, in such abundance from the east had caused the city to blossom. Avatria rose higher and more magnificent into the sky of the Southern Steppes above Tjarlas. The Governor of the province at that time, a Third Estate elf by the name of Ju'kali Sha-Vishau, commanded the reconstruction of the central city following its destruction by a manticorian and dwarven attack three centuries before. He tore down part of the old fortification walls so as to expand the burgeoning city and established a design for the center of Tjarlas that, remarkably, remained in effect down the years afterward. With the wealth and power afforded by the strong flow of Aether from the distant provinces beyond, the city was rumored to rival Rhonas itself in splendor and beauty.

Someday, K'yeran thought, she might spend enough time in this city to admire it. She was determined that time not be right now.

K'yeran turned right, passing along the outer edge of the Heroes Circus and onto the Vira Planetia. There were a number of shops here of the Fourth Estate lining both sides of the road. Several groups of warriors were ogling goods through the windows of the shops. K'yeran chuckled to herself as she shook her elongated head. None of the warriors had enough Imperial coin between them to be allowed through the front door of those shops, let alone purchase anything from them.

The broad avenue curved around to her left. She narrowly avoided being run down by a large wagon and accidentally bumped into a pair of young elves laughing by the side of the road. They immediately started shouting at her and then swallowed their words when they saw the robes of her office. They mumbled their apologies and quickly tried to get lost in the crowd.

The Vira Planetia was recognized by everyone as the line that separated the Fourth and Fifth Estates from the First, Second and Third Estates. The lower castes lived and did business mostly from the outer side of the Vira Planetia all the way to the city wall while the higher castes were most often found inside the circle of that avenue. It was evident as she continued her way down the road for on the right side she was passing the Darmoneti Guild House where the workers of the Fifth Estate would gather. On the left side, however, toward the city center, the impressive Theatre Calesti rose amid delicate flying buttresses. It was an amphitheater that catered largely to the Third Estate. Banners for its current production fluttered slightly in the breeze but K'yeran could still read the script proclaiming the title: "The Tragedy and Triumph of Shebin Sha-Rhonas."

K'yeran shook her head in disgust.

The road opened up ahead of her to pass on both sides of the Emperor's Garden but the Iblisi Inquisitor turned to the right side of the square. There stood a modest sized subatria and an unassuming avatria floating above it. The carved inscription above the main gate proclaimed it to be "Serenity House."

On either side of the entrance, however, stood two warriors in elven armor. They waited watchfully with their hands resting on the hilt of their swords. A third warrior, shorter than the other two, stood to one side holding a standard.

K'yeran recognized it at once as that of Ghenetar Praetus Betjarian.

*Never trim the leaves when you can dig at the roots,* she was fond of saying to herself.

It seemed that the Praetus believed the same.

# CHAPTER 26

## *Unavoidable*

THEY WERE KNOWN AS THE MADRAKAS RILLS, although they were properly a series of gullies that sliced down through the surface of the Chaenandrian Plains. They had been formed by an off-shoot of the Sak'tok River north of Tjarlas and had cut eastward across the fluvial plain, digging channels into the soil which over the years resulted in a jagged series of shallow ravines running north to south nearly five miles to the east of the city. They were, for the most part, capped by vertical cliffs of soil, their steep sides made slippery by the gravel and sand. There were exits from the Rills; steep, narrow ravines that led back up onto the plains, but only a few of these were passable. The Rills were tempestuously dangerous, prone to flooding during the late season rains which frequented the Chaenandrian regions of the Southern Steppes.

They had three primary virtues, Drakis mused

as he stood on a slope just below the crest of the Rills. They were a fine place for a fold if you wanted to keep your arrival secret; they were an excellent place to hide your army if you wanted to remain undetected; and they were within an easy march to lay siege to his prize.

The Rills below Drakis held a river not of water but of warriors. They had streamed through the newly invigorated portal folds, moving in stages from the Prophet's Camp—as they now called it—in the southern reaches of Ephindria. Their incursion into the lands of the southern chimerian families had set them in disarray, or so Ethis had informed them. It was not enough to dislodge the rebel chimerians for they still had a number of Wells remaining which they could draw upon to support their Aether-fueled addictions but Queen Chythal was now prepared to move against them and retake her throne.

"All we need to do is take this one city," Drakis muttered to himself. He looked down, his hand feeling the rough cloth of the crimson cape hanging from his shoulders. "Then I can stop this madness. Then they will leave me alone."

"Drakis," said the deep, rumbling voice behind him.

Drakis turned. "Yes, Belag."

"I am sorry to disturb your reveries," the enormous lion-man said in a surprisingly gentle tone. "They are asking for you at the outpost."

"That's fine," Drakis nodded, but he hesitated. "Belag?"

"Yes, Drakis?"

"Do you remember . . . Do you remember how things were before all this started?"

The manticorian raised his flat muzzle up in thought. "Yes, Drakis. I remember everything."

"How did we come to this, old friend?" Drakis asked quietly. "We were brother warriors of House Timuran. We lived our lives in an obscure House at the edge of a forgotten province. Very few knew us; fewer still cared. How did we come to stand here against the Empire we once served?"

"We came because you led us here," Belag said simply.

"Did I?"

"Yes, Drakis," Belag said, his feral eyes bright and focused on the human's face. "It was our destiny."

"Nothing is inevitable, Belag," Drakis said, looking again over the army that moved about the floor of the gully preparing as best they could for the battle they knew was coming. "We have a choice."

"I made my choice the day we were freed from the enslaving Devotions," Belag said. "I remember everything. I remember my brother dying and my wanting to die with him. Most of all I remember seeing you and knowing that my brother's death had meaning because you lived—because you would bring meaning to all our lives and purpose with every breath. We are here because we could not be anywhere else and matter."

Drakis drew in a breath before he spoke. "Show me to the outpost."

Belag nodded and turned, moving quickly and far more silently than Drakis up a steep ravine that brought them up out of the Rills. Belag crouched down slightly, moving along the depressions between a series of mounds. Drakis followed him with some difficulty; these were lands that were home to the ancient manticores and moving across them was natural and easy for Belag. Within a short time, however, they came upon a dugout in the side of one of the mounds. Belag quickly pushed aside the dust-laden canvas covering the entrance and stepped inside.

Drakis followed and was surprised to see that the dugout actually was much larger than he expected, with a tunnel leading deeper into the ground. His eyes had not yet grown completely accustomed to the darkness but he could make out Belag in front of him and plunged ahead.

The tunnel traversed beneath the hill to the western side. A larger room had been carved out of the hill. Several manticores and a pair of chimerians stood watch by a wide opening, supported by timber framing, that looked out over the flat steppes to the west. Through it, Drakis could see the eastern peaks of the Aeria Mountain Range, their caps still bright with snow. Their foothills flattened out into the unobstructed plains of the Southern Steppes.

There, at a bend in the Sak'tok River, stood the gleaming towers of Tjarlas.

Drakis could make out the walls of the city, and he studied it closely for any advantages they could gain. The fortifications facing them on the east were of older construction. Those would certainly be thicker and impossible to breach. There were gaps in the old walls that now were filled with newer construction. These would be Aether-enhanced and, while more difficult initially than the remaining ancient walls, would be more easily breached once the Aether Well was inverted.

Drakis considered the forest of gleaming avatria towering above the center of the city and frowned at the thought. Braun assured him that he could invert the Well in such a manner as to keep the avatria floating and the Devotions of the Impress slaves in the city intact. It was essential to Drakis' plan and, he thought, to his sanity as well.

"Drakis," Belag said. "This brother has a report which I think you need to hear."

Drakis turned from the observation opening and was surprised to see a young manticore in his family armor standing before him. "May I know you?"

"Grakeag, son of Jagrak." The young manticore bowed slightly, looking anxious and somewhat in awe of the human. He spoke the Imperial tongue but not well and with a manticorian accent so thick that Drakis had difficulty following it. "Son at honored *hoo-mani* Drakis call. Hearing of your words and I obey."

"He is of the clan of Hravash," Belag said with some emphasis.

Drakis did not need the hint. He recognized the clan name at once as the same as another manticore he had known. "Your clan is known to me . . . a most honorable clan who has earned great honor in my sight."

Grakeag drew up tall, pushing out his chest. His mane was barely growing in—a sign of his just reaching maturity. "*Hoo-mani* Drakis speaks well! I will hunt you!"

Belag cleared his throat. "He means . . ."

Drakis gave a weary smile. "I know what he means. He means to say that he will hunt *with* me . . . that he has accepted us as a friend and ally."

"Friend of *Hoo-mani!*" the young manticore declared.

Drakis nodded. "You have something to tell me?"

The young manticore tried to straighten even more. "Sirs! We watch the warriors of Rhonas. They leave the City of Gold and Light on magic trails but we know their ways and watch their magic doors across the plains to the north. For seven suns their warriors leave the City of Gold and Light but for three suns since, no warriors have been seen."

Drakis' eyes narrowed in puzzlement. He glanced at Belag.

"They've been watching the Northreach Folds," Belag explained. "An army of Rhonas has been passing through Tjarlas for over a week. For the last three days, no warriors have been seen leaving Tjarlas through the fold system."

"The army has moved on," Drakis nodded with

understanding. "They've left Tjarlas to its own defenses."

"They believe we are in the north," Belag nodded. "They do not expect us here. Our surprise
will be complete."

Drakis closed his eyes for a moment in relief.
"Then we proceed just as we did in Port Glorious.
You will attack the Northreach Gate and lay siege
to the Old East Wall. Once you've drawn whatever few defenders remain in the town to the wall
defenses, we'll fly in on the dragons, find the central Aether Well in the city and land Braun and
Jugar there. Braun will invert the Well and the
gate should be yours for the taking."

"Just like Port Glorious," Belag observed.

Drakis nodded. "All we have to do is follow the
plan."

K'yeran Tsi-M'harul stepped through the subatria
gates of Serenity House. The garden was a modest
one as befitted an Order that preferred to keeps its
public profile as low as possible.

Assesia Jak'ra stood in the garden, his hands
tucked into the sleeves of his robes. Seeing the Inquisitor enter, he hurried in her direction. "Ghenetar Praetus Betjarian is awaiting you. He asked
specifically for you to meet him in the Hall of the
Duets, Inquisitor."

K'yeran nodded as she turned and walked purposefully toward the third level access shaft. "Of course he did."

"Will you need assistance with this audience?" Jak'ra asked with an anxious inflection in his voice.

"And what help could you possibly be in the Hall of the Duets?" K'yeran chuckled.

"I . . . perhaps I could wait outside in case you needed assistance."

"No, thank you," K'yeran answered dryly as she stepped into the open shaft and immediately began to rise toward the avatria and its matching shaft hovering above. "I think I can handle a single Praetus."

K'yeran drifted upward, slowing atop the gentle force of Aether that propelled her to the third level of the avatria. She stepped gently from the duct onto the floor of the antechamber then, without missing a beat, walked through the arched doors that opened before her and into the Hall of the Duets.

The room was actually a small rotunda with a peaked ceiling. There were, as per its design, only two chairs in the room each of which faced the other. K'yeran heard the door she had just stepped through close. She glanced at it and was satisfied. The door had vanished, sealing the room for their conversation.

The room was designed to allow only two elves within its confines at a time. Once the door sealed, what was said between those within the Hall of the Duets would remain between them so long as they held one another's confidence.

Which, K'yeran mused to herself, was seldom very long.

Ghenetar Praetus Betjarian rose from his chair. He was wearing a cloak over a simple tunic, the only embellishment being the symbol of his House embroidered in gold at the neckline. He wore sandals rather than his usual boots and a pair of riding breeches. Everything from the crown of his elongated head to his feet was dulled by a fine layer of dust. "Inquisitor K'yeran Tsi-M'harul, you are late."

"So are you, Betjarian," she replied as she moved to her seat. "Are you not supposed to be waging some war far away from here?"

"I am," Betjarian replied, sitting down once more on the opposing chair, a momentary thin veil of dust falling from him. "I have two Legions of mine stuck in this town until I can get the rest of my forces up from Zhadras. This whole nonsense about trouble in the eastern Wells has the Occuran nervous. They said it was a temporary problem but it has been three days since they've closed off the northern routes. They say they will not be able to operate both the north and south folds until they can sort the problem out so they won't open the north folds again until the rest of my warriors arrive through the south."

"When will that be, Praetus?" K'yeran asked casually. Information was her stock in trade. One never knew when it could be useful.

"Tomorrow by noon they tell me." The Praetus shrugged. "We can start moving my last two Legions out of the city then but that will take us a full extra day. It's terribly frustrating. Do you have any word from Xhu'chan? You were attached to his command for a reason, as I recall."

"Yes," K'yeran replied with an enigmatic smile. "He is taking the two Legions even farther north and with some haste. He believes he has an opportunity to discover this Army of the Drakis Rebellion and secure the honor of defeating him on behalf of your command and your Order."

Betjarian shifted uncomfortably in his chair.

"Does that not please you?" K'yeran asked.

"Half of my Legions sitting in this city while the rest of the army rushes north without us?" the Praetus frowned. "No, I am not pleased!"

"You think his force is in danger, then," K'yeran asked. "The warriors under his command are of the same type and strength as the army that this rebel army destroyed."

"The fall of those Legions was because the Aether channels were disrupted," Betjarian said with a casual and dismissive wave of his hand.

"Perhaps as the Aether is now being disrupted in the east?" K'yeran suggested.

"The Occuran do not think so—although why I should take council from *that* lot is a mystery," the Praetus said as much to himself as to K'yeran. "The Legions fell before the rebels because their Devotions were interrupted. When the Devotions failed among the Impress Warriors the Legions dissolved into chaos. We've taken steps in the last month to deal with this sort of thing; Devotions altars that function specifically for the Legions and can maintain Devotions for almost ten weeks should there be a disruption in the flow of Aether. We won't lose control of our warriors like that again."

"Then relax, Betjarian," K'yeran said with an easy smile. "You and your Legions may yet find your war. In the meantime, you are in Tjarlas the Beautiful for tonight. Take a bath and find something clean to wear. You can move your armies northward tomorrow."

"It was not part of the plan," the Praetus frowned.

"Nothing *ever* goes as planned," K'yeran said, giving the Praetus her best sharp-toothed smile.

# Book 2:

## The Tide

# CHAPTER 27

## *Dawning*

$T$HEY ROSE UP OUT OF THE PLAINS with the dawn.

Word had gone out to each Legion of the Army of the Prophet through the night with orders and objectives for each. Drakis had reformed the army into ten Legions, utilizing the god names of the Encampment for each. While each was called a Legion, by elven standards they were terribly under strength; each one being comprised of just over three thousand warriors compared to a full strength Rhonas Legion of eight thousand. These ten "Legions" had shifted up and down the Rills during the night to form three army groups. Group North was commanded by Belag and comprised of three Legions: Jurusta, Quabet, and Elucia. Their objective was to assault the Northreach Gate and secure it as soon as the Aether Well was inverted.

Group South was under Hegral's command.

They were to mirror Group North's actions, flanking the city wall on the south side and move against the Emperor's Gate. Also like Group North, they were three Legions in strength: Abratias, Heritsania, and Aremthis.

Center Group, under Gradek's command, was the largest of the three. Comprised of four Legions—Aegrain, Khorithan, Tyra, and Pythus—their task was to lay siege to the Old East Wall of the city and breach it when possible. More importantly, they were to draw any remaining garrison troops to the wall so as to leave the way clear for the dragons to assault the center of the city.

Each of the Legions was made up of manticorian warriors in the lead elements with mixed troops behind. Each was supported by three Aether Mages—all that could be spared.

It was a fine plan. Every warrior who marched up the ravines out of the Rills that morning knew it as they formed up on the steppes. Properly arranged, they marched forward toward the city in the morning light. The Rhonas Army, they believed, was three days' north of their position with only the city garrison left to stop them. They could already taste the victory on their lips.

Over thirty-two thousand warriors set out across the flatlands toward the city.

Jugar stood next to his dragon atop a small rise.

Before him was set the entire vista in the morning light. The shining towers of Tjarlas lay across the flatlands at the foot of his mountains.

*His mountains.*

The dwarf's eyes shifted over the spectacle before him. Eight thousand or so warriors of the Army of Drakis marching as one across the flats so that they might tarnish that jewel of an elven city forever. It was a superb moment.

*You are the last king of the dwarves,* Jugar thought to himself. *How can you question what you have resolved to do with your every breath?*

The dragon could not hear his thoughts and, not for the first time, Jugar was glad.

*All of this because of a naïve Bolter slave.*

The truth was that Drakis had been a gift from the gods though Jugar had not recognized it at first. When the dwarf had emerged from the treasure hole beneath his throne, Jugar had latched on to the human more out of desperation than out of cunning. Yet the pieces had fit so well with the myths he knew about the humans and their ridiculous prophecy that he had not only been able to save his own skin but had come to realize that he could use this man as his best weapon to exact vengeance on the elves.

Not just the elves, he thought as he watched the troops marching westward in a great line toward the city. Vengeance on all of them. Vengeance on the manticores who sold their honor out to the elves and dwarven sovereignty with it. Vengeance on the chimerians and their reclusive queen hiding behind their silent forests. Vengeance on humanity for failing to stop the elves when they had the chance. All of them had conspired in their own selfish ways against the Nine Thrones under the mountain. But the dwarves survived deep in the roots of the world. And when the world was in ruins and tearing itself apart, the dwarven nation would emerge and have the last word over all the other races.

The old world was teetering on the point of a needle in a delicate balance that Jugar had worked hard to achieve. All the pieces were in place. All he had to do was tip it in the right direction and it would all start crashing down. It would set in motion the collapse of the Rhonas Empire as well as the destruction of the rebellion. Order would leave the world above and only the dwarves of Aerkan would remain to pick up the pieces.

A tear came to Jugar's eye. It was such a beautiful vision.

Jugar saw the three dragons of the other riders approaching his hilltop flying low over the Rills from the southeast.

A moment of doubt entered his mind. Drakis had been a gloriously fortunate accident and the dwarf had no love for the humans as a whole, but he had come to feel some fellowship with the human he had so thoroughly deluded over the past few months. He felt no real connection to the Sondau clanswoman and that chimerian Ethis was certainly not to be trusted but Braun . . .

Braun was a strange case indeed. The human as often as not infuriated Jugar with his knowledge of a force of magic which the dwarf had never supposed to exist. Their relationship was a rock-strewn road at best, yet there was something of a kinship between them; a bond forged in the magic which they were both struggling to understand. That Braun's and the dwarf's objectives were at complete odds—the human to master it and the dwarf's to destroy it—had led them on parallel courses. The dwarf grudgingly admitted that he had come to feel an appreciation and something like a brotherhood toward his nemesis.

"No going back now," the dwarf muttered to himself through a frown. "For my kingdom and for my people. That's all that matters."

The dwarf grabbed the harness around the dragon's neck and pulled himself up, swinging his leg over and settling into the saddle harness. He laid his hand against the dragon's neck and urged him into the air to join the others in flight.

Ghenetar Praetus Betjarian eased into the steaming bath with a sigh.

The Vash Barracks maintained a modest but well-appointed avatria adjacent to the barracks for the use of visiting members of the Imperial Court. It not currently being in use, the Praetus decided that he should occupy the suite of rooms for the single night of his stay. It featured an impressive bed and a parlor of sufficient size that he was able to meet with his command staff without descending from the floating structure. It held a library and a private Devotions altar, both of which Betjarian availed himself.

But it was the private bath that beckoned him the most. His aide saw to it that the oversized pool was filled with properly warmed water and a number of scraping implements of assorted sizes and shapes. Betjarian was an old campaigner for his military Order and he suspected that the onerous realities of the road ahead would make such luxuries as a cleansing bath only a fond memory in the weeks to come.

All the more reason to avail himself of it now. There were hours left in the day before he could finally lead his Legions northward out of the city. Plenty of time for one last scraping of the skin and to let the hot water relieve the aching in his joints.

He carefully leaned back, trying to ease the tip of his elongated head onto the polished stone surrounding the bath.

The doors of the bath banged open.

Startled, Betjarian slammed the back of his head against the stone.

"Praetus!" Tribune Galoch rushed into the room. His face was paler than usual, the veins on his long forehead pulsing nearly to the back of his skull. His mouth kept working but only formed the same word over and over again. "Praetus! Praetus!"

"By the gods!" Betjarian cried out, thrashing about in the water for a moment before his hands gripped the sides of the pool, steadying him. "I'm

here! Have you lost your senses? What could possibly excuse . . ."

"Praetus! We are under attack!"

"Attack?" Betjarian tried to wipe the water off
his face. "What are you blathering about?"

"An army is approaching from the east," the
Tribune said, his words rushed despite his obvious effort to gain control of himself. "They are
moving quickly and in formation."

"How many?" Betjarian asked at once, reaching
for his robe at the side of the pool.

"We count ten Legions . . ."

"TEN Legions???" Betjarian turned and stared
with disbelief at the Tribune.

"There are ten Legion divisions in the approaching army," the Tribune answered, correcting himself. "They appear to be about half strength—or
perhaps less. Perhaps forty to fifty thousand total
warriors."

"Could they be Chaenandrians?" Betjarian
spoke his thoughts aloud. "Perhaps they're trying
to take advantage of the displacement of the Legions."

"It's a mixed force, Praetus," the Tribune responded. "Manticores in the lead elements but
there is also a mixture of chimerians, goblins, and
gnomes. There is also a rather large proportion of
humans among them as well . . ."

"The Army of the Prophet!" Betjarian exclaimed
in wonder.

"The Drakis Rebels?" Galoch gaped. "How, by
all the gods, did they get *here*?"

"It doesn't matter how they got here!" Betjarian shouted as he wrapped his robe around him, cinching the sash tight. "Muster the warriors, Tribune, and on my order! I want both Legions in the city mounting the city wall and the defenses at once . . . at once, do you hear?"

"Yes, Praetus!" The Tribune bowed. He started to rush from the bath then stopped suddenly. "Should we sound the city alarm?"

"By all the gods of my House! The Emperor *himself* would have demanded the alarm be sounded before you ever reached my rooms!" Betjarian screamed as he rushed to gather his uniform. "Go! Do it now!"

"Glodock!" Belag shouted, trying to be heard over the rumbling march of the Legion arrayed before him. He wore Chaenandrian battle armor that had been presented to him by Ethis although where the chimerian got the armor Belag knew better than to ask. It was beautifully made and fit the manticore with near perfection but Belag felt awkward in it. Manticorian armor is handed down from generation to generation and is part of their heritage and their honor. That Belag should go into battle wearing the honor of another clan was unsettling to him.

More than that, it was considered an ill omen.

"Yesss, Grahn Aur!" hissed the goblin as he urged his the wyvern saddled beneath him closer to the manticore.

"Get word to the Jurusta and Elucia Legion commanders to form ranks on either side of Quabet Legion about two thousand yards out from the Northreach Gate," Belag said as clearly as he could and slightly slower than he normally would. Glodock was a fine and dedicated messenger. He would always guarantee that the message would get through although his understanding of the Imperial language was not good and the message often arrived a bit less clear than it originated. "They are to wait there for my signal to charge the gates. Standard Chaenandrian formation."

"Chaenandrian . . . what?" the goblin squawked.

"Manticores in the front, pike and sword warriors advancing after them with archers behind in support," Belag explained quickly. The walls of Tjarlas were getting closer with every step. "Have them keep the mages with the archers. They are not to use the mages or archers until the charge begins. The signal will be a single bolt of flame cast toward the wall by my mage."

"But, glorious Grahn Aur," the goblin stammered, apparently confused. "If the mages are not to cast their fire until the charge begins and the charge can only begin if a mage casts fire . . ."

An unnerving wail, low in pitch but then rising abruptly split the air with a piercing clarion call. The manticores all winced, instinctively ducking from the horrible noise that rolled out over the walls of Tjarlas to wash through the air over the steppes. It suddenly was choked off only to begin again . . . and again . . .

"I guess they must have seen us," the goblin chuckled darkly.

"We're a bit hard to miss," Belag replied without humor. "Deliver the orders and then ..."

Far to the south, a gout of flame leaped into the air, arching toward the city wall. The flame exploded above the city wall in a blinding flash. The report followed three seconds later, a clap of thunder that startled the manticorian ranks at the front of his central Legion.

"Gragrach!" Belag swore. The forward manticores of the central group were already charging toward the wall. "Not yet! It's too soon!"

Already the manticores of his own Jurusta Legion to the north were charging forward in a ragged line, eager for glory and battle.

"Release the charge!" bellowed Belag. His command of the army was coming apart, slipping out of his hands and dissolving into the bloodlust of the warriors' charge. More arching balls of fire trailing heat and flame took flight behind him from his own mages. One landed short of the wall, exploding in a blossom of flame and dirt thirty feet into the air. The second was long, plunging down beyond the wall. This vanished for a moment before erupting in a cloud of fire and smoke. The fire continued to burn beyond the wall, its dark, greasy smoke roiling up among the avatria towers of the city and blemishing the achingly blue sky.

"Charge! Charge!" Belag cried as he ran forward, following the manticores as they gripped their blades in their teeth, clawing across the ground on all fours with tremendous speed.

Still, the Grahn Aur glanced to the skies.

*Where is Drakis? Where are the dragons?*

The muffled whooping cry of the city alarm penetrated the deepest rooms of the avatria in Serenity House.

K'yeran bolted from the lounge, instinctively snatching up her Matei staff as she went. She had been halfheartedly reading a book—a rarity in itself—from the archives of Serenity House with little interest. It had been an exercise in passing the time only until she could approach the Occuran Foldmaster at the Emperor's Gate fold and, at last, start making her way south with her prize. Now the book was discarded and forgotten as she ran with long strides through the library doors and down the short, curving hallway. She threw open the doors to the balcony and stepped outside, the alarm suddenly blaring as it echoed between the towers and through the street below.

K'yeran gaped at the vista before her as she leaned against the ornate railing of the balcony. The avatria of Serenity House floated, by design, high enough so as to present an unobstructed view of much of the southern part of the city below and, more especially, the plains to the east and south.

The streets below were filled with panicked

elven citizens of the Second, Third and Fourth Estates. Their slaves followed them as best they could but there was nowhere for any of them to go. The city gates were locked and barred and the Occuran Foldmasters had sealed the folds into and out of the walled city.

But it was the sight beyond the city walls that drew her breath in through clenched teeth.

"By Anjei's Eyes!" Jak'ra swallowed in wonder. "Is that . . . ? Could that be . . . ?"

"Yes," K'yeran said, her anger barely held in check as she spoke. "The Army of the Prophet is paying us a call and it looks as though they mean to stay whether they were invited or not."

"Mistress, Inquisitor," Indexia Chik'dai called, rushing to join them on the small balcony. "Look to the east!"

"Where?"

"There, moving just south of the sun," Chik'dai said, pointing with her right hand as she held her left up to shade her eyes. "Flying just a finger's width above the horizon."

K'yeran held her own hand up, peering into the distance. At first she could only make out the dark shapes moving across the sky and thought for a moment it might be just a trick of the light.

She suddenly dropped her hand, taking a step back from the balcony. "Are those . . . ?"

"Dragons, yes, Inquisitor, I believe they are," Chik'dai answered. "How do we fight dragons?"

K'yeran rocked back and forth, her head shaking in thought. Suddenly she screamed in rage, the sound cutting above the shrill alarm as she brought both her fists down in frustration against the railing.

She spun around, facing the Indexia.

"What do we do, Inquisitor?" Jak'ra asked, his words sounding more like a plea.

"We do what we have to do," K'yeran said. "How charged are the Matei staffs?"

"The Matei staffs are all fully charged," Chik'dai responded. "We were prepared to leave for Rhonas at your word."

"Then have each member of the Quorum collect their Matei staff and come up here at once," K'yeran ordered. "We are hunting dragons this dawn."

# CHAPTER 28

## Siege

DRAKIS LEANED FORWARD on the back of the
dragón Marush, trying to see what was happening below. The beating of the enormous wings
straining forward to scoop the air regularly prevented a view of the ground but what he did see
during the interval when the wings swept down
and back had him worried.

The forward lines of the Army of the Prophet,
so clearly and neatly drawn the night before on
the map had dissolved in the chaos of battle. Drakis could see that the manticores in the center and
northern forces were already charging toward the
wall yet the southern group had not begun their
run. Worse, the charging manticores were suffering under a withering bombardment of spells of
every kind cast down upon them from the city
wall—a wall that looked to be manned shoulder
to shoulder with defending warriors, Impress

Warriors, and Proxi mages. Eruptions of flame and smoke, lightning flashes, and cyclone winds cut across the approaches to the city, obscuring the devastation they were certainly wreaking all along the still charging manticore line. Counter spells from the few mages of Group North flashed toward the city. Those spells were powerful but inaccurate, often falling short enough to endanger their own advancing warriors and more often still arching beyond the city wall and bursting within the city. Smoke from several fires inside the city, especially one large conflagration on the northern side of the central city, billowed upward, marring the clear sky and filling the interior of the city with a hazy pall.

He glanced back. Urulani was there off to his left riding her dragon, Kyranish. Seated behind her was Braun, clinging tightly to the harness. To his right, perhaps two wingspans away, flew Jugar on the back of Pyrash followed closely by Ethis astride Wanrah.

Already, Drakis could see the flash and crackle of folds opening up behind the lines of Group North. The Rhonas warriors were emerging there, moving against the rear of his army's formations.

The ground attack had launched too soon, Drakis realized with a grim shudder. They were running out of time.

*Braun has to invert the Devotions and invert the Well*, Drakis thought. *Once he does, it's over. Once he does, I'm free.*

*Now in the dawn of a dreadful day*

*Into the city of death*
*North and south flying*
*Great cities dying . . .*

Marush banked toward the left with Kyranish following him into the turn. Drakis watched as Pyrash and Wanrah soared away from them to the right.

*Two dragons from the north and two from the south,* Drakis thought. *We find the central Well and leave Braun to his work. It's a good plan. Stick to the plan . . . and I'll be free.*

Jugar knew he had two advantages over his companions. The first was that he already knew where the Aether Well of the elves was located in the city. The dwarves of the mountain knew its location and were able to provide it to him before he left the mountain.

The second was that he knew their plans whereas they knew nothing of his.

Jugar reached down with his wide hand, laying it against the neck of Pyrash. Dawn vanished into sunset. He could still see the armies arrayed below but they looked like moving toy warriors. The fires flared inside the city on the northeast side but strangely he could no longer see the smoke.

"Plans have changed, dragon," Jugar said to the monstrous winged beast. "We fly straight for the wall of the city as fast as your wings can bear us. Do you see that curved bit directly ahead of us?"

"Yes, dwarf, my sight is quite good," Pyrash answered.

"Take us directly over the outermost point of that wall. There will be a field beyond and then many elf buildings. Continue on directly to the west and you'll see a park—a green space. Fly to the left there and follow the road around as it curves northward. That's where we'll find our prize."

"And what is our prize, master dwarf?" Pyrash asked.

"A tall, floating building of the elves," Jugar answered. "Black-and-white marble gilded with silver trim."

"And what do we do once we find it?" Pyrash continued.

"At all cost, we must get me to the Aether Well beneath it," Jugar said. "And we must do so before anyone else follows us there. So, fly, Pyrash . . . fly as I have told you, as fast as you can!"

"What is the dwarf doing?" Urulani pointed as she yelled back at Braun.

The cerulean-blue-and-violet dragon to the north was beating its wings furiously, pulling quickly away from its black-and-rust companion, Wanrah. Ethis was urging his dragon onward but already Pyrash was well away and driving straight toward the wall.

"I don't know," Braun yelled back. "Perhaps he sees something we don't."

"Do we go after him?" Urulani asked.

"No, we stay with Drakis," Braun answered. "If the dwarf can find the Wells for us before we cross into the city then so much the better. Follow Drakis and we'll be fine."

Urulani nodded and looked up and to her right. Drakis continued flying Marush to the southwest. They were supposed to cross into the city above what Belag called the "Manticore Gate—" a smaller and far more modest opening in the southern wall than the Emperor's Gate farther to the west.

K'yeran and her Quorum of Iblisi rose from the balcony platform, their Matei staffs glowing with power. They drifted into the smoke-hazed air above the Vira Planesta. Below them were the shouting, panicked crowds of Tjarlas' citizens, trying to push their way toward the Emperor's Gate. The thunderous sounds of magic coming from the Old East Wall and the dark, thick columns of smoke they could see rising from the northeast quarter of the city had pushed the elves and their Impress slaves around the center of the city. Yet with Legions moving westward along the southern city wall, the Emperor's Gate was now sealed and the only avenue left for escape was the Emperor's Fold.

"I'll bet you that Occuran Foldmaster is wishing he were somewhere else right now," Indexia

Wheton remarked as he floated next to K'yeran, pointing toward the Emperor's Fold. They could barely glimpse the platform and fold between the towers of minor avatria but it was evident that the fold was being overrun by the terrified and near-rioting mob.

"And I'll bet you that we all will be making that same wish before the day is done," K'yeran said in return. "Jak'ra and Phagana . . . you're with me over the Old East Wall. Wheton, you take Uchari and Gushai with you above the Northreach Gate. Chik'dai, you take Qi'tos and Meratsoi above the Emperor's Gate. The dragons will most likely be attacking along the wall, either trying to make a breach or to clear the way for the warriors on the ground. Either way, we are the only ones here who can meet them in the air."

"But how can we bring them down?" Assesia Qi'tos asked.

"I'll let you know after I've killed one," K'yeran replied. "Stay out of the way of magic and arrows from the ground and I'll meet you back here when it's done. Now GO!"

Ghenetar Praetus Betjarian looked out over the Northreach Gate from the balcony of a most displeased Third Estate patron by the name of Clydis Sha-Tupukt's House avatria. The patron had been living a relatively peaceful and lucrative life until earlier that morning when the door of his subatria was unceremoniously broken down and his entire home—whose upper levels afforded a rather splendid view of the Northreach Gate and the steppes beyond—was confiscated in the name of the Emperor and by the Emperor's Will. So it was that the patron found himself, his family, and his Impress slaves standing on the Vira Gardalis outside their own palace while the War Council of the Army of the Imperial Vengeance hastily set up their command in the master bedroom suite, throwing the large bed and several interfering pieces of exquisite and antique furniture over the balcony railing in order to make sufficient room for the war-mages.

Below and before him was spread the chaos of war. The city wall to the east of the Northreach Gate was of newer construction than the Old East Wall and not nearly as well fortified. It had been rebuilt there following the Northern Conquests and its practicality as a defense had been secondary to esthetics. By that time, no one had expected the new wall to ever see an invading army let alone have to repel one. The Army of Drakis had managed to breach the wall east of the gate through the use of some infernal magic of their own but three Centurai had been rushed forward from where they had been placed in reserve in the Stadia Emperious. Three attempts by the manticores to breach those lines had been repulsed but the losses among the Centurai there had been heavy. The Proxis along the top of the wall were also suffering casualties from the mystical bombardment flying from the secondary lines of the attacking army. The residential district directly north was in flames but there was little he could do about that except leave it to whatever local authority still existed. He knew to be careful in the use of his reserves, since he thought they were outnumbered more than three to one but he was about to change all that.

"Tribune Ngiu'kah!" the general snapped. "Did you dispatch the runner up the Northreach Folds?"

"Praetus!" Ngiu'kah answered. "The runner was dispatched with your orders for the army to answer your call to battle here in Tjarlas. He left thirty minutes ago."

"How long before the Army arrives?" Betjarian asked.

Ngiu'kah was a veteran Tribune having fought in a number of campaigns in Lyrania before joining Betjarian's command a season before. Still, he hesitated to make his report. "The Army of Shebin's Vengeance has been moving steadily north in pursuit of what they believed was the main force of the rebellion. Our own Legions may by now be as far northward as the Mournful Mountains . . . possibly beyond . . ."

"How *long*, Tribune?"

The Tribune swallowed before answering. "The first elements are not expected to return for two days, my lord. The core of the army may be expected in four days given open access to the Northreach Folds and a forced march."

"Then we have to hold out for two days on our own," the Praetus nodded grimly.

"Yes," answered Tribune Ngiu'kah, unable or unwilling to venture any further opinion.

"Tribune Gaeus!" Betjarian shouted. "Why do we not have more warrior displacement to the rear of the enemy?"

"Praetus!" the Tribune responded at once. "The war-mages tell me that they are having trouble propagating the folds. Something is interfering with the Aether behind the lines. We are getting some Octia placed behind the lines. They are engaging the enemy with success but we cannot get sufficient numbers of Octia there to establish a foothold against their rear elements."

The avatria shook violently. Plaster from the exquisite crown moldings crashed to the marble floor.

Betjarian leaned against the doorframe as the avatria steadied itself. "Then find a way to get them there! Impress every Occuran in the town and put them to work on the front lines establishing folds. We have to break the back of their army if we're going to . . . what are you looking at, Tribune?"

The Tribune pointed through the archway out beyond the balcony.

Two enormous monsters out of his worst nightmares flew above the battlefield, their leathery wings beating the air with power and speed. Both seemed to be rushing directly toward the Ghenetar Praetus. Their shapes were the stuff of legend, their scale-covered bodies flashing in the morning light.

"Dragons!" Betjarian breathed. "War-mages! Direct all the Proxis to . . . wait!"

Four black shapes streaked through the haze around the avatria, rushing toward the Northreach Wall.

Betjarian's face split into a savage, sharp-toothed grin. "The Iblisi! Remind me to pay a call on the Keeper when I get back to the Imperial City. Her Inquisitor lackeys would seem to have some uses after all. The Iblisi will have a clear shot at that beast once he turns to attack the wall, then we'll . . ."

Betjarian stared in amazement.

The dragon did not turn nor even slow. It plunged through the floating Iblisi, banking slightly as it passed the avatria and the astonished Praetus. The elven commander caught the impression of someone riding on the back of the blue-and-purple dragon, flashing by in a blur of motion, followed moments later by all four of the Iblisi flying after it into the heart of the city. Then, to Betjarian's shock, a second dragon—bearing different markings and a taller rider—flashed past his balcony, following the Iblisi with its own meteoric speed.

"The battle's out there!" the Praetus shouted after the Iblisi tearing after the dragon. "Where do you think you're *going*?"

# CHAPTER 29

## Dragonflight

JUGAR'S EYES WERE WIDE despite the wind and the smoke.

Pyrash drove with determined speed across the city wall of Tjarlas and plunged between the soaring avatria that made up the inner city. The dragon had misunderstood the dwarf's directions and now was banking first left, then right to avoid collisions with the buildings that floated around them like a forest of stalagmites threatening to spear the sky above them on every side.

Beneath them, the panic that had gripped the citizens of the city erupted into blind terror as they passed close overhead. Jugar knew that dragons had long been the fabric of cautionary tales told by the elves to their children. He enjoyed the idea that he and Pyrash were a nightmare incarnate to the elves below.

He would have relished it more, however, if he were not so terrified himself at the moment.

The various avatria of the central city speared the sky all around them. One of them, a spindle-shaped tower of jade contoured like a spiral of reeds loomed directly in their path. Pyrash banked hard to the left, his wings almost vertical to the ground, pressing the dwarf hard down into his saddle harness as the dragon turned.

Abruptly, there was a flash and a deafening clap of thunder. The dragon rocked under Jugar as the dwarf instinctively turned toward the sound.

Lightning was still crackling around an enormous, charred hole in the side of the reed-shaped avatria behind them. A ball of heat and smoke drifted upward from the gaping scar as flames took hold of the interior structure of the avatria and began burning furiously. Unexpectedly, Pyrash dropped out from under the dwarf, diving toward the ground. Jugar remained with the dragon only by virtue of the harness that connected him to the saddle. He reached forward in a panic, grabbing the tanned leather straps with a white-knuckled grip. He could hear the screams of terror from below mixed with the rising rush of the wind as together the dwarf and dragon plunged down the face of a large theater building, turning sharply to the right and pulling up just above the now rioting elves of Tjarlas packed into a long plaza below them. The dragon soared at enormous speed over the heads of the elven families and their Impress slaves, its foreclaws pushing off several statue columns in the center of the plaza.

Thunderous explosions sounded twice more behind Jugar. The dwarf twisted around in his saddle, looking back between the beating wings of Pyrash and past his long, barbed tail. Fire, stone, dirt, the dead and, worse, the injured blasted upward from the plaza twice in succession where moments before the dragon had passed. The crowd below was running madly, mindlessly, in their desire to be anywhere but the plaza. Jugar could see a number of bodies lying still on the cobblestones in the wake of the insane stampede.

Then he saw them rushing through the air behind his dragon. Elongated heads and black, lifeless eyes, black robes, Matei staffs—the Iblisi!

"The Inquisition wants to play, eh?" Jugar sneered. "More sauce for the feast."

He had little time to enjoy the thought, however. Pyrash banked right again and plunged back into the thicket of shining elven towers floating just above the center of the city.

"Where are they?" Ethis shouted in frustration.

"They are before us," Wanrah answered. The dragon was rushing through the central section of the city. The reed-shaped avatria before them was nearly engulfed in flames. "Pyrash's trail seems to be clearly marked."

"Keep going," Ethis urged, craning his neck forward. There were more fires in the plaza ahead. "We've got to catch up with Jugar."

"Do you think the dwarf needs our assistance?" the dragon asked.

"No," Ethis answered. "I think he needs to be stopped!"

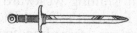

Searing light tore through the air just below Kyranish's right wing. Drakis heard the sizzle of its passing moments before the thunderclap of it slamming into the onion-shaped avatria ahead of them. The force shattered the structure, breaking it in two large sections and several smaller ones. The subatria held below it, however, and the pieces of the building, flames now igniting in various places, remained floating before them.

Urulani grimaced as Marush, flying just three dragon's lengths ahead of her, pulled in both his wings. The dragon counted on his momentum to carry him through the debris with Drakis on his back. Kyranish rolled over the top of the shattered avatria, righting herself and dropping again to follow behind Marush.

Still the black shapes behind them remained in fanatical pursuit.

"Who *are* they?" Urulani yelled across the wind and tumult from the back of Kyranish.

"An Iblisi Quorum," Braun answered, clinging to the harness. "Rather impressive, don't you think? They seem to be adapting quite well in the face of the impossible."

"If we survive them, then I'll be impressed later," Urulani said as Kyranish banked suddenly left and then right again. Twin bolts seared the air, rushing past them and out over the city wall. Urulani could see the Legions under Hegral beyond the city wall, shifting westward as they moved toward the Emperor's Gate. The bolts fell over Hegral's Legions, cascading forks of lightning down among the warriors below. Urulani noted the elven warriors, in full battle armor, as well as their Impress Warriors filling the top of the city wall, shifting westward with the movement of the invaders on the plains beyond.

"I thought the Imperial Army had deserted this city," Urulani yelled more out of frustration than a desire to be heard or answered.

"Find the Aether Well of the city and get me to it," Braun shouted back. "Once the Well is inverted, it won't matter if the city is filled with Rhonas warriors or not."

Kyranish banked left with Marush. A plaza beneath them was strewn with dead elves and slaves of several other races as well, a series of large craters pocking the cobblestones. Marush plunged back among the avatria of the city with Kyranish following only seconds behind.

*It wasn't supposed to happen this way!*

"What do you mean it won't matter?" Urulani asked.

"Once my own Devotions spell is functional

and the Well is inverted, the Legions will be robbed of the Aether," Braun explained, his voice growing hoarse from yelling over the wind. "We'll have done what Queen Chythal asked. We can leave and the Legions of Rhonas will either stay behind these walls or be forced to walk home."

"Then where is it?" Urulani demanded of the heavens, her eyes darting between the avatria towers flashing past her in a bewildering array.

"That's it!" shouted the dwarf, his hand to the neck of Pyrash. The world around them had once again become surreal but the elegant black-and-white marble of the Farlight Palace with its beautiful silver trim was clear to his eyes. "Can you rid us of those pests behind us?"

"For a short time, master dwarf," Pyrash answered. "They are most persistent."

"Long enough to get me safely into that subatria garden?" Jugar asked.

"I believe so," Pyrash chuckled. "So long as you do not care *how*."

"I'm not particularly finicky about your methods, beastie, just so long as . . ."

Pyrash suddenly opened both his wings flat against the wind. The sudden halt in the air pressed Jugar forward, his hand slipping from the dragon's neck. Desperately, he tried to grip the harness straps ahead of him. They both shuddered to a near complete stop in the air, their momentum and the curve of Pyrash's leathery wings carrying them slightly upward.

The Iblisi behind them were caught off guard. They flashed past the dragon and wavered in the air. Their concentration had been so completely on following the monstrous creature of the air that they were suddenly disoriented, their course wavering among the avatria forest around them.

Pyrash, on the other hand, knew exactly what to do.

The dragon beat its wings in great arcs reaching through the air, holding its position as it drew in a great draught of air, blending it with the gases belching up through its throat. In an instant, the gases mixed with the dragon's exhale, igniting into a blue stream of plasma fire shooting from the dragon's gaping maw. It engulfed one of their pursuers, who fell from the sky trailing smoke from burning robes and screaming in agony.

But this had not been the dragon's target. Pyrash's blue flames swung back and forth with the turning of his head, bursting through the shells of several avatria surrounding them. Each flashed into flame and smoke at once, filling the air around them with acrid smoke and heat.

Jugar began to cough and panic. He was used to darkness but this was different—this was a smoke so thick that he could not *see*. He struggled to reach forward with his hand, to find the dragon's neck and give him a piece of his considerably upset mind . . .

The air suddenly cleared, the wind carrying

Jugar's tears from his stinging eyes. Jugar grinned.

There, before them, was the black-and-white tower of the Farlight Palace.

He placed his hand on the dragon's neck. The world was suddenly bathed in a salmon hue of sunset in the dragon's other world but the tower remained before them. "No chances, dragon! Take us straight in below the avatria and land in the subatria garden. That's where the central Aether Well will be found. That's where I've work to do."

He lifted his hand from the dragon's neck, reaching for the pocket of his coat. He rested it for a moment on the hard bump beneath the leather then, reassured, gripped the harness once more.

The Heart of the Aer was still with him.

Jugar knew it was one thing to bring down some small Aether Well of an obscure House on the edge of the Rhonas Empire but an entirely different matter to bring down a central Well of an elven city. He would have to demonstrate some delicacy in arranging the collapse of this Well.

Pyrash dove down toward the shadows beneath the avatria of the Farlight Palace.

After all, Jugar reasoned, he wanted to live to see the terrible results.

Ethis pulled his dragon skyward. The smoke and haze filling the city was making it difficult for him to see. He had managed to drive one of the Iblisi into the wall of an avatria, crushing the elf. Somehow he had managed to lose the remaining three Iblisi agents for the time being.

Wanrah had been injured by a pair of the bolts from the Iblisi Matei staffs. There were slight tears in the membranes of both her wings; nothing that wouldn't heal with time. But Wanrah could still fly, and so Ethis continued to seek Jugar and Pyrash, peering at the city below them.

"There you are!" he breathed.

He could see the blue-and-purple markings of Pyrash climbing up through the center of the city from the west side. Streaks of lightning flashed behind the dragon from his own set of pursuers.

Wanrah saw them, too, diving painfully down to help protect his fellow dragon.

Marush and Kyranish wheeled around an enormous coleseum in tandem, Marush cutting to the left as Kyranish turned sharply to the right. Their paths crossed over the coleseum, giving the Iblisi behind them a moment's hesitation over which of the dragons they should follow. Kyranish then banked hard left again, diving down over the crowded street below and toward a plaza featuring a series of columns. The citizens below were mad with fear. Urulani wondered how they might be comforted. This was not their fight—not their war—but they were caught up in it nevertheless. They would be the ones who would suffer the most and suddenly the raider captain felt compassion for them.

"On the left!" Braun shouted into her ear. "That's the Palace! That's where I'll find the Well!"

"What do you want me to do?" Urulani called back.

"Land me on the subatria wall," Braun grinned. "I'll make my way into the garden from there. Once the Well is inverted, come back and get me."

"But Drakis," Urulani said. "I can't see where he's gone!"

"Put me on that wall!" Braun urged. "Once the Well is inverted, then the battle's won and we can all go home!"

*Is that not what Mala said to me?* Urulani thought with a chill.

But she answered with a nod, her hand to the dragon's neck. In moments the dragon altered course slightly to the left and the black-and-white marble structure quickly grew large before them. Kyranish opened her wings, slowing as she approached the wall, the long talons of her hind legs reaching for the stonework. Kyranish's grip shattered the marble but the masonry held. Braun slid down the foreleg of the dragon, landing hard atop the wall. His legs gave way and the mage fell on his back.

In that instant, a brilliant shaft cut through the dragon's wing. Kyranish howled, her outrage matched by her pain.

"Go!" Braun shouted, waving Urulani away. "Go now!"

The dragon did not wait for Urulani's answer. Kyranish spread her wings, pushing them both straight up into the sky, desperately clawing at the air for altitude.

But the Iblisi had anticipated this. They circled around the dragon, their Matei staffs flaring, bolts of blinding magic piercing the dragon as it fought to regain the air. Urulani held on as it climbed higher into the sky, its tormentors climbing with it, their bolts carving holes in the dragon's wings and perforating her scales and hide. Kyranish thrashed desperately looking for an avenue of escape, but the Iblisi wheeled around her on all sides and there was nowhere for the dragon to go but higher. Flight is a predatory response in dragons for they instinctively know that there is safety for them in the clouds.

Kyranish saw the sun as she climbed upward among the burning avatria of Tjarlas. Then her membranes shredded from her own desperate beating of her wings and, now high above the towers of Tjarlas, she fell from the sky for the last time.

And Urulani, still in her harness, fell with her.

# CHAPTER 30

## Collapse

U RULANI FELT KYRANISH SHUDDER beneath her. Flaring bolts of light lanced the air from every direction. Then, with a terrible roar, the dragon rolled backward in the air and plunged toward the city below.

"Kyranish!" Urulani screamed in outrage, the wind howling in her ears. She pressed her hand against the dragon's neck but nothing changed; she was not transported to that otherworld of the dragons and, in that moment, she knew the dragon she had known was no more. Tears welled up in her dark eyes, pushed back across the smooth, night-black of her skin before being whisked away with the rushing wind of their fall. She could see the towers of the avatria below her now as onrushing spears threatening to impale them. "Kyranish! Wake up!"

But the dragon did not respond, twisting

lifelessly in the air. They began to roll and tumble, slowing in their fall, the world starting to spin madly about them.

She realized she was not alone.

Two dragons were falling out of the sky.

Urulani saw Marush plunging downward next to her. She thought at first that the Iblisi had killed him as well but then realized that the other dragon's wings were pulled in against its body rather than flailing in the wind. She glimpsed Drakis, still on the back of Marush, looking at her, yelling and gesturing at her wildly.

"*Jump!*" he seemed to shout.

*Jump?* she thought. *Jump to where?* But the ground was coming closer by the moment and there was no time for questions. She reached down and desperately yanked against the leather straps securing her to the harness. *Too long to undo.*

She pulled out the dagger at her waist.

They were already falling between the avatria towers.

She pulled at the securing straps with her left hand but her grip slipped along the leather. She wrapped the hand around it then pulled them both tight, the dagger sawing at the harness.

The small plaza below with a fountain and a number of subatria shops around it grew larger by the moment.

The straps gave way to the sharp blade. Urulani had been pushing against the harness with her feet to keep the leather straps taut. Their sudden release caught her off guard and she was flung from the back of Kyranish, suddenly falling freely through the air.

She closed her eyes.

Talons wrapped around her.

She heard the sickening sound of a terrible crash and collapse. The pretty little plaza was certainly no more and, most likely, many of its surrounding buildings had shattered beneath the crushing mass of the dead dragon.

Urulani realized in that moment that she was still alive.

She opened her eyes and regretted it.

The street of the elven city rushed past her with sickening speed. The talons around her body were a little too firm in their grip, making it difficult for her to breathe but she had no intention of asking the dragon to loosen its hold on her. They were flying far too low and too fast for comfort or safety. A tower on a corner shop building rushed in her direction. Urulani instinctively held her arms in front of her face to shield herself from the deadly collision but the dragon suddenly moved her sideways with a jolt, swinging her around the structure as they flew past it. The floating avatria of the central city were now everywhere above them. Marush twisted his course down several streets before finding a large open plaza.

The dragon, still flying at tremendous speed, pulled up over the screaming, panicky elves of the plaza, roaring into the sky. Straight up the dragon rushed, vaulting once more above the avatria towers. Their upward speed slowed until the dragon came nearly to a stop in the air, its wings extending. Urulani felt as though she were floating in the air, neither going up nor down in that moment as Marush reached up, bringing the Sky Mistress toward Drakis.

He grabbed for her with both his arms, taking hold of her hands just as the dragon released her at the top of their flight.

Drakis pulled Urulani toward him, swinging her around behind him.

"Hold on!" Drakis bellowed to her.

The dragon once more pulled in his wings, craning his great neck downward.

Urulani wrapped her arms around Drakis' waist in a viselike grip. Below them, she could see the Iblisi already rushing up toward them.

The dragon plunged downward, wings tight. They were once again headed into the thicket of avatria towers below.

"They know how to stop us!" Drakis yelled over the rising gale around them. "Is Braun at the Well?"

"Yes!" Urulani nodded.

"Then I hope he hurries!" Drakis shouted as Marush dove directly through the onrushing Iblisi and sped once more among the twisting chasms between the avatria of Tjarlas.

Ethis could see Jugar on Pyrash below him. The dragon was weaving between the avatria in the central city with three of the Iblisi closing at his heels.

Ethis urged Wanrah downward. The dragon dove in from behind, barreling through the Iblisi. The elves scattered among the towers in their surprise. One of them, to Ethis' satisfaction, misjudged his turn and smashed directly into an avatria.

Ethis knew that the dwarf had to maintain contact with the dragon in order to give him any instructions. Ethis reached down with his own hand and touched his dragon's neck.

The avatria somehow became enormous trees towering into the sky. *Perhaps the dragons are more comfortable among thickets than cities,* he thought.

"Jugar!" he called out.

The dwarf turned around in surprise. "Well, you're a fine sight on a dark day!"

"I'll give you a *very* dark day if you ever leave me behind like that again," Ethis shouted back.

"Sorry, lad! I was just a wee bit too enthusiastic. It shall not happen again, I assure you," Jugar smiled. "Let's find the others and leave."

"Leave?" Ethis said, just as both dragons banked out of the central cluster of floating towers. They were on the north side of the city again. The Sak'tok River glistened in the morning light beyond the city wall. Below them, the elven Legions still manned the defenses. Beyond, the Army of the Prophet was in trouble, with a number of Centurai appearing behind their lines. "What do you mean leave?"

"The job's good as done," Jugar beamed. "Any

minute now the whole thing should come crashing down and we'll have our victory."

"I'm surprised you have that much faith in Braun," Ethis admitted. "I'd have thought you would have demanded to be at the Well with him."

"With him?" Jugar scoffed. "He doesn't even know where the Well is! Besides, the job's already done."

"That cannot be. Braun's at the Well now," Ethis said. "I just saw Urulani land him there not three minutes ago. Hey, where are you going?"

Jugar had pulled Pyrash around, making a hard turn back in toward the city.

"He's done it again!" Ethis groused, turning his own dragon back in pursuit.

The garden was hot.

Braun wiped the sweat from his forehead as he moved across the floor of what had been a subatria garden. The plants were charred, some of them still burning and the ground was warm under the soles of his boots. The inverted dome that formed the bottom of the Farlight Palace hung over his head but the surface of it was charred and blistered. The walls surrounding the remains of the garden were most curious as there were a number of places along the wall where the soot outlined the shapes of humans or, perhaps, elves. They were like inverted shadows: patches where shapes had somehow shielded the wall from heat and flame. There was debris beneath each of these strange shapes outlined on the wall but Braun was not keen on investigating too closely.

Besides, he told himself, he could ask his questions later. There was important work to be done.

He turned toward the Aether Well and gasped.

The Aether Well was not a single monolith of crystal but three spaced around a central altar. More than that, Braun had never seen Aether Well crystals of such size before. Each was nearly thirty feet tall, extending upward from the garden into a hole in the center of the avatria overhead.

*Something is wrong*, Braun realized.

The color of the Aether Well crystals was a strange green that pulsed upward from the ground, forming brilliant green trails along jagged fracture lines. Aether spilled out from these lines, radiating in irregular flashes from the fissures. Between the three crystals, the Aether collided, twisting and writhing. As Braun watched, more fissures began to appear in the Well crystals, each spilling more of its power over the ruined garden.

*They're cracked. Broken*. Braun thought. *I've got to fix them.*

Braun hurried to the center of the garden, moving his feet quickly over the heated ground.

*Perhaps that is what happened to the elves here*, the mage thought as he rushed toward the altar between the crystals. *All I need to do is mend the cracks, make the crystals stable again. Then I can maintain the Devotions at the same time I flip the Well from the altar.*

Braun reached his hands out for the altar. He could feel more Aether running through it than he had ever before believed possible.

Braun smiled as he touched the altar.

*All I have to do is . . .*

The Tjarlas Governor's Well vanished in a flash of heat, power, and madness.

Braun simply ceased to exist, entirely consumed by the power he had unwittingly released.

The avatria of the Farlight Palace with its beautiful black-and-white marble exterior and its intricate silver trim vanished too, pulverized by the upward blast and flashing into a ball of purple flame as its structure and contents were instantly consumed by the supernatural heat and power. All this fueled the conflagration as its disintegrated mass was added to the explosion. Fingers of smoke and fire drove into the sky even as a dome of light and compressed air rushed outward.

The surrounding avatria were engulfed in the resulting ball of flame, shattered and instantly ignited as well, adding to the fire climbing above the city.

Then, the Aether died.

The burning towers fell. Bereft of their Aether, the avatria of the High Estates dropped from the sky. Already pushed from their foundations by the force of the Well's explosion, the burning towers crashed downward onto the city below. Some simply collapsed, crushing those who were in the streets beneath them. Others fell over on their sides, their flaming structures cutting a swath of destruction in their path.

The once glorious skyline of Tjarlas had, in a matter of minutes, vanished forever beneath a pall of fire, smoke, and ash.

With it vanished the Aether Well that gathered Aether from and supplied Aether to the Northmarch Provinces, the outposts in Chaenandria and the vast Wells in southern Ephindria.

# CHAPTER 31

## Consequences

DRAKIS AND URULANI BOTH TURNED toward the sound of the blast. Smoke and flame burst upward from the ground, engulfing the avatria above the center of the detonation and igniting the falling avatria around it. Pieces of debris, trailing flame and smoke, soared upward, far above the tops of the tallest avatria in the center of the city, arching over in every direction.

Urulani instinctively clenched her arms tightly around Drakis.

"Marush!" Drakis shouted. "There's a . . ."

The air was suddenly pressed out of Drakis' lungs. The expanding wave of the blast slammed into them with frightening speed. It caught the extended wings of the dragon, vaulting him and his passengers suddenly forward and upward. Marush tumbled once, managed to steady himself for a moment but then was caught by an updraft of tremendous heat and spun, tumbling again.

The smoke engulfed them. Drakis choked and gagged on the smoke and dust, his face stinging with bits of miniscule debris. He could not see in the sudden darkness. He lost all sense of direction as they continued to tumble, blind and gasping.

Suddenly they burst into brilliant sunlight once again. Marush was laboring to keep them in the air. Drakis could hear the wheezing sounds coming from the dragon. They were still among the avatria of the city.

A city that was falling.

The floating avatria everywhere around them were crashing down hard onto the foundation subatria beneath them. Few of them settled straight down but began tipping sideways, their slender, exquisite shapes collapsing into each other, shattering and raining down on the crowded streets below.

The mad, insane streets below. He could hear the screams, the wails and the roar rising up from beneath the destruction—a howl that called him to join them.

"It wasn't supposed to happen this way!" Drakis shouted to the streets below, to himself, and to the sky. "I didn't want this!"

"Get us clear of the city," Urulani urged Marush from behind Drakis, reaching forward and pressing her hand against the dragon's neck. "Fly us back to the Rills. Quickly, Marush, before a building falls on us."

The dragon worked his wings with a will, slipping between the collapsing avatria and bursting over the city wall, turning toward the east.

Tears streamed down Drakis' cheeks, blown back by the wind. "It was not supposed to happen this way! What have I done? What have I done?"

Five hundred and fifteen leagues to the north of Tjarlas, Legate Xhu'chan stood on the field of victory known on the map only as the Flat's Gap. It was a wide, featureless place with little to commend it. Those few who had tried to settle here soon moved on to lands that were more forgiving and bountiful. The goblin raiders occupied the better, more elevated lands to the west. The Mournful Mountains could barely be made out on the eastern horizon.

All that remained was the carnage of battle that disturbed the landscape, the most peculiar part of which now rested in a colossal heap on the ground before him situated atop what appeared to be the only mound within a hundred miles on the plains.

A dragon. An actual dragon.

It lay where it had crashed to the ground. The shattered form—charred in several places—no longer retained the grace of its flight that the Legate had marveled at when first he saw it rushing through the sky over the scattering, panicked ranks of his Legions and yet he still had to admire the power the beast represented even as it lay broken here on the plains. The dragon had engaged his foremost Legion—over eight thousand warriors—with a ground force of barely more than seven hundred ill-equipped rebels. Yet this single creature and its seven hundred had held his Legions at a standstill for three days. It had cost Xhu'chan nearly a full Cohort of warriors and nearly half a Centurai of Proxis before his army managed to bring it down.

Xhu'chan shook his head slowly in wonder.

Magnificent as the dragon was, it was the small figure of a human woman cradled in the crook of the dragon's foreleg that held his wonder and attention. Her wispy, almost white hair shifted in the wind. She was a slight girl as humans go. She wore a patchwork of armor over a long coat of padded leather.

"Tsaj, you are sure this human girl is Drakis?" Xhu'chan asked.

"Yes, Legate," Tsaj replied with a sharp bow of his head. "As you requested, we captured several of the rebels during the battle. All of them were kept apart from one another. Each one was brought here in turn to identify the body before their execution."

"They all named this youth as Drakis?"

"Each of them swore to it," Tsaj reported crisply. "Several of them shed tears at the sight of her."

Xhu'chan considered the young woman more closely. The wounds to her body were evident—the blistering of her right leg from the Aether magic cast against the dragon as well as the four arrows piercing her left side and back.

The Legate stepped back quickly.

"My lord?" Tsaj asked with obviously feigned concern.

"Her face," the Legate said. "It bothers me somehow."

Tsaj leaned forward for a closer look. "I don't see anything unusual, my lord. Just the face of a human—perhaps more comely than some by human standards but . . ."

"No, Tsaj," the Legate frowned. "There is something about it that—that haunts me. She is smiling. She is smiling in death as though she had greeted an old friend. As though she is the fortunate one and I am left here to deal with . . ."

"Legate Xhu'chan!"

The Legate closed his black, featureless eyes for a moment. He reached back and scratched the point of his elongated head before he acknowledged the war-mage. "Have you found the main force yet, Kleidon?"

"No, Legate, but a far more urgent matter has come to our attention." The aging war-mage wheezed slightly from his exertions in coming. "The Aether—it has vanished!"

"Vanished?" Xhu'chan exclaimed. "The Occuran will pay dearly for this! They assured us that the magic would flow without interruption to the front of the army advance!"

"No, Legate, you do not understand," Kleidon said, anxiety showing in the throbbing veins sticking out along both sides of his long, bald skull. "The Occuran were not part of the Army. They do not receive their Devotions from our new altars but from their own altars linked to the folds. Now the folds have vanished to such a terrible extent that the Occuran have all fallen out of their Devotions. There were over sixty of their numbers attached to our advance. In each case they have gone either mad as Bolters or nearly unresponsive. There are only a handful of them left who are answering questions at all."

"What about our own Devotions?" Xhu'chan asked quickly.

"They are holding," Kleidon nodded though his grayish brow was wrinkled in concern. "But I have checked and they, too, are no longer receiving Aether from the folds. They are discharging into the army as they were meant to do—but we have no Aether for the war-mages or their Proxis on the battleline."

"Then we must withdraw," Tsaj interjected.

"How?" Kleidon snapped. "We've no Aether with which to charge the folds and, it seems, no Occuran capable of opening them even if we did!"

"Tsaj!" Xhu'chan barked.

"My Legate!"

"Have the Legion commanders get their troops in order and prepared to march," Xhu'chan ordered.

"March?" Kleidon blurted. "March *where*?"

"Back to Rhonas," Xhu'chan replied.

"That's over five hundred leagues!" Kleidon said in disbelief. "Without the folds?"

"Without the folds, if we must," Xhu'chan said,

shrugging his shoulders. The armor was beginning to feel heavy already.

"And how long will that take?" Kleidon asked.

"Not more than two months," Xhu'chan answered.

"Two *months*?"

"Why? Are you in a hurry?" Xhu'chan asked with a calm that he did not feel. "Cheer up, old mage. Drakis is dead. We have a victory and all we have to do now is return within two months to claim it."

"Why two months?" Tsaj asked behind the Legate.

"Because, Tsaj," Xhu'chan answered. "In two months' time, the Aether charge on those delightful new Devotions altars will expire and there won't be any army left to march anywhere. Whatever has happened to our Aether, I believe it will be restored by the Will of the Emperor long before then and you'll be toasting our victory in the halls of the Emperor himself not a day afterward."

"And if not?" Kleidon asked quietly.

He looked once more down on the gentle, peaceful smile of the dead woman in the arms of the dragon.

"Then this may well be the last march for any of us," Xhu'chan answered.

Ghenetar Praetus Betjarian was on the walls of Tjarlas when the Well exploded in the center of the city. He watched in horror as the power of the blast climbed higher and higher over the skies of the city and the spindle-beauty of the hundreds of avatria crashed down, collapsing and falling over. The fires in the center of the city merged into a single terrible storm of flames.

But it was the sound that unnerved him the most. A chorus of rage, laughter, fear, and madness echoed up from the streets behind him. The chaotic uproar of an entire city suddenly fallen out of Devotions. It took only minutes for the crowds to emerge from the streets, clutching whatever weapons they could find at hand.

And all their rage was directed at the warriors of their own Legions.

Betjarian did not understand why but realized almost at once that knowing why was not of immediate importance. What *was* important was that his army was now being attacked both from without the walls and within. His instinct as a warrior and a leader of armies dictated his actions.

He had to save his Legions.

At once he ordered the Legions within the walls to establish a front against the slaves and the citizens, both groups now enraged, insane, and desperate to attack their own army. The Vash Barracks within the city became their defense. Communication with the other Legions stationed around the city had failed completely and the war-mages were suddenly without connection to their Proxis in the field. Betjarian was forced to send runners with messages, ordering that all Legions converge on the Emperor's Fold at the southeast part of the city. As long as the Devotions held his army together, he felt confident that he could retain command and get them out through the Emperor's Fold back toward Zhadras. There he could regroup and determine how best to proceed against the rebel army.

He sent word out through the Legates, the Tribunes, the Centurai, and on down toward every warrior in the field to retreat back inside the city walls and make their way toward the Emperor's Fold.

It was a good plan, based on everything Betjarian knew from his long years of experience.

Belag's roar rose up with the fireball over the city. He lifted his arms above his head, the blood-soaked fur shining in the morning light.

The attack had fallen into desperate straits from their first charge at the gates. They had expected to be largely diversionary; trying to remain outside the range of the wall Proxis' direct fire and feigning attacks until the Well could be brought down. But then the charge began too soon and at different times. Worse, the flipping of the central Aether Well had not taken place as expected. Belag could see from the battlefield the occasional flight of the dragons among the spires of the city as well as the flashes of magic following them. He could not make out what was pursuing the dragons but he had the sinking realization that they might not be able to count on the inversion of the Well at all; that they might have to take the city by force.

Then the gates had opened and Belag had almost despaired. The city was not only defended but apparently in force, contrary to everything they had thought the night before. Ranks of Rhonas warriors issued from the Northreach Gate. Worse, folds began opening behind them, pouring more of the Emperor's warriors into the back of their lines. The front dissolved into a confused and desperate melee battle between different Octia and Groups folding across the lines, each trying to get a superior position over the other from both the Army of the Prophet and the Rhonas Legions. The elves made concerted efforts to push Belag's Legions closer to the city wall and within more accurate range of the Proxis casting spells from the battlements.

Belag raged in frustration as his army began to dissolve under the force of so many enemy Proxis and their withering magic . . . but then all the world seemed to stop as the great city was engulfed in one, unthinkable cataclysm.

The thunder continued to roll out from over the city walls and down across the battlefield. The buildings of the Rhonas Empire dropped out of the sky behind the city wall, adding to the continuous rumbling shaking the ground under their feet.

"Kugan! Megash!" he yelled. "Re-form the line! It won't be long now!"

The two manticore warlords gave the order, which was rapidly passed across the field. The manticorians pushed forward, coming shoulder to shoulder against the Rhonas warriors, who were stepping back from the battle line.

"Look at the wall!" Belag commanded but his words were unnecessary. The eyes of everyone were already raised to the city. "They've stopped! The Aether is gone ... and the walls are silent! Their magic no longer rains from the sky! Drakis has robbed them of their might!"

The Legions of the Rhonas Empire were hastily retreating back through the gate.

"Belag!" Kugan said, his voice filled with hope and pride. Belag had appointed the manticore warlord of Jurusta Legion the week before. "The Rhonas Centurai behind our lines have been stranded. Their folds are no more. Our warriors have surrounded them. They are dying as we speak. And the Rhonas Legions before us are re-treating toward the gate."

Belag stood tall, straining to look over the tops of the warriors, a grim smile on his lionlike face. "That sounds very much like an invitation to me. Let's follow them in. Sound the charge!"

Belag's ancestral blood surged hot inside him. His was a great warrior race. He could not deny himself the glory of this charge. Despite the council of his warlords, Belag rushed to the front of the battle line of Group North. Quabet Legion was behind him. There were only one thousand, nine

hundred of their original three thousand who remained to make the run for the gates.

Belag led them all the way across the bloodied
ground. He expected the gates to close as they approached; they would have to bring their own
mages up to assault the gates and break them
down. But the gates remained open.

Belag raised up his hands, slowing the charge
and brought them to a halt before the open gates.
Unworldly sounds rolled out from beyond those
gates—sounds that would forever be remembered
by those of the Quabet Legion.

Alone, Belag entered the gates.

Alone, Belag returned a few moments later
closing the gates behind him.

"Close all the gates," Belag ordered in a quiet,
dry voice. "Seal them shut. Let no one in. Let no
one out."

The word was passed to Group Central and
Group South.

The city was sealed.

Many asked Belag what he had seen within.

He remained silent.

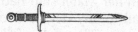

The Theatre Calesti was burning furiously as
K'yeran staggered onto the plaza known as Emperor's Gallery. The screams, howling, and insane
laughter rang in her ears. Smoke filled the plaza,
making it difficult to see very far. This filled her

inexplicably with fear: not because she was afraid of attack—she could bring to mind any number of ways to deal death—but a fear of being *seen*.

She was afraid someone would see her for who she was.

She jabbed her fist into her thigh, hoping the pain would somehow bring clarity to her thinking. It made no sense to her. *Why should she care what people thought? Why should she feel this terrible dread and—could that be guilt? Is this what shame felt like? She was only doing her job,* she told herself. *This terrible, bloody, shameful job . . .*

She closed her black eyes with her hands, leaning back against a broken wall, trying to rub the images from her mind away from her sight. But the images kept coming to her. Death, torture, pain—she had meted them all out without a second thought. Now each incident boiled up in her memory in shocking detail, and she felt physically ill at each recalled incident and image.

*What is wrong with me?*

She had barely managed to save herself when the Aether Well tore itself apart. Only the remaining charge in her Matei staff had allowed her to arrest her fall to any degree and even that had been a near thing. The avatria fell around her like stone rain. She had survived by training and instinct the terrible fall of the city.

*But how will I survive the fall of my own mind?*

She felt almost paralyzed by her own remorse. *It must be the magic of the humans,* she thought.

*They've done this to me, conjured some spell to inca-
pacitate me . . .*

*Incapacitate me from inflicting more pain . . . more
evil . . . more lies . . .*

She cried out in rage. She needed help and she
could only think of one name that had any experience with the human magic. He could free her
from this curse. He could take away her guilt.

She needed Soen.

She rushed across the ruins of the plaza. The
ground was carpeted with the dead. She could
hear the insane wailing beyond the curtain of
smoke and could only hope she did not encounter
anyone in her flight to the door of Serenity House.

The avatria was missing entirely but the façade
remained largely intact. She pushed through the
bent gates, feeling her way around the left-hand
corridor. She tripped over someone who groaned
in the darkness, and she tensed in fear but continued to move past.

She found most of the kitchen intact. She sped
through the kitchen and into the pantry beyond.
She fumbled for a moment, trying to trip the release but she found it at last. The hidden panel
swung open and she ducked inside.

There, in repose, stood Soen Tjen-rei with a ball
of light illuminating the chamber from where it
floated in the center of the room. He appeared the
same as when she had captured him. He stood in
his weathered and faded robes, his Matei staff
gripped in his hands.

K'yeran hesitated for a moment, staring in wonder at the globe of light glowing overhead. It was the most common of spells cast with Aether but to see any magic after it had failed so completely was shocking to her.

She took a breath and stood back. Her own Matei staff, still clutched in her hand, was useless now as Soen's had been.

"Did you really need to capture me?" Soen asked quietly. "That was hardly worthy of you, K'yeran. So I am back at the Keep, am I?"

"No, you are in Tjarlas . . ."

"Tjarlas?" Soen snapped and then looked up, noticing the wailing, distant sounds. "What's happened? What's going on?"

"You have to help me," K'yeran said, rushing forward, the desperation raw and open on her face. "The Well has fallen and much of the city with it. The Devotions have failed and . . . and they've done something to me. They've cursed me with their magic and you're the only one that can undo this!"

Soen looked at her in silent contemplation.

"Soen, I meant something to you once!" K'yeran pleaded. *I've never begged in my life!* "And . . . and you meant something to me, too. Please! You've got to take this curse off of me. I hate who I am . . . everything I've done . . . you've got to take this away from me!"

Soen spoke quietly. "I can't."

"You can't?" K'yeran blinked, the despair threatened again to engulf her. "Or you *won't*?"

"You haven't been cursed—at least, not by human magic," Soen said. "I cannot take this away from you because this is who you are and who you have been. This isn't magic, K'yeran. This is something else . . . and I'm going to help you find out what it is."

"Why?" K'yeran asked. "Why would you do that for me?"

"Because if we cannot find the answer," Soen said. "It may mean the end of everything for us all."

# CHAPTER 32

## Between Evils

"LORD DRAKIS," BELAG ANNOUNCED, his leo-
nine face lifted in an expression that Drakis
could only interpret as smug. "I beg leave to present before your council Gragh-Krigan, King of the
Chaenandrian Prides!"

Drakis tried to wave in acknowledgment but he
could not stop his hand from shaking, so he
merely nodded.

He sat at the focal point of a large, if hastily
erected canvas pavilion on the steppes east of the
still burning Tjarlas. It had been three days since
the city had fallen to them and the fires had continued unabated. He specifically asked that the
Prophet's Guardians set the presumptuous chair
with its back toward Tjarlas. Tsojai Acheran and
most of the other members of the Council of the
Prophet believed that Drakis' choice for the position of his victor's throne was a savvy political

move designed so that all who approached him would be forced to observe also the city in the distance behind him and thereby be reminded of his power and evident destiny.

Drakis alone knew the true reason he had insisted the chair be placed in that position.

He could not stand to look upon the burning, fallen city.

Instead, he sat on this ridiculous throne feeling utterly and frighteningly alone with his pain in the midst of a mob.

Urulani stood next to him, her dark-hued face also looking over the assembly. She eschewed her dragon-rider coat in favor of the leather vest and sleeveless homespun shirt she had worn when Drakis first saw her in Vestasia. She had remained next to Drakis at every meeting of the council since they had returned on the back of Marush from the horror of the skies over Tjarlas. The smooth skin of her arm, dark as midnight, hung within inches of Drakis' hand but he could not bring himself to reach out to her. He feared what she might have to say to him, believing he was deserving of her reproach.

The Council of the Prophet was arrayed on either side of a large carpet laid lengthwise before his throne. Tsojai Acheran, the elf on the council, and the female goblin called Doroganda were both beaming in their delight at the victory. Ethis sat on the opposite side of the carpet from them, looking impassive, the most common expression among his race of shapeshifters. Jugar sat next to the chimerian, still in his padded flying coat that now showed considerable wear and damage. The dwarf and his dragon had been closer to the center of the Well's destruction than anyone. The dragon, it appeared, was now somewhat deaf from the experience and Jugar . . .

Drakis frowned. There was something different about Jugar that he could not quite comprehend. The dwarf was quieter than he remembered and, most unnaturally, reticent to talk. Drakis had tried several times over the days since Tjarlas fell to speak with Jugar. Drakis had hoped to unburden himself as much as help the dwarf, but Jugar had turned away with some excuse or other. He found himself longing for the days not long past when he could not get the dwarf to keep silent for more than a breath at a time.

Drakis sat in the midst of an army singing his praises, surrounded by councillors ready—no, more than ready, *demanding* to follow him into death—and faced a parade of dignitaries all espousing their allegiance to Drakis and his victorious cause.

Here, in the midst of all this adoration, Drakis felt alone in his grief.

He had been haunted by the ghost of Mala since she had left him among the lost citadels of Drakosia to go to her death but that burden was now overwhelmed by the cries of Tjarlas rising up from within the walls of the fallen city. He had heard their shrill, shrieking wails even as the spindly avatria had come crashing down on top of them. The roar of the wind in his ears had not drowned out their keening nor did the smoke stinging his eyes hide from him the images of horror that erupted in the streets beneath Marush's wings. An entire city fallen at once into madness, vengeance, pain, and death. Belag had ordered the gates closed. They had not opened for these last three days. The terrifying sounds had diminished but not ceased entirely. Now, three days later, the sentries posted on watch about the city still had to be changed hourly for their nerves could not stand the howling insanity that continued from behind the city walls.

Drakis' hand still shook.

He quickly clasped his hands together, lacing the fingers and pressing them down into his lap.

He realized that Belag was still speaking, translating for the manticorian king.

". . . before great Drakis of the Prophecy. The justice of his warriors is now proven in their conquest over the coward elves and their unholy usurpation of the lands of our fathers . . ."

*Blood flowed down the Vira Gardalis like a black river*, Drakis remembered. *It gleamed in the rising light of the day. The civilized elves of Tjarlas had worn daggers and swords as ornaments to their elegant dress that morning, never suspecting that they would spill the blood of their own friends, slaves, masters, and strangers not hours later.*

". . . All the Prides of Chaenandria offer the claws and fangs of their warriors to Drakis, Man of Prophecy, that he might fulfill his destiny on behalf of all the great and noble races . . ."

*They had returned on the second day to see if they could help. Flying over the city walls on Marush with Urulani again behind him, they had circled the Theatre Hydris on the eastern side of the central district. The amphitheater was open to the air above. At first it looked as though the theater was packed and Drakis had hoped that these people had somehow managed to come here for refuge. The he noticed that none of them were moving except for the single performer on the stage . . .*

Drakis became aware of an awkward silence in the pavilion. Belag was looking at him with a questioning expression while the Chaenandrian King frowned.

Drakis drew in a shuddering breath as he sat up straighter on his throne. "I am most grateful to the King of Chaenandria for his support."

Gragh-Krigan looked at Belag expectantly.

Belag cleared his throat. "What the King of the Chaenandrian Prides has asked is when Drakis intends to move against Rhonas Chas?"

Drakis closed his eyes. *One last battle . . . it was supposed to be the last battle and he would be free.*

"Please tell the great Gragh-Krigan that Drakis has not yet determined the next move in his campaign," Urulani said from her place next to the throne.

Tsojai Acheran raised a thin eyebrow over one of his featureless elven eyes. Doroganda let out a low growl.

Belag nodded and began his own native speech to the Chaenandrian King. Gragh-Krigan nodded attentively and then responded in a series of low rumbles, hisses, and throaty calls. The words made no sense to Drakis but he did notice the ears of the other manticores in the room swiveling forward, all of them shifting their stance and becoming more attentive.

"The King of the Prides offers as a gift to the mighty Drakis the knowledge of the Northern Prides," Belag translated. "The despised Legions of Rhonas—nearly the full strength of the army that passed through Tjarlas over this last week—has been tracked by the cunning and swift warriors of the Hrumach Clan. They bring word by the swiftness of many runners that the Legions of Imperial Repression are no longer traveling between the winds."

"Traveling between the winds?" Doroganda blurted out.

"He means they are no longer using the folds for transport," Belag said. "The runners report that the entire army is *walking* back."

"Then we must attack!" the dwarf shouted.

The unexpected outburst startled Drakis. "Jugar, this is not the time . . ."

"It *is* the time," the dwarf said, red-faced in his determination. "We've been given an unprecedented, miraculous victory over the jewel of the entire elven empire. Tjarlas itself has fallen to us in a triumph beyond our hopes. We have the might of arms at our disposal to bring to its knees the heart of evil Imperial dominion. All we need now is the *will* to use it, to make the elves pay for their past atrocities and ensure that never again will they rise up to commit more atrocities in the future!"

"Would you inflict this on all the elves?" Tsojai Acheran said in a quiet voice. The events of the last three days had affected him deeply. His words had lost their strident tone. "Would you plunge the elves into death and madness because of the Imperial Will?"

"If it will burn then let it burn," the dwarf asserted. "Did the Imperial Will have mercy upon the dwarves in their own halls? Did the Imperial Will hold back its blades of death when it was held at the throat of all the humans of Drakosia? Did the Armies of Conquest allow the manticores of Chaenandria to keep their honor? Did they spare the Ephindrians the poison of their Aether? The Imperial Will has condemned the Empire and all those who serve it! We want justice!"

A number of cries in support erupted from the crowd around the tent.

"This is not the time or the place to consider this," Ethis said. "The Council of the Prophet . . ."

"The Council of the Prophet serves Drakis and his cause," Jugar asserted. "It is his destiny to bring justice to Rhonas and make it pay for its crimes! It is his destiny—our destiny—to destroy this corruption for all time!"

Cheers rang out both within and outside the tent.

*Rhonas Chas in flames. Tjarlas was a tenth the size of the Imperial City. Now Braun was gone and none of the acolytes knew how to maintain the Devotions as*

*Braun had claimed was possible. An entire Empire plunged into madness, chaos, and death.*

"Our army's blades are bright and sharp," Jugar continued. "They stand ready to assault Rhonas itself and the prophecy demands it. We must not wait! We must not debate! We *dare not* delay! To war, I say! To war NOW!"

Thunderous cheers and applause greeted the dwarf's final words though not from any of the other council members present. As the noise died down, Jugar turned to Drakis, the dwarf's eyes fixed on him.

"Well, Drakis . . . Man of the Prophecy," the dwarf said through a gap-toothed grin. "What would you have your army do?"

Drakis stared at the dwarf.

He thought he could hear the cries of the city in the distance behind him but wondered if they could be heard only in his mind.

"Will Lord Drakis hear me in this matter?"

Drakis looked up sharply.

Urulani caught her breath.

Drakis rose at once, wary at the unexpected figure making his way into the pavilion.

An elf pushed carefully through the crowd. His Iblisi robes were a shambles, torn in many places and their original color almost completely obscured by dust and stains. He held his Matei staff in his hands, gently using it to part the assembly in front of him. Behind Soen walked a second Iblisi, a female elf with her head bowed slightly. She, too, carried a Matei staff and by the markings on her robe, she, too, was an Inquisitor.

"Soen," Drakis barely managed to speak the name.

The former Inquisitor opened his arms with his slight bow. "I am pleased you remember, having so carelessly forgotten me once before on the plains to the north. But I have come to add my knowledge to this assembly and its deliberations . . . for we are a delegation from within the walls of Tjarlas."

"You were there?" Drakis whispered.

"Yes, Drakis, I was there," Soen replied. "I have seen too much, heard too much, and learned far too much. I watched as the Legions of Ghenetar Praetus Betjarian fought the very citizens and slaves they were sworn to protect down the length of the Vira Planesta. I saw them stopped by the fallen ruins of the Farlight Palace's avatria and forced to enter the narrower maze of streets to the west of the High Estates, desperate to reach the fold near the Emperor's Gate. Not one of them emerged from those warrens alive—not that it would have mattered if they had. The fold had already collapsed, the Occuran Priest having torn both the fold and himself apart long before the Legions attempted their escape."

"What are you doing here?" Ethis demanded.

"It would be better to ask what I've *been* doing there," Soen said.

"Very well, then," Drakis said. "What have you been doing?"

"Restoring sanity," Soen smiled. "Including my own."

The elf moved in front of Drakis, casting his glance over the council before continuing. "The Iblisi Order have long professed themselves to be the guardians of what they believed was the truth. But Braun, the Master of Aether, believed in me when others did not. He believed that I would be a hope not only to the other acolytes that studied beside me but also to the devout believers in Drakis and beyond . . . as a hope for the elves who suffer under the oppression of the Imperial Will as surely as the slaves oppressed in turn by them."

Soen turned to face Drakis. "Braun needed his secret kept safe with someone that he knew could do so. That is why Braun taught me what he knew about inverting the Aether Wells . . . and how to uphold the Devotions at the same time."

"No!" the dwarf shouted. "Are we now to entrust our conquest and justice into the hands of an elven Inquisitor? He lies!"

"Braun taught me truth—a new truth," Soen spoke loud and clear so that his voice would carry throughout the pavilion. "What I once thought was true is no more. Braun believed in Drakis and gave his life for that belief. I now offer myself in his place—to do what he promised."

Soen swung his Matei staff in front of him, grasping it with both hands. He raised his knee, planting it against the shaft.

"I choose a *new* truth," Soen shouted. "I choose Drakis."

Soen pulled hard. The Matei staff splintered in two with a terrible crack. Soen tossed the shattered pieces at Drakis' feet.

"The dwarf Jugar is right," Soen said in a clear voice raised to be heard by the crowd in the pavilion. "We must attack Rhonas at once. The Legions have all rushed northward, drawn there in the belief that you and your army are there. Now, because Tjarlas has fallen, they are stranded without the use of Aether or their precious folds. It will take them months to return on foot. All that stood between you and the Imperial City itself were the Legions that remained in Tjarlas and now they, too, are gone. The Iblisi were to have returned to Rhonas with a call for aid but the city fell too quickly and no word was sent. *Nothing* stands between you and the Imperial City—a city that does not suspect your approach."

"Then we have them!" Jugar shouted, his joy unrestrained. "The prophecy of vengeance shall be fulfilled and justice will be ours! The treasures looted from the world will be taken back and we shall glory in the suffering of our enemies!"

Another great cheer rose up from the warriors in the pavilion. It rolled beyond the canvas and out into the Clan-Legions of the Encampment until the members the Army of the Prophet were all cheering the call to make war against the throne of Rhonas itself.

Drakis became pale. He sat back on his throne. His hands began to shake again.

# CHAPTER 33

## *Nothing At All*

SJEI-SHURIAN, GHENETAR OMRIS OF the Order of Vash leaned forward on his high-backed chair, his face coming dangerously close to the light. "Nothing? You know nothing? Is it possible that the Keeper of her Order has such a desire to insult this council that she might stand before us and tell us that she knows *nothing?*"

"I am the Keeper of Truth!" Ch'drei Tsi-Auruun, Keeper of the Iblisi, stood uncomfortably bent over in the column of light cast down from the circle in the domed ceiling of the Modalis chamber in Majority House. "This council knows well my calling is defined by the Will of the Emperor and I answer to his authority alone. I have come here in my capacity as Keeper for the purpose of ascertaining that truth—certainly not to be lectured or questioned by a spear-carrier whose discipline rankings at the Vash Squires Academy were the worst of his class!"

Ch'dak Vaijan, Minister of Law stifled a laugh as Liau Nyenjei, the Minister of Thought, coughed nervously from his seat across the rotunda.

Sjei pushed himself back against the chair in frustration.

"Perhaps," came the smooth, lilting voice to Sjei's left, "the Keeper could enlighten us with that which she does not know."

Sjei turned in the shadows bathing his throne to look at Shebin even as Ch'drei turned in the light to do likewise. Shebin had taken to her role on the Modalis council with relish and, Sjei had to admit, the young woman had a flair for intrigue. Her placement next to the Emperor was invaluable to the Modalis but Sjei could not lose the feeling that she was no longer under anyone's control—perhaps even her own.

"Shebin, favored daughter of the Emperor," Ch'drei bowed her head slightly in acknowledgment. "It is what we do not know that we fear the most—especially regarding the war being undertaken in your most illustrious name. We do not know what has become of the north. We have lost all contact with any of our Quorums operating in conjunction with your Army of Shebin's Vengeance. Indeed, we have had no communication with any of our order in Tjarlas nor any point beyond, either in the Eastern Provinces or those to the north. Ghenetar Omris Shurian, have you had any word from Praetus Betjarian?"

"No," Sjei grumbled.

"Nor from any of his command?" Ch'drei asked.

"We have had no word from anyone in Tjarlas," Sjei acknowledged. "In truth, we were desiring your aid in contacting them."

"Restoring contact is the province of the Occuran, I believe. Is that not right, Master Xiuchi?" Ch'drei said.

"We cannot reestablish the fold in Tjarlas," Kyori-Xiuchi said, clearing his throat. "Our attempts to do so have met with repeated failure over the last three days. Worse, the flow of Aether from the Northern Provinces and the Aether farms in Ephindria as well as the Southern Steppes has stopped altogether. We are having to draw more Aether from the Western Provinces as well as the Southern Reaches. I feel sure this is just a temporary problem . . ."

"A temporary problem quite like the 'temporary problem' that obliterated our northern armies by these Drakis Rebels before," Sjei said, his voice raised. The elven warrior was frustrated and angry. There was a strange feeling in Rhonas Chas, a perceptible tension that made the skin on the back of his pointed skull itch. "We lost a Legion then—are we about to lose an army now?"

"We need to send for the southern Legions at once!" said Arikasi Tjen-soi. Sjei could hear anxiousness in the Minister of Occupation's quivering voice. "Bring them north into the capital as a precaution."

"And leave our southern borders open to Lyrania?" Sjei scoffed. "Even if we did strip the southern defenses it would take them a week just to arrive. By then, whatever this problem is may well have been resolved and we will have left the defenses of the Empire in complete disarray!"

"The honored Ghenetar of the Vash knows well that there is but a single Legion garrison in Rhonas Chas—only one," Arikasi responded with such vehemence that spittle flew from between his sharp teeth. "Everything else was committed to the north!"

"They are still there, I tell you!"

"Where? You don't even know where they are . . ."

"There is no point in this endless speculation," said Ch'dak Vaijan. The normally calm Minister of Law made his own frustration evident as his raised voice echoed through the round hall. "We need truth—not wild imaginings! I thought that was the purpose in speaking with the Keeper today. We cannot act on fantasies and pretend our decisions are wise. If the Keeper will indulge us a bit longer, we might secure her aid and that of her most capable Order in determining the truth which all of us so desperately . . ."

The large doors to the rotunda banged open, slamming against the walls so loudly that it startled everyone in the room.

"By Mnearis' Cloak!" Sjei swore, leaping to his feet. "Who dares disturb the deliberations of this council?"

An Iblisi Indexia ran unceremoniously into the shadowy hall. She completely ignored Sjei's demand as she rushed across the polished stone floor directly toward the amazed Keeper. The Indexia came to a stuttering halt and leaned over at once to speak into the Keeper's ear.

Ch'drei suddenly straightened her back in surprise, staring with her flat, black eyes at the Indexia before her. "Are you certain?"

"Yes, Keeper," the Indexia replied. "They await you now."

Ch'drei turned to address the shadows that surrounded her in the hall. "Councillors of the Modalis—citizens of Rhonas all—I must beg your leave on a matter of—of some urgency."

"Our deliberations have not been concluded, Keeper Ch'drei," Sjei said, his black eyes narrowing.

"The council asked for truth from the north," Ch'drei responded. "And when I return, I may have what you ask."

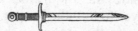

Ch'drei Tsi-Auruun sat on her throne beneath the low ceiling of her audience hall, her long, bony fingers moving anxiously along the shaft of the Baton Seal of the Iblisi Keeper.

*It started here,* she thought. *It seems like a lifetime since I sent him on this chase. Here we are safely beneath the ground, but we are not nearly so deep as he will soon be, nor so safely hidden from the world above along with all the other truths entombed here. How sad that it must end this way.*

The double doors at the end of the low, onyx hall opened.

Ch'drei lifted her head.

K'yeran Tsi-M'harul strode into the hall. The Inquisitor confidently swung her Matei staff as she approached. Her robes were still covered in ash and soot and torn in several places but she held her head high.

Ch'drei barely noticed her.

It was the bent and shackled figure behind the confident elf woman that held the Keeper's fixed gaze.

"Soen, my son," Ch'drei sighed.

Soen shambled into the hall. He no longer had his Matei staff. His robes were faded and filthy, ragged in places. His gaze was fixed toward the floor as he approached.

K'yeran stopped before the throne of the Keeper, standing straight and proud. At last, Soen arrived beside the Inquisitor, still not having raised his eyes to face the Keeper.

The doors to the audience chamber closed at the back of the hall.

"You have done well, K'yeran," Ch'drei said quietly, her eyes still fixed on Soen.

"No, Keeper, I have not. I have failed you entirely," K'yeran answered. She turned to Soen. "Will you be all right?"

Soen rose up, a sly grin forming over his sharp teeth. "I believe I have never been better, K'yeran. Thank you."

The shackles instantly vanished from Soen's wrists and ankles.

Ch'drei stood in a rush with unexpected agility

for an elf of advanced age. She raised the Baton at once, aiming it squarely at Soen's chest.

Nothing happened.

The complete absence of the deadly Aether discharge was more shocking to the Keeper than if the bolt had found its mark. She staggered backward, falling onto her throne.

"K'yeran," Soen said with offhanded confidence. "Would you mind leaving the Keeper and me alone now? We have so much to catch up on."

"Of course, Soen," K'yeran replied, casting a glance toward Ch'drei. "As it turns out, I have business to attend to. I'll just leave you two alone."

K'yeran turned and, with quick strides, moved back toward the entrance to the hall.

"Oh, K'yeran?" Soen called over his shoulder.

"Yes?"

"Please see to it that we are not disturbed," Soen smiled, his eyes fixed on the astonished Keeper.

"By your will," K'yeran replied, slipping between the doors and pulling them closed behind her.

Ch'drei blinked, her blank black eyes shining. The lips that curled back from her sharp teeth were quivering.

"I'm home," Soen said in lusterless tones. "Miss me?"

"Soen," Ch'drei began. "My son . . . I . . ."

"Getting in was, of course, the easy part," Soen said, stepping over to the nearest of the wide pillars supporting the low, stone ceiling. He leaned back against it, his arms hanging loosely at his sides. "I mean, when all of the Iblisi Order has been tasked to bring you in, who would question when one of their own Inquisitors showed up with the very elf everyone wanted captured. No, the difficult part was in contriving the time to drain that charmingly powerful artifact in your hands of all its power before you decided to use it."

"The shackles," Ch'drei nodded as she turned the now useless Seal in her hands. "The slow, beaten walk to my throne."

"I knew you would appreciate the performance." Soen shrugged.

"I should have killed you the moment you entered the room," Ch'drei said, shaking her long, pinched head.

"How sentimental of you not to," Soen sighed.

"You have done it, my son," Ch'drei said, looking up from her throne. There was relief in her aged features, as though a great burden had been lifted from her. "I had always hoped it would be you."

"Indeed?"

"I sent the best after you," Ch'drei said with genuine admiration. "And you survived every test, every hunter. You've proven yourself, my son. You are worthy of this chair."

"Ah, my dear Ch'drei," Soen smiled. "Why would I want to pull the chair out from beneath you?"

Ch'drei's eyes narrowed. "You are surprising as always, Soen. What do you want?"

"What I have always wanted," Soen replied. "What *you* said you wanted; not to save the Empire—which we both know is going to fall— but to determine that the fall happens in a way that will benefit us both."

"And how do you propose to do that?" Ch'drei asked quietly.

Soen cocked his head to one side. "By taking the Emperor's place."

"With just that much ease?" Ch'drei said, arching her thin brows.

"Well, I could use a little assistance in the matter," Soen acknowledged. "In particular, *your* assistance."

"Indeed?" Ch'drei turned the now powerless Seal over in her hands. "And what assistance would that be?"

"Why, nothing at all," Soen said.

"Nothing?"

"Nothing," Soen continued, stepping away from the column and approaching Ch'drei on her throne. "In fact, I *insist* on you doing nothing. Recall every member of the Iblisi—every Assesia, every Indexia and especially every Inquisitor located in and around Rhonas Chas into the Keep before nightfall tonight. You will barricade the members of our Order in here, answer no summons no matter who issues it, and remain here—in the Keep doing *nothing*—until I send word for you to come to the Imperial Palace."

"And just what will be happening while I do nothing?" Ch'drei asked.

"Rhonas Chas will be under siege by Drakis' Army of Rebellion," Soen replied in tones so matter-of-fact that Ch'drei thought for a moment she might have misunderstood him. "They will arrive before morning, through folds they will open on the outskirts of the city. Their Legions suffered in the fall of Tjarlas but their victory has brought the Chaenandrians into this rebellion on their side. They are a reinforced army of more than five Legions, with magic that nearly matches our own, and dragons."

"Tjarlas fell?" Ch'drei gaped.

"It is a burning ruin," Soen nodded. "The Aether from the Northreach and Southern Ephindria has been usurped by the rebellion for their own use. This Drakis Army slipped behind the northbound Legions and cut them off. Xhu'chan's Army of Shebin's Vengeance have no folds to transport them back to defend Rhonas Chas and no other armies can reach us before Drakis' forces are at our gates."

Ch'drei's eyes widened. "How can you stop this?"

"I can't. Nothing can stop them now," Soen said, stepping up to the Keeper's throne. "*But* I will arrange it so that I will take the Emperor's place, make it appear to be a victory for the rebellion, and that I have taken the government in the name of Drakis."

Ch'drei raised her bony chin. "Won't this 'Drakis' have something to say about this?"

"Not much, I think," Soen answered with a nod. "You see, he'll be dead."

"Ah," Ch'drei sighed.

"Every great cause deserves a martyr," Soen said. "Don't you agree? Besides, Drakis is what holds this rabble together. Without him, who will they follow? Their rebellion will fall apart amid petty squabbles . . ."

". . . And we will still be here," Ch'drei finished.

"And we will still be here," Soen agreed.

Ch'drei considered Soen's plan in silence. It was dangerous but if it failed, she could already think of a number of ways her absence could be explained to the Imperial Court—especially if the city were under siege. Furthermore, if Soen's plan failed and the rebellion succeeded in taking the capital city, she might be able to strike a bargain with the invaders based on her Order's refusing to resist them during the battle.

But if Soen succeeded, her Order would take control of the Empire. She decided in that moment that if Soen were to succeed, she would have to do more than nothing.

"Soen," Ch'drei said, rising from her throne. "Come with me, my son. If you are to be Emperor, there is one last truth that you will need to know."

# CHAPTER 34

## *So Far to Fall*

"SHEBIN, AWAKE."

"Go away," murmured Shebin Sha-Rhonas, daughter of the Empire. She kept her eyes closed tightly in the hopes that the lovely dream she had been having would continue. "It is too early."

"No, Shebin," insisted the female voice. "It is too late."

Shebin groaned, feeling the ire rise with her consciousness. Whoever was responsible—and for that matter any number who weren't responsible—were going to suffer for their presumptuous inconvenience to her sleep. She pushed herself up from the warm comfort of her bed, turning to glare at the first chambermaid to come into sight. "I left no instructions to be disturbed! I am the Emperor's chosen daughter and will not be treated in this insolent manner by . . . !"

She stopped her rant short, disappointed as she

sat up in her bed. The elegant bedchamber with its arching panels of interlacing petals shaped from white coral that surrounded her was devoid of the usual bevy of servant girls that she demanded rush to her first call each morning. The pale, delicately carved doors on either side with their opal windows remained shut. The enormous bed, finished to a gleaming white, floated above the polished floor—an avatria in miniature—but no servants, anxious or otherwise, pressed against it.

The dark, hooded shape of a woman in a black robe stood in silhouette against the brilliant morning light streaming into the bedchamber from the sitting room beyond. The curtains to the balcony were open, allowing the dawn to intrude around the standing figure that held a Matei staff in her hand.

Shebin suddenly felt her head pounding. She had been somewhere the night before—she could not remember where or with whom just at the moment—but she knew of a certainty that she needed more sleep. The pounding was distracting. "Who are you? What do you want?"

"My name is K'yeran Tsi-M'harul," the woman said, pushing back her hood. "I am an Inquisitor of the Iblisi."

"I can see that by that dreary robe you're wearing," Shebin answered, rubbing her bony hand down her pinched face, hoping it would help the pounding go away. "What are you doing here? Who let you into my presence?"

"I let myself in," K'yeran answered, "but that is

not important. Why I have come is to save your life."

"My life?" Shebin sneered in disbelief. "The Guardians of the Imperial Palace are tasked with my protection!"

"And yet I stand here in your bedchamber," K'yeran observed. "You must dress quickly, Shebin, and come with me if you wish to live."

Shebin realized that the pounding was not coming from within her head. It was coming from beyond the sitting room, beyond the balcony overlooking the Imperial City.

Shebin slid out of her bed, snatching a robe from where it lay draped over a chair next to one of the doors. She pulled it over her gaunt shoulders as she rushed past K'yeran. Modesty did not come naturally to her but politics did: appearing on a veranda of the Cloud Palace of the Emperor unclothed would be to invite trouble. She barely managed to tie the robe closed before stepping onto the balcony.

Shebin caught her breath.

Her apartment was situated on the northwestern side of the Cloud Palace, affording her an extraordinary view of the Imperial City. The Vira Rhonas, curving slightly to the north from the Garden of Kuchen directly below her was clogged with elves and their slaves, the roar of their shouts and screams coming like the crashing of waves up to her. The mob shifted and moved like wheat stalks or the surface of a pond in a wind, all desperately pressing toward the south. Through the avatria she caught glimpses of the Paz Vitratjen and Paz Rhambutai, both of their plazas choked with frantic people as well. God's Bridge to the Isle of the Gods across the River Jolnar was crammed with desperate citizens as well.

The reason was obvious. Flashes of light broke against the city wall to the north of the Guild Quarter. The muffled pounding of their impact came to her a few seconds later. Several columns of smoke were rising from fires within the city this side of the Jolnar River.

"Drakis is at the gates," K'yeran said.

Shebin drew back, any color in her face drained and she became deathly pale. She pulled her robe tighter around her. "No! It is impossible!"

"Nevertheless," K'yeran said, "Drakis is at the gates."

Shebin turned to face K'yeran. "He will come for me. He fights for *me*. I know it. He wants me. He's coming for me."

"He is coming to kill you, Shebin," K'yeran said, taking a step back.

"Yes, but he *is* coming!" said the daughter of the Emperor, a strange, crooked smile breaking over her sharp teeth. "Don't you see? They said he left me but he never did. I've brought him back to me, don't you understand? He will love me. I've *made* him love me."

"Then we must keep you safe from harm until he comes for you," K'yeran said slowly, holding out her arms to the young elven woman. "Come with me, Shebin, and I'll take you somewhere no one can threaten you again."

Ethis slid down the scales on the side of Wanrah's neck, pleased to have his feet on the ground once more, and looked around in amazement.

The Army of Drakis had grown considerably over the last few days with the addition of the considerable forces offered by the Chaenandrian Prides. Each were once again organized into their Legions according to the ancient gods of Drakosia and prepared before the mages opened these last folds to the fields outside of Rhonas Chas. The Legion commanders were especially drilled in their duties by Belag, who impressed on them how they would each follow the battle plan as given to them or he would hunt them down afterward with the emphasis on the word hunt. The orders given them were not to the liking of the younger Chaenandrian manticore warriors who were anxious to earn their honor on the field of battle in a glorious charge but Belag had managed to convince them that they must wait until the proper time for their charge against the city—and that he alone would tell them when that would be.

Now their army was marching out of the fold portals stretching for almost a mile wide across the fields northeast of the Imperial City. Ethis stood next to the dragon as it lowered itself to lie on top of the trampled crops. And, to the south-west, the chimerian gazed over the heads of the ranks of warriors whose rhythmic footfalls shook the ground and saw the collection of spindle towers, minarets, and domes shining through the haze of distance that was the Imperial City.

*How have we come to this?* Ethis thought, his four hands balled against his hips and his elbows akimbo.

They were the victims of their own success, he decided. Ethis had been one of the D'reth for as long as he cared to remember. His purpose had been to serve the family of Ephindria and especially Queen Chythal after the sundering of the Houses and the resulting civil war. The sickness of elven Aether had infected the body of Ephindria and the chimerians were nearly destroyed because of it. In his duty to his Queen and to his people, he had seen Drakis as an opportunity. At first it was a vague chance that he might be used as a distraction for the Empire. But as Ethis journeyed further with the human, it became clear that he could be so much more useful in the cause of Queen Chythal. The proposal to use the Army of the Prophet to free Ephindria from the grasp of elven Aether had been a logical one and with few risks to Ephindria itself—using someone else's army to besiege the elves in Tjarlas long enough for Queen Chythal to reclaim and reunite her kingdom and her family.

Yet Drakis had managed in the most spectacular and terrible manner imaginable to utterly destroy one of the greatest cities of the elves. His purpose had been to capture the city's Well, deprive the elves of Aether, and bargain for a homeland for his followers.

Instead, he had plunged a city into madness and been forced to watch while it tore itself apart. Then, apparently victorious beyond anyone's dreams, he had been trapped into continuing the war that now threatened to bring down the Empire and, Ethis feared, plunge the entire world into the same madness that had consumed Tjarlas.

*It seems,* he thought, *there was such a thing as too much victory.*

And now he felt powerless to stop it.

Ethis frowned. A familiar, dark-robed elf was approaching him.

"You were missing all night," Ethis said. "Your absence has been of some concern."

"And yet our paths have come together once more," Soen said. "Travelers on the same road again, are we not?"

"That depends upon our destination," Ethis replied. "Although I believe that road is a short one."

"I believe it is the Cloud Palace, if I am not mistaken," Soen nodded. "A place which I know very well."

"If the Emperor's Well falls then madness will grip the entire continent," Ethis said. "That will be a long fall, indeed."

"Then we must prevent that fall, Ethis," Soen observed. "And I will need your help to do so."

"Indeed?"

"Urulani rides with Drakis," Soen said as he turned to look back on the soaring towers of Rhonas Chas. "I will ride with you while the dwarf rides alone—in so many ways."

Two dark shapes were approaching from the northern sky.

"Drakis is coming," Ethis said.

"Come a little way down the road with me, Ethis," Soen urged. "And perhaps we can shorten this fall."

"And what do you have in mind?" Ethis asked.

"By all the gods of Kiris! Where are the garrison Cohorts from the Krish and the Nekara?" Ghenetar Omris Sjei-Shurian bellowed. Dust sifted down from the rafters as another concussion rocked the Battlebox chamber beneath Majority House. "We called for them an hour ago!"

"They cannot move through the streets," complained Ghenetar Omris K'don Usk'dasei, the supreme commander of the Order of Krish. "The citizens have panicked and are trying to leave the city through the southern gates and folds, but there are just too many of them."

"We gave the order and they are trying to comply, but there's no way for the Cohorts to get to the northern wall," Ghenetar Omris Qi'sei Nu'uran of the Nekara Warrior Order concurred. He pointed down at the mystical sand table that was the predominant feature in the center of the underground chamber. "The Vira Rhonas is completely impassible and that effectively cuts the city in half and keeps either of the other two warrior Orders in the city from reaching the battle for the northern wall."

Sjei gazed down at the sand table. The sands had been transformed by the war-mages to replicate the Imperial City in detail. Sjei had imagined many different terrains and locales that might be represented on this table but never had he expected to see Rhonas Chas here. The sand table recreated in miniature the reports that came into the Battlebox from the war-mages and their Proxis. It was intended to give the Modalis a clearer picture of the course of the overall battle but if what Sjei was looking at were an accurate depiction of the state of the battle then he was genuinely concerned. An armed, mixed force began pouring from a line of twelve fold portals on the northern outskirts of the Imperial City about two hours after dawn. The rebels did not hesitate, forming up quickly and moving at once against the northern city wall while more of their warrior ranks continued to emerge behind them. Within the hour, the opposing army numbered almost four full Legions, assaulting the northern wall of the New City east of the River Jolnar and around to the Patrician's Gate. An army of more than forty thousand against a combined garrison force of less than two thousand, five hundred—and a third of those he could not bring into battle because of the panicked populace. "Then we need to clear those streets. Ch'dak Vaijan!"

"Yes, Ghenetar Omris!"

"You're the Minister of Law," Sjei snapped. "Can you do something about this?"

"I fear that law has very little to do with this," Ch'dak answered, swallowing hard. "The entire city is in dread."

"Listen, I don't need *all* these streets cleared," Sjei argued. "Just a few avenues so that we can move whatever Cohorts we have through the city."

"I—I'll try to enlist the Ministry of Security and the Ministry of Interior," Ch'dak wiped his long forehead. "I'll see if we can get some help from the Paktan Guildmasters and the Daramoneti Order of Workers as well."

"Do that," Sjei demanded then turned to the Ghenetar Omris of the Nekara. "Qi'sei, what about your southern command?"

"We've dispatched urgent orders to Cohorts stationed in Pronas, Vadratsi, Djuban, and Port Rhemalas," Qi'sei answered too loudly. "We also have sent word to the Legion of Rhonas Fire to decamp and rush to our defense."

"How long, then?" S'jei asked.

"Assuming the Occuran provide us the fold portals without any delays, the first of the Cohorts may be arriving before nightfall," Qi'sei answered as he looked away, his voice quieting. "The Legion could arrive in two days."

"What about the Krish?" Sjei asked, turning to the thick-bodied elf standing on his left.

"Our Legions are not at strength and many of those used in the Nine Crowns War were taken from the local Houses," answered K'don, the thick-bodied elf to Sjei's left. "We have called for everything available—about six Cohorts—but they cannot be here sooner than two days' time. We are trying to muster the provincial Houses as well, but that will take more time."

"More time," Sjei muttered through his clenched teeth. "I need more time."

Something caught his eye on the board. Something he had never seen before.

"What is that?" Sjei asked, pointing toward the sand table.

Three strange shapes formed out of the sand, floating above the other sands and moving quickly toward the northern wall of the city.

"I don't know," K'don said, leaning forward. "I don't think I've ever seen . . ."

"Dragons!" shouted a war-mage from the upper gallery.

Sjei's head snapped around. "What?"

Several more war-mages turned at once, their voices on top of each other.

"Dragons . . ."

"Three flying creatures . . ."

"Wings the length of ten elves . . ."

Sjei turned back to the Battlebox, his eyes fixed on the strange shapes. They moved with incredible speed toward the wall. He could see several explosive spells loosed skyward in the direction of the forms but they seemed unaffected, their darting, weaving courses still closing toward the city.

"What do we do?" K'don stammered. "How do we stop these things?"

"We knew they had dragons," Qi'sei said. "We defeated them before."

"That was three hundred years ago!" K'don said.

"So what did we do then?" Qi'sei growled.

"Legate Ordis!" Sjei shouted.

"Yes, my lord!" the Legate said, stepping up smartly. His armor was polished for parade and would be entirely useless in the battle now raging against the north of the city.

"Have you sent for the Keeper?"

"Yes, my lord," the Legate nodded eagerly. "Two hours ago."

"What was her reply?" Sjei barked.

"We have not yet received a response," the Legate answered.

"Then send another runner!" Sjei demanded, then turned back to the sand table, his eyes fixed on the dragons as they passed over the wall. "Where are you, Ch'drei? Where are the Iblisi?"

# CHAPTER 35

## By a Thread

SOEN STARED DOWN AT THE SCENE BELOW in amazement from his perch behind Ethis. Between the broad black-and-rust-colored neck of the dragon Wanrah and the sweep of the beast's enormous wings, he could see that they were approaching Rhonas Chas down the length of the River Jolnar from northeast of the city. The Army of the Prophet below them and to their left was trampling flat the fields north of the Fourth Estate District. They were approaching the Benis Gate of the Daramon Wall but Soen knew that they were there largely to draw out any of the elven garrison remaining in the city. Their orders were to hold short of the walls and defend themselves as they waited for the fall of the Emperor's Well before they made a move against the city itself.

*The poor fools*, Soen thought. He tried to calm himself. He was feeling uncharacteristically anxious and upset, attributing the feeling to the Conjuration Aether that was surging through his bones. He had completely drained one of Braun's Aethereon altars of its Aether, absorbing the magical energy into himself in preparation for their assault. The power surged wildly through him, seeking release and form. *Soon . . . soon I'll unleash you, and then I can only hope you are enough.*

Soen looked back down the length of the dragon's black-and-rust-marked back and beyond its sweeping tail. The green-and-yellow Marush flew behind them, so close that Soen could not see the tips of either of the dragon's wings within his field of vision. Urulani and Drakis appeared periodically behind the enormous bobbing head of the dragon straining with the urgency of their flight through the thick air close to the ground. The blue-and-purple Pyrash followed in the rear. Soen knew that Jugar rode on the back of the third dragon although he was having trouble seeing the dwarf at all.

Soen frowned. The dwarf was up to something. Jugar had emphatically insisted on the necessity of his coming on this mission, only to reject any suggestion of bringing a second warrior or— better still—one of the acolyte mages with him. He alone would bring Pyrash into the battle and not even Drakis could persuade him otherwise.

Soen leaned around the chimerian as Wanrah rushed over the Kiris and Anjei Bridges, both falling quickly behind. They were over the confluence of the Jolnar and the Havrar Rivers, rapidly approaching the Sentinels. Those towers on either side of the river protected the ends of Tjujen's Wall. They were the boundary between the lesser estates and the central district of the Imperial Capital.

Aether-driven fire, lightning, and ice flew at them from the towers and the walls on either side. At least some of the war-mages and Proxis of the garrison had managed to get to the walls. It had been expected, however, and had largely dictated their approach to the city. The magic exploded behind them in their terrific rush through the air, the Proxis unable to get their spells ahead of the dragons charging through the air at speeds too fast for the war-mages to anticipate.

With the magic fire behind them, Soen saw the Isle of the Gods directly in their path with God's Bridge on the left.

"Is that the third bridge?" Ethis shouted into the howling wind around them.

"Yes!" Soen shouted back to be heard. "That's it!"

Wanrah followed Ethis' command and banked left just as they passed over the tip of the Isle of the Gods. Soen faintly heard the horrified cries of the elves packing the bridge below as the dragon, followed by two more of its kind, wheeled overhead seemingly close enough to touch. Soen cast a glance at the Old Keep as they turned, its squat ramparts on the opposite side of the river from the Isle of the Gods.

"Stay silent, Ch'drei," Soen wished. "For just a little longer."

Wanrah began to climb above the scattering, frightened mobs surging in the Vira Rhonas below them. The avatria towers were a forest around them as they clawed their way higher into the morning sky. The Imperial City passed under them, its familiar maze of streets, alleys, and avenues filled with terrified elves and slaves, all growing smaller in Soen's eyes as they fought their way higher into the air. They had avoided the war-mages and their Proxis' expected fire from the walls, but the cost had been in velocity and altitude. Now they fought desperately for both as the dragons beat their colossal wings through the air above the Vira Rhonas toward their goal.

The Cloud Palace of the Emperor, like a mountainous ornament dwarfing all the floating elegance around it, hovered like a prize above the Garden of Kuchen directly before them.

"How far up?" Ethis demanded, all four of his hands gripping the saddle harness so tightly Soen thought the straps might break.

"Do you see the main platform that leads to the towers?" Soen called out.

Ethis nodded.

"Four levels above that you see those petal-shaped balconies? That's the level of the Emperor's Devotions," Soen continued. "That's where we'll find the altar and the Well."

"What about the Cloud Guardians?" Ethis asked. "Won't they object to our dropping in, so to speak?"

"Most emphatically," Soen said. The Cloud

Palace was growing larger to their eyes by the moment. Soen could already see Guardians rushing
out onto the platforms at the various levels. Soen
shouted, "Right! Right then left!"

Ethis and Wanrah obeyed. The dragon flipped
suddenly to the right, cutting across the face of the
Cloud Palace, then reversed itself into a left bank,
a gentler turn that permitted Soen an unobstructed
view of the balconies surrounding the avatria.

*Let it be enough,* Soen thought in a prayer to any
gods who might be listening.

He reached out with his left hand.

The Aether in his bones responded.

Marush was flying directly behind Wanrah when
the first dragon turned hard to the right. Marush
instinctively turned left, desperate to avoid both
the Cloud Palace and the other dragon. He swung
away from the Cloud Palace, circling back out into
the sky, carrying Drakis and Urulani with him.

A brilliant blue wave shot through the Cloud
Palace and beyond the far wall, dissipating in the
air above the city.

"That's it!" Drakis shouted. "Now, Marush! Get
onto one of the balconies!"

Marush continued his turn. One of the petal-
shaped balconies presented itself before the
dragon as a likely perch. Marush cupped his
wings, caught the air, and slowed.

Drakis unbuckled his harness as they approached. He could see the slumped form of three Cloud Guardians lying on the veranda, a coolly lit hallway leading into the palace beyond them. "Stay close to me, Urulani. Soen knows what he's doing!"

"Yes, but do we know what Soen's doing?" Urulani rejoined.

The claws of Marush's hind legs reaching out to catch the edge of the terrace.

Drakis prepared to jump down from the dragon's back. "What choice do we have but to . . ."

An explosion suddenly filled the air around Drakis with dust, smoke, and debris. Drakis jumped toward the opening beyond the platform. He landed hard, rolling into the curved hallway. Choking, he struggled to his feet as the dust cleared.

The balcony was gone. Drakis looked down over the shattered edge. Soen may have taken care of the Guardians on this level but several of their ranks several levels below remained unaffected. A war-mage among them had obliterated the landing from under them just as the dragon came to rest. Suddenly deprived of his expected perch, Marush fell out of the sky with Urulani still attached to the saddle harness, both tumbling down the face of the Cloud Palace along with the shards of the balcony. Drakis stared in horror as the dragon spun, his wings beating frantically at the air as he fell. Fortune favored the dragon, however, as it fell faster and faster down the sheer face of the palace, its wings finding purchase in the air with its renewed speed. Marush suddenly righted himself just above a lower level, skidding slightly in the air before suddenly soaring outward from the palace and over the city. More bolts from the war-mages below pursued them as they swung around in the sky.

Drakis gritted his teeth. He could not wait for them. It was only a matter of time before the Cloud Guardians from the unaffected lower levels made their way up to the Emperor's Devotions. They were running out of time and opportunity.

Drakis drew his sword and darted down the curving hall.

The interior was a curving maze of corridors as Soen had instructed them before they took flight. Soen had also said that once they understood where they were on the Devotions level, finding the Emperor's Devotions would be simple. The problem was that Drakis had no idea which of the terrace entrances he had come in and nothing in the multiple intersecting arched corridors afforded him any recognition of his location.

A voice hissed behind him. "Is the Man of Prophecy lost?"

Drakis wheeled around, weapon readied in his hand.

Soen arrested Drakis' sword hand in a powerful grip, his wide, sharp-toothed grin frightening. "There's no time for games. Follow me!"

Soen led Drakis around a long curving corridor, then down a series of shorter corridors. Drakis was suddenly uncertain about the path back. In each successive passage, Cloud Guardians lay slumped to the floor. Several looked almost blissful as they lay in a heap against the walls or sprawled on the polished marble underfoot.

"What did you do to them?" Drakis asked.

"A little something I learned in a most embarrassing manner," Soen said as they turned into yet another corridor, "from Braun."

This corridor opened into a wide, curving gallery extending thirty feet above their heads to buttress arches bending toward the inner wall. The gallery looked as though it might form a huge circle in the center of the palace avatria. A number of additional Cloud Guardians lay along the length of the gallery in both directions, mixed with a number of comatose courtiers in different types of dress. Drakis guessed that their outfits must have been highly significant in terms of their official positions in the Imperial Court, but he was completely unfamiliar with what Orders or Ministries they must have represented.

"Here!" came the deep, echoing voice from their left. "This way!"

The dwarf waving his ax was just visible around the curve of the gallery. Soen and Drakis ran quickly toward Jugar, finding him standing next to a pair of ornately carved onyx doors more than three times the height of the dwarf.

"Well, so you've finally come! I've been waiting here for an unreasonable count of time but your triumph being so near at hand, I wanted to wait until Drakis himself arrived to confront the

Emperor and let him feel the just results of his crimes!"

"You mean you could not open the door," Soen said.

"Oh, and I suppose you can?" Jugar fumed.

"Yes, as a matter of fact," Soen affirmed.

"Right, then," Jugar snarled. "You open the door, we go in, separate the Imperial head from its Imperial body and end this thing once and for all!"

"No!" Soen said with vehement conviction. "Whatever happens, do nothing to harm the Emperor until I've got control of the Devotions altar. It is critical that an elf take control of the altar first."

The dwarf sputtered. "Why, that's the biggest nonsense . . ."

"Remember what happened at the Citadels, Drakis?" Soen asked. "You couldn't open the Well because you needed *humans* to make it work. This is no different: the Emperor's Devotions altar was created only to accept elven control. You may not need an elf to invert the Well, Drakis, but you certainly need one to take control of the Devotions."

"Is that where Braun went wrong?" Drakis demanded. "He couldn't command the altar in Tjarlas and so *that's* why Jugar couldn't save him?"

A roaring sound echoed down the gallery. Drakis felt a sudden flash of heat.

"It's the dragons," Soen said. "Trying to keep the Guardians occupied."

"We're wasting time!" Jugar urged.

"Very well, Soen," Drakis said. "Be quick!"

Soen nodded, reached toward the center of the onyx door and pressed the release.

The door slid downward, vanishing into the floor. Soen slipped quickly through the opening. Drakis and the dwarf both followed him with their weapons in their hands.

Drakis was dashing into a meadow surrounded by towering forests. A sweet, fresh breeze filled the air, blowing across a small pond at the edge of the meadow. Six snow-capped peaks pierced the sky in the distance all around the glade. In the center of the meadow stood a small, grass-covered mound.

Atop the mound, sat the Emperor of Rhonas in serene repose.

"I've had about as much of that as I can take!" grumbled the dwarf. He pulled from his pouch his strange, dark stone.

"The Heart of Aer!" Drakis said in surprise. "What are you going to . . . ?"

"See a little more clearly," the dwarf answered.

As he raised the stone, it seemed to Drakis to emit a pulsing darkness that began to eat away at the beautiful mountain scene. The meadow dissolved into a black stone floor. The lush forests gave way to dark columns of red marble. The pond vanished altogether. The mound was transformed into a raised dais that supported a throne of granite shot through with veins of glowing crystal. The darkness from the dwarf's stone reached higher into the octagonal hall. The distant mountains became six enormous Aether Well crystals, six feet across at their base where they plunged into the stone floor, each of which converged fifty feet directly over the throne.

"The Well of the Empire," Soen whispered in awe. He turned back toward the onyx door, once again closed behind them. He pressed a release and the door locks slammed hard into place.

"The Well, yes . . . but where's the altar?" Drakis asked.

"*That's* the altar!" Soen took a hesitant pair of steps forward, eyeing the dais. "The throne is the altar."

"Well, then, *do* it," Drakis urged. He gestured toward where the Emperor sat with his eyes closed in quiet repose. "Take control of the Devotions while the Empire sleeps!"

Soen ran his tongue over his pointed teeth, hesitation in his dull, black eyes. "We never anticipated the spell would penetrate this far. We certainly didn't think it would work here in the Well of the Empire. We need to . . . consider this for a few minutes . . ."

"Consider it!" Drakis hissed. "The Guardians will be here at any moment!"

"You're right," Soen nodded, looking back toward the sleeping Emperor. "I'll have to . . ."

Suddenly Soen's eyes flew open wide. The elf's pointed skull snapped backward, his spine arching as he drew in a gasping breath.

"Soen?" Drakis asked in alarm.

The elf pitched forward, falling to the ground.

A dwarven ax was lodged squarely in Soen's back.

"Jugar!" Drakis cried, stepping back.

The dwarf stepped forward, reaching casually down for the handle of the ax lodged in Soen's split rib cage.

"I wouldn't worry about one dead elf," Jugar said, and then his face broke into a gap-toothed smile. "There's going to be a lot more of them by nightfall."

Drakis thought he heard the Emperor stir behind him.

# CHAPTER 36

## Endgame

"JUGAR, WHAT HAVE YOU DONE?" Drakis gasped out in horror.

"What I've had to do." Jugar was having some difficulty extracting his ax from Soen's back. The dwarf placed his boot against the elf's spine, yanking on the handle as he tried to dislodge the blade. "What I swore I would do with every breath since the elves took my crown. We never thought they would bother with us. We were under the mountain and thought, 'Let the elves conquer their neighbors and all the world under the sun for all we care.' But ruling the light wasn't enough for them. They had to have the dark as well. My dark. My stone. My kingdom. I watched the Nine Thrones fall one after another until none were left . . . none but mine."

"Yours?" Drakis stepped back, raising the tip of his blade in front of him.

"Yes, mine!" Jugar grimaced, twisting the handle and pulling hard again. "Sorry to disappoint you, Drakis, but while you were so intent on taking the Crown of the Ninth Throne you never thought the dwarf you killed wearing it could be anything but the king. Who would have expected a jester to wear the crown? But the crown was nothing—the Heart of Aer was everything! *That's* where the true King of the Ninth Throne was during the battle: below your feet and out of sight and mind. While you killed each other over the crown, all I had to do was wait under the throne with the true prize until you all chased each other out."

"But I was still there," Drakis nodded.

"Yes, lad," The dwarven ax blade suddenly came free with a sickening, sucking sound. "I may have been wearing the jester's costume but *you* got to play the fool."

"This has been your plan all along?" Drakis' mouth had suddenly gone dry. "To kill the Emperor?"

"Kill the Emperor?" Jugar jeered. "No, Drakis, I'm not going to kill the Emperor—I'm going to kill his Empire. I'm going to free all the world from these damnable Devotions all at once, utterly destroy Aether magic, and then watch the Empire plunge into madness and drag all the rest of the sunlit world down with it into its own death throes."

The dwarf spun the ichor-covered ax skillfully in his hands. "You can come watch, too, if you like. It's the least I can do for the human that made it all possible."

"No," Drakis said, shifting his stance to place himself between the dwarf and the Imperial Throne.

Jugar's broad grin faded slightly, menace in his eyes. "Do you really think this wise, lad?"

"Don't do this, Jugar," Drakis said. "It doesn't have to end this way."

A sudden pounding sounded at the onyx door behind the dwarf. Muffled cries could be heard coming from the other side.

"It was *always* going to end this way!" Jugar growled. "Get out of my way, boy!"

"No, Jugar, please . . . Don't make me stop you . . ."

"STOP ME?" The dwarf charged forward, his ax swinging quickly in his powerful hands. Drakis barely managed to counter the blow with his sword, the blade scraping down the shaft just below the ax blade, deflecting it to the side. "You can't *stop* me! You're *nothing*!"

Drakis took another step back. He shifted his sword, anticipating another swing of the ax but Jugar shifted his grip, thrusting the top of the ax straight at Drakis' face. The blunt top of the ax slammed against the human's forehead. The pain exploded above Drakis' eyes, sending him reeling several more steps before he could regain his footing.

"I'm Drakis!" the human said, his breath ragged. "You said I was the Man of Prophecy."

"Because I *made* you!" Jugar shouted as he quickly closed again with Drakis, his ax now arcing high above his head. Drakis managed to set his stance barely in time to intercept the haft with the hand guard of his sword, arresting the swing and binding up both weapons. "You were no one—a slave among slaves who just happened to have the right name."

Drakis kicked with his right foot, planting a blow against the dwarf's chest. The blades of both weapons rang as they separated.

"I molded you, shaped you, forged your worthless life into a legend," the dwarf raged. "I sold your story to the gullible because they had to believe in *something*. They don't believe in you because you're great, Drakis. They made you great because *I* swindled them into believing in you!"

"But you helped us!" Drakis cried out. "You even tried to save Braun in Tjarlas!"

"I didn't try to *save* him," the dwarf bellowed. "I was trying to *stop* him!"

The dwarf charged again, his ax flashing in the light of the six Aether Well crystals towering above them. Drakis' own blade danced quickly to counter the blows raining down on him in rapid succession. The razor-keen edge of the ax connected with Drakis' shoulder plate, glancing downward into his left arm. Blood welled up from the wound as Drakis cried out but he managed to spin around, clouting the dwarf in the head with the hilt of his blade. The dwarf toppled sideways from the blow, rolling twice across the ground.

The pounding on the doors was becoming more pronounced.

Drakis' left arm hung limp at his side, his sword

held in his right hand. His breathing was ragged as he strode toward the dwarf. "I've always thought I was a fraud—but not today. I may not be the Man of Prophecy but *someone* has to be that man here and now—and I guess it has to be me."

The dwarf pushed up away from the floor with a terrible cry, snatching his ax up as he stood. Drakis ran directly toward him, his sword clutched in his right hand. The dwarf howled, throwing the ax with both hands directly at the charging human. Drakis saw it coming, swung his sword and connected with the heavy ax in flight. The force of the blow made him stumble, halting him a dozen feet from the dwarf. Drakis shifted his gaze back from the ax to the dwarf.

Jugar was grinning at him though there was a hint of sadness in his eyes.

The ax had been a diversion.

The dwarf was holding the Heart of Aer in his left hand, his right arm extending as a spell formed on his lips.

Drakis reacted at once from his instincts as an Impress Warrior. He fell to his knees, sliding across the polished floor toward the dwarf. He could only hope that the spell would somehow miss him.

Jugar looked away from Drakis, his attention now on the throne, his eyes suddenly wide.

"NO!" the dwarf screamed.

Drakis plunged the tip of his sword into the dwarf, the blade sliding expertly up under his ribs. Drakis drew the weapon free of the dwarf, pitching to one side.

The Heart of Aer tumbled from the dwarf's hands as he fell to the ground. The dwarf's blood welled up from under his body, flowing around the dark, strange stone.

Drakis, now face down on the floor, raised his head to see what had distracted the dwarf.

The lifeless body of the Emperor laid sprawled down the steps of the dais.

On the Throne of the Emperor's Devotions . . . sat Soen Tjen-rei.

"Where are we going?" Shebin asked, darting glances around her. A sign fixed to the side of the narrow alley declared it to be the Atje Hranoshei, a name that struck Shebin as being longer than the passage was wide. Walls of subatria crowded in on either side and ran between the foundations in a wandering maze. Shebin had some vague notion that slaves and members of the Lesser Estates may have used these same routes in the course of their duties to the Empire; duties that were far beneath her notice let alone her station.

"Not much farther now," K'yeran repeated the answer she had given only minutes before.

At least these alleys were abandoned. She could still hear the muted sounds of the mobs and the almost constant rumble of war-mage magic in the distance beyond the narrow canyons of the alley walls. The Vira Rhonas proved impassible, as was the Vira Condemnis. The Iblisi woman that had rescued her from the Cloud Palace had managed to get them out of the Garden of Kuchen before the horde closed around them. Somehow they had crossed the Vira Condemnis into the alleys just north of the Forums of the Estates. She could still see the tops of the towering Forums minarets barely visible to the east above the subatria walls around her.

The Atje Hranoshei ended abruptly at a cross alley whose weathered sign declared it to be the Atje Nyelo. Shebin had never heard of these names before and was thoroughly confused about where they were. She determined to see K'yeran punished in the most painful manner, and not for the first time since meeting her that morning.

K'yeran turned to the right almost immediately through an arched, dark alleyway that opened into a plaza so small that Shebin doubted whether the name Pazi D'hin could even properly be applied to it. It seemed more like the accidental space created by several subatria foundations that didn't quite fit together and had left this space abandoned and useless. The plaza was filled with dried and rotting leaves and dirt accumulated for uncounted time. It remained in the perpetual shadows of the shining avatria piercing the sky around it.

Shebin had lost sight of the Iblisi, giving her another reason to see the woman tortured, and she moved quickly toward the obvious exit: a wall opening to the left. The moment she had turned into it, however, she realized that it had been sealed closed and now appeared to be only an alcove.

"Do you hear that, Shebin?"

The daughter of the Emperor spun around. K'yeran was standing next to the entrance to the Pazi D'hin, leaning back against the wall, her arms folded across her robes.

"Do you hear it?" K'yeran asked again. "Listen, Shebin. Listen so that you will always remember the sound of it."

"I don't hear anything," Shebin said, striding toward the arched exit from the Pazi.

K'yeran moved sideways, her body blocking the opening. "That's right, Shebin. You don't hear anything. Where is the thunder of Imperial war-mage magic being deployed against the invading army? Where are the cries of the rioting mobs? Where is the roar of dragons circling the Cloud Palace? Do you hear them, Shebin?"

Shebin tilted her tapered skull, straining with her long, pointed ears to hear the sounds that moments before had been pushed to the back of her thoughts.

"They're gone," K'yeran said. "They have stopped because the Emperor is dead."

Shebin stared at K'yeran, taking a careful step back.

"Long live the new Emperor," K'yeran smiled.

"Indeed," Shebin agreed, blinking her eyes. "Long live the new Emperor. He should know that I am a servant of the Imperial Will and most anxious to support his cause. My death would be a mistake for the citizens of the Empire consider me a cherished treasure—and my influence on his behalf . . ."

"The Emperor is deeply appreciative of your service to the Empire," K'yeran interrupted as she took a step toward Shebin. "And believe he knows how best you may continue in that service. To this end, he bids me bring you a gift."

"A gift?" Shebin released her fear in a laugh. "Well, I am most honored!"

"Yes," K'yeran said. "A gift he most heartily believes you deserve."

Shebin's smile faded slightly over her perfect, sharp teeth.

K'yeran stepped forward, her Matei staff in her left hand. With the right the Iblisi grasped Shebin by her shoulder, driving her forcefully down to her knees. Shebin cried out but K'yeran ignored her, the Matei staff glowing as it touched both shoulders of the Emperor's daughter and the back of her pointed skull. Then, K'yeran bent over and kissed Shebin on the front of her long forehead just above the eyes.

K'yeran straightened up.

"Good-bye," said the Iblisi. Then she turned and began walking away.

"That was it?" Shebin said, struggling to her feet, the hem and front of her dress now dirty from the ground. "What gift was that?"

K'yeran continued to walk down the narrow, arched passage that led back to the Atje Nyelo.

"You will answer me!" Shebin shouted, striding up the shadowy alley. She gripped the shoulder of the Iblisi and spun her around.

K'yeran's backhanded blow split Shebin's lip

and drove her head forcefully against the wall. Dazed, Shebin lost her footing and fell.

"So many elves suffer under the Devotions of the Emperor," K'yeran snarled, leaning down over Shebin's prostrate form in the dim light of the covered alley. "They have no idea of their guilt. They were kept as slaves to the Imperial Will just as surely as any of the Sixth Estate! But *you*, Shebin, fell out of Devotions when your father's House fell. *You* are not a slave to the Imperial Will because of Devotions . . . you *chose* to do evil!"

"So you are going to murder me, then?" Shebin rubbed her hand across her bleeding and bruised lips.

"Quite the contrary," K'yeran said. "The Emperor decided that a living curse would be more appropriate. Something you can carry with you wherever you go."

"Curse?" Shebin asked. "What curse?"

"Wherever you go," K'yeran said, "no one will be able to remember you."

Shebin blinked and then blurted out a laugh. "Remember me? I'm Shebin Sha-Rhonas! Plays have been written about me! My name is in music from one end of the Empire to the other! Armies march in my name! My name will live forever!"

"But not for you," K'yeran said, shaking her head. "No one who meets you will remember you from one day to the next. You will never be able to form attachments long enough to ever harm anyone again. Survival alone will be a challenge, for no matter how many creatures surround you in the throng, you will be profoundly and eternally alone."

K'yeran turned again, walking back out of the alleyway.

Shebin started to laugh. "That's all? A lame curse and Drakis thinks he can walk away from me? I have armies in my name! I have the love of this people! I am more powerful than he can possibly imagine! I am Shebin Sha-Rhonas and I will carve my name on his tomb!"

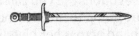

The banging on the doors had stopped.

Drakis struggled to his feet, his blood-streaked sword still in his hand. He looked at Soen sitting on the Throne of Emperor's Devotions then turned to stare back toward the onyx door.

Soen, too, lay there face down on the floor but as he watched the figure began to change. Two arms flowed into four and the sharply defined lines became more fluid.

"Ethis?" Drakis stuttered.

The chimerian slowly managed to pull himself over to the wall and then sit up. "Yes, Drakis . . . it is me."

"Are you well?" Drakis asked. "Do you need help?"

"I'll survive," Ethis said, his lips twitching as he struggled to keep his features solid enough to properly form the words. "Although it may be a while before I attempt anything like that again. What about Jugar?"

Drakis looked away. "Dead."

"I'm sorry, Drakis, truly I am," Ethis said. "I suspected him, but . . . not this."

"What do you mean?" Drakis asked.

"He means the plan was for Ethis to impersonate me in order to distract the Emperor," Soen said from the throne. "We had not anticipated that my Aether spell would include the Emperor as well. The dwarf did not know of the diversion and very nearly ruined it all."

Drakis nodded then rose and walked over to Soen, who was still sitting on the throne. "Then it's time, Soen. Take control of the Devotions and reverse the Well."

Soen drew in a deep breath.

"I'm sorry, Drakis. I can't do that."

"What do you mean, you can't do that?" Drakis asked quietly, his eyes narrowing.

"I mean I never could do it," Soen answered. "Neither could Braun for that matter, no matter what he believed or told you. Devotions are tied to this Imperial Throne and the Aether that flows through it. It is impossible to reverse the Well and maintain Devotions. The only way to gain control of the Devotions is to become the Emperor."

"And that's you, I take it," Drakis sighed. "So what happens now?"

"Now comes the best part, my friend," Soen said. "Now comes the part where Drakis gets to die."

# CHAPTER 37

## *Something to Believe In*

BELAG STOOD ON THE NORTHEAST FIELDS, surrounded by his army. The acolytes had managed to keep the worst of the bombardment magic
away from the battle line but he knew that the
Athereon altars were being drained with the effort. If Drakis and his dragons did not affect the
fall of the city soon, there would not be enough
Aether remaining to attack the city. As it was, he
felt certain there was insufficient remaining to en-
able them a proper retreat.

The walls of the Imperial City and its shining
towers beyond were tantalizingly close. His
army was overwhelmingly manticorian now due
to the insistence of the Chaenandrian Prides on
joining the Army of the Prophet in their conquest. The lion-men were everywhere on the
front lines of the army's Legion formations. Belag could feel them straining to be released, to

charge the walls and bring down the great city in glorious combat.

"Kugan!" Belag shouted to be heard over the tumultuous noise coming from the rolling explosions of fire, lightning, and ice over the front lines. "Keep those assault manticores in line! There will be no charge until I give the word." Belag then turned to Edra, the slight human woman who stood at his side. After the debacle of Tjarlas, Belag had made certain that an acolyte had been attached to each of the Legion commanders in order to relay his commands directly. It had cost him precious conjurers for the attack but it was the price of maintaining control over warriors all hungry for the kill. "That goes for every Legion down the line. They are to hold position no matter what happens in front of them until they get the release directly from me. I don't want any . . ."

"Grahn Aur!" Kugan called out, standing tall and pointing toward the city. "The magic has ceased!"

Belag strained to see the city. The magic breaking in wave after wave against his Legions had gone silent.

A tremendous cheer rolled like a storm from the Army of the Prophet. The Legions roared in triumph and derision of the city whose defenses had suddenly gone silent.

"Now, Grahn Aur?" Kugan begged, war lust in his eyes.

"Why are the avatria still flying?" Belag murmured.

"Grahn Aur?" Edra asked, uncertain whether this was something she was supposed to relay to the other warlords of the Legions.

"The avatria," Belag said, his feral eyes narrowing beneath his fur-covered, knitted brow. "The city has gone silent yet the avatria are still flying. Inverting the Well always causes them to fall . . ."

"Do we charge to victory, Grahn Aur?" Kugan urged.

"NO!" Belag roared. "Hold here! Wait for my word!"

Drakis moved into his combat stance, the blade of his sword held at the ready before him. He could feel his breathing slow, the air drawn deeply into his lungs. This would be his last battle and he was at peace.

"I'll fight you, Soen," Drakis said. "I know who you are and how capable you are of killing . . . but I would rather die than see my people or your people fall back into tyranny and . . ."

"Drakis," Ethis coughed behind him. "You've won."

Drakis glanced at Ethis, leaning back against the wall of the Emperor's Devotions. "This isn't the time for . . ."

"He is quite correct, Drakis," Soen said as he stood up from the Throne of the Emperor's Devotions. "You have conquered the Emperor and brought down his tyranny. Be still. For the first time in your life, perhaps, there is no one chasing after you, no footfalls to fear and death does not stalk you."

Drakis could see now that there were three onyx doors that gave access to the chamber. Soen raised his hand and the locks on all three clacked free. The doors opened quietly. Drakis turned, expecting the Cloud Guardians to plunge into the room but there was no charge of elven warriors, no flood of death . . .

. . . Only the exquisite dark figure of Urulani.

"The Guardians have fled," she said in astonishment.

"They've gone?" Drakis gaped in amazement.

"Marush and I were circling the palace. We saw them leave," Urulani rushed to where Drakis stood. "But that's not all. The attacks from the lower levels have also ceased and, so far as we can see, the war-mages have stopped their magical attacks all along the perimeter. I decided it was safe to perch Marush and come find you." She glanced around at the dead dwarf, the wounded chimerian, and the fallen Emperor. "What happened here?"

"I'll tell you exactly what happened here," Soen said, stepping down from the dais. "Drakis, the Man of Prophecy and his loyal companions Jugar, Ethis, Urulani, and Soen—the Inquisitor who had come to believe in Drakis . . ."

Soen bowed slightly with a smile at this phrase.

". . . flew the dragons Marush, Wanrah, and Pyrash through the defenses of the Empire and brought their justice to the evil Emperor cowering in the heart of his fortress palace. Urulani had failed to enter the palace but Drakis, Ethis, Soen, and Jugar came as one to the Chamber of Imperial Devotions and discovered the Emperor on his throne."

"Here, they attacked the Emperor at once," Soen gestured at the room surrounding them then lowered his long-fingered hand to point at the dwarf lying in his own blood on the floor.

"Jugar, the brave dwarven companion of Drakis, saw that the Emperor had singled out the Man of the Prophecy for death," Soen said, standing over the body of the dwarf. "Jugar imposed himself between the Emperor and Drakis in order to save his friend. The Emperor's bolt found Jugar instead, and Jugar sacrificed his own life for the cause of the Prophecy."

Drakis glanced at Ethis.

Ethis chuckled painfully where he lay against the wall. "Listen to him, Drakis. He tells particularly good stories."

"Ethis did likewise as they charged across the room," Soen continued, now gesturing toward the fallen chimerian. "The Imperial dark magics were unleashed against him, wounding him greatly but, being a chimerian, only caused him to fall. His wounds were not fatal to his kind . . ."

Soen paused, casting a questioning glance at Ethis.

The chimerian chuckled. "Yes, I'll survive."

Soen nodded and then continued. "It was in this

moment that Drakis realized the destiny the gods intended for him: that he would free not only the slaves of Rhonas but the Rhonas citizens themselves from the Emperor's tyranny. He knew in that moment that his destiny was to build rather than to destroy. He threw himself on the Emperor, casting him from the throne, killing the Emperor and . . ."

"Conveniently leaving the throne open for Soen Tjen-rei to become the new Emperor," Drakis sneered.

"No," Soen shook his head.

"No?" Drakis questioned, his eyebrows lifting.

"Let him finish, Drakis," Ethis urged.

"Drakis killed the Emperor, but not before he was mortally wounded himself—cursed by the dying Emperor's final spell," Soen said, his hand gesturing toward the Emperor's body.

"A *withering* curse?" Ethis suggested.

"Ah! Yes, a *withering* curse," Soen nodded in thanks to Ethis. "Terrible curse, that withering curse: causes the body to completely decompose and become unrecognizable."

"Good curse," Ethis agreed.

"Which is why," Soen concluded as he stepped up to Drakis, fixing his blank elven eyes on the human, "Soen Tjen-rei—*former* Iblisi of the Rhonas Empire held the dying Drakis in his arms and heard his last testament to his people. That Soen should present the throne of Rhonas to the Council of the Prophet, surrender the Empire to their rule and will them to establish a Republic as existed in Drakosia of ancient days. With his last breath, Drakis—as the last Emperor of Rhonas—granted all slaves and people everywhere status in the Sixth Estate; everyone was henceforth to be a citizen of the Rhonas Republic."

"But it's not true," Drakis said quietly.

"No, it's better than true," Soen said. "Ethis will confirm the story and no one else remains to contradict it. Belag's council will take control of the Empire and its Legions. I will work with Braun's acolytes to reduce the Devotions over time and eliminate them altogether when it is safe to do so."

"Why?" Urulani asked.

"You of all humankind should know," Soen said, drawing in a deep breath. "When I was in Tjarlas those three days, I spent much of my time trying to restore the peace of Devotions to those who were not too far gone to be helped by it. I came to suspect a truth which, only last night, was confirmed for me by the Keeper of the Iblisi—a truth which was kept most hidden of all: I learned *why* those who fall out of their Devotions so often go insane. Braun suspected it . . ."

"Braun didn't trust you," Drakis said.

"No, but Braun trusted something more than any of us or even the Aether or Aer magic," Soen said. "There were, it seems, a few things which he kept from me in our time together but he also knew that there was one thing he could teach me and ask me to keep safe for him—for all of us. And that is how I came to learn this great truth: that the Devotions were not used only to control the slaves but to control all the citizens of Rhonas as well . . ."

"That was no secret!" Urulani shook her head. "Tsojai Acheran could have told you that . . ."

"But the Devotions were not just to control our thoughts within," Soen said, "It was to keep other thoughts out—other influences that were, shall we say, against the Imperial Will."

"Yes," Urulani breathed in sudden awe. "I see!"

"See what?" Drakis demanded.

"The gods," Urulani replied. "They kept out the gods!"

"How do you banish gods?" Drakis scoffed.

"The Devotions made it so we could not remember the truth," Soen replied. "The gods were not banished but the Aether magic made us deaf to them. The inner light of conscience was extinguished, that spark of the divine kept at bay. All our Aether, all our power, all our government and our resources were channeled into the self, aggrandizing the self and maintaining the self. Who were we elves before we did this to ourselves? What could we have accomplished without Devotions that served the will of the few through the suffering of the many? We were once a beautiful race creating beautiful things. What could we become again if our hearts and our souls were restored to us?"

"But why not just destroy all the Wells?" Drakis asked. "If you restore the influence of the gods . . ."

"Guilt," Urulani sighed. "It isn't just about what has been done to them—it is what they realized, in a devastating moment, that they had done to others. They could not face who they truly were."

"But now that we understand that truth," Soen urged. "We can bring them to that knowledge gently and the Empire—pardon me, the Republic can heal."

Drakis stepped around Soen, staring down at the lifeless Emperor. "I actually tried to save him."

"Then save his people instead," Soen urged.

Drakis turned around. He stared at his sword for a moment and then slid it back into its scabbard.

"Withering curse, you say?"

Soen's lips split into a wide, sharp-toothed smile. "Well, people will believe anything if you tell them it was magic. So, where do you think you'll go?"

"Go?" Drakis asked.

"Drakis is dead," Ethis observed, struggling to his feet. "You are free to go wherever you like."

Drakis drew in a breath. Here, in the heart of Imperial Rhonas, where the lifeblood of the oppressive Empire's Aether had kept the gods at bay, he realized that he was not only free of the Empire, but of Drakis, the Man of Prophecy as well.

"North," Drakis said with watery eyes. "Back to Drakosia. Somewhere I can build a quiet life of my own."

"And I'll take him there."

Drakis looked at Urulani in surprise.

"That is," the raider woman said, "if he doesn't mind."

# CHAPTER 38

## Pyres

THE STREETS OF RHONAS CHAS were deserted of its citizens. The warriors of the Imperial Garrison, with trepidation at first and grim duty afterward, had cleared the avenues and alleys of the Imperial City, urging its citizens—largely with patience and occasionally with force—to return to their homes and to remain there until the army heralds summed them from their homes the following morning. It had taken the better part of the day to restore order in the city but by early evening Ch'drei received word from Soen that she should come to the Cloud Palace.

Ch'drei walked across the God's Bridge over the south branch of the River Jolnar. She left instructions with the members of her Order to remain within the Keep until she returned. Only one Inquisitor accompanied her: K'yeran Tsi-M'harul who had come to summon her.

"It is so quiet," Ch'drei said as they walked down the Vira Rhonas past the marketplace. "I have wondered sometimes if Rhonas Chas were spoiled by so many citizens but now I find this silence discomfiting. It feels like the city is waiting to die."

"Or perhaps it is holding its breath," K'yeran observed. "Waiting to be born."

"What an odd thought!" Ch'drei glanced at K'yeran. "You always could find a different way of looking at things, K'yeran!"

"I prefer to see new opportunities, Keeper," K'yeran offered. "It is better for a tree to bend than to break, is it not?"

Ch'drei nodded but remained silent. They passed the Vira Coleseum with the Great House of the Myrdin-dai on the corner. *How strange,* Ch'drei thought, *that they should have been so powerful for so long and been brought low by this Drakis. Change was the one constant in the Empire,* she thought, *and perhaps that was good after all.*

They came at last to the Garden of Kuchen. Ch'drei naturally moved to the Tower of the Third Estate. A pair of Cloud Guardians stood watch at its entrance but the access to the Cloud Palace was otherwise completely deserted.

"Soen is taking no chances, I see," Ch'drei observed.

If K'yeran heard the Keeper, she offered no reply.

They both drifted upward in a column of light until they reached the platform surrounding the base of the avatria of the palace itself. K'yeran walked before Ch'drei, bringing her across the polished granite to the twenty-foot-tall, delicately inlayed doors that led into the grand reception hall. K'yeran opened the door slightly, the light within spilling out across the platform. Ch'drei nodded in acknowledgment and stepped inside.

The Keeper took two more steps into the hall before coming to a halt.

The enormous room was familiar to her. Its sweeping pillars reached high into the dome overhead. There, at its apex, the Aether-driven fauxsun still shone down and illuminated all below in its radiant light. The Emperor's platform still floated above the floor although now barely a few feet above the level of the polished floor.

What was different was that the hall was largely deserted except for a number of key figures of the Imperium. All of the Modalis was represented. Sjei-Shurian, the Ghenetar Omris of the Vash and Sinechai of the Modalis, stood at their head, looking thoroughly miserable. Kyori-Xiuchi of the Occuran stood behind him but would not look at the Keeper at all. Minister of Thought Liau Nyenjei, Minister of Law Ch'dak Vaijan and the Minister of Occupation Arikasi Tjen-soi stood with their heads bowed down.

Ch'drei frowned. There was another member of the Modalis, she thought, but she could not remember the name right now nor even picture a face.

But it was not just the Modalis that was present.

Ghenetar Omris Qi'sei Nu'uran of the Nekara and Ghenetar Omris K'don Usk'dasei of the Krish were both present as well. That constituted the command of all the elven Legions. Pak Getsok and Pak Temenosh of the Paktan and Daramoneti Guilds represented the workers of the Fourth Estate and a number of other major and minor functionaries.

Soen had gathered in the reins of the entire Empire.

Yet this was not what stopped the Keeper of the Iblisi in fear.

It was the manticore seated on the Throne of the Emperor. On the lion-man's right, he was flanked by Soen as well as another elf unknown to Ch'drei and an unkempt mud gnome. To the manticore's left was a chimerian—Ethis, she thought—and a female goblin who could not seem to keep herself still for her delight.

K'yeran closed the door, her voice echoing through the immensity of the hall. "Council of the Drakis Republic; allow me to present Ch'drei Tsi-Auruun, Keeper of the Order of the Iblisi."

Ch'drei spun around to the Inquisitor holding the doors closed behind her. "What is the meaning of this, K'yeran?"

"It means the Prophecy has been fulfilled," K'yeran said with a thin, satisfied smile crossing her features. "It means that the Empire has fallen—long live the Republic."

"But . . ."

"The wind is blowing, Keeper Ch'drei," K'yeran

whispered. "Will you bend or will you break against it?"

Ch'drei straightened up and turned. Slowly, she walked the length of the audience hall to stand before the Council of the Prophet but she faced Soen.

"So I am the last one brought to grovel at your feet?" Ch'drei asked.

"You were the last called here," Soen acknowledged, "but your surrender will not be to me."

"But you *were* Emperor, weren't you?" she said.

"All I ever wanted was to be an Inquisitor in the service of the truth," Soen answered. "And I still am. You are being given a great gift, Ch'drei. Not only will your Order remain intact, it is going to play an essential part in what is to come. The Order has been hunting down the truth and burying it from its inception. Now we're going to put it to some living use."

"And where is Drakis?"

"Dead, Keeper," Soen answered. "I bequeathed the Empire to Drakis . . . and Drakis gave the Empire to the people represented in this council."

Ch'drei considered this for a moment, sighed, and then turned to face Belag.

"How do I address you?" she asked.

"I am the Grahn Aur," Belag replied.

Ch'drei painfully knelt down on one knee. She felt her age as she did, wondering if she had lived too long after all. "Grahn Aur, in the name of the Order of the Iblisi, I offer our allegiance."

"To the Rhonas Republic," Belag prompted.

"Not to Drakis?" Ch'drei asked.

"No," Belag said. "He wanted it this way."

Early the next morning, the Army of the Prophet charged the walls of Rhonas. They met with no opposition but were allowed to break down the Benis and Patrician's Gates as well as the Meducean Gate that led directly onto the Vira Rhonas. It was largely for the Chaenandrian manticores who desired honor in their conquest. The fact that the city and the Empire as a whole had fallen the day before would be forgotten in the stories they would tell upon returning to the Chaenandrian Steppes.

Later that morning, the Army of Drakis organized itself in a triumphant march into the city. The citizens of Rhonas Chas watched in some confusion at their conquest but were comforted in some part by the quick assurances of the Council of the Republic that the occupying army was not bent on revenge or looting.

It was later that same afternoon that word came to the warriors in the city that Drakis had died on behalf of their cause. The victory of the morning was tempered by the knowledge that the symbol of their freedom had given everything for them. The story of his final moments spread like lightning from post to post and camp to camp. That evening, at sunset, all of Rhonas looked up in wonder. Urulani was on the back of Drakis' dragon, Marush. They were told that she was flying northward with the remaining dragons; Pyrash of the dwarven hero Jugar, and Wanrah, freed by Ethis in memory of Drakis' sacrifice. Many tears were shed on behalf of Drakis as the dragons flew northward and some watching claimed that they saw a second figure seated behind Urulani as the dragons flew higher into the northern sky.

"Perhaps," some said, "it was Drakis' soul rising up to meet the gods."

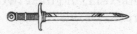

Jugar Edorak Aerkan, King of the Ninth Dwarven Throne, was returned to the dwarves beneath the Aeria Mountains with all the honor and respect that the elves could afford a hero of the Republic and the dwarf who died trying to save Drakis. In his name, the elves withdrew from the dwarven halls they had conquered, abandoning them to the dwarves once more. With Jugar's body, the Rhonas Republic also returned to them the Heart of Aer as a token of their goodwill.

The dwarves accepted both with thanks and wisely remained beneath the ground, unseen by man or sun.

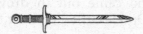

The exhausted, ragged remains of the Army of Imperial Vengeance in time returned to an Empire that no longer existed. Nevertheless, the Republic welcomed them and even sanctioned a parade of victory in their honor. They were then quietly absorbed into the new Republic—and could no longer remember why they had gone to war in the first place.

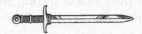

Ten years later, Urulani returned to Rhonas Chas. She came with her husband, a builder and conjurer from Drakosia, and their two children on the back of Marush, Drakis' dragon who had never left her.

There was a week of celebrations in her honor. Though the midnight color of her face was now showing a few wrinkles at the corners of her eyes, she was heralded as the most beautiful sight in the entire Republic. She kept her family apart from the official celebrations and allowed only two visitors into their private chambers in the Cloud Palace of the Grahn Aur; Iblisi Keeper Soen Tjen-rei, the architect of the Republic's Enlightenment, and Ethis, the Ambassador of Ephindria.

Marush proved to be a celebrity equal to Urulani. He lolled about the Garden of Kuchen beneath the Cloud Palace to the delight of the citizens who came out in droves to see the dragon of Drakis curled up near the tomb of his master.

It was to that tomb, at the end of their sojourn in the City of the Republic, that Urulani came to pay her respects with her family.

"It is rather impressive," Urulani said as they walked slowly up the wide steps to the tomb. "What do you think of the likeness?"

"I think they have made him rather too tall," her husband chuckled. The bronze-and-steel statue of Drakis atop the granite tomb was over thirty feet in height, his sword somewhat incongruous above the peaceful garden around them.

"He was a great hero," Urulani said, wrapping her arm around that of her husband. "The greatest I have ever known."

"Yes, I believe he was," he responded. He reached down, gently taking the flowers from his son and daughter. He stepped toward the tomb, knelt down, and laid the flowers beneath the name.

## DRAKIS
## MAN OF PROPHECY

"Thank you," he whispered. "I did the best I could in your name. You took everything from me and gave me everything in return. Whoever or whatever you are, Drakis, I had to be you for a while. Someone had to be Drakis—I hope you understand that I did the best I could."

He stood up and stepped back from the tomb.

"Drakis!"

He turned toward the screeching sound.

"Drakis!"

It was a shriveled, cadaverous elf. Her frame was so emaciated that it was barely possible to tell that she was a female. She wore tattered rags for clothing; her hands were like callused claws reaching out for him.

"You've come back for me!" Her voice was like a rusted hinge. "You remember me! You *must* remember me! You loved me!"

He stared at her without comprehension. Urulani pulled her husband back to her. A pair of Cloud Guardians at the corners of the tomb noticed the frantic elf woman and quickly approached.

"It's me!" the woman wailed as the Guardians gripped her arms, pulling her away. "Shebin! Your Shebin!"

"My apologies, Flight Mistress," one of the Guardians said as he struggled with the elf. "There's always some insane elf woman coming around the tomb, going on about Drakis."

"No! Let me go!" the elf woman howled. "Drakis has come back! He's come back for me!"

"Does this happen often, Guardian?" Urulani asked, gathering her children about her.

"Every day, Flight Mistress," the second Guardian answered as he tried to pull the clawing elf woman away from them. "That's why we we're stationed here, to take care of these deranged elves as kindly as possibly."

"Are there many of them?" her husband asked.

"Don't know," the Guardian shrugged. "We never seem to remember them once they're gone."

"My thanks, Guardian," Urulani nodded then looked down at her children. "Do you think it's time we fly home?"

Both children cheered.

Urulani turned her children around and started walking down the broad steps from the tomb. Marush was already attentive, stretching his wings over the garden before them and inviting them back to the sky.

Urulani turned to her husband and spoke in quiet concern. "She said her name was Shebin."

"Common enough name," her husband replied.

"Didn't we know a Shebin once?"

"Yes, many years ago, as I recall."

"You don't think it's actually her, do you?"

The man once known as Drakis shrugged, then smiled at his wife. "No. I just don't remember her, Lili."

The family climbed up onto the dragon's harness. Marush gave a great push with his wide wings and together they vaulted into the sky, sailing between the avatria on either side of the broad avenue once called Rhonas but since renamed as the Vira Drakis.

Forgotten entirely was the elf woman far behind them who was being dragged by the Guardians from the garden as they had unwittingly done every day for a decade. In a city still struggling with its dark past, it was a kindness to this elven female that they should care for her. In her madness, she had not yet embraced the healing and compassion brought by the Iblisi enlightenment. So they would be understanding of her and gentle, even as she kicked at them and whispered in endless repetition . . .

*"Drakis is returned! Drakis is returned!"*